The
Been a Little Incident

ALICE RYAN grew up in Dublin. After moving to London to study at the LSE, she spent ten years working in the creative industries, holding roles in publishing, film and TV. She was Head of Insight and Planning at BBC Studios before returning to Ireland. She now works at the Arts Council of Ireland and lives in Dublin with her husband Brian and their daughter Kate.

Find Alice on Twitter at @Alice_Ryan

Alice Ryan
Enjoy!

There's Been a Little Incident

Alice Ryan

An Apollo Book

First published in the UK in 2022 by Head of Zeus
This paperback edition first published in 2023 by Head of Zeus,
part of Bloomsbury Publishing Plc

9 7 5 3 1 2 4 6 8

A catalogue record for this book is available from
the British Library.

ISBN (PB): 9781803284095
ISBN (E): 9781803284057

Typeset by Divaddict Publishing Solutions

Printed and bound in Great Britain by
CPI Group (UK) Ltd, Croydon CRO 4YY

Head of Zeus
5–8 Hardwick Street
London EC1R 4RG

WWW.HEADOFZEUS.COM

To James, Caroline and Matt for a wonderful beginning.

And to James and Matt for beginning again – and for all the wonderful times since.

BLACK FAMILY TREE

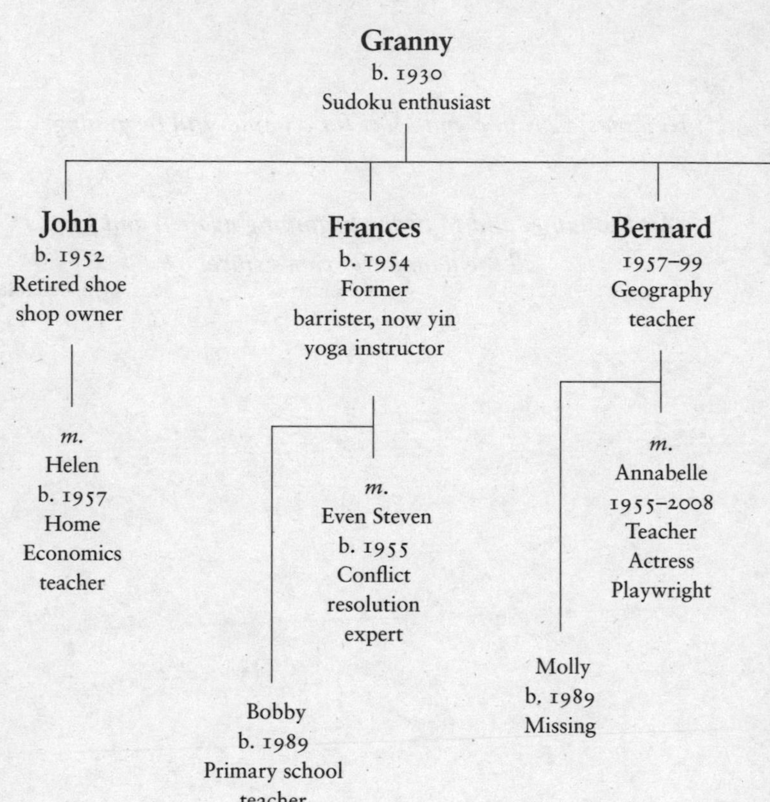

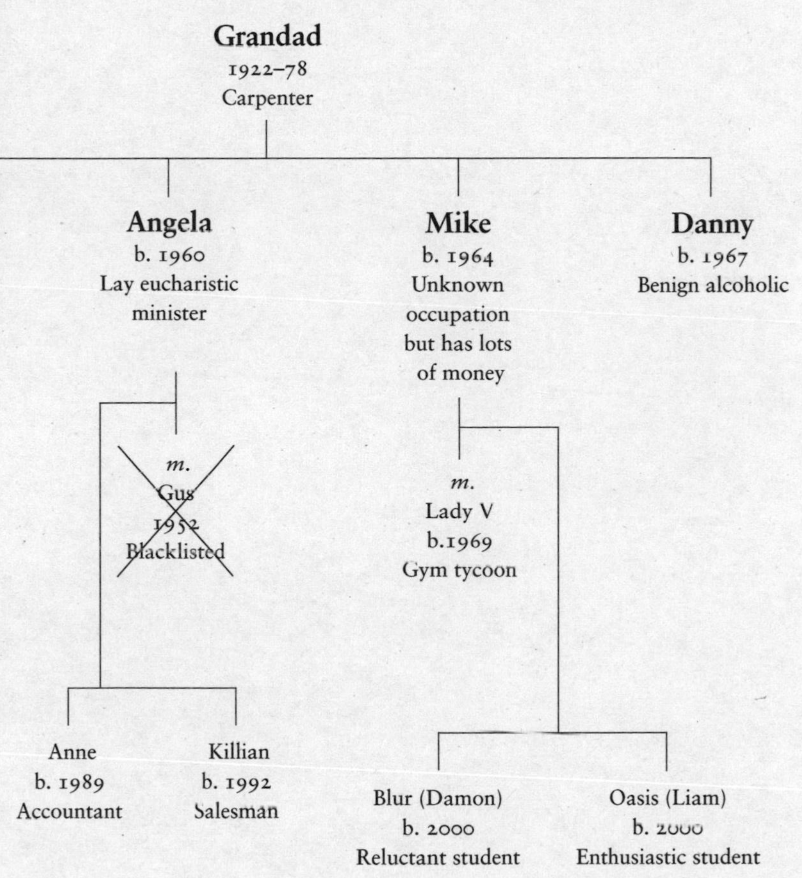

Grandad
1922–78
Carpenter
Angela
b. 1960
Lay eucharistic minister
m.
Gus
1952
Blacklisted
Mike
b. 1964
Unknown occupation but has lots of money
m.
Lady V
b.1969
Gym tycoon
Danny
b. 1967
Benign alcoholic
Anne
b. 1989
Accountant
Killian
b. 1992
Salesman
Blur (Damon)
b. 2000
Reluctant student
Oasis (Liam)
b. 2000
Enthusiastic student

PART ONE

PROLOGUE: MOLLY

Islington, London, Friday March 1st 2019

Someone opened the back door to the roof. It wasn't really a door, but a big window that people were climbing through, spilling onto a damp tar surface, grasping the opportunity for fresh air. For days, it had poured from the high heavens; pelleting pavements, battering umbrellas and flooding roads. The rain pounded at a rate that made Molly's pulse accelerate. She loved a mild crisis like dramatic weather, which upended everyone else's beloved routines and temporarily shifted people to the space she operated in: reactionary, improvised, spontaneous.

But she didn't feel any of those things tonight. Tonight, she felt like the last person at the party even though things were just getting started. Even though shots of tequila were being handed around and previous attempts at being quiet for the neighbours were losing ground, she felt like something was slipping away.

A piercing yell emanated from the roof. Someone was attempting drug-fuelled parkour. As B sprinted through the living room to stop the impending catastrophe, Molly made for the front door. Despite the booming party, when she closed the door behind her, the street was quiet. She sat on the wet doorstep and tried to breathe.

Molly thought about grief like a cut. When you accidentally grazed your finger with a knife there was a moment of grace where no blood emerged. All was white and it looked like you had made it out OK. But when Molly stayed still, the blood began to rise to the top of her finger. Grief was always coming for her. Waiting until she couldn't move. Until there was nowhere to hide.

So, she ran. She ran from boyfriends she accidentally acquired, from religions she accidentally joined, from laws she accidentally broke, but mainly, she ran to keep ten steps ahead of her grief. And for the most part, she had managed to escape it. She had waitressed in Manhattan, picked fruit across Australia, changed sheets during the day and skied at night in France. But all that time, she was never truly alone. Up until now, she had always had B. Now B was moving in with his boyfriend and for the first time in a long time Molly would be on her own.

She'd glimpsed it at Christmas. During her ill-judged, mismanaged, sick-as-a-dog grey London Christmas, the grief had caught up with her and since then it had sprouted shoots, a springtime bonanza of loneliness. She'd been struggling to sleep, losing weight – losing her footing. It was beginning to feel as if, despite all the adventures and all the friends, at the end of the day, Molly didn't really belong to anyone.

She counted upwards in fives, and for a while, she was not spiralling. For a while, all she could feel was the wet from the step seeping into her jeans and the sound of her quiet breath.

Dublin. She didn't know if she could still call it home but that's where she would go. Her aunts and uncles had been busy lately, her cousins too, but they'd be there for her, they always were. And if the grief caught her there, then at least there was a safety net to keep it from engulfing her.

She stood as the rain started again, the respite brief this time. At the other end of the street a couple were arguing. Their muffled voices rose as the rain quickened. The girl draped her arms around her boyfriend's neck pleading forgiveness for something. As they stumbled under a street-lamp, light shone fleetingly on the man's face and Molly realized who it was.

He removed the girl's lithe arms from his neck like he was letting her down gently. Molly watched her ponytail swing as they disappeared around the corner. The girl walked like she weighed nothing, almost bouncing, and Molly wondered when she herself had stopped bouncing. Why her feet suddenly felt like lead; why what was once possibility all around her had suddenly started to feel like traps for grief to catch her. The blood was rising to the top of her finger; it was time to run again. She'd catch the first flight to Dublin in the morning.

She turned on the step and slipped into the pounding rain, safe in the knowledge that although she was running again, this time it was towards home.

1. THE FAMILY

Ten days later, Dublin, March 11th 2019

'There's been a little incident.'

Uncle John stared at us gravely. We had attended enough family meetings to know that the incident could be that he'd discovered a small bomb at the underpass of the dual carriageway. Equally we could have run out of mini-quiches.

He ushered us into the den. A map of Europe stretched across the wall. Red thumbtacks marked Molly's movements like the Allies' progress during the Second World War – if the Allies had moved between damp flats in North London. At the centre of a corkboard was the note she had left her best friend B. The note didn't say where she was going, just that she loved us, but she had to run. Maybe a romance had escalated inconveniently. Maybe she was just bored. Either way it seemed as if – this time – the incident was that Molly had disappeared again.

Uncle John called for silence, but we couldn't help groaning as all thirteen of us squeezed in on top of each other. Oasis and Blur's endless limbs sprawled across the floor like delinquent daddy-long-legs, and we all craned to avoid Blur's athlete's foot. Angela's rosary beads almost strangled her daughter Anne, who no one realized was huddled under a table.

Somehow in the midst of the chaos, Lady V luxuriated on an armchair in her exercise gear, her eyebrows arched like a Tasered cat. Her nails were painted a lovely pink like she was friendly and fun, and not a villain from a 1980s movie about a gymnastic competition gone too far.

The rest of the aunts were perched on each other's knees like schoolgirls and Granny sat on the printer. Blur was sending documents to print from his phone and the tangle of limbs on the floor erupted into laughter when curse words appeared from under Granny's layers. Between that and the fact that Uncle John was wearing a pair of strange military boots for the operation, it was hard to take the whole thing seriously. Besides, half the people in the room were jealous of Molly's jaunt and the other half were happy to see the back of her.

'Does everyone present understand the distinction between strategy and tactics?'

Uncle John was short, so he shouted loudly across the tiny room, fearful of losing our attention. Spit landed on the front row. Halfway through his explanation of the extraction plan he got worried that we would see how much he was enjoying himself, so he bashed the map of Europe and shouted, 'This is serious. Our Molly is missing.'

'Our Molly is off her face, having the time of her life in London, while we are planning black ops with a sixty-seven year old former shoe salesman in suburban Dublin.' (Lady V)

'Is off her face the same thing as mindfulness?' (Aunt Angela)

'Off her face means on drugs, Angela. I'm actually trying a mindfulness course myself but last night half the class fell asleep. What I want to know is: why did they sign up for the class if they find it that easy to fall asleep? Some of us have genuine anxiety issues.' (Cousin Bobby)

Uncle John detested the hecklers and glared at them accordingly. He started bashing the map again even though the rest of us were much more interested in cousin Bobby's anxiety. He was such a tall strapping former rugby player, it was hard to visualize him meditating. A delayed quarter-life crisis would certainly explain the revolting moustache he was cultivating.

'It all started with Brexit.' (Even-Stephen)

Even-Stephen wore those shirts with no collar that made him look non-threatening like an acupuncturist or a sculptor. He was a conflict resolution specialist so that was probably part of the ploy, like when therapists smile politely at you but they're actually frantically writing in their notebook how crazy you are.

'It started when she didn't come home at Christmas. We should never have allowed that.' (Uncle John)

'It started when she killed that squirrel in Bushy Park when she was five.' (Uncle Mike)

'That rock was much more powerful than expected, and you know it. Molly is a rare being. She isn't cut out for this relentlessly commercial world.' (Aunt Frances)

Aunt Frances used to appear on the news as an expert on criminal law. Now she wore a cape. She used to smell like she bathed in Diorissimo. Now she smelt like grass left to fertilize too long. She updated you on her aura and told you what kind of energy you were giving off (not as positive as hers). Half the family thought this was 'fantastic – good for you, Fran!' (Angela and Helen). The other half thought it was a total charade (Bobby and Mike).

'I, for one, envy Molly. I would love nothing more than to abandon my life.' (Aunt Frances)

'That's good to know, Mum.' (Bobby)

'If only we could get her into the Sudoku.' (Granny)

'It wouldn't kill her to pick up a phone.' (Uncle Mike)

'Emotionally, it might. Technology is an insidious beast.' (Aunt Frances)

'Emotionally my arse. Look what she is doing to her poor aunts. Angela looks like she died and then came back to life but just barely, like your man Lazarus. Excuse me, Angela. I know that was harsh. Can the young people not find her on the internet?' (Uncle Mike)

Uncle Mike bashed his elbow into Bobby's ribs to make his point. Some of us worried that this might worsen Bobby's newly revealed anxiety. But Bobby took it well, probably out of sympathy, observing, as the rest of us did, that Uncle Mike hadn't realized that he wasn't one of the lads anymore and was far too large a man to sit on the floor. His whole body was squirming to keep upright.

'Apparently, she hates the internet.' (Uncle John)

'The internet has made young people cocky little nippers, hasn't it?' (Uncle Mike)

'I thought the internet was tracking us all whether we like it or not.' (Even-Stephen)

'It is if you use it, but I believe Molly has – as we call it in military terms – "gone dark".'

Uncle John was delighted to be at the centre of things again and he wasn't going to lose the floor. He started telling the aunts and uncles about the dark web, describing it like a place on the map just beyond the Dublin Mountains. Aunt Helen used the opportunity to unveil another round of miniature scones and miniature sandwiches and miniature buns that she had hidden under a bookshelf. A cucumber sandwich fell butter-side down onto Anne's pale clean hair, but she didn't make a fuss.

'Who will come with me to find her?' Uncle John got to the point of the meeting.

He was met with silence. When it came to Molly, there were no logical allegiances. The family was made up of new-aged hippies, religious nuts, alcoholics, former shoe salesmen, delinquent youths and Sudoku enthusiasts so it was hard to detect a pattern. There wasn't a split by gender or age. Hippy Aunt Frances? Pro-Molly. Raging capitalist Uncle Mike? Anti-Molly. Old but mysteriously liberal Granny? Pro-Molly. Leisure centre tycoon Lady V? Anti-Molly. Religious nut Aunt Angela? Prays heavily for Satan Molly. Even-Stephen? Fucking even. Oasis and Blur? Pro-Molly. Bobby and Anne who were closest in age to Molly? Mixed.

Molly had left both Bobby and Anne high and dry too many times to count. But before TV was seen as the lesser of screen evils, they had spent endless hours on the street playing rounders, setting booby traps and doing knick knacks. They remembered Molly in luminous cycling shorts. They remembered her hair tied in bright pink scrunchies and her teeth obscured by braces. They remembered her parents dying.

'When the time comes, that is? I realize we are not there

yet, but should this continue I think we should mount an operation to find her.' (Uncle John)

'How many times do we have to go find Molly? What about that time you had to spring her from that prison in Poland?' (Uncle Mike)

'It was a local jail cell, and it was terribly well appointed.' (Uncle John)

'Remember when she went to Mexico to liberate those strippers and the police wouldn't let her back into California?' (Blur)

'And she'd lost her shoes.' (Oasis)

'What if she's been abducted like that girl from Galway? Sheena something? God rest her soul.' (Aunt Angela)

Aunt Angela had been normal enough until uncle Gus left her. Then she'd drunk a pulpit of holy-water-flavoured Kool-Aid. Now she was one of those people at mass who is allowed to give you the cardboard snacks. When Anne and Killian had friends over, she used to make them close their eyes and sit in a circle holding hands saying the rosary. When they were one round in, Killian used to slowly disentangle his friends' hands and help them out the window without Angela noticing. One night he climbed out the window himself and went to Australia.

'Molly hasn't been abducted. She's on goddamn holiday.' (Lady V)

But Aunt Angela was already saying the rosary in the corner. We tuned her out like a radio station we wouldn't choose but tolerated because it was already on. Even-Stephen started on about how Molly was like all of us – a mixed bag. The rest of us wanted to vomit at how reasonable he always was. Uncle Danny let out a snore over by the sustenance station. His face looked like an ashtray. Uncle Danny was an alcoholic. But a benign one. He was like the caramel barrel in a box of Cadbury's Roses – he bothered nobody.

'Is this like the stint in Greece with the one-armed carpenter where it will sort itself out, or more like what happened in Poland with the mayor where intervention is required? What does B think?' (Even-Stephen)

'B is busy with his new book and his new boyfriend from Galway who is a billionaire from selling imaginary money on the internet.' (Uncle Mike)

'He isn't a billionaire, and for the last time, Dad, Bitcoins aren't imaginary.' (Oasis)

'That might be what set Molly off – losing B and to a billionaire.' (Aunt Helen)

'I will get a mass said for her in Glenmalure.' (Aunt Angela)

'Is mass still a thing? I thought we had a referendum and got rid of it.' (Blur)

'Is Molly missing? Or is she looking for attention as usual?'

But nobody heard Anne's quiet question because Granny took a tumble and activated the printer. It beeped like NASA preparing a rocket for lift off. Paper flew high into the room. Her children jumped to help her. John in his army gear, Angela clutching her rosary beads and muttering novenas under her breath, Frances in her cape, Danny smiling serenely and Uncle Mike groaning, unable to get up off the floor. Granny used to say that if she hadn't given birth to all six of her children, she wouldn't have believed they were related. Eventually they settled her down.

'When was the last time anyone actually saw or talked to Molly?' John's voice was low.

The room turned quiet. No one seemed to remember. At the time, the rest of us hadn't thought much about how Molly hadn't made it home for Christmas but maybe Uncle John was right; maybe something had been building and we'd missed it. Maybe if we'd seen her then, we'd know whether or not to take her latest vanishing act seriously.

'I want everybody to go home and look through your last texts from Molly – see if there were any hints.'

Outside, a pale darkness lingered over the cul-de-sac. A car turned its headlights on and beams of yellow momentarily lit us up, crowded together in the den of the semi-detached house in Leopardstown. None of us had spent enough time in the den previously to notice the décor. The curtains were a furore of 1980s pastel and tassels that took up half the room. They were categorically disgusting but warm and cosy, and together with the slow drip of the radiators coming on, John and Helen's house felt infinitely safe. Standing in front of us eating a mini-quiche, Uncle John himself looked decidedly suburban and harmless no matter how much he shouted. It was hard to imagine London or missing people or anything other than the quiet safety of the den as we ate mini sandwiches together. Together except for Molly. Maybe the silence was because we were nervous. Not just for her, but for us too. Who were we without Molly?

No matter how exasperating she was, somehow Molly had a special connection to each of us. Molly and Blur shared a history of minor crime and rescued each other from dodgy situations without alerting the wider family. She and Oasis led marches to government buildings about the environment. After babysitting late one Easter weekend, Molly accidentally got hooked on the Masters, and ever since, she and Uncle Mike compared notes on all the Majors – a more unlikely golf fan there never was. Molly indulged Aunt Angela by attending 7 a.m. mass, although unbeknownst to Angela, Molly spent the time alternating between meditating and singing the soundtrack to *Evita* in her head. Molly brought Anne to life, was more reasonable than Even-Stephen and ate Helen out of house and home. Aunt Frances approved of Molly's non-conformist walkabout lifestyle and, weirdly, Molly and Bobby both loved swimming in the rain. And there was a reason uncle John was so worked up – sometimes it seemed like Molly was the daughter he'd never had. Molly had a connection to each of us, but, more than that, she brought us all together – for good reasons and bad. Molly Black was like electricity – sometimes she lit up the world. Sometimes she electrocuted you.

'Did I really have to Zoom in from Sydney for this?'

We had forgotten Killian.

'It's 4 a.m. here and I had to call my family because someone has gone on holiday. I thought Uncle Danny had died. No offence, Uncle Danny.'

'None taken, son.'

Our intermingled limbs shuddered into inadvertent laughter, and we all began to move.

'WAIT, WAIT, DO NOT DISPERSE! What are we going to do about Molly?'

Uncle John held out his hands to stop us, but we were on the move.

'I'll call my pal in the Guards OK?'

Uncle Mike latched onto John's good chinos to try and pull himself up. Blur, Oasis and Bobby all pushed him from behind to help him gain momentum. There was a terrible moment when it looked like Uncle John's trousers might come down, but his belt clung onto his hips for dear life.

'It will be embarrassing when she rocks up in a week with a new hairdo and another tree-surgeon boyfriend, but the Guards will tell us what we need to do, OK?'

Finally on his feet, Uncle Mike put his hands on Uncle John's shoulders. At first glance he looked like he was reassuring his brother, but his copious panting indicated that he was just taking a rest.

'Now, I presume there is lasagne?'

Helen sprinted to the kitchen to take industrial-sized lasagnes out of the oven. Several of us followed Bobby into the lounge to ask him about his anxiety. Lady V pulled out of the driveway in her Land Rover like the house was on fire, Anne slipped out the front door without anyone noticing, and no one remembered to hang up on Killian.

2. LADY V

Molly Black. Friday 11.01.2019

Happy Birthday Auntie V!!! Can't believe you are 50 – you don't look a day over 30! Miss you all – be great to chat if you are free some evening? Know you are busy so whenever suits! Lots of love x Mol

Veronica Black. Saturday 12.01.2019

X. V

Molly Black. Thursday 24.01.2019

Just heard Boyzone on the radio!! Was it Stephen Gately? Is that why you won't tell us? RIP

Veronica Black. Thursday 24.01.2019

No. Can't say.

Molly Black. Saturday 09.02.2019

Thinking of joining a gym! Might be good for the old endorphins, what do you think? Hoping B will join too… although… he hasn't raised his heart rate since the last series of Love Island. Anyway, hope you're well, let me know if you're free to chat soon! X Mol

Veronica Black. Sunday 10.02.2019

Good for you. X.V

Dublin, March 11th 2019

It was rumoured that Lady V had a tattoo. Some said it was a V, others thought it was the symbol for 'ruthless' in Chinese. It was actually a balloon floating away but V would rather lose fifty gym members in one day than show the Black family her tattoo. Even though the tattoo was on her ankle, as she drove away from her in-laws, she pulled her hood over her jet-black hair, as if the family still had their eyes on her. She needed to drive fast to get their chaotic bluster out of her system. She pulled out on an amber light, just as it turned red, and sped towards the M50.

If she had to spend her evening stuck like glue to her in-laws in a fake war room, then she'd at least like it if they could be truthful about the situation. Nobody wanted to tell the truth because Molly's parents were dead. Very sad. Very, *very* sad. But Molly's upbringing before that had hardly been a remake of *The Waltons*. Molly's mother Annabelle was a wild and eccentric drama teacher turned playwright. Her most successful play, *Peas*, was a comedy about a cashier at Crazy Prices who chopped up her boss and hid his body parts in various sections of the frozen food aisle. Molly's dad Bernard was a kind man, but he had no drive. They never made a penny more than their teachers' salaries, which they spent on opera and Italian biscuits (gross things with no chocolate on them). Bernard died of a heart attack when Molly was nine. Then Annabelle died in a car crash ten years later, probably driving like the lunatic that she was. That left Molly an orphan at eighteen. Of course she was going to be a bit of a fuck up – why was no one prepared to acknowledge this?

To be fair to the Blacks, they had raised that girl like their own. John – who had never set foot in a university – practically did her sociology degree for her. He stayed in the library late after work writing essays on Durkheim's theory of social solidarity, then bored them all to death talking about it for years after. Her cousins were devoted to her. Her aunts were all nut jobs in their own way, but they tried their best. Molly was nearly thirty now. If she needed to go off for a few months to take drugs and sleep with foreigners, what was the big deal? By the time she was in her early thirties, V had opened her own gym with a twin hanging out of either side of her and nobody had been much concerned about her mental state. Nobody, except for Annabelle. V experienced an unusual twinge of guilt but quashed it by driving faster.

She flipped on the radio. A woman was giving out about asylum seekers being rehoused in her estate. It was the asylum seekers V felt sorry for. Some of those places beyond Kildare were worse than Syria. V switched it off again, her frustration reaching boiling point. She flew through another amber to get to the motorway. Of course, the family would say that V didn't care about Molly because of the incident with the car.

When Molly was eighteen, she was minding the twins

for the day. V had insured her on the new jeep (a custom-made Toyota Land Cruiser). V wasn't even off on a leisurely break herself; she was up to her eyes testing new sports equipment at a conference in Birmingham when, halfway through the day, Molly's friend B sent V a text saying:

'Would it be worse if Molly broke your car or your babies?'

V knew full well that that message could only mean that Molly had crashed her car so of course she wrote back:

'CAR.'

The Blacks thought this was a ghastly response even if it was a joke. It had tarred her for life in their eyes and she had been growing into her reputation ever since. She knew that behind her back they called her Lady V and thought her cold and heartless, but it wasn't that she didn't care about Molly. She just didn't think it was normal for an entire family to lose their minds over a woman who was nearly thirty going away for a few days. They had double standards when it came to that girl. For instance – who knew what Killian got up to in Australia? It was well known among the younger half of the family (which V actually happened to fall into) that Killian was a total MAN ABOUT TOWN in Sydney. She saw it for herself on Instagram. She kept tabs on all her nieces and nephews that way. Bobby was having a post-break-up identity crisis, and if Anne had a life, she'd be off somewhere doing SOMETHING with SOMEONE instead of ironing shapeless men's shirts for herself on Saturday nights. V looked at the gauge and found she was 20 kph over the speed limit. She forced herself to slow down. This unsettled feeling wasn't about the Blacks and she knew it. It was about the words that had crawled under her skin yesterday and taken root, spreading through her like an infection.

'She's of an era.'

V was used to the men who came to the gym whispering in hushed tones when she passed them in the weights room or in middle-aged huddles by the bikes and it wasn't always PC. She had heard much worse about herself. Tits and arse and all the things they'd like to do to her, so she couldn't understand why this comment had rubbed her up so badly.

V was used to being talked about, because she used to be someone. She'd appeared on the cover of *IMAGE* magazine, on ads for cereal and the ESB. She was that girl from the Kerry Gold ad who remembers to pack butter for her husband on their honeymoon. She had been a regular in the small number of fancy restaurants that existed in Dublin at the time and was on first name terms with at least two members of The Corrs. Before Mike, she had even dated a member of Boyzone (for legal reasons she can't reveal which one). When she'd been someone, columnists had said she was a stuck-up bitch, they said she'd married Mike Black for his money, that she was sharp and unapproachable. But they'd never questioned her looks. No one had ever questioned that Veronica Black was anything other than categorically, clinically, provably attractive. Not until this jumped-up top knot in a vest with a towel around his neck like he was Rocky Balboa tagged her with a best-before date like gone-off milk.

'She's of an era.'

There was something about being stuck in time. As if when the 1990s had ended, she'd ceased to exist, evaporated into irrelevance. Top Knot went on to tell the older man he was lecturing that V was plucked and preened. Modern girls were natural. They had messy hair and imperfections and that's what made them beautiful. He ended every statement with a questioning tone like the man he was talking to was too stupid to get it. People of V's generation? – he explained patiently to his dad or his uncle or a random stranger he'd accosted to make his point – wore make-up to the gym? It was embarrassing? She was embarrassing.

In the jeep, V glanced towards the rear-view mirror. Everything about her was set. Her eyebrows arched, her cheekbones high. Everything in its place. Like Top Knot said it was. Girls today were all over the place with their beanie hats and their exposed freckles. They wore jeans up to their ribs that did nothing for them. In V's day nobody would have looked twice at you if you were a mish-mash like that. She pulled off the motorway into a petrol station, slowing to a stop in a parking space by the shop, a thought occurring to her. They might be suburban nobodies dressed up in hipster jeans, but they were of their era.

On a poster in the window of the petrol station, a bright-eyed, ponytailed girl beamed at her. Her eyebrows were twice as thick as V's and her smile was broad and open, none of the pouting V's agent had trained her to perfect. On the poster, there were multiple photos of the same girl. At a music festival, her arms were naturally lithe in the way that only youth could account for and no amount of 'Banish Bingo Wings' classes could retrain. In another picture the girl wore a nurse's uniform. A gaggle of girls in white tunics and unflattering navy trousers had their arms tight around each other like they wanted to squeeze each other's insides out. Even in her youth, V's friendships were never like that. She and her friends didn't hang out of each other and tell each other secrets. They were contained, formal and highly competitive.

V knew this girl. She knew this girl well and it took a few moments for her to register that, actually, she didn't. She only knew the images that had sprung up across the city, in newspapers and all over Facebook. In the final photo, Sheena Griffith was on her own. Even in a static photo you could tell that her high honeycomb ponytail had been swaying. Her eyes were alive like she was staring right at you. She'd have made a great model. But chances were, she was dead.

They were always dead – isn't that what the crime shows said? It was all about the first twenty-four hours. You had to act fast. V shivered as she thought about Molly. But Molly wasn't really missing, was she? She pictured the note Molly had left B. Molly Black didn't go missing. Molly Black ran away.

V got out of the jeep. Maybe Molly was right to keep running. Eventually she would end up in one big traffic jam trying to pay off an astronomical mortgage, wearing yellow Marigold gloves and scrubbing a kitchen floor. Despite herself, V smiled at the thought of Molly out there somewhere running wild. With her messy hair, no make-up and raucous laugh, Molly was of her era. Let her have it. Let the girl run wild before some nobody decided that she was past her best-before date.

3. JOHN

John. Friday 08.02.2019

MAX APOLS I missed your call Mol. I was up with Granny, she locked herself into the bathroom and Danny has gone walkabouts. I'll try you again, but you are most likely out – it being Friday night! No pressure but you might look into that job I sent you – I know temping is great RE flexibility but it might be good to consider something more permanent? Best wishes, John.

Molly. Friday 08.02.2019

Ha ha thanks Uncle J, I'll look into it. You'd love to have me settled down!! I'll call you Sunday? It would be good to chat, I miss you x

John Black. Sunday 10.02.2019

Dear Molly, great to chat. A number of follow ups from our call. 1) You need to get a DRAUGHT EXCLUDER for your front window. This comes in the form of a foam adhesive and is very easy to apply. Available in any hardware shop. 2) Your throat sounded scratchy; make sure you go to bed early tonight. Sleep is the best medicine. 3) I've looked it up and you are quite right, Beyoncé is indeed married to Jay-Z. This changes everything. More thoughts on this as they come. Best wishes, John.

Molly Black. Sunday 10.02.2019

Thanks Uncle J, what would I do without you? X Mol

Dublin, March 12th 2019

To an independent bystander, it might seem that Molly's disappearance was the best thing that had ever happened to Uncle John. At the very least it was good timing. Retirement had been tricky. The feud with Proinsias Murtagh had picked up pace since they'd both retired but it wasn't a full-time occupation. There were still spare hours where he shuffled around the house hoping something would break so he could fix it. He hated golf, crosswords, watercolours and anything else Helen suggested. He hated the modern-day scourge that seemed to afflict his peers: lycra-clad middle-aged cycling packs. But in particular he hated lunch. Leisurely lunches were for layabouts. Every day at 1 p.m. he ate a ham sandwich and drank a cup of tea. He stood at the kitchen counter listening to the news on the radio. He was done by 1.15 so time stretched out around him. He couldn't pick up the crossword now, even though he'd like to give it a go, because he had made such a song and dance of hating the thing. Molly's disappearance certainly filled a void. If only it had happened sooner.

John stood on his lawn waiting for Proinsias Murtagh

to cycle by. Sometimes the environmental fascist yelled out something about John not following the recycling rules correctly, or the emission levels of his Skoda, and John had to be there to call him a jumped-up eejit. But just as the eejit pulled out of his drive, the phone rang in the front hall and John had to make do with a scowl, before scampering back into the house to answer it.

'What colour hair does Molly have?'

John was about to tell Mike not to be daft but suddenly he wasn't so sure either.

'Brown or blonde.'

'That's the trouble. The Guards want us to clarify.'

'She is always going back and forth between the two, isn't she? Can't you tell them browny-blonde? And it's long. Tell them that when she gets home, we'll be hinting heavily that she needs to cut it.'

'Great. I'll tell the guards that when they find Molly, the first thing they're to do is bring her to the hairdresser. What's B's real name again? All I can think of is how he says, "B – please don't use my dreaded full name – Eustice." Is it Bartholomew or Breffnie or something? I bet you it's Breffnie.'

'Drat. It's slipped my mind. How could I forget the boy's name? Maybe Bobby would know?'

'I doubt it, they aren't really the same type of gay, are they? They'd run in different gay circles.'

'Mike, that is an offensive comment. What a completely old-fashioned backwards way of thinking about sexual orientation. When I was helping Molly with her sociology degree—'

'I'm going to have to stop you there, John. I'll let you

know when I've spoken to my pal down at the station about next steps. I'm late for a cycle and these shorts are squeezing the bollocks off me.'

The phone went dead and John was left with this distressing image. All these older men in spandex were completely unbecoming. If you saw Mike in his cycling gear, you'd consider calling the police to report indecent exposure. Men their age shouldn't be squeezing into tights and panting around parks. It was terrible to admit this, but John got a slight pang of something not unakin to pleasure when he read in *The Irish Times* that one of these super-fit men in spandex had had a heart attack while running and died on the side of the road. He liked to store their name for the next time Helen pressured him into exercising.

As he replaced the receiver, it rang again. He looked at it for several seconds like there must be some mistake. He had just *had* a phone call. It was most likely a post-phone call error, like the phone was burping after a big meal. Nonetheless he picked it up.

'May I speak with Mr John Black?'

The English accent on the other end of the line threw him, and he immediately straightened up like he had arrived at a job interview or joined the army.

'This is he.'

'You are the next of kin for a witness we are looking for in a missing persons case. Molly Black is your niece?'

Everything clicked into place, and John snapped into action.

'Yes, our Molly is missing. I didn't realize the guards had linked up with Scotland Yard so quickly. People complain about their efficiency. Well, I'll be the first to sing their praises from now on. I have an entire operation ready to go at our end. Photos, last known locations, a detailed description – although funnily enough her hair colour is proving tricky. Have you ever heard of this – where a person knows what someone looks like very well – so well they almost can't describe them?'

'Sorry, Mr Black, I think there has been some confusion. The missing person we are investigating is Sheena Griffith. Am I to understand that your niece Molly is unaccounted for?'

The mention of Sheena Griffith silenced John. Molly didn't know the Griffith girl. Molly had nothing to do with her. What was happening with Molly was a mix up; it wasn't serious like the Griffith girl. Her face was on the nine o'clock news every night. She was in trouble or dead. Her family were pleading for information. Their Molly couldn't be connected to something serious like that.

'Well, we haven't heard from her for a few days but she's most likely just taken a holiday. She's not a great one for staying in the same place for long.'

John's heart began to race. The Griffith girl was a good-natured, decent person. You could tell from her face. Neat blonde hair, small blue eyes and a bright smile. She was a nurse. She ran marathons. Dread filled him as he imagined what her parents must be going through. He couldn't have an inch of that. Not a centimetre.

'Molly attended a party the night Sheena went missing. A few people we've interviewed mentioned that Molly left early – around the time Sheena Griffith was last seen on the same street in Islington.'

'What does that mean for our Molly?'

'We are extremely keen to talk to her. We would like to know if Sheena was with anyone, if she was on the phone, if there was anything strange happening on the street. How long has Molly been missing?'

'Just a few days. It's really more of a city break or a romp in the country.'

John had never used the word romp in his life. He had no idea why he had inserted the city break option. His heart was racing, beads of sweat dripped down the back of his polo shirt.

'OK, sir. Could you keep us informed should you hear from your niece?'

The detective recited his phone number and hung up. John stood listening to the dead dial tone, frozen in the hall. His first thought was to call Molly. They had tried that, of course. Her phone was in a drawer in that draughty house in London. But in his mind, she was still within arm's reach. She was still in the ether, like when someone leaves a room, but you can still smell their perfume. It had been a slight bit of a bother up until now, but if he could just speak to her and tell her that there was this other serious business with the Griffith girl, she'd be back in a jiffy. Wouldn't she?

Outside, the sound of a wheelie bin rolling on gravel snapped John from his shocked reverie. Through the frosted glass of the front door, he could make out Proinsias Murtagh's hi-vis vest as he searched in John's bin for forms of plastic that were not actually recyclable. John hadn't put something wrong in the recycling bin for months. Not since that Swedish girl with the pigtails got everybody up to speed about how bad things were. He even washed recyclable containers out fastidiously. But Murtagh was bent double, halfway into the green bin searching for an offending item. Not for the first time John wondered how someone who loved the environment so much could be such an arsehole. John had always presumed environmentalists would be peaceful types whose worst offences were putting vegetables in lasagne. But Murtagh was using the environment as an excuse to behave like a tyrant. He had to be stopped. John placed the receiver down and stormed towards the wheelie bins, grateful for the distraction.

4. ANNE

Molly. Monday 04.02.2019

Iceland!

Anne. Monday 04.02.2019

Why are you watching University Challenge?

Molly. Monday 04.02.2019

First time for everything!

It reminds me of you – I miss you!

Anne. Monday 04.02.2019

Do you need money?

Molly Black. Monday 04.02.2019

No – but thanks again for last time.

Why does the captain of the Oxford team keep ignoring the girl? She has all the right answers!!!

Anne. Monday 04.02.2019

They do that sometimes, it's frustrating.

Molly. Monday 04.02.2019

Why is Paxman so mean to them?

Anne. Monday 04.02.2019

If you buzz in before he finishes the question, you really should know the answer, Molly.

Molly. Monday 04.02.2019

Interesting that the women seem more hesitant to buzz in…

Anne. Monday 04.02.2019

Bunsen Burner

Molly. Monday 04.02.2019

Bunsen Burner!!!! This is fun!

Anne. Monday 04.02.2019

Yes, women generally do tend to be more cautious with the buzzer, but as you see, we both just lost out to the boor from Cambridge because we didn't buzz fast enough. It is a fine balance between tenacity and patience.

Molly. Monday 04.02.2019

Just like life really…

Boor. Fantastic word.

He's a handsome boor though, isn't he?

Anne. Monday 04.02.2019

You say these things to annoy me.

Molly. Monday 04.02.2019

It's true. I do!

Are you free for a call? Be great to catch up! I'd love to hear about work and how everyone is!

Anne. Monday 04.02.2019

I'm about to go to bed.

Molly. Monday 04.02.2019

OK! No problem! I'll catch you again!

Lots of Love! X X X

Anne. Monday 04.02.2019

Mussolini

Molly. Monday 04.02.2019

Mussolini!! I could really get into this!

Dublin, March 12th 2019

It wasn't Molly's fault that Anne had locked herself into a toilet cubicle. But it wasn't *not* her fault either. Ever since the family AGM, Anne had felt the gravitational pull of Molly's mess clutching at her. It clawed at her chest and she struggled to get air past her throat where it lingered. She was so focused on not getting sucked down the Molly sinkhole that she couldn't focus on anything normal. Molly's latest mess had brought Anne right back to her fourteen-year old self, leaving her insecure and on the defence. That was why she'd attacked Alastair Stairs and had to run and hide in a toilet cubicle. So in that way, Molly was at least partly responsible for her predicament.

I am not Molly. I am Anne. I am NOT Molly. I am Anne. She had been repeating this mantra over and over for the last twenty-four hours. On the way home from the family AGM, every time the bus pulled away from an empty stop on the dual carriageway and lunged closer towards the city centre, she was less Molly and more Anne. I am not Molly. I am Anne. I am NOT Molly. I am Anne. It was important to remember that because that's what Molly did to you. She wasn't just someone you knew. Someone you were related to. Somehow, she got inside you. She embedded parts of herself in you. So that eventually you felt responsible for her. You became her conscience so that she didn't have to have one. But Anne was done with that now. Anne was a grown woman with a high-powered job and an apartment. She wore pencil skirts. She audited insurance brokers. She had a lodger called Joel. She drank coffee. She recycled. She made meals and froze them. She even made her own stock, for Christ's sake.

Anne kept inadvertently touching things in the cubicle – leaning back against the wall, almost touching the toilet then jumping in fright at the thought of all the germs. Thank Christ her barricade had started just after the facilities had been cleaned, so the calming smell of bleach dominated. In a moment of uncharacteristic frivolity, she thought to hell with the environment and folded layers and layers of toilet paper into a cushion so that she could sit on the closed toilet seat and take stock of her situation.

The Black family fell into two groups. Those who adored being squashed up in a tiny room with each other (Uncle John). And those who paid cognitive behavioural therapists to work through being squashed up in a tiny room with each other (Anne and potentially now Bobby). Her therapist said that Anne must stop reliving past conversations and events. But if only everybody knew how impossible Molly was. If they could just open their eyes and see what Anne saw, they'd stop thinking of Molly as a lovable rogue to be humoured and see her for the contagious mess that she was.

Anne didn't know what made some people attractive and others not. She'd studied it like she studied everything else but could detect no clear pattern that explained the impact Molly had on people. Molly's draw would have been easier to understand if she had one standout feature that nobody could argue with like Annabelle's auburn hair, Bobby's sharp jaw or Lady V's symmetrical face. But there was nothing particularly striking about Molly's appearance.

On paper Molly was pretty. She had sweet freckles across her nose, blue eyes and hair that changed naturally between brown and blonde like those mood rings they'd had as children. She was lithe and smiled often – but so did lots of women. Anne had watched and watched trying to pinpoint what made Molly so appealing, whether it was how she moved or what she said. The only conclusion she reached was that, on paper, Molly was nice-looking, but when it came to real life, she was a magnet whose force field knew no bounds.

Anne, on the other hand, had the perfect features for blending into a wall. Her pasty face could redden if the paint in a room called for it. Saying she was fair was a polite way of conjuring up an image of any colour at all. Non-existent eyebrows and eyelashes meant that when she closed her eyes, she could almost feel herself slip out of people's minds.

Still, that was Anne's lot. She wasn't jealous or pining for what she didn't have. She just didn't want to have to carry Molly through life as well as be outshined by her.

Molly's parents dying was HORRIFIC. Worse than horrific. But at a certain point you had to grow up and deal with the hand you were dealt, not float from one narrow existence to another until you fell off the map. Anne had no idea what it was like to lose both her parents, but it wasn't like things with Angela and Gus had been a barrel of laughs.

When Anne's dad had left her mum, he had left her a list of all the things that were wrong with her. Number 12 was that Angela insisted on wearing a cardigan that she KNEW Gus found itchy when it brushed up against him. Number 41 was that no matter how much he instructed her, Angela refused to coil the hose correctly to ensure irreparable kinks didn't develop. She thought it wasn't a big deal, but it was causing PERMANENT damage to the hose.

Anne had thought that the tense house and final accusatory note were bad, but, if possible, the religious fervour that followed was worse. Just when the rest of the country was being sprung from the chokehold that religion had them in, Angela saw a set of rules – any rules – and decided that's what would save her. Anne didn't have a thing against religion – religion wasn't the problem. It was how her mum used religion as a way to give up. Angela had given up smoking, drinking, eating meat on Fridays and doing anything but pray on Sundays, but more than any of that, she'd given up thinking. She didn't have to. After Gus left, if the kids came to her with a problem, a worry or a fear, Angela had two responses: first search the Bible for guidance, and second pray on it. It was as if she had been set free from the burden of having to exist. Gradually it had built a wall between them all until they each survived but on their own. So, it wasn't *Little House on the Prairie* but Killian and Anne had found a way to cope. Like the rest of the human race, Molly had to face her lot and work through it. No one could keep life from her. As much as Uncle John and the rest of the family would like to.

Beside her on the layers of toilet paper, Anne's phone was brightening like the Northern Lights as her family analysed

Molly's latest disappearance. As instructed, Anne had read her most recent messages from Molly. She didn't understand why Molly had to send multiple messages one after the other like a rolling brain dump instead of compiling her thoughts into a single message like a normal person. If you have numerous things to say, just wait to put them all in one message. But beyond the formatting issues, there'd been nothing unusual in them. Anne had sent them on to John; she'd played her part in Molly's latest saga and, right now, she had her own issues.

Six minutes ago, Alastair Stairs had stopped by Anne's desk. He was wearing a navy suit and a blue shirt, and he still hadn't gotten his glasses fixed. He kept pushing them up his nose to between his eyebrows where it was now red from wire and Sellotape. What was wrong with the man? Why was he hovering near her all the time? And why couldn't he just get his damn glasses fixed?

There was a moment before he said anything. Seconds maybe, but it was long enough for Anne to run through the multiple things she could have done wrong to merit this encounter. Had she left something in the printer? He didn't have any paper in his hands. Why didn't he have anything in his hands? It must mean it wasn't work-related. Panic escalated as she realized it could be a social visit. Alastair was from England. He could want any manner of interaction. Did he want to go to the pub for a pint? They were always going to the pub in *Line of Duty*. Because he was an outcast too, maybe he wanted to 'team up'. Anne didn't want to 'team up' with anyone. She'd spent her life actively *not* teaming up. But then another thought struck her – had she forgotten to give money to a collection for a co-worker? Alastair Stairs was forever organizing those things, probably trying to make people like him. Who was leaving/had a birthday/got married/had a baby recently? Anne might not even know the offender. Would Alastair think less of her if she didn't put in money for someone she had never even spoken to before? Or should she just put in the money to placate him? But that would be downright silly. Why should she put money in for a present for someone she didn't even know? She was beginning to get a little angry with him for even coming over to her about it. But then a flash of dread shot through her – maybe it was even worse than a collection for someone she didn't know. Maybe he'd found an error in one of her audits. The insurance broker in Ennis from last year? She'd been strung out, she wanted to tell him. Even if he'd found one thing, it wouldn't necessarily transfer to the entire audit. Would he believe that?

This was what thinking about Molly did to her. I am NOT Molly. I am Anne, she repeated again, firmly this time. She was not couch surfing across flee-infested dives in London. She was one of the best auditors in Leinster. She was on the road to partner. She didn't have to answer to a man with perpetually broken glasses who wanted her money to buy frivolous cards and who questioned how good she was at her job.

'Whatever it is, Alastair, I don't want to hear it.'

Anne had turned on her heel before she could process that he had in fact asked her if she wanted a cup of tea. There was almost time to stop the next comment, but then before she could pause, it was already out.

'And get your goddamn glasses fixed, you fool.'

People said that Molly's zeal for life was infectious. But Anne hated infections.

5. BOBBY

Molly. Wednesday 13.02.2019

What was the name of that guy on your rugby team who would eat the head of an anchovy for a fiver?

I just saw him in the big Sainsbury's in Camden. His trolley was full of concerning items.

Bobby. Wednesday 13.02.2019

Gerard Whitehead. What constitutes concerning?

Molly. Wednesday 13.02.2019

Multiple packs of jelly.

Personally, haven't had jelly since the 1990s.

Would actually like some now but can't as don't want to be associated with Gerard Whitehead.

What man in his late 20s eats jelly?

Bobby. Wednesday 13.02.2019

The kind of man who eats the head off anchovies for a fiver.

Molly. Wednesday 13.02.2019

Do you keep in touch with any of the old rugby gang?

Bobby. Wednesday 13.02.2019

Nope. Too much jelly at the alumni events.

Molly. Wednesday 13.02.2019

Ha ha!

Do you fancy a chat?

Bobby. Wednesday 13.02.2019

Like on the phone?
Is everything OK?
(besides the jelly
emergency)

Molly. Wednesday 13.02.2019

Yup! Just wanted to chat!

Bobby. Wednesday 13.02.2019

Its 2019 Molly, phone calls are reserved for emergencies. Leave me a voicenote. I'll listen to it while I'm running, I'm heading out now. PS What flavour jelly?

Molly. Wednesday 13.02.2019

Voicenotes are a scourge on humanity.

Enjoy run, I'll try you another time. x

PS Lime

Bobby. Wednesday 13.02.2019

Jesus, lime jelly. Sad to see things go so wrong for someone.

Molly. Wednesday 13.02.2019

Ha!

Miss you x

Dublin, March 13th 2019

Bobby walked through the gates of the stadium as dark was falling on the pitch. He wasn't sure why he'd agreed to come. But here he was; back in the place that had made him, and somehow seemed to have broken him too. The last of the players were heading for the changing room. A short little round guy kept dropping things. First his water bottle, then a towel, then his rugby boots, which for some reason he'd taken off. Bobby almost wanted to run towards him and help but he knew better. Instead, he walked to the side of the stadium and up the concrete steps. He looked out on the pitch and pictured the mud, sweat and blood – he almost missed it.

He tried to remember how it had felt to be that person. To race through a gap in the line that no one else seemed to see. To feel hands grabbing at the air near you but just miss every time. To never look behind because you knew now that you were through, that you were free, and all you had to do was run like the wind or kick for a drop goal. In his memory the roar of the crowd came almost before the ball was through the bars; sometimes it seemed to come even before his foot touched the ball, as if how he performed was only ever a result of where the crowd was at that day, their mood, whether they willed him on strongly enough. He was their vessel. He'd never really been his own. He'd only ever been theirs.

He tried to remember if he'd been happy – hearing the stadium erupt and feeling the vibration of the whole school leaping to their feet. Working hard for something and winning. Being the hero. But all he could remember was scanning the stands until he found Jack. And then later, scanning the stands and remembering that Jack was gone.

Jack had been easy to spot because of his hair. When all their friends had bleached their hair at fourteen, how close you got to Jack McCarthy's naturally blond hair deemed how close you were to perfect. He hadn't understood then but now Bobby could see why the boys in his class had attempted those awful bleach jobs. Why they'd pierced their ears or worn flamboyant shirts to the disco. Because everything else about them was painfully inconspicuous. When they weren't in actual uniforms, they had their informal ones; O'Neill tracksuit bottoms, rugby shirts, Adidas runners. They all chased after the same girls; blonde, fake-tanned, Ugg-boot-wearing clones. And somehow, even though they were the last ones who wanted it, he and Jack had been the poster boys for it all; the rugby, the clothes, the girls. Bobby looked down now at his boots and leather jacket. Even with all the wins, his name on all the trophies, he'd always felt out of place here and now he looked it too. He'd worked hard to build a persona as far away as possible from the one he'd once had. And yet, even he could see he'd just traded one uniform for another.

Despite all the private junior school job offers, Bobby

taught in a school across the city where no one knew him, where they prized Gaelic football – something he was no good at. And the great thing about eight year olds was that they had no interest in who you were outside school. They just wanted more time in the yard at lunch and to do Art on a Friday afternoon instead of Maths. When Bobby was in the classroom, there was no one else he could be other than the person he was in that moment; making the children laugh as he howled like a dog telling them how Setanta became Cú Chulainn by killing a fierce dog, quizzing them on counties and struggling through Irish lessons, hoping none of them noticed. But when he left the miniature chairs, snotty noses and smiling faces, he was lost again, trapped between multiple versions of himself – unsure which one was real, if any of them were.

In the dim light of the stands he almost wished he could go back to that other person – the captain of the Senior Cup rugby team – and play a role he was good at. All those years he had thought it was hard pretending to be someone else. Now he saw that it was much harder to be himself.

'Bobby Benson captains the school to a THIRD Senior Cup final in a row.'

Uncle Mike appeared in the middle of the pitch. He wore his trademark shirt and blazer but his jeans were stuffed awkwardly into a pair of Ireland rugby socks. The funnelled socks made him look too heavy on top like he might keel over – like the rotund ringmaster of a circus. He smiled widely as he made his way across the pitch, a giant banner in his hands.

'He's fast, he's handsome, could he be Ireland's next captain?'

Mike's voice echoed around the stadium. The junior team were making their way to the gate now. They looked up at the madman on the pitch and politely averted their gaze. Bobby tried to smile but something was constricting in his chest and he felt the urge to flee. Mike must have sensed he was on the wrong track because he dropped his booming voice to a near normal decibel.

'Could you give me a hand with this, son?'

Bobby made his way down the steps and out onto the pitch. His feet sank into the soft grass and immediately he thought of the recent rain and pitch conditions and the havoc it would wreak. But that wasn't his problem anymore.

Mike was unfurling the banner which seemed to advertise manure, but he kept tripping in the holes for the rope. Bobby wasn't sure how Uncle Mike was involved with the club. He was panting after a slow walk across the pitch so clearly he didn't play. Presumably he kept the whole thing afloat financially. Bobby supposed that even raging capitalists had causes. He took the rope off his uncle and began looping it through the holes.

'Thanks for coming, son.'

'Sure.'

With Bobby taking charge, Mike seemed to relax. He leant against the railing and out of nowhere produced a grease-laden paper bag.

'Battered sausage?'

He waved the half-eaten sausage at Bobby. Bobby began lacing the banner around the railing.

'Jesus, Mike, get that thing away from me. What would V say?'

'Why do you think I'm hiding in a rugby stadium in the dead of night?'

Bobby laughed. He half wondered why Mike hadn't asked Blur or Oasis to help him, but it was nice to have been asked. It was even nice to be in the quiet stadium, lacing a banner to a railing, with no one else's eyes on him. Not searching the stands for someone who'd died a long time ago.

'Could I talk to you about something, Bobby?'

Bobby held his breath. Presumably Mike was about to re-hash the same old speeches; what could have been, what Bobby had lost when he left rugby, the sense of community, the lifelong drinking buddies and how there was still time to get it all back. This wasn't a crime; Mike – no one – could understand how viscerally being back here reminded him of Jack.

Nobody talked about Jack. Especially not Bobby. He wasn't stupid, he knew that was unwise, that it would coil up inside him and erupt somehow, but that didn't make it any easier to talk about it. That vault was sealed and locked, and it couldn't be opened, or everything would fall out. Just the thought of someone saying Jack's name sent palpitations through his entire body.

Bobby felt his fists clench as he laced the last length of rope around the railing. Here he was in the same place where his whole identity had been defined when he'd made a surprisingly good kick to touch at twelve years old. He'd always thought that the real him was just in there waiting to get out, but it turned out that the real him disappeared when Jack did, and nothing had ever been the same since.

'The tash has got to go, son. It is violently distressing.'

Bobby looked up.

'Don't get me wrong, I know what you're doing. What you *have* to do. Good-looking guys like you and me we have to do something to lower the temperature, right? Me? I use this ring of fat.' Mike took a firm grip of his love handle through his shirt. 'It's not even real, you know? It's an implant. Very difficult to maintain.'

Bobby felt his lungs expand as breath filled him and he laughed. The relief at not having to talk about Jack was physical, and Mike wasn't that far off. In a way Bobby *was* trying to camouflage himself from other people's idea of good-looking. But he kind of liked the moustache. Or at least he liked how much everyone else hated it.

'You're trying your hand at being ugly. It's the polite thing to do. For society.' Mike took a last bite of his sausage and crossed one leg over the other. Bobby could see now that the rugby socks were funnelled into Italian leather brogues.

'It's an honour to get advice from the family style icon.' Bobby pointed at Mike's feet. Uncle John would have had a heart attack if he saw the clumps of mud stuck to the thin Italian soles. Laughing, they walked back towards the stands and sat down.

'There is one other thing.' Mike shifted his large behind on the cold concrete. Bobby realized that Mike was nervous. 'I know you've been asked to coach before, but everyone knows I'm your uncle – probably because I tell them.' Mike broke into a sweet, almost childish smile. Bobby was touched at his uncle's admission. 'So the club just wondered if I'd mention it to you again. I know you left rugby suddenly and that you've had some tough times but, Bobby, you were brilliant. The best this country has ever seen. Except maybe Dricko and Sexton or Woods, but you see my point. Or actually that young lad James Ryan is very promising, but you know – you loved it, I think?'

Someone turned the pitch lights off and the blue haze of evening suddenly turned black. Bobby felt an inexplicable relief at being plunged into darkness. He thought of the short little round guy he'd seen at the entrance, of all the hopes and fears he'd had at that age, fears mainly. It seemed to him now that he'd been afraid of everything. But not on the pitch. On the pitch it was like he could breathe. Mike was right, he had loved it. And Bobby did want to help kids like the short little round guy feel that way, but the irony was that he was almost afraid to. He couldn't watch anyone get hurt like he'd been. It wasn't rugby. It wasn't this club. It was the depth of the grief that sat here, in every seat around him. He was grateful when Mike changed the subject.

'Sure, maybe you'd think about it. How's the love life? Any lads on the scene? What happened to the last lad? That extremely nice black lad?'

Bobby wished Mike would stop incessantly saying the word lad. It made him feel like Mike was referring to a group of football hooligans. They hadn't had a conversation in ten years where his uncle hadn't mentioned what a great LAD Gareth Thomas was or that he supported Leo Varadkar – a multi-talented medical AND political LAD.

'He wanted kids.'

'But *you* want kids.'

Just when he was beginning to relax, here they were again: the unseen, unnamed assumptions about himself that everyone else knew about – was dead certain about – but him. He stayed silent.

'I mean, I just presumed. You love kids. Sure, you're a primary school teacher.'

Bobby almost laughed. As if he didn't know what he did for a living. And as if not having children meant you couldn't love them. He took a deep breath.

'I had better head home.' As Bobby stood, he felt the air change between them, and he was sorry. He knew Mike meant no harm, but the familiar feeling of being trapped in a version of himself he'd no control over was creeping up on him and he had an urgent need to get away from his uncle and this place.

'Of course, son. Thanks for your help with the banner. Do you want a lift home? You could come over for dinner? You could be my excuse for takeaway? I mean, another one.'

'Next time.'

They walked in silence towards the gates. Mike scurried over to a bin with the greasy sausage wrapper like he was hiding evidence of a crime. His BMW was pulled up in front of the clubhouse where it looked like a few old timers were drinking. Bobby recognized some of them from the sidelines of his own games years ago. They'd followed him, advised him, cheered him on like he was their own son. He wondered at their lives, if they'd been here ever since.

'Will you give the coaching a think? And for the love of Mother Mary and all the saints above will you please shave that tash?'

Bobby hugged his uncle. When they broke apart, he almost said something. About all the things that just didn't feel right. How it wasn't rugby, it wasn't the club or the stadium, it was just this person he felt trapped in and couldn't find a way out of. It was like he had to live a different life now, a contained life just to keep afloat, he couldn't get too involved in the world or it would let him down again. But instead, he smiled and made his way to his bike.

At the gate he turned to take one last look at the pitch. With the lights off and the stands empty it felt safe. He almost considered going back to sit in the stands for a bit longer but then a roar came out of the clubhouse. The old timers began spilling out and he remembered that it was never his. It was always theirs, like he'd never really been his own. He'd only ever been theirs.

The BMW pulled up beside him and Mike rolled down the window.

'Bobby? Scrap the tash but don't get rid of the leather jacket. It's sexy as hell – an absolute magnet for the LADS.'

6. B

Dublin, 1996

Molly's mum's eyes were not on the road. They roved from the tape deck to B and Molly in the back to the occupants of neighbouring cars. Annabelle observed the journey like she had nothing to do with it. As if she was a passenger on the Orient Express, instead of a suburban mum, driving children home through Rathfarnham. A breeze from the open window blew her layers of shawls, causing constant movement in the front seat. Her earrings jingled as she shook her head, indicating to the kids that they still weren't getting it right. In the back, Molly and B sat quietly, unsure exactly what it was she was asking them to do. As they pulled up to a red light, Annabelle pressed rewind on the tape deck. She unplugged her seatbelt and turned her full attention to the backing vocalists.

'You need to find a way to connect more deeply to the lyrics. Picture this – you've been sleeping with this guy on and off since the seventies, right?'

B's jaw dropped.

'You aren't asking him to marry you.'

Still open-mouthed, the backing singers looked on in shock.

'But you aren't getting any younger, are you? There are less and less roles for actresses past thirty. SURE it picks up again when you're old and directors want kindly grannies who in real life aren't a day over fifty, but what are you supposed to do until then?'

The lights turned green and anxiety rose up through B's perfectly knotted school tie as Annabelle showed no signs of turning around to resume driving.

'Should you hang around waiting for this mediocre playwright with a fake limp to take things to the next level or should you cut your losses? That's what you want to know. That's what you NEED to know. So, take all that, pour it right down your lungs and let's get to the heart of this.'

The back seat let out an audible sigh of relief when Annabelle plugged her seatbelt back in, but the anxiety returned when she put her foot to the floor to catch up with the traffic. The lazy disco notes at the beginning of the song were becoming increasingly familiar to B as Annabelle pressed play on ABBA's 'The Name of the Game' for the fifth time. Cold air poured through the open window as they flew down the road in the Toyota.

Around them, the suburbs were grim. Various shades of grey melded into each other as they passed a concrete shopping centre. Stray trollies rolled aimlessly, and plastic bags floated towards the Dodder River. The sky was done for the day, lowering a depressing ash colour around them.

The sultry voice that emerged from the front seat was

unnervingly emotional compared to B's own mum's demeanour. Waiting for B at home with her yellow rubber gloves and her tight brown perm, Pamela seemed appealingly dull in comparison. B willed the mortifying journey to be over. He would eat his fish fingers and beans and never be mean to Pam again.

Annabelle seemed unperturbed by the confused glances from other cars as snatches of her performance floated out the open window. B was silently calculating how many sets of lights there were to his house; three. When they were flying along like this, Annabelle's eccentricity was OK, but should they be stopped for enough time to be spotted by someone from their school, it wouldn't bear thinking about.

'The musical interlude is the most important part, don't switch off here. Of course, you want to look like you are respecting the musicians at this time, so you are doing a serene yet benevolent sway, but remember YOU are the star. People have paid to come see you. They are watching your every move.'

Molly let out a laugh. Then, as quick as if it had never happened, Annabelle winked at B in the rear-view mirror. Suddenly B caught on: Molly's mum wasn't serious. It was all a game. The performance was for them. For him. To make him laugh.

Annabelle stretched behind her to give the mic to the backing vocalists. Giggling, they leant over her balled-up fist.

'Louder!'

Molly and B knocked their heads against each other as they leant closer to the mic, yelling from the bottom of their lungs.

'Bravo on the improvisation, B!'

B realized he was swaying his hands. Molly was clapping and the wind was flying through the car as they passed out of the traffic of Rathfarnham leaving the stray trollies and grey shopping centre behind them. Annabelle sang out at full volume, asking if she should trust in some mysterious force beyond the Dublin Mountains.

'Because that's all we really want to know in this mixed-up world, isn't it?'

Annabelle turned to them, her auburn hair cascading around her smiling face. In contrast to the grey around them, Molly's mum was a ball of colourful pashminas and unstoppable energy.

'If we are brave enough to trust someone – will they let us down?'

Her blue eyes glistened, and B knew the answer. Annabelle wasn't cooking fish fingers or arranging endless summer camps like other mums, she didn't stand at the school gates and swap recipes and offer advice and tell you to put your hat on. But she was there, and she'd never let him down.

7. B

Molly. Friday 01.02.2019

Wait for me, I'm coming!!

I'm literally on our front steps.

B. Friday 01.02.2019

That's interesting because I too am on our front steps.

Molly. Friday 01.02.2019

I'm on the steps figuratively.

Emotionally.

Psychologically.

On a deep philosophical level I'm on those steps with you.

B. Friday 01.02.2019

The party started an hour ago. I'm getting in an Uber if you are not PHYSICALLY here in 5

4

3

2
Is that what you're wearing?

1
To be fair, you were always a fast runner.

Molly. Thursday 07.02.2019

Fancy takeaway? We could go to the mean Greek man?

B. Thursday 07.02.2019

Sorry didn't see this sooner – at a tasting. Hope you enjoyed souvlaki without too much trauma. Staying at Jeff's tonight. x

Molly. Saturday 09.02.2019

Should we join a gym?

B. Saturday 09.02.2019

What a preposterous idea.

Molly. Saturday 09.02.2019

What about endorphins?

B. Saturday 09.02.2019

What about Pizza?

Molly. Saturday 09.02.2019

This seems wise. Extra cheese to counter my earlier bout of madness please

B. Saturday 09.02.2019

Will have you checked by psychiatrist.

Molly. Tuesday 12.02.2019

Can you pick up milk on your way home?

(And Skittles and Ribena)

Asking for a friend

B. Tuesday 12.02.2019

Out with Jeff, won't be home till late but there will be milk in the fridge when you wake up.

(And Skittles and Ribena for your friend)

Molly. Tuesday 19.02.2019

Are you home tonight?

We have to finish The Crown. We've already left it very late. They might throw us out of the country.

B. Tuesday 19.02.2019

That Lord Snowdon is such a minx. See you at 6. Jeff coming too.

Molly. Friday 01.03.2019

Uber from ours to the party tonight? I SWEAR I won't be late this time.

B. Friday 01.03.2019

Ha ha, coming from Jeff's. See you there

B. Friday 01.03.2019

Did you leave the party already? You snake. See you in the morning.
X X X

Missed call from B. 02.03.2019 13.10
Missed call from B. 02.03.2019 13.20
Missed call from B. 02.03.2019 14.00

London, March 14th 2019

The publishing house was on the top floor of a skyscraper near Euston Station. Emerging from the elevator, B stepped into a book-lined corridor. A man with glasses was returning from a coffee run. He placed a flat white on the receptionist's desk, and she handed him several jiffy bags. They laughed about his afternoon of proofreading.

B froze in the elevator door. The stacks of proofs, the man with the glasses; it was all too real. What if something happened to snatch it all away? What if his book was a colossal failure? What if – worse – nobody even noticed it? A lifelong dream was coming true and for a moment he wanted to step backwards into the elevator to save himself from it. Distractedly, the receptionist asked if she could help.

'My name is B. Eustice? I have an appointment.'

'B!'

Belatedly recognizing him, the receptionist jumped from her swivel chair and bounced around to the front of the desk. It looked like she was about to hug him, but he must have scowled his genuine horror at this prospect because at the last minute she settled for an animated wave.

'We are so thrilled to be publishing your blog! We all love you so much.'

B wondered if it was his nationality or his personality which made him instantly suspicious of this. He wanted to pull her bony elbow towards him and ask – Do you really? What's your favourite recipe? Do you ever read the nasty comments below? And if so, do you get a whiff of racism underlying the potato accusations levelled against me? Yes, my recipes rely heavily on potatoes but that is the point. We NEED to reduce our dependence on meat. Potatoes are a great way of feeling satisfied without killing the planet. Nobody criticizes Ottolenghi for shoving chickpeas down our throat and the man cannot move past that legume. Instead, B settled for thank you.

The receptionist showed him into an office with floor-to-ceiling windows. The view was largely made up of cranes and smog, but the scale was impressive. He rarely saw London from up high. He was used to navigating the busy pavements and getting bashed through tube stations. Up here, the city felt contained below him. Safe at a distance.

He wandered further into the room. There on the desk was the first copy of his book. In bold across the top, it read 'The Eco-Friendly Meat Eater' followed by 'B. Eustice' in italics along the bottom. In the photo, he was standing in Jeff's kitchen, the turquoise Moroccan tiles behind him, arms folded, a tea towel thrown casually over his shoulder and a relaxed smile curling at the side of his mouth. He looked confident, like he didn't have overactive sweat glands or sleepless nights. He looked like the person he had always hoped he would be. It was half thrilling, half terrifying. How had he created this person and how did everybody believe he was real?

Not long after he'd come out, he'd been watching TV with his family. Their favourite contestant on *X Factor* had revealed that they were a dyslexic orphan with three weeks to livc (or something along those lines). B's mum was wailing into a faux fur cushion. His dad turned to him and said approvingly, 'You're not an emotional gay.'

This was questionable. B had spent most of 1998 crying in his bedroom listening to 'My Heart Will Go On' wondering why no onc had taken icebergs more seriously. But at the time his dad's comment had seemed like a compliment – some sort of a salute. It didn't matter whether or not it was true – it gave him a framework for who to be and he was so grateful for the steer that he'd made it true. He had embodied it, built his identity around it.

That strategy had got him through his teens, but he'd moved on since then and knew that suppressing emotions was nothing to celebrate. And yet when tears rose to his eyes now there was still a part of him that tried to quell them. He wasn't an emotional gay. He picked up the book but almost didn't open it. If he saw her name, he might crumble. He risked it.

'For Annabelle.'

People expected you to be scarred when you lost a parent, they advised therapy and were endlessly patient, but what if the parent you'd lost wasn't yours but your best friend's? How could you explain to anyone the seismic gulf of losing the person who'd made you who you are? And now that all his dreams were coming true the one connection he had left to Annabelle had pulled a runner.

Molly would come back. He knew that. She needed time to adjust, to let B go. It might take them a while, but they'd find a way to be each other's everything without having to have nothing else in their lives. He had complete confidence that Molly would come back and yet his heart lurched for her in this moment. It was Molly who'd encouraged him to set up the YouTube channel in the first place. Molly who'd sat up late at night tasting recipes and making up online profiles to leave him endless five-star reviews. She had decided that the term PA was too 1990s – so she curled up in her pyjamas in the damp flat in Finsbury Park emailing sponsors and suppliers and press claiming to be from B's 'team' like B was Kim Kardashian. She made phone calls too – her accent a wild creation that if asked about she leant into, claiming to be from a remote part of Québec and googling details of small towns as she spoke, delightedly telling whoever was on the other end of the line how she could only get home via a milk route that takes twelve hours from Montréal.

He missed Molly in his bones. For better or worse, she was his everything and now she was in some dive in Camden. Or she'd tapped back into the Landscaper Lad cabal and was drinking green tea with a tree surgeon. Either way she'd disappeared so that she wouldn't have to watch him go first. He was half grateful, half furious.

B stuffed the book into his tote. He couldn't discuss a digital marketing campaign now. He didn't want to hear how many billboards his face would be on. How many people would see the cover of his book in the next few weeks. The only two people he wanted to see it couldn't; one was too busy running and the other had crashed into a truck and gone from the most alive person on the planet to stone-cold-dead leaving those around her to wonder if they'd ever get over it.

Making his way out, he explained to the receptionist that he needed to reschedule the meeting. She was strangely relaxed about it, like he hadn't been expected in the first place. Avoiding the elevator, he raced down stairwell after stairwell until he reached fresh air.

He saw the daffodils first. Bunches and bunches of daffodils obscured Jeff's face, but it was definitely him. Jeff's light brown curls bounced in the wind, and he looked shy. Nervous almost. He glanced around him like he was out of place, despite having lived in London for even longer than B had. He wore a pair of jeans and a polo neck. B wondered if Jeff knew that he had been weaning him off hoodies. B had filled their wardrobe with an array of polo necks. This one was dark green, and if B did say so himself, it beautifully highlighted the hint of green in Jeff's brown eyes.

B himself wasn't good-looking. But he could do you one better. He was profoundly self-aware. He knew his best features (soft skin, not too hairy, tall enough) and his worst (strawberry blond and corresponding pale pallor, chubby cherub-like face that is great at nine, less so at twenty-nine). He knew what he was good at (blogging, being on camera, cooking and tweezing stray hairs with only his fingers) and how good he was at each of these things (top tier, middle tier, lower middle tier, unparalleled). He knew his strengths (chameleon-like adaptation skills in social situations, even-keeled in an increasingly over-effusive society) and his weaknesses (Terry's Chocolate Orange and being too even-keeled in an increasingly over-effusive society). He knew who liked him (mums, Lululemoners and anyone with a dark sense of humour). He knew who didn't like him (die-hard vegans, unsuccessful vloggers and for some reason Molly's cousin Bobby). He even knew how to meld to those who didn't like him. But he never melded for Jeff.

He had never felt the need to impress Jeff. For the first few weeks they were dating, B saw him as a nice but boring numbers guy. Until one day he woke up and realized that all the other guys he'd been chasing – minor celebrities, other vloggers, and medium-tier chefs – all paled in comparison to this polite, innocuous financial wizard.

The daffodils parted and Jeff's face broke into a smile. His beautiful eyes blinked three times before he was able to shake off his tic by holding his eyes shut and counting for five seconds. Looking at Jeff scrunch his entire face, B felt a rush of blood giving him tingles all over. Jeff was his curly-haired, daffodil-bearing man. A man with a nervous tic who had waited in this unseasonably wet March to bring him flowers. B's partial fury at Molly gave way entirely to gratitude. She wanted him to have this. She was giving him a grace period and he needed to take it. His face was on the cover of a book. He was the Eco-Friendly Meat Eater. He was the man in the kitchen with the turquoise Moroccan tiles. He stepped forward into the life he had always wanted.

8. DANNY

Dublin, March 15th 2019

A light mist coated the grass and he realized that it must be nearly morning. The mist made him feel safe, like there was nothing beyond the blur of white in front of him. He stopped on the gravel path and wondered what part of the park he was in. He knew he'd come in the Parkgate Street entrance, but everything was different in the dark. Whole nights, long journeys, parts of the city disappeared when he walked. That's why he did it. To make everything disappear.

Most days, he left the house at 5 p.m. He arrived at the pub with the after-work crowd, nestled into a corner and listened to their complaints, their advice, their consolations and their triumphs. On certain days he knew to expect certain groups. On Thursdays the place filled with the shirts and ties from the bank across the road. On Fridays it was the graphic designers who wore brightly coloured jumpers and drank pale ales.

The graphic designers spoke a language he didn't recognize. They compared recipes for hummus and recommended podcasts like they were giving each other a kidney. Even though they had their own vocabulary, they were warm and carefree in a way that was addictive to watch. They were relaxed in each other's company and unfailingly polite. He saw them on the rare occasions he was out in the daytime too; queuing outside cafés for brunch, cycling colourful bikes, drinking non-alcoholic beer. They ran marathons and cooked for each other. They were light and bubbly and kind. They weren't scared or shame-filled or downcast. They weren't alcoholics.

No matter the group, the pub was always empty by midnight and that's when Danny walked. He walked for hours, crossing the city in the dead of night. He walked midweek to soak in the silence. He had made it clear across the city to the North Bull Island, he had walked the entire length of Clontarf Road. He'd walked the South Circular, past the dregs of partiers on Camden and Leeson Street. He had wandered the leafy suburbs imagining the people curled up in bed inside. He'd followed the canal until it reached the docks. He'd passed through the clusters of glass apartments at Grand Canal, wondering at this city he'd grown up in, not recognizing it and wondering if it recognized him.

In the Phoenix Park, he realized that he was still standing in the same spot. Underfoot he could feel that the sole of his shoe was about to give way. He felt the faint pain of the tiny pebbles that had inserted themselves into crevices. The drink must have worn off because he hadn't noticed a single second of the last five hours, but now, all of a sudden he was completely aware of everything. The pebbles in his shoes, the dark sky, movement at the edges of the trees, and the mist. The mist no longer felt safe. Suddenly, it was encroaching on him, coming for him. He wanted to be back in his mother's house but remembered he had no idea where he was. He would be able to find his way back when the sun was fully up, but it wouldn't be light for another two hours and that felt like a lifetime. Still, he was used to it. Waiting was all he'd ever done. He lay down on the nearest bench and closed his eyes.

When he woke, a rough hand was shaking his curled-up body. Almost immediately it came for him; desperation filling his whole being. The familiarity of the feeling didn't make it any less painful. Despair was like the cold, it came from within and once it took hold it was all encompassing, hard to imagine you'd ever be warm again.

Danny expected to see a guard about to tell him to move on, but when his eyes adjusted to the light, a man with a weathered face and wiry white hair was pointing across the grass, whispering loudly.

'Look.'

Standing in the mist, a stag was staring directly at them. The mist came almost to the stag's bony knees and his chest was wide and broad. He was close enough that Danny could make out his caramel eyes and serious expression.

'Shove over.'

The gangly white-haired man nudged Danny upright on the bench, pulling his purple nylon tracksuit up at the knees and sitting down beside him.

With all his might, Danny willed the man not to say anything else. He clenched his fists tight like they could block the man out because he wanted to stay in this moment with only him and the stag before the dread took over. Somehow, staring into the stag's eyes was keeping the despair from enveloping him. The man must have sensed this because it was sometime before he said anything. When he finally spoke, his voice was low and deliberate.

'My name is Frank and I know who you are.'

Danny wasn't going to engage. He was going to stay silent until this dawn-walking old man with his wiry white hair and his weathered face – weathered hands, weathered everything – left to go bother some other poor soul.

'I know who you are because I used to be you.'

Frank's voice was still low, but any tentativeness was gone, replaced with a measured authority.

'A drunk. A drunk who thinks it's all over.'

Danny turned to look at the man. He wasn't just weathered, he was weather-beaten. His face was a ruddy red and his hands looked like they'd recently mixed cement. His knees jiggled on the bench.

People had tried to save Danny before. His family, the odd friend from a building site – although most of them were alcoholics too, if not professional then highly qualified amateurs. He wondered what this old haggard man in a purple nylon tracksuit knew that they didn't.

Danny couldn't be saved. The best he could hope for now was to cause as little bother as possible for the rest of his days.

'Someday. Not for a whole day or even for an hour, but for a few minutes someday you will consider getting your life together, and when you do here's my number.'

Frank handed Danny a tattered piece of paper with a phone number on it, as if he kept it in his pocket for just this purpose. Danny didn't tell him that he didn't own a phone. That the multiple phones his siblings had bought him sat unopened in drawers in his mother's house because a phone would tether him to the world in a way that he wasn't able for. Frank stood and broke into a speed walk in the opposite direction, moving his elbows violently into the early morning sun.

Danny turned back to the stag. Any second now the broad-chested animal would move, and the moment would be lost. But instead, it was the sun that moved. It began to wash the stag in a weak yellow. Danny caught the animal's eye again and for a few minutes the despair wasn't swallowing him whole. He took a deep breath and tried to hold on to the brief respite as long as he possibly could.

9. LADY V

Dublin, March 19th 2019

People were always surprised to find out how much V loved Mike. Or maybe they weren't surprised that she loved him, but they were surprised to discover that she showed it. When he had walked into the hospital yesterday, her whole body relaxed. Her shoulders released and she let go of a tiny bit of air she didn't even know she was holding. His large frame enveloped her tiny one and she could see the nurses trying not to stare. Mike's face had remained full of concern until he was allowed to wheel her to the door of the hospital and scoop her into the Land Rover. Being so well-minded had made the whole ordeal almost pleasant but the meds must have been strong too because when she woke this morning her ankle was on fire and she was in a foul humour. The only thing for it was to get to work.

V hadn't thought through how to shower or wash her hair in the cast so the whole thing took over an hour. By the time she was up and ready it was already eight o'clock, two hours later than her usual departure time. She was grabbing her keys when Mike appeared at the top of the landing.

'Where on earth do you think you are going?'

'To the gym.'

'To do what?'

'Work.'

She was confused by the smile on Mike's face as he walked slowly down the stairs. He was buttoning a white shirt over his greying chest hair. He smelt like sandalwood from the aftershave she had gotten him for his birthday. He was stocky with a tyre of fat around his middle, but somehow he pulled it off.

Last night he had asked exactly how she had broken her ankle and instead of telling him the embarrassing truth, she had managed to blame someone else: that stupid girl with the clogs who really did leave too much soap on the floor when she mopped. She just happened not to have been mopping anywhere near the treadmill at 5.45 when V tripped and fell.

It wasn't even just a trip, it was like something you'd see on *You've Been Framed*. For some reason she'd lost her focus and then in a split second she'd lost her footing and done all the things that the signs – she herself had written – told you not to do. She desperately tried to grab at something, but the machine was running at level eight and it flung her across the room. She bashed backwards into dumbbells and landed with her ankle sticking out in all the wrong places like a scene from a gory horror movie. She lay there feeling something she hadn't felt in a long time. Besides the acute pain of her most likely broken ankle, she felt frightened. She thought of what that fool in the top knot had said about her being past her prime and now here she was on the floor, unable to move, having fallen like an old woman. She couldn't tell anyone. She had to find a way to downplay it. It was the girl in the clogs who'd found her. That's what gave V the idea to blame her.

'And how do you think you'll get to work?'

Mike placed his hands on her hips. She had completely forgotten the nurse's warning that she wouldn't be able to drive in the hard cast. The nurse had mentioned a period of time so long that in her morphinesque state V had thought she was joking.

'I can wait for you to drop me.'

Mike was still smiling as he kissed her forehead.

'I will be doing no such thing, V.'

Being housebound wasn't so bad at the beginning. She hung around while Mike got ready and humoured him as he tried to build her a pillow fortress on the couch, from which she immediately escaped after feeling a genuine pang of claustrophobia. Then the twins emerged.

Despite the pain and the impending boredom, she smiled as she watched them run for the bus, Liam admonishing Damon for delaying them and Damon serenely absorbing being yelled at while eating a cinnamon bun. Such was her joy at witnessing them grab their backpacks at nineteen just like when they were five, the thought occurred to her that maybe she should stay home more often. But that was at 10 a.m.

By 11 a.m. she had organized a painter to repaint the railings, paid the gas, electricity and next semester's college fees, she had cleaned the fridge and done an online food shop. She spent the next hour devising a new Strength and Conditioning workout that weaved a course of burpees, box jumps, prowler, shuttle runs and squats. She sent it to the head trainers at every gym for their input. It was now midday and she was starving. But she avoided the kitchen because food was going to pose a problem.

Now that she couldn't exercise, she would have to reduce her food intake drastically. This wasn't new; she was used to starving herself. Before the twins, she'd never set foot in a gym, none of the models back then had. They had subsisted on cigarettes, gin and narcotics (but V likes to ignore that part of the 1990s). If she couldn't exercise, she couldn't eat, and if she couldn't eat then she would need a plan for the next four weeks until she could get a soft cast and presumably at least do upper body exercises. She would need a distraction. A project. Something to count. Something to measure. Something that would give her the sense of achievement that she had enough self-awareness to know she was slightly addicted to.

She could call a friend. She had friends. Nicely contained friends who she had lunch with. They met once a month in a cocktail bar for a glass of Champagne before heading around the corner to Marcel's for an entirely liquid lunch. The topics up for discussion were new kitchens, new cars and new husbands (in that order) and detailing anything awful that had happened to their nemeses that could be celebrated. Mike called them the Botox Bettys. But Liam said they were more like the Schadenfreude Sheilas.

Everything was fuelled by competition. Whose husband was more successful, whose children were most popular/sporty/good-looking/smart (the latter was less interesting). They each found wonderfully creative ways to boast. The secret was to wrap the boast up as a major catastrophe. At the last lunch Camilla had told the girls she was desperately worried about her daughter Afric; the entire Irish rugby team wanted to marry her; what would Camilla do?

They were so competitive that they'd each been known to postpone the lunch to coincide with major deals that the others would have to congratulate them on. Imelda had asked to meet the Saturday after her kitchen extension was featured in *The Sunday Times*. Camilla had moved the lunch to after her modelling agency got bought up by Elite. Jacqui had rescheduled for just after she'd opened a new boutique, and even V had postponed it until after she suspected she might win Business Woman of the Year last year (which she did). She wasn't going to call them now that she was down. They'd phone each other behind her back and speculate on whether she'd fallen because she had an incurable brain tumour – or, worse, was ageing badly. It was a generational thing, she told herself. Her generation hadn't known about non-competitive, vulnerable friendships the way girls now did and it was too late to start.

She hobbled into the living room and lay on the carpet. She did round after round of pelvic floor exercises. She might end up smelly and forgetful in a nursing home, but she wouldn't be peeing herself and that was something. She stretched her arms over her head and counted as she pulsed her biceps. The day ahead seemed endless and she'd no concept of how to fill it.

Did she really spend this much time at the gym? And how could she possibly be this hungry? She figured she was only hungry most of the time because of all the exercise, but she couldn't afford to be this hungry without being able to work off anything she ate. A flare of anxiety shot through her. She turned on the radio and tried to ignore a rising panic. When the house phone rang, she dived for the receiver.

'Mike?'

'No, Veronica, it's John here. I was just looking for Mike. I'm terribly sorry to hear about your accident. That woman with the clogs sounds frightfully irresponsible. What was she doing wearing clogs in this weather anyway? As a shoe expert I can tell you they are wildly unsuitable for Ireland's temperate maritime climate. You were very good not to fire her immediately. Wet floors are a LETHAL business. You could have DIED. But I digress. How ARE you?'

Usually V avoided John like glazed doughnuts but now his voice was oddly reassuring. She was comforted by his outrage on her behalf and almost felt outrage herself despite the fact that it was a complete fabrication.

'Good, John, good. Look, I've been thinking. Do you need any help with this Molly thing?'

There was a silence uncharacteristic for any of the Blacks.

'That's why I was calling. Truth be told, Veronica, I'm very worried.'

V wasn't prepared for this response. She'd brought it up on impulse, thinking that maybe she could ring around some of Molly's friends, keep herself busy. She wanted a project, not a late middle-aged man to have a nervous breakdown on her watch. She waited for him to say more but he just breathed slowly at the other end of the line. Lord have mercy.

'Look, John, leave it with me. I have a few ideas.'

'Do you?'

'I'm very good at stalking people on the internet. Let me see what I can do.'

V hung up the phone, her momentary pang of fondness for her brother-in-law already dwindling. The clan-like mentality of the Black family was oppressive. They lost the plot when one of them peeked beyond the pale. The girl had most likely shacked up with one of those bearded chaps who wore far too much gingham or fallen in love with some eejit in a bedsit in Brighton. V was already regretting volunteering for the task. It would draw her into a web of people and communication she'd rather do without. She had worked hard to live a life of clean lines, of functional relationships based on a perfectly calibrated level of distance, and the Black family had generally left her to it. Except Annabelle. Annabelle hadn't known the meaning of the word distance. Even now, V got a strange feeling when she thought of Annabelle, ill at ease like she was out of her depth. Like Annabelle knew something about her that she didn't know herself.

Jumping up to distract herself from this uncomfortable thought, V forgot her broken ankle and nearly tripped over herself. Pain shot up through her cast and she cursed all the expletives she could think of. She dragged herself into the kitchen and got a pen. At least now she had a project.

V would find Molly. Once she'd tracked her down in some depressing hellhole, V would fly to London. She would stay in Claridge's, put her foot up, have Molly over for afternoon tea and give her a talking to about B moving in with this billionaire. She would tell her how unhealthy it was – being in love with a gay man. It was holding her back. They would get their nails done. Maybe a blow-dry. V would be the hero. She sat at the kitchen table and made a list of all the potential information sources she could use to track Molly. But in the end, it only took seconds. Ten days ago Molly had been tagged in a photo by someone called Ned Fortune. The location was so far from home it sent shivers down V's spine.

10. JOHN

Dublin, March 19th 2019

There were plenty of stationery shops near Leopardstown but heading into town made John feel purposeful. Town was more professional. And the place on Baggot Street was a cut above the rest. They took stationery seriously. They allocated you a booth where a stationery specialist gave you a one-to-one consultation on your stationery needs. Today John's needs were multi-fold. He took out his pen on the 46A and began to make a list.

He planned to buy thirteen mini-notebooks for each member of the family. Spiral bound at the short edge side would seem to make sense, but he would take the specialist's advice on the best product in the small notebook range. The primary purpose of the notebook would be for everyone to jot down the last time they had heard from Molly but he'd also like them to note down anything they remembered her saying in the last few weeks. People she'd mentioned, parts of England she'd like to visit. He'd heard the Lake District was very nice, could she be there for instance, holed up reading some Jane Austen? Even John had to admit that seemed unlikely. Either way, John himself would trawl through the notes and collate anything of interest for the Guards.

The guards had been very sympathetic but not at all concerned. They kept repeating that Molly was a grown woman and that she had left a note. It turned out that people who were nearly thirty were allowed to run away. According to one sergeant, all the college-educated yuppies were climbing Machu Picchu – had they tried there? Climbing Machu Picchu was just what you did these days, he said, like in their day when you got a job.

John had probably popped down to the station one too many times and he could tell now that they thought he was a sad busybody with nothing better to do. But what about how she might have seen Sheena Griffith that night, he kept asking? Apparently, they had a new lead on that case and John hadn't heard from the UK police since. When he'd been at the station yesterday the Guard at the desk hadn't recognized him, so she'd asked him if he was Molly's dad. After all these years, John still hated the moment when he had to say no.

He thought of it as a room. The room was filled with all the things that would have happened if they'd been able to have children. Not toys and clothes. More like the types of people they might have become. For instance, maybe he and Helen would look different. Maybe he would have gone bald from all the worry and Helen wouldn't still have such a small waist. Maybe Helen would have given up teaching by now and maybe John wouldn't have sold the shoe shop but had a daughter in there running the place.

He never pictured sons because his own father was so hell bent on them. Instead, he pictured a smart-as-a-button daughter who surprised them at every turn. A no-nonsense lawyer who threw her eyes up to heaven when he and Helen asked her about getting married. Or a sporty daughter who was always out practising something or other, coming home red-faced with strands of hair stuck to her cheeks. The sporty one would always be starving. And maybe because of that, because of them, John would have learnt to cook. And maybe on Sundays when the lawyer and the sports star came home John would be a different person, pulling shepherd's pies out of the oven as the girls threw their arms around him for a hug.

It was best to keep it all in one room. To watch these thoughts come and let them into the room. Not locked away or shut up or anything as dramatic as that, just in the one place so that it didn't hurt in multiple locations. And the truth was – he could be happy about that room. He often smiled imagining it. It wasn't the end of the world to have these thoughts. It wasn't tragic or morose. More often than not it was heart-warming. Maybe these girls existed in some parallel universe and when he thought of them it was like he was just paying them a visit.

Of course, now he wished they'd adopted when they'd been young enough to. People thought they hadn't because they'd just kept hoping it would happen for them, and that was true, but the real reason was fear. His fear. Not Helen's. John was terrified that the powers that be would look at his finances, at the business or even just at him, at his lack of education, at his background and find him wanting. He was terrified that a tight-lipped, well-educated man or woman from the government would arrive at their door or issue a letter confirming to John what he knew already – that he wasn't good enough for the lawyer or the sports star.

So, it was his fault. And the thing about Helen was that she hadn't a bone in her body that could hold it against him. She loved him so thoroughly that it was like it had been her decision too. And sometimes that made it worse. But mainly it just made him count his lucky stars that he was blessed to marry a woman as wonderful as Helen.

And as well as a happy marriage, he'd had his work. He'd made his way up from working as a clerk to buy the whole shoe shop. That wasn't something to be sniffed at. He'd sold shoes to half of Dublin – and many celebrities. There was Claudia who did the traffic for the AA on the radio. She came in every October for a pair of brown leather boots. All the TDs for the local constituency knew not to bother knocking on doors if they weren't wearing a pair of Black's loafers and one time John even fitted a man who looked very like the man who might have murdered that woman in Mayo. He'd fitted many criminals actually. One quite distressing murderer who'd burnt his wife to a crisp but also some lovely minor criminals. Every year he sent a pair of smart loafers to an Englishman who'd fled to the Caribbean to avoid being arrested for tax fraud. He'd stolen millions from Her Majesty's Revenue and Customs, but Harold always paid for postage.

John looked out the window and saw that it was about to rain again. The country was just recovering from two weeks of battering. They'd been hit by storm after storm and John half wondered if the weather was what had stopped Molly from coming home in recent weeks. Maybe she'd wanted to, but flights had been cancelled because of the storms.

Since Molly had left that note, all he could think about was Christmas. It had always been a landmark. No matter how long Molly was away, at least they knew they'd see her at the end of the year. Inadvertently, John shook his head. It was his fault. His mother was deteriorating and taking up more of his time and he'd been caught up with stupid Proinsias Murtagh. He should have got onto Molly earlier, booked flights for her if she didn't have the money.

He knew that she'd enjoyed being on her own and that she'd strolled all of London on a crisp Christmas Day – but still, he needed to lay eyes on her – they all did – just from time to time to make sure her small frame was managing to hold all that grief. He didn't care that she was nearly thirty. Why did people keep telling him that? Danny was fifty-two and John would never *not* be looking in doorways, hoping against hope that passed-out heaps were not his baby brother.

'You hear about that doctor?'

John hadn't noticed the two women who'd sat down in front of him. The younger one was scrolling through her phone, despite impeding gigantic blue nails.

'There was loads of texts on her phone from a doctor in the hospital where she worked.'

'It's clearly him that done it. It's always the creepy doctor. Where is he from, Pakistan or somewhere?'

'Mam, you are some racist you are. He is actually from Roscommon. Red hair and all on him.'

'Sure that's worse. I'd take a handsome Indian-looking fella over a Culchie any day.'

John jumped as his phone rang. He thought he had

been caught listening to the racist. He desperately wanted to know more. Any time he heard Sheena Griffith's name mentioned he felt the blood drain from his head with terror. He picked up the phone when he saw V's name flashing across the screen.

'Veronica, you must be calling about thc development in the Sheena Griffith case. This doctor sounds very dodgy indeed.'

'John, Molly is in Bangkok.'

John's heart seemed to stall but his brain was already racing.

He knew all about Bangkok. He'd seen a documentary which detailed the sex workers and drugs and full moons and exposed elcctrical wires all over beaches and something to do with ping pong balls that he couldn't get his head around.

'You can't be scrious.'

But already he knew that she was.

11. MOLLY

25th December 2018

Molly hadn't planned to spend Christmas alone. At first, she didn't have the money for the flights – she'd spent it on a pop-up restaurant. Then the flights had shot up and by the time she had money again, even the boat back to Dublin was sold out. Being alone for Christmas couldn't be that bad – it was two or three days. B wasn't flying until the 23rd and other friends would be back in the city by the 26th. It might even be nice to have the place to herself.

She figured she'd walk. Christmas Day itself would be crisp and cold but bright and sunny. She'd start off early and go straight down Farringdon Road until she hit the river. Then she'd walk along the Thames until Waterloo Bridge. She would wind up through Covent Garden, strolling all the squares, Bedford, Russell, Gordon and Tavistock. Maybe there would be other people out, and in a brief exception to big city rules they'd nod at each other, even say Happy Christmas. She thought she would march until her nose was cold and her feet sore. But in the end, she wasn't even able to stand, let alone walk.

She'd fallen asleep on the couch in the living room and in the dead hours of Christmas morning, sharp pains stabbed at her sides. Immediately she pictured the previous night's takeaway. The spicy prawns she'd thought were different enough to take advantage of her first Christmas Eve alone. A dull light shone from the TV and a draught she wasn't used to shuttled in from the front windows. She started for the bathroom but didn't make it. The prawns came up in a pale pink mush punctuated by green chillies and flecks of red pepper. She heaved into the dark until it felt like there was nothing left, but still she retched. The TV flashed in her peripheral vision, blurring as her knees gave way. There was a moment before she fainted when she thought, how strange it was that this was happening in the deep stillness of Christmas morning.

When she regained consciousness the smell of vomit hit her, and she tried to sit up. She tried to clean up the sick, searching for kitchen roll, but her knees were kindling now, and they kept bending without warning until she lurched for the bathroom. This time she managed to make it to the toilet. After retching bile, she slumped down the side of the toilet and rested her cheek on the cold tiles. She knew she should try to drink some water but moving was beyond her, so she lay on the cold tiles alternating between vomiting and falling in and out of an eerie semi-consciousness.

In her dreamlike state, she found herself at home in her childhood house in Rathgar. She couldn't see them, but her parents were there too. There was no talking but familiar movements and noises and even smells hovered in the rooms near her – just out of reach. She had ten years longer with her mum, ten more years of memories, and yet when she dreamt of home, she always dreamt of both of them. Her dad wasn't always visible, but he was always there because there was a togetherness about them that couldn't be splintered. What was hazy and unclear sometimes became vivid and real.

At one point, Molly was sitting at the kitchen table. Her mum was sitting opposite their neighbour Kimberley. Kimberley's parents were undertakers, and her father had run away with the mortuary cosmetologist. Annabelle had an open-door policy for all of Dublin (especially for people with interesting stories that involved mortuary cosmetologists) and Kimberley was often there, at the kitchen table trying on hats or asking advice.

This particular night Kimberley's boyfriend had asked her to marry him. Kimberley was sitting in a feather boa drinking a cup of tea mulling over whether or not to say yes like she had been asked to go to a movie. Annabelle was out of sight. At one point it seemed like she was washing up, at another she was pruning a plant. But from somewhere she asked Kimberley if she loved her boyfriend or not. Kimberley paused as if she'd never really much thought about it. She reached out for a digestive biscuit.

'Well, I do like seeing his clothes hanging beside my clothes in the wardrobe.'

There was a cackle of laughter and the sound of Annabelle climbing the stairs. After a few moments rustling in her bedroom Annabelle placed an old corduroy jacket of Bernard's on the table.

'Stick this in your wardrobe and then see how you feel.'

Molly still couldn't see her mum's face, but she could hear her riotous laugh and she knew that Kimberley had laughed too. It had seemed funny and ridiculous and light at the time – but in her dream, Molly knew that it wasn't. It wasn't funny at all.

Kimberley had someone else's clothes hanging in her wardrobe. Her life was intertwined with someone else's. Someone reminded her to take out the bins. Someone knew what time she'd be home at. Kimberley wasn't wrong, Molly wanted to scream – over the digestives, into the soft light she wanted to roar that it was the small things that made you belong to someone else. Molly awoke to a feeling of trepidation as if she knew something in her dreams that she had yet to realize in real life.

She'd been very sick before. She'd the flu for a week on an air mattress one sweltering summer in New York. Her stomach had churned for much of her travels through South America. And yet somehow lying on the cold floor of the bathroom in the early hours of Christmas morning, this didn't feel like those other times. The other times had been awful and depressing but she knew they'd pass. Everything passes. She tried to tell herself that this would pass too, but as she lay there, it didn't just feel like food poisoning, it felt like running out of rope. In six months she would turn thirty. Thirty year olds had lives. They had careers and children and houses. They could, at the very least, mind themselves.

She knew that in a few hours her phone would start ringing in the other room, that Uncle John and B would call, and Bobby and Anne would text. Other friends would share heart-warming Christmas ads, and at first, she thought it was energy stopping her. She thought that when she had the energy, she'd call John and tell him what had happened – but she knew in her heart that it wasn't just the sickness she wanted to tell him about.

She was used to asking for help – she'd asked for money, for flights home, for John to speak to landlords and the police and anyone else she'd gotten on the wrong side of. She was used to being wild Molly, exasperating Molly, cheeky Molly, but still after all these years she hadn't found the words to be sad Molly. She would have felt more comfortable calling her family to say she'd been arrested than that she was lonely.

She had all the words in the world. More than her fair share, but somehow she couldn't talk about loneliness; couldn't make the words come out seriously. No matter how hard she tried, she couldn't seem to make them honest and not wrap whatever she said up in a joke that would make everybody feel better. So, she joked and did all the things that people said made her so easy, so light, so fun. But she knew now that she was running out of steam. The sands were shifting and what seemed before like a big broad landscape of friends and adventures was beginning to feel like a gaping hole; an empty wardrobe with nobody's clothes but her own. After retching once again, she slid down the side of the empty toilet bowl and willed herself back to Rathgar.

This time, Kimberley was gone and the end-of-day light was splintering the kitchen into bright and dark patches. Molly was standing at the sink. Down the back of the garden, the old treehouse slid sideways down the oak tree. Beside an incomplete patio, carefully placed stones marked out two circles of flowers. She could hear her mum moving tools and operatizing pop songs. A high-pitched version of 'What if God Was One of us?' Echoed around the garden. Her dad was somewhere in the house, in the front room marking papers or upstairs reading, and for a few seconds she held them; one in front of her, one behind her. She let herself feel the warm glow of safety that came from belonging to someone.

When she finally woke again something had changed. The darkness had lifted and there was a weak grey light hitting the tiles. Her body felt different too; she still felt weak but the power of the food poisoning– the visceral control it had had on her – had lessened and she knew what she had to do. She stumbled unevenly into her room. She found her phone in the crumpled bed sheets, and she used every emoji she could find to send love to her uncles and aunts, to her friends and to B. She told them about the beautiful winter walk she was about to embark on and all her plans for the day. She sent smiles and kisses and tried to be what she'd always been – light and easy. She threw the phone back on the bed just before the retching began again.

12. ANNE

Cork, March 18th 2019

There are well-known behavioural patterns that should be adhered to on work trips. For starters you never ever booked a seat right beside your colleague. You politely let them know which train to Cork you would be on. You might even chat to them over coffee if you happened to meet in Heuston Station. Then you gave them a polite but closed-mouth smile/nod and told them you'd see them at your final destination. If by some complete disaster you ended up right beside them on the train, you made small talk until you were just past Inchicore, then you nodded towards your laptop and said, 'Back to the old grind.'

Alastair Stairs was not complying with the etiquette. He had squeezed into the seat right next to Anne, and by Portlaoise he had told her so much about himself, she wondered if she had inadvertently asked him for his life story – either way, she got it. Alastair Stairs was an only child. It was just him, Mum and the dogs. Mum loved *Strictly Come Dancing* and still could *not* believe the son of a shop assistant had become an accountant. But his interests were not limited to accountancy. He was passionate about model aeroplanes and pork – pulled pork, stuffed pork, some sort of Vietnamese caramelized pork that his granny makes – the ways in which pork is undervalued in society, and reading histories of middle England. He felt strongly that no one talks enough about the plague. The plague took between three and five days to incubate in people before they got sick. Then, it was another three to five days before (in 80 per cent of cases) patients died. Did Anne know that it had killed an estimated twenty-five million people in Europe alone? He continued to talk about the plague from Portlaoise to Templemore. This part was actually quite interesting because at least Anne learnt something transferable. Learning that Anton Du Beke was born in July was of no value to her.

'What about you?'

'I have a brother in Australia.'

When it came to family, Anne always led with Killian. He was simple to explain. He was a salesman. He had a socio-behavioural condition that people referred to as charm. If she talked about her brother, then she didn't have to explain her missing father or religious zealot mother. Or worse, her extended family.

At some point in their lives, each member of the Black family had received a badge. Molly was fun. Bobby was a sports star. Blur was wild, Oasis a scientific genius. Uncle John was the family hero. Uncle Danny the family disappointment. These oversimplified caricatures of aunts and uncles at least had decades to form, but for the nieces and nephews it happened in an instant. They'd been permanently marked by something they'd said in the back garden when they were three years old, which completely determined who they were going to be, according to the amateur child psychologist aunts and uncles drinking Chardonnay on the lawn.

At its most positive, Anne's badge was competence. In reality, she knew that the family saw her as fastidious, tightly wound, annoying even. Anne led teams of auditors, she gave major presentations to CEOs, she ran workshops and even on occasion advised the government. Out here in the world she was somebody. But then a family birthday rolled around or the annual haiku competition ramped up and she found herself sitting on the floor, washing dishes in the kitchen or doing someone's tax return for them.

Sometimes she felt like she was suffocating under the weight of a family who all seemed to slot so easily in with each other. She could see them glaze over when she spoke, all the while presuming that she would always show up. Instead of competence being a helpful trait to have, it seemed to deem her uninteresting and for some reason to preclude her from having any other personality traits. She was a safe bet – that was all. No one ever had to worry about Anne – if they ever thought about her at all. Anne gazed out the train window considering whether and how to nip this personal chit-chat in the bud but for some reason she continued.

'I have a cousin who always runs away.'

'That's an interesting hobby.'

'Not for those who have to find her. She's run off to Thailand now.'

'Wow. That's something. Will you go find her?'

Anne stared out at the passing fields wondering the same thing herself.

'What is she like?'

Anne almost did a double take; what was Molly Black like? She realized that she might never in her life have been asked that question before. Everyone she knew well, knew Molly and she didn't talk about her family to anyone else. She didn't talk about anything with anyone else. Alastair was smiling politely at her, but she didn't know where to start.

Somehow by Limerick Junction, Anne was telling Alastair about the time Molly had convinced the family that she'd won the Lotto. The jackpot had rolled over for weeks until it was the biggest amount in Irish Lottery history – €18.9 million. The minute the numbers were drawn on Saturday at 7.55 p.m., Molly went straight to the shop and asked for the exact numbers that had just been announced. Helen and John were hosting a summer party, but the rain had abruptly ruined the event. Drenched in their shorts and sun dresses the family congregated in the Good Room. Molly flicked on the nine o'clock news to check out a particularly grizzly murder she wanted to follow up on. She needn't have said more. The Blacks loved a good murder. She said she might keep watching till the end as she happened to have done the Lotto that week and sometimes the news had a reminder of the numbers called earlier that evening. When the numbers were called out, she stayed silent. One by one the family turned to look at her, pale-faced, as she stared at the ticket. Uncle Mike grabbed it from her hands.

'Holy Mary Mother of God.'

In hindsight it was actually quite a dangerous prank.

Mike was not a fit man, and his brother had died of a heart attack. He pushed the twins out of the way so he could sit down and told someone else to check it. One by one they each checked the ticket. It took a few moments for any of them to become euphoric but once they did it was just like the plague – highly contagious. Champagne was produced and the twins' heads hit the roof as they jumped on the couch. But Molly's performance was only beginning. She silently walked to the top of the room and took the ticket back. They were all watching her, expecting a speech, when she ripped it into eight pieces then threw it into the fire that she'd insisted Helen light.

'Money is a cruel master. I want no part in its mind games.'

The funniest part was that it sounded exactly like something she might have said if she *had* won the Lotto. It took about an hour to explain to every member of the family that she hadn't actually won in the first place. Most people were *furious*. Funnily enough Lady V found it hysterical. She had a chronic fear of becoming too wealthy even though she was well on her way, so she was relieved. In an uncharacteristic burst of nostalgia, she told Anne how the prank made her miss Annabelle. Uncle Mike stormed out of the party and didn't speak to Molly for a month. Helen silently lamented opening the Champagne she'd won in a raffle at the school that she'd being saving for eleven years.

Anne suddenly realized how strange it was to find herself convulsed with laughter on a Monday morning talking to this virtual stranger. She looked up quickly to gauge his reaction. Alastair had taken his glasses off to wipe his eyes.

He was snorting so hard his eyes had started to water. Anne realized she couldn't think of a time when she – Anne Black – had ever made anyone laugh so hard. For some reason she felt like she should pull back in some way, compose herself, but the carriage was next to empty. Alastair was beaming at her now and she could see no reason not to continue laughing.

'You got your glasses fixed.'

'Yes, well, you seemed to feel quite strongly about it.'

The heat rose to her face. Between the hysterical laughter and the sudden embarrassment, she could feel herself begin to sweat. Her hair was surely frizzing and was bound to start sticking to her face. The conductor announced that they were pulling into Kent Station. She stole a glance to see if Alastair was annoyed but he was still smiling, his fixed glasses back on his nose. He caught her eye and for a terrible moment she thought he might kiss her. On the INTERCITY to CORK at NINE O'CLOCK on a MONDAY morning. Shockingly, it was followed by a much worse minute when she realized he wasn't going to. He jumped up to grab his bag and made his way to the door.

13. ANNE

Connemara, June 2002

Anne knew that she had only been picked for the relay team because she was Molly's cousin. She knew that the other girls thought she was an annoying tag-along who corrected their grammar and was terrified of being caught speaking English. But she only did that because she thought they were here to learn Irish. It took her several days to realize that they were actually at Irish College to think, talk, dream and fantasize about having a boyfriend.

Anne had no problem with boys. She didn't even have a problem with boyfriends. There was a quiet boy from Wexford who had beautiful pronunciation that she had her eye on. But it was like the girls in the house had been taken ill. They shortlisted potential boyfriends in the morning over cornflakes. They whispered about dumping boyfriends on the way to class within earshot of the unsuspecting dumpee. They passed notes to potential new boyfriends in class when they were supposed to be learning proverbs. They broke away in little clusters on the way to the beach to kiss current boyfriends. Groups of boys and girls disappeared behind ditches and re-emerged minutes later red and giddy like they'd drunk a bottle of vodka in a field in the West of Ireland on a Tuesday afternoon.

They were consumed until it pained them. They were so giddy about what drama would enfold the next day that they couldn't sleep at night. And everything had to happen in an exclusionary whispery huddle. Huddles to plan break ups, huddles to decide the next romance. The boys seemed to have no say. Anne lay awake at night, willing herself not to complain about their constant chatter and wondering why she didn't care as much about boys as the huddle did.

Molly didn't care either but for some reason that elicited awe from the other girls. Molly was only six months older than the rest of them, but the other girls followed her around the house like she was a celebrity. They asked to borrow her clothes for the Céilí. They swapped their neat hairdos for her messy ponytail, carefully curating Molly's exact level of mess in the tiny mirror in the corner of the room.

What no one seemed to notice was that Molly's messy hair was held in place by *Anne's* hair bobbins, that the clothes the girls borrowed were *Anne's* clothes, and even the pink runners from Penneys that they passed around like gold dust were *Anne's*. Annabelle had mixed up Molly's luggage with a bag of props so Molly's brightly coloured cycling shorts and scrunchies had been sent to a community theatre in Cork, and when Anne and Molly had opened Molly's suitcase, they were greeted by two machine guns and a bag of cocaine. After the Bean An Tí who ran the house had called the police and the substance was tested by the Príomhoide from the College, the contents turned out to be two startlingly realistic toy guns and several sandwich bags of Persil. (Anne was actually grateful for the latter because she didn't like sending her underwear to the communal laundry, so she used the fake cocaine to wash her knickers in the sink.) But the convenience of the powder didn't quell the pain of knowing that it wasn't her clothes. It wasn't her hair or her shoes – she had all the right things. It was Anne they didn't like; it was Anne who wasn't cool. In those same clothes, bobbins and runners Molly shone; Molly was worshipped. Molly was even friends with the top tier of boyfriend material; the tallest, most joke-making, tracksuit-wearing rabble who were referred to even by the teachers as 'NA LADS'.

Even Anne had to admit they were alluring. They weren't exclusive like the huddle. They bounded around the school like human baby giraffes only getting used to their infinite limbs. They came from all over the country but were identifiable by the blinding yellow of the bleach they had died each other's hair the first week. When it was your turn to dance with them at the Céilí they threw you around the dancefloor no matter who you were. Even Nerdy Gurty who brought the Harry Potter books to the Céilí could be seen smiling when they got her into a spin on the dancefloor. They had been known to get the teachers up, man or woman, the older the better. But just because they were likeable and fun it didn't mean that they should win the relay race.

For three weeks the teams had competed until there were only two left: the huddle including Molly and Anne versus NA LADS. The whole school was up for NA LADS. Then when the first event began it became clear that even the huddle was up for them. The huddle smiled and giggled at every step, using the relay as a platform to flirt on a public stage. The whole thing was just a performance for them. The masses cheered when Bill came back to help Áine when she fell in the sack race. They whooped and hollered when Cian kissed Isabel on the cheek during the egg and spoon. (Anne thought he was going out with Áine but they must have switched during the relay.) Shauna had used the obstacle course to nudge and wink at Fionn like she was having some sort of seizure.

But it didn't matter now. They would lose the relay anyway. It was Molly's stint and she and Tall Paul were in a race around the grounds out of sight from the masses. Anne stood to attention waiting for Molly to come around the corner with the bunch of flowers she was to pick by the church. When those flowers touched Anne's hands, she was allowed to start dribbling the basketball. Anne gripped the ball tight, ready to go, while her counterpart made jokes for the crowd like he was the hyperactive priest in *Father Ted*. To be fair, he was pretty funny. NA LADS had it all. They could be a great boyband, it occurred to Anne, if Louis Walsh got his hands on them. They might end up being famous and Anne would spend the rest of her life telling people she was at Irish College with them.

Suddenly the grassy hill erupted as Tall Paul came around the corner, his long legs making a metre with each step. The *Father Ted* caricature was raising his arms to rally the crowd like it was the Olympics, but then there she was. Molly was sprinting and she had always been fast. Tall Paul had slowed down to a jog to enjoy the crowd and he didn't notice Molly as her messy ponytail whipped past him. He did a double take but it was too late. Molly only had eyes for Anne. She broke into a smile and held out the supposed bunch of flowers. They were weeds. A nettle stung Anne's knuckle but she didn't hang around to dwell on it; she popped them in the back pocket of her jean shorts and started dribbling the ball. She looked towards the hoop. She could hear the slapping of runners on the concrete behind her. NA LADS all had legs like ostriches, and she knew that her competitor would be at the hoop in seconds, so she took the shot.

One solitary roar emerged from the grassy hill. Nerdy Gurty was standing and cheering like Ireland had just won the Quidditch world cup. The rest of the grassy hill were suspended in disbelief unsure what to do. Suddenly NA LADS piled on Anne. Their excess limbs were everywhere, hugging her, patting her on the back, cheering her. She emerged from their tangle, rising high up onto their shoulders. Anne searched for Molly but couldn't see her among the jean shorts and Gaelic jerseys. She felt herself burn red and suddenly regretted everything; taking the competition so seriously, risking the shot. She should have let them win. She could have slunk into the background while NA LADS did a lap of victory fanned by the huddle.

Instead, the whole school had their eyes on her, and she had no idea where to look or what to do. But slowly the crowd began to follow NA LADS' lead. The grassy hill began cheering and Anne spotted the boy from Wexford with the good grammar. He winked at her. And there was Molly, hugging Gurty on the grassy hill.

Later that night, in their furry bathrobes and matching furry slippers, the other girls would sulk around the fire furious about all the attention Anne got, but it would be worth it. Anne and Molly walked home without them, their arms around each other, the countryside miraculous in the late evening sun, their hair sticky from the sweat of dancing all night, out of breath and full to the brim with happiness.

14. B

London, March 21st 2019

'The ironic thing about vloggers is that they often still worship the tangible world of traditional media. Is that true in your case?'

B didn't like Mags from the start. She had shuffled into Foyles late, her satchel overflowing with papers. Her hair was messy, and she wore baggy jeans like it was the 1990s. In B's vision for the night, the journalists interviewing him were serious people, food critics or environmental activists; intellectuals who saw that he was spearheading an entirely new way of living. Instead, the editor had sent an archaic concept – 'A technology reporter'. Mags wanted to talk about how B had come out of the internet into the real world like Pinocchio becoming a boy.

'Absolutely, Mags. Seeing my face on the tube this morning was almost as big a deal for me as reaching my first hundred thousand subscribers.'

B paused to make sure Mags was writing this down. He knew for a fact that he had more subscribers than her entire paper. She *should* be pausing to ask him how many subscribers he had now. She *should* be impressed by his success, but instead she would write another article about there being 'a large community on YouTube' like they were an obscure sect in middle America and not the rest of the entire world.

Mags droned on about how interesting the internet was and, despite himself, B felt a physical void beside him. Where once he'd been mortified by any attention, terrified by what others thought of him, over time he'd built a curated public version of himself who could operate in the world; who could do interviews and come across as calm, collected and charming. But Molly had always been with him, the two of them treating the whole thing like a game. When *The Sunday Times* had done a feature on him, Molly had joined him and the reporter for brunch; after his interview with *Glamour* they'd brought the reporter to a cocktail bar and stayed out until 4 a.m. Molly would chime in with anecdotes, she'd remember zeitgeisty facts about him that he'd forgotten. As he struggled to know how to behave with Mags, he realized that Molly had co-created this person with him and now that she was gone he wasn't quite sure how to pull off the performance.

'I'm sorry to interrupt.'

B vowed to kiss whoever this was right on the lips. Until he saw that it was the peppy receptionist from the publishers. He was suspicious of her relentless positivity, but still, her intervention was worth a smile. He signalled to Mags that he must run and followed Peppy up the stairs.

The launch party was starting to fill up, but he needed a minute. He stepped into the small annex he'd dropped his satchel in earlier. He wandered towards the tiny window and looked down the street. He told himself that he was looking at people generally. He wasn't looking for Molly.

'You have to let her go.'

Jeff had been cracking eggs for a carbonara last night. The ironic thing was that Jeff was actually a much better cook than B. More intuitive, less structured.

'You have this whole new adventure in front of you. Molly is allowed to have one too, you know?'

B had looked in Jeff's soft brown eyes. He was uncharacteristically worked up. Usually easygoing – he was firm about this; he didn't want B to chase after Molly.

As Jeff held his gaze, B realized that he rarely had his nervous tic. It filled B with warmth to know that Jeff wasn't anxious at home. Jeff returned to cooking and B hugged his back, resting his forehead between his shoulder blades as Jeff continued to stir.

Jeff had bought a new shirt and tie for the event. He'd had his light brown curls cut. He always seemed so self-assured but then there were these glimpses of insecurity; that he wanted to be noticed just like everyone else. He had crossed off the days on the calendar until the launch like a child before Christmas. Molly, on the other hand, had decided to give B so much space she'd fled the country. Was she being frivolous and adventurous or was she a major pain in the fucking ass who lost her mind when things weren't about her? And then somehow still managed to find a way to make it about her in the end? He couldn't spend the rest of his life as her sidekick, dropping everything when she broke up with another tree surgeon.

'If a guy had gone to Thailand, do you think there'd be a search party? Molly is her own person. She has a right to do what she wants, even if that is disappear for a while.'

Jeff always had such an even tone; he sounded like an independent arbitrator – a therapist who told you truisms you didn't want to hear. But was he right? Was Jeff the voice of reason? Or were they turning into that smug couple who reinforce each other's thoughts about everyone outside their precious duo? It was strange to think of Molly as outside of anything to do with B.

Molly's laugh was wide and raucous – it gave you a fright if you weren't used to it. Molly's lack of organization meant that she looked at you when you were talking to her because she was completely incapable of being anywhere else. She didn't plan shopping lists or think about what she might say next, she was just there in that moment. The fact that she was unconstructed made some people nervous – what did she want? What was she striving for? Not being able to place her freaked people out. But Molly as good or bad didn't exist for B. She was a part of him.

Her stringy hair, neither brown nor blonde but somewhere in the murky middle and always tied up with something unorthodox – elastic bands, wire or surprisingly often a sock. Her scruffy hands which always had dirt behind her nails from her incessant (and unasked for) weeding of public parks and patches of grass beneath bus stops. Her clothes that never quite fitted but somehow came together like the chaos had been curated. The utter junk she ate; at twenty-nine, her favourite tipple was Ribena. Her idea of a classy dinner was a round of brie melted in the microwave eaten whole with breadsticks held as chopsticks. Her beauty routine that consisted of soap, or Fairy Liquid in a bind. None of this existed outside B. He was far too close to see any of it.

When B thought of Molly, he pictured her in her red coat at the bottom of his driveway the day her mum died. It was spring and far too warm for a winter coat. But it was the last thing her mum had bought her and somewhere along the way she'd decided to put it on over her pyjamas. It turned out she needed it too because, despite the heat, she had shivered all day, staring blankly out the window as B drove them out of the city. Would it have been less painful if Annabelle had been a less alive person? If Annabelle had been a pleasant albeit humdrum person? He knew in his heart it wouldn't have been less painful, but still, Annabelle dead was a complete oxymoron.

Staring out the small window of the top floor at Foyles, B saw a couple on the street. They were a while away from each other but, despite the throng, they had spotted one another. He was wearing a stylish dark green raincoat and tortoiseshell glasses. He held a grey umbrella like a walking stick. She was actively unstylish – short and encumbered by wet paper bags. Her raincoat was old – black with white polka dots. Inexcusably dirty white ASICS peeked out from beneath her frazzled load. She stopped dead in the street. B craned his neck to see why. Suddenly she started waving frantically. She was making a total scene, waving her hands wildly, even though the stylish man could clearly see her. At first it looked like he was embarrassed but then B realized that he had broken into a wide smile. They were laughing. On a rainy Thursday night in central London after dreary days in offices and commutes on trains, she had found the energy to make him laugh and he was grateful. The stylish man had reached her now. He bundled her short frame and excessive baggage into him. She was still pretending to wave as he scooped up all her wet bags. B watched them all the way to the tube. The door knocked and B felt a rush of kindness for Peppy. Her whole face was lit up with hope.

'Would it be OK if you came out now? The editor would like to introduce you.'

There was no world in which Molly was outside B. He realized now that he had known all along what he would do. After the promotion for his book was done in a few weeks, he would go to Thailand to find her. He would just have to hope Jeff could understand.

'Of course, and Elizabeth, I want to thank you for everything. You have been most helpful.'

B smiled as he walked past her out of the room. She beamed despite his realization in the doorway that her name was most definitely not Elizabeth.

15. B

London, 2016

B's phone vibrated beside his bed. He reached to grab it beforc it fell onto the floor.

'Sorry to bother you.'

Molly's voice was hoarse, and B vaguely wondered what time it was. The sun was streaming in through the shutters but there was no noise from the street and the rest of the house was still. He wondered what it would be this time: money, clothes, keys, Lucozade? (She'd rung him once from the bedroom next door wondering if he'd get her an avocado because she had a desperate craving. He'd told her she was probably pregnant and hung up. It had backfired when she'd coming running into his room in a panic and they'd had to go to Boots for a pregnancy test.) He had a vague hope now that she was just standing on the doorstep, but her tone indicated that her problems were more severe than lost keys.

'Where are you?'

'Stoke Newington Common.'

'I'm coming.'

He swung his legs out of his warm bed and shivered. Reluctantly standing up, the thought occurred to him that he should have congratulated her for not having lost her phone. That was a first. Molly lost so many phones that B had long ago stopped memorizing her number. The only phone number he remembered was the landline that she'd scrawled on a piece of paper as a child – a number he couldn't seem to forget even though the line and the house were long since someone else's.

Molly had asked B home to play on the first day of primary school. From the outside, her house was a perfectly normal suburban home like his, but inside was like a Turkish bazaar. At first, the blood-red hallway seemed to engulf you in darkness but when you stepped inside and closed the door behind you the colours emerged. Year-round fairy lights circled the mirror and gold-flecked purple and orange saris hung from the ceiling. He didn't remember meeting Annabelle or Bernard that day, or what they ate or what games they played; all he remembered was following the uneven ponytail on the top of Molly's head through a maze of masks, books and rugs.

He often wondered why Molly had decided on him. Because that's how it felt. She'd come out of nowhere in her bright pink everything with a messy ponytail on top of her head, homing in on him like she only had eyes for him. One night, years later, sitting on the steps outside the dregs of a party, he'd asked her why she'd been so determined to be friends with him. She told him that she'd heard Bill Ryan and Tim Doherty slagging his school bag and she couldn't bear it. He'd laughed; it was the most Molly reason he could imagine. He'd made a drunken mental note to thank

Bill Ryan and Tim Doherty. They'd done him a pretty big favour.

Now, he stretched his arms high into the sky as he went into Molly's room to find some clothes. He was aware that his selection was less than desirable, but his own hangover was beginning to hit, and he needed air, so he gave up mid-scavenge. As he made for the door, he unhooked one of their roommate's padded coats from a coat hanger. At the very least she'd be warm.

Google maps told him where to go and he followed blindly, glad the suggested route was a bus not a tube so he wouldn't have to test his hangover underground. He got onto the empty double decker and looked out at the silent city. They'd already been in London several months but still it felt like a maze. He missed the numbered streets of New York where they'd lived in a walk-up above Chinatown. Or the wide streets of Perth where the city had felt tiny and they'd mastered it, popping down to wine tastings in Margaret River at weekends. Still, there was something about London that felt familiar – like it could be permanent.

He was almost afraid to admit it to Molly. To tell her that he thought he might be done moving. After years of sub-editing he'd begun to get by-lines and now that his blog was taking off he thought he might finally take Molly's advice and set up a YouTube channel. Molly seemed to like London too but B worried that it was because of the pace. There were so many parties and club openings and brunches, she never had to stop, never had to be alone, never had to look too closely at what she was running from. And now there was Jonas.

Jonas was the head of the agency where Molly was

temping. He was from Stockholm and in order to impress him Molly had been using the IKEA catalogue to learn Swedish. Across their sitting room, yellow post-its crawling with black permanent marker were dotted on tables, chairs and vases. *I AM KLINGSBO*, asserted the post-it stuck to the coffee table. The sink informed them it was KATTEVIK. Jonas was forty-five, and although admittedly handsome, he looked inordinately like a vampire. He was paler than snow, had pitch-black hair and, B was not exaggerating, fangs. But that was fine, if you wanted fangs then fine. But B had stalked him online and was pretty sure that Jonas the Vampire had a wife, two kids and a dog named Mimmi back in Stockholm.

He ambled into what he figured must be the common. It was distinctly unplanned, uncertain of its boundaries like an unfinished back garden. Overgrown chunks of grass were bisected by the railway line. It had a more authentic feel to the pruned and preened parks he'd visited so far, and the few people dotted around seemed equally unplanned; tired parents trundling strollers, people on their way home from last night.

Molly was sitting on a bench. A pair of silver earrings encrusted with fake diamonds dangled from her ear lobes. Two Hasidic Jewish men passed in front of her, their long curls seemingly immune to the wind. One raised his hand to his hat to keep it from blowing off while the other tried to balance a large cake box.

'You were right. He's married.' Molly looked up as B approached her. He put his hands in the pocket of his hoodie and sat down at the other end of the bench.

'The guy with the hat or the guy with the cake?'

Molly laughed at B's attempt at mock confusion. Last night's dark eye make-up was slightly smudged, but she still looked pretty. Her lack of self-consciousness meant her looks could take you by surprise. A tiny bit of eye make-up or a new dress and she became someone different, someone who suddenly outshone everyone in the room.

People thought Molly was invulnerable. That just because she was easy-going and light-hearted, she could never have a low moment, she could never be down. But B had learnt that it was the opposite. People who give out that much good energy, who are breezy and jovial and try their best to be happy and positive all the time, have a far greater capacity for getting hurt than those who put up a defence. Molly had no defence. She was an open book. She let anyone in and sometimes – increasingly often – she got hurt.

They were under a row of trees heavy with droplets. It wasn't clear if they were better or worse off here: protected from the wind but sprinkled on when it blew. He realized that Molly was shivering. He reached for the bag to find something to keep her warm. In the harsh light of day suddenly its contents looked like he'd swapped bags with one meant for a charity shop. He pulled out the padded coat while he searched for a pair of flat shoes. He could only find one patent loafer. Molly laughed.

'God, things aren't that bad, are they?'

She pointed at the padded jacket. A large buckle jangled from the middle, and a strip of luminous orange stretched around the centre of the white and navy padding. Somehow, in his haste to get out of the house, he'd brought her a life jacket.

'Is this an intervention? Is my uncle John here hiding in a

bush somewhere?' They both began to laugh as she peered behind the bench.

A gust of wind blew droplets across their legs and they let out a yell. They jumped to their feet and started walking towards the gate.

'Hey, at least you learnt something.'

'Not to sleep with Swedish vampires who have wives and children and a dog called Mimmi?'

'I was going to say the name of every piece of furniture in Swedish but, yeah, that too.'

'That's the best bit – it turns out IKEA don't name furniture by its Swedish name. They name furniture after things like rivers and islands and towns. Apparently, I walked into his living room with a smug smile on my face and did the equivalent of pointing at his couch – "Blackpool" – nodded knowingly at his coffee table – "Hull" – then sat down, chuffed with myself, in his armchair slowly repeating "Luton, Luton, Luton".'

B couldn't control his laughter. He stopped on the path to get his breath. Molly wandered ahead into the grass. She'd taken off her heels and was walking barefoot.

'B, will I be OK?'

Molly turned to face him. Suddenly she looked small and vulnerable, like in first year of school when she used to trip over her long kilt running excitedly around the prefabs pretending to be Boo Radley.

'Oh Mol, of course you will. And no matter what happens you've always got me.'

B began stuffing the life jacket into the bag, but Molly reached over and took it from him. She glanced up at him and they shared a smile.

'What? It looks warm.'

She began strapping the life jacket tightly around her, motioning to imaginary exits. They sauntered across the uneven footpath, the wind blowing rain from the trees on their heads, or maybe it was just raining. Either way they didn't mind.

16. BOBBY

Dublin, March 23rd 2019

Bobby's greatest fear was losing the use of his arms and legs. He'd thought it all through: if he lost his arms he could still run, if he lost his legs, he could learn wheelchair basketball, but if he lost both and had no way to exercise out his anxiety, he didn't know how he'd cope. He could feel his thighs on the bike now and they were colossal. He could almost picture the muscles at work beneath his skin like the diagrams they showed you in Biology class. The psoas major weaving behind the rectus femoris. He'd done a year of sports science before he'd realized he'd needed to get further away from his past than a lecture hall filled with former rugby players.

Now as he cycled out to the sea, he let his thighs do the work. He let his body take over. His body was smarter than him. It knew what to do, if only his mind would just let it, and then the endorphins would start and no matter what was happening, if he could run or cycle or swim, he would be OK. He could lose one or the other, he just couldn't lose both his arms and his legs. He held the handlebars tighter and pushed his legs extra hard.

Cycling was all he and Jack had ever done. They cycled to the beach, swam almost the entire bay then cycled back, dry before they reached home. People yelled at them to get off the motorway when they cycled to the Sugar Loaf. They would sprint up the mountain then cycle home without breaking a sweat. Nothing in the world felt as good as days like that; his whole body would ache, and he knew that he would sleep that night, that he'd used up every ounce of energy, there'd be none left to feed the nervous thoughts that crept up on him at night.

Jack existed in perpetual summer. When Bobby thought of Jack, they were always in t-shirts and there was always too much time. Boredom was the ever-present enemy; there was never anything to do so they had to be inventive. As well as cycling as far as they could, they got odd jobs. They had washed cars for a while, Jack had mowed lawns and Bobby had coached rugby at summer camps. But then they'd discovered sailing. Some of the wealthier boys in their class were members of sailing clubs; they even had their own boats and fancy gear, but neither Bobby nor Jack had ever been out on a boat before. Unless you counted the ferry to France. One day they'd cycled up to the sailing club and every summer after that and even weekends into November they'd taken sailing lessons until by fifteen they were teaching the little kids.

It was a fall off a boat that sent everything spiralling. It had been a beautiful summer's day and Jack and Bobby were confident out on the sea by now. They sailed around Dublin Bay, racing boys from their class who had sailed all their lives and trying not to be smug when they beat them. It was only a small knock, but Jack had bled so much that the instructor insisted on taking him to the hospital. It all happened so quickly that Jack had forgotten his backpack, so Bobby had cycled to his house later that night, one bag strapped to his front and the other to his back. He would always remember that cycle, how even though it was late, the blue of the sky was refusing to relinquish to black. His legs felt light and the air was warm around him as he cycled the Strand road in a dark blue hue, unaware that everything was about to fall apart.

It was Jack's sister who answered the door and told him that the cancer could be back. Bobby struggled to connect the word to Jack. Leukaemia was something that happened to brave bald eight year olds who were visited by Princess Diana. It didn't happen to a healthy, fully formed fifteen year old who could cycle for miles, whose hair flopped into his eyes and whose walk you tried to imitate in the full-length mirror of your mum's bathroom. Bobby knew Jack had been sick as a child but that wasn't a threat. That was just something you knew about your friend like that they used to wet the bed, or they'd had a dog who died. It was over, it couldn't come back to haunt you like this. But it did and Jack was dead within the year, just a few days after his sixteenth birthday.

Bobby pulled his bike up to the sea. It was just starting to rain, which was when he liked to swim best. But he needed to catch his breath. He would never be as fit as he was at fifteen, he would never have as much energy, he'd never be as fearless. Sometimes he wondered if he'd ever be as happy.

He sat down on the patch of grass that looked over the

small sandy inlet and looked out at the sea. The cycle had already calmed his nerves and once he got over the initial cold, he knew the swim would do the rest. He would swim and swim until he ached and then he'd cycle home and hope that he'd done enough to stave off the shadows that followed him.

His phone rang on the grass beside him and he glanced at the screen. His heart sank. Bobby knew his anger towards his mum was unfounded. She was entitled to change but he couldn't help it – the new her drove him up the wall. She was once the most sought-after criminal barrister at the Bar. She wore Chanel night, noon and morning. She had driven her Audi like she could afford to total it and drunk red wine late into the night, sneaking cigarettes outside the back door. She was somebody. She was herself.

Everyone else thought it was cool that Frances had jacked it all in for spiritual enlightenment, but Bobby knew that it was just one more thing she could be ferocious about. One more thing she could be the best at. She didn't just take up yoga. She travelled to India for several months to train with teachers she insisted on referring to as gurus. She meditated for hours on end and posted about it on blogs. It annoyed Bobby no end that he had given her the liberal souvenir of the decade – a gay son right in time for the gay marriage referendum.

But apparently, he wasn't doing it right. When Bobby told his mum why he'd broken up with his last boyfriend, she had insisted four times that it was the other way around. She kept telling Bobby that his ex might change his mind, refusing to understand that it was him; it was him who didn't want children. It wasn't that she even wanted a grandchild – she didn't even like children that much – it was just another of the preconceived notions that she and everybody else seemed to have about Bobby that he couldn't seem to escape. He sometimes wondered if there was a manual; if he'd come with a manual about who he was and everyone else had read it but him.

Bobby looked out at Sandycove. There were other, longer beaches but when they broke the kids and their friends out, Annabelle and Frances always brought them to this tiny inlet past Dun Laoghaire pier. Parking was a nightmare for anyone with morals but luckily Annabelle was happy to drive right up on the kerb and block three entrances. Bobby, Jack, B and Molly raced into the sea while Anne carefully took Killian's hand and guided him slowly to the water. Their mums changed into one-pieces and took it in turns to swim for Ireland across what seemed like the whole bay. They must have been cold. An accurate memory would include shivering and subsequent headcolds, but all Bobby could remember was warmth. Jack swimming and swimming and swimming and only stopping from exhaustion. Smiling wide-eyed, his sandy hair catching the light. The sun on their faces, the debates about what toppings to get on their ice creams at Teddy's and the coarse towel his mum wrapped painfully tightly around him.

She'd been there. His mum had been there, she'd been present and loving, and Bobby wondered how so much had built up between them. Bobby thought about Molly and Annabelle, how they hadn't just got on – they'd filled each other's worlds. They seemed able to enjoy each other in a way that Bobby wondered if he'd ever had or ever would have with his own mum. He wondered if that was how it worked – Molly and Annabelle had been in sync, perfectly together, and so Annabelle had died. He and his own mother couldn't keep from rubbing each other up the wrong way and so they were destined to do so for the rest of time.

The phone stopped ringing and immediately he felt guilty. It could have been important. It could have been about Molly. Bobby had thought he'd get off lightly this time, that he wouldn't have to chase her halfway around the world because his work was non-negotiable. Teachers couldn't just take time off during term time, but due to an unseasonably late Easter, he had two weeks off coming up. Conveniently Molly had decided to disappear just before the Easter break. He almost laughed at the thought of Molly thinking the timing through – at the thought of Molly thinking *anything* through.

He stood and began to take off his clothes. He had to move quickly or he'd start to think about the cold, he'd anticipate the pins and needles, so he ran. He sprinted down the steps and dived into the sea, just as the rain began to pound all around him.

17. MOLLY

June 22nd 2007

Her name was Lucinda Vanessa Smith-Byrne and it wasn't even her birthday. Her birthday was in January, but she'd always dreamt of having a summer fête, so she was hosting a white tie and sparkles extravaganza on the 22nd of June. Which just so happened to be Molly's eighteenth birthday. This was probably why Molly was the one person on the planet who wasn't invited.

Molly sat against the cold radiator in her room with the door locked. She could hear her mum pottering around outside, so she turned the radio up louder. She knew all the things her mum would say. About not caring what other people did or thought. About being your own person, about treading your own path, but right now she didn't want to hear it. Molly always did that. She always trod her own path and tried not to care what others thought – but just once, just for this one night on her eighteenth birthday, she wanted to sit in her bedroom and wallow.

The window was open, and she could hear the sounds of the neighbourhood ramping up for a rare sunny evening.

People were out on the street unloading shopping, setting out garden furniture, getting ready for barbecues and saying chirpy hellos to each other. Molly turned the radio up louder. Up until this point the music had all been upbeat and summery but now The Fray's 'How to Save a Life' came on and Molly was delighted. She'd just learnt the word for this; catharsis was B's new favourite word. He went around saying it night, noon and morning, trying it out for size. Annabelle had intervened to tell him that no, running out of bananas when you've a craving for banana bread was not cathartic.

Lucinda Vanessa Smith-Byrne had brought seven of her closest friends to Portugal to get a tan for the party. Apparently, they had a strict schedule of oil applications and turning to ensure even sun coverage. They had been told in advance to bring various shaped bikinis including at least one strapless top to maximize tan and ensure uniform skin cancer. Kylie Murphy-Slattery had fallen asleep on the first day and gotten sunstroke. She had to stay inside for the rest of the trip. The word was that she had been bumped from the dance that the Special Eight had planned for the party. A choreographer from Pineapple Studios in London had been flown in to teach it to them before the trip and they spent every night after tanning practising while the housekeeper videoed them for mistakes.

Of course, Molly didn't want anything to do with the party. She wasn't insane. But sometimes she felt it. Sometimes she felt like she lived in an alternative universe where all the things she thought were fun and cool were seen as eccentric and strange and all the things everyone else wanted seemed completely nuts to her. There was no planet in which she wanted to spend her eighteenth birthday watching the Special Eight (were they the Special Seven now?) dancing to 'Hips Don't Lie'. Obviously, she didn't want to be there. But she didn't want to be sitting against the cold radiator alone in her room on her eighteenth birthday either.

The door knocked. She wondered what her mum would suggest now. Molly had already said no to going to Uncle John's house so a ragtag group of aunts and uncles could be scraped together to throw her a pity party. Molly had refused to call B. She couldn't deny him the opportunity to see the Special Seven. He really wanted to see what they'd been practising and tell anyone who'd listen that their dance was a form of catharsis. Killian had made it very clear that being invited to the party despite being two years below them in school was the greatest moment of his life. He'd spent every penny he had on a white suit that made him look like a pimp. Since Jack had died Bobby didn't leave the house except to exercise and Anne was still in deep mourning about the end of the Leaving Cert so there was nowhere to be and nobody to be with.

Molly didn't even feel like driving around listening to ABBA with her mum. Even if they wore their balaclavas. The balaclavas had been Annabelle's idea. She'd had them left over from a play so they'd popped them on one night and started driving around wealthy suburbs blaring 'Money, Money, Money' to see if anyone would call the Guards. Their licence plate had been called in three times (Foxrock, Blackrock and Castleknock) and every time the Guards had found it hilarious. But it was too warm for the balaclavas tonight.

'Come in.'

Her mum stood in the door unusually quiet. Her face was pained, and Molly knew that her heart was broken by not being able to fix this. Her hair fell vibrantly around her timid face like even when she was trying to be subdued her hair couldn't comply.

'I've just had a call from the theatre, the props guy fell down the stairs again. He's the guy who throws himself down the stairs every time his wife tries to leave him – you know, Jerry?'

Why her mother hires these people is beyond Molly. But she had to admit her mum had her attention now.

'Is there any chance you'd come in and help me? It's only passing hats to the actors and helping them with their wigs.'

Annabelle's plays were no longer held in community centres. There were no longer bit parts for Bobby and Molly and B. Anne was no longer the stage manager. Her plays had appeared at the Abbey, the Gate and The Gaiety. They had been reviewed by the *Guardian* and *The New York Times*. They'd appeared on the West End and there was talk of Broadway for the latest. It was about a man who buys six cooked chickens in a supermarket and over the course of one night dismantles them for a giant stock. Each chicken represents a woman in his life. As he breaks the chicken bones he screams their names wildly into the theatre: BRIDGET! PAULA! MAIREAD!! Maybe that was catharsis.

There were countless people who'd kill for the opportunity to work with Annabelle Black. She still taught drama and her students adored her. They'd drop anything to give a hat to the man breaking up the chickens. Annabelle didn't need Molly. It was clear that she'd just run out of ideas. The idea of her mum running out of ideas was tragic enough to rouse Molly.

'Only if I don't have to change my clothes.'

Molly pointed down at the denim pinafore that she wore over a loose white t-shirt of her dad's. She knew it made her look about twelve but it was cool in the heat and the truth was she felt about twelve right now; vulnerable and small in a world she couldn't make sense of.

The roads were empty, but laughter floated out of beer gardens and parks, reverberating into the air like the slight shaking of an amp. In the shops, which weren't quite closed yet, bored shop assistants gazed out of windows checking their phones for when they could leave.

It was a while before Molly noticed that they weren't heading for the theatre. Parking there was a nightmare so perhaps her mum had found a spot elsewhere. But Annabelle pulled up outside the Guinness Storehouse and told Molly she needed to pick up a prop. She ran in, leaving the car pulled up unevenly on the footpath. Molly sat patiently for a while until the heat got to her. Eventually she stepped out of the car and paced the cobblestones. They felt smooth under her pumps and Molly had an urge to lie down on them. To feel their coolness on her bare skin.

She knew what had happened. Her mother had one job. Probably to get a keg for an after party or actually Greg (that was the name of the chicken disassembly man) did drink a pint on stage after chicken number four but now Annabelle had met someone. She'd be having a loud raucous chat and she'd forget the time and the play would start and the director would be losing his mind. Molly looked at her watch. It was nearing seven o'clock and the play started at half past. She left the unlocked car and made for the door.

The cool of the storehouse was comforting but its vast cavernous emptiness was not. Molly couldn't see or hear anyone in any direction. There was a glass elevator in the centre, but she didn't even know what floor she was looking for. She called her mum's name, but it echoed into the wide space and it was clear she was alone.

She was used to this of course. Molly had long accepted that she had to share her mum with the world, that that was part of the bargain. That her mum ran into distant friends and old piano teachers and neighbours' chiropodists and fans and that not stopping to chat was not a genetic possibility. But for today, just today, she wanted her mum to be hers alone or at the very least for her mum to have left her be, sitting against the cold radiator in her bedroom listening to sad music. Just tonight she didn't want to be trailing her mother around as she'd done all her life, getting left in pubs, meeting larger-than-life characters and hearing wild stories.

She got into the elevator and pressed every button. At every floor there was emptiness. At every floor her voice echoed. When she reached the top, the doors opened onto an entirely glass room. Despite the still bright sky, lights pinged on in the streets below.

'She's here!'

Molly peeked out the door of the elevator and the first person she saw was Jerry. Both his arms were in casts and one leg too. To be fair to him, his strategy seemed to have worked: beside him his wife was nursing a large gin and tonic. Molly began apologizing thinking that she'd stepped into a pre-show party but then the music started and B's voice came over the microphone.

'Ladies and gentlemen, may I present the Special Five.'

Uncle John and Uncle Mike bookended a five-person line-up, with Blur and Oasis in boyband poses on their hunkers and Killian standing front and centre in his white suit. The Backstreet Boys blared into the room and B struggled at a mixing desk to turn it down but that didn't stop the Special Five. Uncle Mike was pulling his elbows back and forth indicating some sort of sex move, Oasis was doing cartwheels into tables knocking over drinks, Blur was attempting the worm, Uncle John had his arms straight down by his side, fists clenched, Irish dancing on the spot, and Killian was singing 'I WANT IT THAT WAY' at full volume, climbing the bar with a mic in his hand.

Molly didn't want to laugh. She didn't want to have to be made to feel better, but the room was lit up. Hundreds of little fairy lights hung from the roof and a banner across the bar read HAPPY BIRTHDAY MOL! It wasn't just her family either – all her friends had come, even the ones she suspected secretly wanted to see how the Special Seven's tans had progressed. And they were all up now, dancing and hugging Molly, asking if she had a clue what her mum was planning and whether Bobby would show up. Her mum hung back. Molly could tell that she wasn't sure she'd done the right thing. She made her way out onto a balcony and Molly followed.

'I thought you'd run out of ideas.'

'Ideas? Nah, that's never the problem. Choosing the right one, though – that's tricky.'

Despite the warm night there was a breeze this high up and her mum's auburn hair blew into her face.

'I'm sorry about Jerry. He was just at such a low ebb I felt I had to invite him.'

'Falling down the stairs seems to have done the trick, though, right?'

They both laughed.

'I know I always tell you not to care what other people think, Mol. To be your own person. But it's not always easy.'

'I didn't want to go to her party.'

Molly leant her head on the railing and looked down at the city below. The steel was cool on her chin and the light breeze was the perfect temperature.

'I know that. But maybe it would have been nice to have been invited?'

Her mum tentatively reached her arm around her, and Molly fell into her. She hadn't thought she cared. She hadn't thought she'd felt left out. She hadn't thought she'd wanted her own party. But her heart was filled, not by the party, but by her mum understanding how she felt when not even she herself had.

Behind her she could hear B playing all her favourite songs trying to entice her in. Someone was yelling that Bobby had arrived. Her heart clenched at the thought of Bobby, who was terrified of leaving the house, cycling here. She knew he'd have brought his bike so he could leave quickly if it all became too much but he was here. She had spotted Anne in the crowd too wearing a beautiful pink dress, looking nervously on as her brother tried to do the splits. The thought of Anne going out and buying a dress for her party made her well up.

Molly would drag Anne up to dance and maybe even Bobby, if it wasn't too much for him. B and Killian would showboat, and her aunts and uncles would put Riverdance to shame. Molly felt that familiar sense of excitement rise up in her. She was in her comfiest clothes and comfiest shoes and she could dance all night. But just for this one moment she leant against her mum's soft cold arm and sat looking down at the city with the one person in the world who loved her most.

18. JOHN

Dublin, March 26th 2019

John had been thinking about it all day. He had emptied the dishwasher, put two washes on and popped to the shop for bananas, but all that time, the call had been hanging over him. He was a grown man of sixty-seven. He had made more difficult phone calls than this. He had fired people. He had faced more than one armed robber in the shop. He had been on the jury for a murder trial. But yet he looked for another task to avoid picking up the phone.

He spotted some dust in the front room. What they needed was one of those old-fashioned multi-coloured dusters. People laughed at them now, but his mother had used one to great effect before she'd given up everything to focus full time on Sudoku. He made do with a wet cloth and took a mental note to investigate possible duster options. The wet cloth left a streak on the coffee table, so he had to go back into the larder to source some kitchen roll. Marvellously, one job had doubled into two. But the fact remained that it was his duty to pick up the phone and ring these people.

After all the calls he had gotten down the years from good Samaritans it was the least he could do.

It used to happen about once a month. The phone would ring downstairs in the kitchen. Eventually they had a phone installed in the bedroom. Helen often volunteered to go. She didn't see why John protested so much at this. She loved Danny too, she said one night when John had been particularly exhausted. But it was always him who went.

When people called, they always apologized. John could never get over this. Sometimes they were angry. Danny might have refused to leave their pub; he could be asleep in their car. He might have lost his keys. Sometimes they were sympathetic – people in the parish knew that he'd been the priest's favourite as a child. And no matter how late it was, how inconvenient it was, John couldn't express his gratitude towards these people. On nights when the phone rang, at least he knew where his brother was. What's more he knew that someone was with Danny. A sympathetic neighbour might have let him crash on their couch and just wanted to let John know, or an irate bartender was only waiting fifteen more minutes for John to get there or he was calling the Guards, but either way they always apologized.

People thought the phone calls in the middle of the night must have been hard, but it was the disappearances that were hard. Danny had spent two decades working on building sites in Manchester and Liverpool. When he'd left Dublin in the 1980s, he had been just like everybody else. The Irish lads on the sites worked from 7 to 4, had pints and a carvery at lunch, followed by pints late into the night before a few hours' sleep in a hostel or a bedsit. There had been a crew of them, known for being expert and crucially fast brickies. They could work all night on a job if the money was right and it'd be done well too. It was hard to tell when things started to go wrong, but John knew in his heart that things were already too far gone by the time he and Annabelle finally travelled to Liverpool to get him.

Danny was already homeless. Most nights he seemed to be able to get a bed in a men's shelter but on nights he drank he'd make do with park benches or alleyways. The morning they found him, Danny was asleep in an early house near the docks. They didn't know where any of his belongings were or if he even had anything left. A kindly lady behind the bar said they should try Whitechapel men's hostel and sure enough he had a few plastic bags in a locker there but nothing worth salvaging. John sent Annabelle off with a hundred quid for new clothes and he took on showering Danny.

All he could think as he lifted his brother's limp arm over his shoulder was all the ways he had failed him. It had been too late to do anything by the time John had cottoned on to what was going on at the Christian Brothers. Then he'd let the drinking go on too long. Probably because of what had happened with the priests. In the institutional shower at the shelter Danny's face was weathered red; his eyes were puffy. He stank and he looked ten years older than John, not the other way around. He would never have a life. They would get him back to Ireland, but John knew that Danny's would be a life on the fringes, just about keeping afloat. John had failed once, and he wasn't going to fail again. He'd left it too late with Danny, but he could save Molly. And if he could find Molly, there just might be a minuscule chance that he could save this Griffith girl.

He stood in the hallway and picked up the receiver. He had written the number down on a piece of paper the last time it had appeared on the news. These phone lines were manned by the local police station, volunteers, local agencies. He would simply be giving a small bit of information to a professional, so he didn't know why he was so nervous. There was just something so real about the Griffith girl's situation. He hated that Molly was even mentioned in the same context as her. A lump of dread filled his throat every time he heard Sheena's name on the one o'clock bulletin.

'Hello, I'm sorry to be a bother but I have a small bit of information about a potential witness in the Sheena Griffith case. My niece Molly.'

'Molly Black? The police mentioned her but said they couldn't track her down. Have you heard from her?'

Uncle John was thrown. 'May I ask who I am speaking to?'

'Her dad, I'm Sheena's dad.'

The voice on the other end of the line was husky but in hindsight John wondered if that was just pure exhaustion. John's stomach dropped. He struggled to find his voice.

'I'm so sorry for what you and your family are going through.'

'We appreciate that. Did you say you might have some news?'

'Well, Molly, we've found out that she is in Thailand.'

'Can we call her? Ask her what she saw?'

'She seems to have left her phone behind, but the thing is, we're going out there. We're going to find her and when we do, we can let you know if she saw anything.'

There was silence on the other end of the line.

'Is she OK?'

'Who?'

'Your niece Molly.'

His heart ached at this man – this stranger's empathy. How in god's name did he have the capacity to care about their Molly?

'We hope so. And we are desperately hoping the same for your daughter too.'

He could hear the gratitude in the man's thanks as he hung up. Standing in the dim light of the hallway, a shot of fear ran through John; the same fear he'd felt all those years before. He hoped against hope that this time it wasn't too late.

19. DANNY

Liverpool, 2003

He was angry and it wasn't something he was used to. Usually he was light. Usually he was jovial, but mostly he was numb. He wished that he had forgotten it was today. He wished that he was already on a bender, already gone, but it was today, and he knew it was today, so he started to get dressed. In an upstairs flat, a shower hummed and behind him the boiler rattled. It clinked and dripped, and he found the noise disconcerting. Mid-morning when he was at his most sober, all noises unnerved him. He reached with one arm to the shelf above the cupboard for a bottle. But then he remembered that it was today, so he stopped himself and again he was angry.

He was surprised to find some almost clean clothes in the cupboard. He stood staring at a folded jumper and a shirt that might only have been worn once or twice before. He tried to remember where they came from and how long they had been there. Then he pictured the volunteer. She was young and Irish. But instead of pale and freckled she was blonde and had good skin and she was tall like he imagined Swedish people to be.

He knew the Swedish-looking volunteer had pitied him. They both did. She'd come with a nice young man – English with Irish parents. They'd spent a lot of time talking about where his parents were from. It was funny to hear him pronounce *Ballinrobe* and *Sneem* in his upper-middle-class English accent. Danny knew he'd kept them too long. They had other deliveries to do so he took the parcel they handed him and let them go. Despite their pity, he'd felt their glow for days. The way they smiled and how their eyes were alive. He wanted to thank them and maybe even give them tea next time, but the next few times they'd called he'd been out and then they seemed to stop coming.

He pulled the second-hand shirt over his head and rooted for trousers. When he found none, he knew what he would have to do but he wasn't sure he could face it. He stood in a shirt and boxers looking at the bottle on top of the cupboard. He could throw it all in. He could stand her up. But he knew that if he did that, Annabelle would tell them. She would report back and soon he'd have the whole family on top of him.

They had an unspoken agreement. When she was in London to review a play, she got the train up to see him. She didn't ask too much of him. She didn't ask him about the drinking or if he was working at the moment. She didn't push him to come home. She said she just needed to see him every few months and in return she didn't pressure him. He avoided the others' calls. He put their visits on the long finger, but Annabelle didn't take no for an answer. They had an agreement and he could just about abide it for the moment.

He switched on the electric radiator and took a pair of trousers from the pile at the end of the bed. He stood at the sink and tilted the wet patch under the tap. The smell of urine didn't bother him. He was used to it by now and soon it was overtaken by the smell of the Pears soap. But he was worried that they wouldn't dry in time. He was to meet her at The White Horse. It was only around the corner, but he couldn't remember if it was one or two o'clock. Either way he knew she'd wait.

He was placing the trousers on the radiator to dry when he heard a bang on the door of the basement flat. He stood frozen. He wondered without hope if it could be one of his neighbours. Maybe when he'd run the tap, he'd interrupted their shower. But the upstairs neighbours didn't call in here. Nobody called in here. In his heart of hearts, he knew it was her. He didn't move.

The anger was quick to return and this time even more viscerally. She was breaking their pact. Encroaching on him. He could feel her presence like the walls pressing in on him. She was asking too much and he couldn't cope. He was hanging in. In this small contained space, he was somehow managing to hang in, but he couldn't do any more than this. It already felt like too much. Why couldn't she leave him be? His hands were clenched, and he was startled to find tears rising through his chest. He kept thinking that she would knock on the door again, but moments passed and still there was silence. Finally, he heard her climb the steps to ground level and close the gate behind her.

He watched as the patch of dark grey on the trousers

slowly turned light again on the radiator. This would be the hardest moment. The next five seconds where he could just take the bottle and disappear. Forget Annabelle. Forget their arrangement. Evaporate from everything that was too much. He stood over the radiator and breathed. He waited five seconds, then ten, then a minute.

He would go to The White Horse. Annabelle would be there. They would pretend that she had never come to his door. His gratefulness that she had not pushed too far over the threshold into his life would allow him to be buoyant. He would ask about Molly. He would look excitedly at pictures. On his way there he would think of things to tell her. He might even mention the two volunteers. He wouldn't talk about the charity they worked for; instead he might turn them into neighbours – friends almost. People he saw regularly and did things with. That would make her happy.

He unclenched his fists. He reached for the bottle on top of the cupboard and took one short, sharp swig. There was no toothpaste, so he scooped up some of the foam from the Pears soap and swilled it around in his mouth. Opening the front door, he tried to loosen the material around his crotch where the soap water had hardened on his trousers. An envelope was sitting on the step.

There was no name on it but he knew what it was. He folded the notes into the inside pocket of his jacket. After Annabelle was gone and the supreme effort over, he would spend it. And he would be gone for days.

20. THE FAMILY

Dublin, April 5th 2019

When we found out that Molly was in Thailand we lost our collective minds. Phones buzzed all over Dublin with one-to-one calls and WhatsApp alerts. Landlines were resurrected. Various duos had in-person meetings. Frances met Angela in Avoca. Uncle Mike met Even-Stephen in Neary's. Bobby met Anne in Two Pups, and having so much time on his hands, Uncle John met every member of the family individually at various locations across the city. The news was accompanied by a horrified half giddiness which some of us were ashamed of. Some of us were not.

Rumours escalated. Molly had won a trip to Thailand in an online quiz. She'd done a yoga training course and was now teaching tourists in a fancy resort. She'd followed a married man there. She'd followed a fifty-two year old Israeli lesbian called Rhonda there. She'd become a Muay Thai fighter in the jungle and was now known as Loma. (It turned out the last two theories were the plot of a Netflix movie that had morphed into an explanation of Molly's disappearance.) The only thing that was clear was that Uncle John would get his extraction plan. If only he could get a word in edgeways.

'Very humid place Thailand. But fantastic beaches by all accounts.'

Uncle Mike had borrowed an extendable pointer from his office but had nothing to point it at, so he waved it around in the air. Uncle John was making a big show of being uncomfortable despite the fact that he was sitting in a giant armchair.

Mike had insisted on hosting the family symposium this time and John was deeply unhappy about it. The rest of us were delighted to be in the mansion. Everyone had their own seat in the tasteful mirage of cream and V had ordered in sushi. There were crates of 7up and Coke, and Prosecco was flowing. Aunt Helen was wearing red high heels for the outing and Aunt Frances was already tipsy. Even-Stephen was halfway through a speech about the symptoms of dehydration when Bobby cut him off.

'Forget hydration, how did she get there in the first place? She can barely make rent.'

'Could some young fella have covered her costs?'

Uncle Mike was using the pointer to itch his chin. He immediately revised his point.

'But she isn't one for the moneyed man, is she? She is always chasing after those gardeners.'

'When we find her, she might come and live in Glenmalure.'

Aunt Angela lived in a ghost estate in Kildare and was always trying to get people to move there. Molly would be more at home as Loma, practising Muay Thai fighting in the jungles of Thailand.

'These are the people I have on my list for the extraction team.'

Ignoring the chit-chat, Uncle John produced a piece of paper from his pocket.

'Me and Mike will head the team, obviously. But we'll need some younger members of the family in the mix too, in case there is a nightlife scene we need to tap into. Bobby and Anne, I presume you can make yourselves available?'

It seemed that Uncle John could only read if his glasses were balanced on the very end of his nose. Several of us wondered if he had the wrong prescription. We made a note to mention it to Helen later.

Anne seemed to be muttering something about not using up her annual leave to chase Molly but V cut her off.

'Why are we so sure Molly needs rescuing?'

Lady V's signature exercise gear was rolled up on one leg to reveal her cast. Beautifully painted aubergine toenails poked out the bottom.

'John, you had better tell them.' Mike arched his eyebrows at Uncle John. They looked at each other intensely like they were in a two-man play and one had just revealed to the other that he'd lost the family farm. Uncle John rose from his chair in slow motion to a stunned silence.

'The BRITISH METROPOLITAN POLICE are looking for Molly.'

Over California rolls later, we would all agree that Uncle John could really have clarified the bit about Molly being wanted as a witness. Clearly he was so delighted to be back in the driver's seat that he wanted his contribution to elicit maximum impact. All hell broke loose as we scrambled to understand Molly's latest crime. Blur was loudly shouting

ARSON and MURDER to provoke panic. Even-Stephen kept telling us not to jump to conclusions, which annoyed us no end, and Aunt Angela was gripping her rosary beads, keening like a banshee.

'Could someone dose Angela with garlic?' (Blur)

'That's for warding off vampires not religious nuts.' (Bobby)

In the confusion over Molly being a wanted felon the doorbell rang. Oasis was the only one level-headed enough to answer it. He returned with a smiling Asian man wearing glasses.

'Hi, Anne.'

Heads turned in slow motion and jaws dropped like contagious dislocation had spread through the family. A phone was vibrating on the table, but no one moved to silence it. Aunt Angela inexplicably crossed herself as if the mere thought of her daughter having a friend was a bad omen. No one was more shocked than Anne. She stared steely eyed at this man like he had just murdered her cat.

'You must be a friend of Anne's. You're very welcome, please come in.'

Of all the people in the entire family who could have got it together to greet the smiling man, Uncle Danny was the last person any of us expected. He stood to shake the smiling man's hand and showed him towards a chair. We hadn't even realized Uncle Danny was in the room and most of us hadn't heard him talk unprompted in a decade.

'I hope I haven't interrupted. I should have waited in the car. It's just we're going to the cinema.'

'Not at all, son, we're wrapping up here anyway now.'

'Righty-ho.'

The courteous stranger directed his comments towards Uncle Danny, but the shock was wearing off so now the entire family wanted a piece of him. Uncle Mike used the pointer to illustrate an array of drinks, of which the smiling man chose Coke (full fat like Anne, we all noted). Bobby patted him on the shoulder encouragingly like he was in a boxing ring about to take on a heavyweight. Uncle John started to fill him in on the plan to go to Thailand to pick up Anne's wayward cousin Molly over Easter. He made it sound like she was waiting at a bus stop for a lift, not actively on the run.

'Molly seems like quite the character,' the smiling man chipped in as he took a sip of his Coke. His good-natured take went down very well among the group. There were chuckles and murmurs of agreement. But Anne bolted upright out of her chair. Her pallor vacillated between red and white as vivid as the stripes on the American flag.

'WE CAN'T STAY.'

'I didn't catch your name, son.'

Uncle Mike ignored Anne's outburst and perched on the stranger's chair.

'Alastair Stairs.'

'Fantastic. Alastair – is that a Scottish name?'

'Yes, absolutely it is, well spotted, my dad was Scottish but I'm from England.'

We could all see that it was killing Uncle Mike not to be able to ask Alastair where he was from – *originally*. Thankfully, Bobby swooped in before Uncle Mike got there.

'What are you going to see at the cinema, Alastair?'

'We are very late. We need to go immediately.' Anne was standing in the middle of the sitting room. Her shoulders had risen to within a millimetre of her ears. Fair hairs were sticking to her forehead, which had taken on an almost alarming level of shininess. It was Lady V who realized first that Anne might be having a panic attack. She jumped up on her crutches.

'Of course, Anne, you mustn't be late.'

Mike was protesting about how the young lad had just got there and his Coke was only half drunk but Lady V shot him a look and he surrendered his claim on Alastair Stairs.

'I'll walk you out.'

Alastair followed a limping Lady V to the door, trailed by a visibly shaken Anne as the rest of the room stared on, intrigued. Uncle Danny continued to confound us when he stood again to tell Anne how nice it was to meet a friend of hers. We all rallied a chorus of agreement. We were of course happy for her, but mainly we were *dying* of curiosity. We needed to know everything that could be known about this individual and his relationship to Anne. We waited until the front door shut.

When older people in the Black family were worried that they were about to say something racist they put a positive adjective in front of the word that they thought might be problematic. Uncle Mike got there first.

'Is Anne dating that EXTREMELY NICE Chinese man?'

Bobby rolled his eyes.

'He is quite clearly English.'

'Yes, but I mean *originally*, where do you think he came from originally, Bobby? What was his surname again? Elevator? Or was it Otis? Or are they the people who make the elevators?'

'There is a very strong Catholic community in the Philippines, he could be from there.' (Aunt Angela)

The younger generation tried to ignore Mike as he started googling Thai surnames and Angela as she listed Asian countries with high levels of Christianity. Blur found Alastair on LinkedIn and started reading his CV out loud. Helen was impressed that he listed baking as an extracurricular activity and Frances was delighted that he practised yoga. Uncle John chipped in with his own area of expertise.

'I can tell you that the young man has great taste in shoes. He was sporting a lovely soft leather Italian brogue – €100 at retail would be my estimate.'

The patter rose in excitement, so it was a while before we heard Killian roaring down the line.

'So now you've rung me because my sister is going to the cinema? Fuck's sake.'

He hung up before we could apologize.

21. ANNE

Dublin, April 5th 2019

Alastair couldn't possibly still think they were going to the cinema. He couldn't possibly think they'd ever do anything even remotely social together again. The only reason she was even in the car was that she had been too shell-shocked by the whole experience not to get in. Soon she would find her breath. Soon she would find the words to tell him to pull over. Not to bring her home. Not even to a bus stop. But to let her out on the side of the road. On the dual carriageway. In the middle of the traffic, for all she cared, she just had to get out. Out of the car and out of this minor dalliance that had escalated far beyond its remit.

It had all gone wrong in Cork. Since Alastair hadn't come up through the ranks with Anne, he didn't know about her boundaries. He didn't know what her intake had learnt when they'd trained together, about her routines and her polite interactions that didn't move beyond the beautifully clear lines of the workplace. And if someone had given him the memo, he didn't seem to have read it because he kept asking her for a drink. She wanted to tell him that he seemed great. That he seemed just the job for someone. But she wasn't in the same zone as him. She wasn't doing the same level of interacting that other people were doing. She was in a contained interaction zone.

For Anne, being an auditor wasn't a job. It was everything. It had given her structure when everything else in her life had seemed like a great uncontrollable herd of cattle that could go any direction. She thanked Christ for the safety of accountancy. For the clean lines of Excel. For the beauty of a balanced spreadsheet. For fixed and variable costs. For pivot tables and a world that could be managed. That made sense. That could be solved. She had long ago given up hope of being able to trade in the currency Irish people seemed to value most – an inane chattiness that she couldn't abide. As an auditor she was able to succeed on merit. For being thorough. Diligent. Responsible.

She knew that no one else could understand how much work meant to her. They complained about hours and difficult bosses. They tried to squeeze in drinks with college pals and dates. Anne didn't want those things. What she wanted was her morning routine – arriving at the desk, coffee in hand at 7.30. Flying through emails before anyone else came in. Smiling at colleagues as they pattered in sleepily at 9 – she wasn't a tyrant – she didn't mind what they did. She just wanted to do what she did and do it well. She took half an hour at lunch to walk around the Iveagh Gardens before eating the contents of her lunchbox at her desk and reading the business section of *The Irish Times*. And in her own small way she was happy. Happy and safe in the knowledge that she would make partner, that she would not be conflicted about being late for a boyfriend waiting at home, that children were not in her eye line. But that was before Alastair was transferred from Ealing.

In Cork, every day after lunch he had bought her a Walnut Whip. She'd mentioned that they were tricky to get but she'd said it in passing. She didn't like the walnut on top, just the white gooey part, so he'd taken to eating the nut. On the third day of this routine it was all getting a bit cosy. She didn't like where it was going so she tried not to eat them. She thought a pile of Walnut Whips on the edge of her desk would send a message – a 'don't engage with me on this intimate Walnut Whip level' type of message. But by about 6 p.m. when she knew she'd be there for at least another three hours, her stomach would start to grumble, and she'd rip open the foil. Keeping his eyes on his screen he'd smile and reach over for the nut, but he was smart enough not to say anything for once in his over-talkative life.

It was coming towards the end of the first week of the secondment when she had finally agreed to go for a burger on the Friday night. Usually audit teams were packed up and gone by 4 p.m. on a Friday but they'd both agreed to work the weekend. They had nowhere else to be. Then the next day, it had felt weird in the office with no one else there, so they'd left early. They'd gone to the cinema. The cinema she could get behind. No useless chit-chat and Coke on tap. That last week they'd gone three times. Late showings were the perfect way to wind down from the hectic day.

She thought something would change when they got back to Dublin, but without her realizing it, he seemed to have slipped into her life. She'd gotten used to a Walnut

Whip after lunch. (Where was he sourcing them? Had he bought them in bulk on the internet?) He had even stayed over once - a wildly unlikely slip in Anne's well-defended boundaries. But this fiasco with the family had woken her up. It was one thing for Alastair Stairs to talk to her at work, to join her on her strolls around the Iveagh Gardens and even to entwine his hand into hers terrifyingly close to the office. It was quite another for him to meet the Blacks.

Somewhere along the line he'd gotten the wrong impression of the Blacks. His entire family was one person (and many dogs). No matter what Anne said about them, just the idea of a sprawling extended family who knew too much about each other appealed to him. He thought they were nosy and eccentric but ultimately great. They were not. They were suffocating. They were overbearing. They pigeon-holed you and it didn't matter how you changed or who you became, they could only see you the way they had when they met you first – which was either at your birth or theirs.

Their half-stifled shock at Alastair's arrival this evening had been unbearable. She'd heard them practically squeal when she'd closed the front door. They had no idea who she was or what she did with her time. They didn't want to know. They just wanted to measure her every action against the person they thought she was. The pain was acute.

'PULL OVER!'

Alastair's hands jumped off the wheel and he swerved slightly into the bus lane. 'My goodness. Sorry about that, I got a fright. What did you say?'

Up until this point he seemed to have no idea that anything was wrong. He had been animatedly complimenting everything in Uncle Mike's house. How friendly Bobby was, how kind Uncle Danny was. He had never seen anyone as good-looking as Lady V. Did an interior designer do the house? There was a very complete feel to the style of the rooms which he didn't think he'd be able to achieve if he were to decorate his own house. When he started on about how comfy the cushions were, Anne knew he hadn't a clue about the gravity of what had just happened, the line he'd overstepped. There could be no long-winded discussion. She would have to be completely uncompromising.

'Stop the car now. Not up ahead, not at the lights. Now.'

'Is this about me coming into the house? I should have waited in the car. I got a bit excited to see them all if I'm honest. I'm very sorry.'

'Stop the car. Stop the car. STOP THE CAR!'

'Oh my goodness.'

He pulled over after the turnoff for Stillorgan and she got out of the car. She didn't look back. She walked the whole way to Grand Canal. When she closed the door to her flat, relief flooded her from her hairband to her pumps. She didn't move. She stood with her back to the door, feeling immense safety as the lock clicked behind her. A vase of white tulips sat on the hall table. She had recently brought all her winter coats to the dry cleaner then folded them away, so the coat stand was unencumbered waiting for the raincoat on her back. Her post was ordered on the hall table. Everything was in its place. Everything quiet as a mouse until her phone pinged.

'I had no idea coming into the house would cause so much distress. I'm very sorry, Anne. I know your cousin

Molly irritates you immensely and with good reason – it seems like she walks out on everyone.'

Anne was still looking at the screen when another message arrived.

'But not letting anyone in in the first place isn't the answer either. Best of luck finding her.'

She slid the phone across the hall table. It slid too far and fell off the end into a wastepaper basket. Good. She wouldn't be needing it anyway. She wouldn't be engaging with him again. He was completely off the mark.

She walked into the kitchen and prayed that Joel the lodger wasn't sitting there eating corn on the cob. The room was empty, and she went straight to her safe place: the cupboard under the sink. She pulled on her plastic gloves. She was halfway done with the skirting boards when she remembered what Uncle Danny had said. In that awful, terrifying moment of exposure when the family had barely concealed their giddiness, his eyes had met hers and his words had stopped her in her tracks.

'You deserve to be happy.'

She sat back on her hunkers in a vacant stare. Life had taught her that no one got what they deserved. She saw a fleck of grease she'd missed, and her vacancy returned to focus.

22. MOLLY

London, March 2nd 2019
The morning after the party

Molly's bedroom door opened. She was surprised that B was up so early and slightly worried that he'd impede her escape, but through a squint she realized that it was Jeff standing in the doorway. Topless, he was holding two mugs of coffee. For someone so lanky he was sculpted like a personal trainer. Grey sweatpants hung off his abdominal V where Molly could make out a strip of black boxers.

'You've come to the wrong door.' Molly scrambled over the covers to reach for the coffee. 'The audition for Calvin Klein models from the nineties is next door.'

Pulling the mug back just as she was about to reach it, Jeff smiled. Molly lost her balance and crumpled back into the covers; a pile of tangled hair in an old t-shirt and leggings. Relinquishing, Jeff handed her the mug and sat down on the covers. He inched back until he was leaning against the wall and looked around her room.

She wondered what it must look like to a grown up. To a

man in his late thirties who owned a flat, who had savings in the bank, who probably visited the dentist at regular intervals and had life insurance. Her room was next to bare. She had a rolling lease, but it wasn't just this house. It had been like this in every place for the last ten years. If Jeff looked under the bed, he would find a half-unpacked suitcase that lived there permanently.

Up until recently it seemed like everyone Molly knew was shifting and jumping in some shape or form. Friends who worked in banks had given up their jobs to open cafés or juice bars, people were going back to college to retrain for jobs they actually liked. They were spread across house shares in North London: Camden, Kentish Town, Islington and Finsbury Park. There was always a room going and there were so many of them jammed in together that rent was cheap.

Molly kept meaning to get a permanent job, but temping was so easy. She could work whatever hours she liked and still be available for a last-minute trip to Berlin and to spend every weekend at a different festival during the summer. But there were fewer and fewer people available for gigs now. There was only one house share left and it was beginning to feel like they were the leftovers from other houses, clinging to other times.

And now B was about to fall down the rabbit hole too. He was leaving the dive in Finsbury Park for Jeff's apartment in Soho with the turquoise tiles and the Le Creuset everything – not just pots. It turned out Le Creuset made mugs and egg cups too and Jeff had them all. Jeff's apartment had all the grown-up things like real pasta strainers and so many tea towels you could blow your nose in one, stuff it back in the drawer and it'd be weeks before you'd reach the snotty one again.

Molly wanted to be gone before B. She wanted to disappear. To slip happily into some other reality so that she didn't have to be there while he packed all his belongings and gave her reassuring smiles. He would try to get several dates in the diary with her, asking her to lunches and dinners to make the transition easier for her and it was AWFUL. She had to let him off the hook. He had to go into the future headfirst. He couldn't look back, and if he did, he couldn't find Molly behind him. In the background. Living a life that was over; the last person at the last party.

'Could you do me a favour?'

'Of course.'

'Could you make sure B knows I'm OK? I'm going back to Ireland for a bit.'

Outside a bin truck stopped and started, letting out warning beeps. Molly realized it must be even earlier than she thought. That was good. She had plenty of time to get herself together. To be gone before B woke up. She half wondered why Jeff was up so early.

'I need you to do something for me too.'

Jeff's eyebrows contorted in concern, and Molly knew what was coming. She should have set her alarm for dawn, been gone before she saw anyone. She had disappeared before. This wasn't how you did it. You couldn't engage with anyone else. They would try to convince you to stay. She could immediately see how the day would go. She'd end up having brunch with B and Jeff, they'd convince her to fly later and by then the hangover would catch up with her and she wouldn't be able to resist the couch and a roast. Then she'd never leave. She'd end up hanging around waiting for everyone else's life to move on around her.

'Let me give you some money.'

Molly looked up from her mug, half distracted by the noises outside. It didn't matter how long she had been gone or how far away she was, when she woke early in any city other than Dublin, Molly always missed the seagulls. Instead, the bin men were calling out to each other, their voices reassuring.

'I know you're going to say no but you don't understand. I've got more than I know what to do with. You and B, you've been together since you were four. Now I'm taking him away and it's not guilt. I'm not trying to make myself feel less guilty; it's just that if you are going to go somewhere, go somewhere proper. Don't just go to Dublin. Let me book you on a flight to somewhere where you can clear your head.'

Jeff crawled to the end of the bed and padded barefoot into the other room. She could hear him searching in the living room for his jacket. Molly wondered if he had any idea how much was in her head. How much there was to clear. She'd been on the move for over ten years and still there were drawers in her head that she feared opening. There were thoughts and memories she couldn't let go of, places in her heart she was afraid of. Big things, but small things too and sometimes the small things were the most painful.

Last summer Killian had come home for a wedding and all the cousins had gone for lunch. Anne had ordered a salad and just as the waiter was walking away Killian had asked him to make sure there was no sweetcorn in it. He did it unthinkingly, without question. It was as natural to him as if he was listing his own aversion and Molly thought about it all the time. Anne and Killian were so different. Tall, handsome, cocky; Killian could talk you into paying for a gulp of polluted air. Anne, on the other hand, recorded *Countdown* to watch on Saturday nights while she ironed. They were polar opposites, but they knew each other in some way that transcended having anything in common. They belonged to each other.

Who did Molly belong to now that B was moving on? Who did she belong to so much that sometimes they got confused between her needs and their own? Who knew that her favourite part of the egg was the white? Who knew that when she couldn't sleep, she sang the soundtrack of *Evita* in her head? Who knew that when she couldn't breathe she counted upwards in fives? Even before her mum died B had been that person. But he had to have his own life. She was close to Anne and Bobby, but they'd had to bail her out so many times before. She knew Uncle John would do anything for her, but he already had Uncle Danny to mind and now Granny too. Was she really going to land in on them and upturn their ordered lives with her chaotic one all over again?

Something imperceptible had shifted at Christmas. After the vomiting had finally ended and she'd used what strength she could muster to industrially clean the flat, she'd readied herself for a return to normal – for B to come back, for the next adventure, for her spirits to rise – but in the intervening months she couldn't seem to keep the creeping tide at bay. She was thinner than she'd ever been – a nervous anxiety eating her from the inside. The grief was coming for her and there was no party, no brisk walk, no new distraction that could stop it from engulfing her. She was beginning to think that everyone had a certain number of allocated coupons. Coupons to make mistakes; to fuck everything up but still come home. Part of having parents was having limitless coupons. But orphans don't have coupons. Orphans have running shoes.

Jeff came back into the room, his phone in one hand and credit card in the other. He was already on Skyscanner. She let out a soft laugh.

'It's a nice thought, thank you.'

'I'm deadly serious. Let me do this for you. What about Thailand?'

Jeff's brown eyes had a tinge of green she had never noticed. He looked exactly like what he said he was: deadly serious. He hadn't blinked since he'd come into her room and she wondered if some days it just never started. If some days his reflexes forgot to be nervous. She felt a pang of warmth towards him. For the immense effort he made with her. And she wondered if maybe he just wanted some time with B. It can't have been easy having her around the whole time. Maybe it wasn't just her family she was running out of coupons with.

She would come back. In two or three months when summer was kicking off. They would start a new routine. One that placed a bit of space between them. She sensed a fog clearing. The darkness of the last few weeks was lifting, and a burst of excitement rose through her. She wouldn't be the last person at the party, she wouldn't be left behind. Because she wouldn't even be here.

'How soon could I leave?'

Jeff smiled as Molly jumped off the bed. She pulled up the covers and dragged out the half-empty backpack. She poured it out onto the desk under the window. Bills and council tax notifications scattered across the floor, but behind them, a tumble of summer clothes. Her hair was falling in swathes across her face, so she leant the bag against herself while she looked for something to tie it up with. She pulled a sock off her foot and knotted it around her hair in a bun. She swiftly put all the bills directly in the bin and began to roll up the crinkled summer clothes. She couldn't care less what she brought. She just wanted to be gone.

'Have you ever wanted to disappear?'

Jeff's words stopped Molly dead in her tracks. She turned to look at him. His loose brown curls flopped to one side of his forehead, glinting with streaks of silver, which only served to make him more attractive. His bare chest wasn't tanned but it wasn't white either; it glowed a pale yellow. He held her gaze and somehow in that moment she felt like he had seen deep inside her. Like he knew something about her that she didn't even know.

'In Thailand, there's this community. I don't know where. Some island. It's mainly yoga retreats, ashrams, that kind of thing. But sometimes people go there to disappear. They leave their phones, their personal belongings, everything, and just walk into the forest. They can be gone for months, years even. I don't know. Sometimes I understand it.'

She looked up at him. Jeff was so sure of himself – quietly confident. How could someone like that ever want to disappear? Someone with a boyfriend, a flat, a good job. Someone who didn't have anything to run from. His admission felt like an act of great kindness. If even life-insured, mortgaged and regularly tended teeth type people wanted to disappear sometimes then maybe she wasn't so crazy. But she'd never go that far, would she? She took a sip of the coffee. It was lukewarm, but she was already burning inside, alive at the prospect of running again.

PART TWO

23. SHEENA

London, January 10th 2019

Sheena Griffith was a good person. She had no idea why she was in the dispensary of St George's about to cross a line she could never have imagined even coming close to, up until right now when she was standing on it.

Sleeping tablets, he'd said, preferably zopiclone. Some codeine if she could get her hands on it. All she had to do was mark them down for patients who'd already been discharged then remove the labels so they couldn't be linked back to the hospital. No one would ever know. And she'd be really helping him out.

Staring at the rows and rows of labels she wondered if she loved him. If that was why she had agreed to throw everything away for some sleeping tablets. But it wasn't real love, she knew that. It was a phony half love that just about staved off the crippling loneliness that had crept up on her from behind after what happened to the baby.

She tried to weigh up if it was safer to take a full box or one tray of tablets from several boxes. Deciding on the former, she slipped the zopiclone in her top pocket. Totally visible, she would hide them in plain sight. She might not even take them home. She might drop them back. She might put them in the bin or laugh about accidentally grabbing them at the nurses' station later. Or she might bring them home and throw her life away simply because she was lonely.

'Jesus.'

Closing the door to the drugs cupboard, Sheena crashed into a white coat. She relaxed when she heard the accent. The Irish doctor leant in towards her.

'Jesus is more effective than oops, isn't it? But less offensive than, well, fuck.'

He whispered the last word and looked left and right at the doctors and nurses passing in the hallway to make sure no one had heard. It took Sheena a moment to adjust. To realize that he hadn't seen her. That so far, she'd done nothing wrong. So far it could all be an honest mistake.

'I'm Conor, by the way.'

He was in gastroenterology. She knew about him, they all did, because he looked like a caricature of an Irish person. One of the other nurses had gone up to him at the Christmas party and pointed at his mop of red hair and freckles and asked him if his ancestors had survived the famine. He said he guessed they must have. She had reported back that he was from Roscommon.

'I'm Sheena, it's nice to meet you.'

'You're the smiley ICU nurse.'

'Sorry?'

'That's what the gastro team call you.' His face reddened and it looked for a second like all his freckles were about to join together. 'I hope it's OK that I said that. I'm sure you take your work seriously. It's just when the team consult on the ICU ward, they say you are happy, I mean, nice to work with.'

He held his hands up in the air like he was trying to stop an impending accident. Sheena smiled and felt her heels rise from the ground in her usual unwitting bounce.

People thought that Sheena was tall but on second glance she was just athletic. They thought she was tall because she was all limbs and couldn't help but bounce as she moved. She bounced on the wards, she bounced around the town at home, she even bounced on the tube where people looked at her like she had lost her mind. At twenty-five, her ponytail still swung like a little girl. She swung, and she bounced and swivelled on the balls of her feet until she stopped. Until the last few weeks when she couldn't get any distance at all between her and the hard ground.

It started with the baby. She had treated babies before. She had even treated a baby in the ICU before but not like this. Not so close to saving her. The baby girl was out of danger. She had made it. After weeks of watching her like a hawk all through Christmas, weeks of excruciating near-misses and incredible catches, the baby had survived. She would be fine. The baby's beautiful mother who looked like death at the end of three months on the brink would sleep again. Her handsome dad who slept on the floor outside the ICU because he was too tall for a chair could go home. They were all going home, until they weren't. Until Sheena came in for an early morning shift after New Year's to find the baby dead. Dead and gone and no trace of her or her ghostly mother or her aching-backed dad and instead a chart of new patients equally as dire. The Christmas lights were still hanging up but the period of hope was over. Sheena wasn't the baby's mother. She wasn't even her aunt or her cousin. She couldn't fall apart. She had to help the five year old who had come in in the early hours of the morning with meningitis and now might not live through the day. All her life she'd wanted to be a nurse but now she was here and maybe she just couldn't do it. Maybe she just wasn't able. But who would she be if she wasn't a nurse?

'It's nice that people think I'm happy.' Sheena felt her shoulders release. 'Not think. I mean, I *am* happy. Sorry, god, long shift.'

'Tell me about it. If you ever want to grab a coffee, that'd be really nice.'

Sheena looked up at him in surprise. She couldn't remember the last time she'd done anything other than work, sleep or shower. The doctors always seemed so old, but Roscommon Conor couldn't be much older than thirty. And he had suggested a coffee. Not a drink in a bar that she'd have to try to stay awake for. Maybe she could talk to him. Maybe she could tell him about baby blue. Roscommon Conor was reddening even further like he was holding his breath and she realized she hadn't answered. She let out a laugh.

'Yes. Absolutely. Yes, I'd like that.'

Her ponytail swung as she walked away from him, his number in her phone. She smiled for the rest of the shift. She was in bed drifting off to sleep that night before she remembered the sleeping tablets in the breast pocket of her uniform and the line she'd inexplicably crossed.

24. MOLLY

Postmarked Bangkok, March 8th 2019
Arrived in Dublin one month later, April 8th 2019

Dear Uncle John,

I hope that you and the family are well.

As you know, I've been running for a long time now. I think that while I moved from place to place, I could pretend on some level that Mum and Dad weren't fully gone. That maybe Dad was still stocking his wardrobe from the lost and found at school, rolling up the sleeves on his latest fleece to show me on the map where Greenland was, smelling of green tea and chalk. That Mum was still driving around Dublin singing ABBA at the top of her lungs. That her face would light up if I came home like it did when I got back from school every day. I could imagine that I still had a home to go back to.

I've been trying to find a way to stop running for a while and I think I might finally have found one. It means being away from you all for a bit, but that's OK. I'm OK. Or at least I think I will be. You don't need to worry about finding me anymore.

Love always,
Molly x

25. BOBBY

British Airways Flight, April 13th 2019

The other passengers would have been hard pressed to guess that the six Irish people on the British Airways flight from Heathrow to Bangkok were travelling together. Lady V was in first class. She claimed she got randomly selected for an upgrade when they saw her broken ankle, but she arrived at the airport with a pillow, an eye mask and a carry-on bigger than Uncle John's checked-in bag. She was in a foul mood because Mike had abandoned her to his family and was making up for it with complimentary gin. Down the back of the plane Uncle John had accidentally overdosed on Xanax. Ironically this induced a panic attack in Anne who feared John might die from the Xanax and, on the other side of the aisle, B was indulging an air stewardess who claimed to be his BIGGEST fan.

In the middle seat of the middle aisle, Bobby was attempting to practise extreme mindfulness but it wasn't working, so when Anne jumped out of her seat to apologize for Uncle John stretching his legs over the stunned elderly couple sitting next to him, Bobby slid out behind her, with no plan other than to be anywhere on the planet except in seat 32E. In an alcove between the bathroom and the galley Bobby sank into a squat and felt the blood rush to his legs for the first time in hours. He placed his head against the plastic window and closed his eyes.

The Black family had countless flaws. They were nosy and judgemental. Their collective sense of direction was so poor that more than one of them had gotten lost on the way to their own home. They cared about the stupidest things and thought you did too – did you know there are roadworks on Leeson Street? What do you think they are for? Did you hear sirens today? Where did you think the guards were off to? Did you know that Martin down the road had a triple bypass? Ah for god's sake, of course you know Martin. You've known him all your life, albeit not well, but you know he has the red car and the wife with the dog and the hairdo? Well, he nearly died anyway. What do you make of that? You didn't make anything of it. All you wanted to know was whether it was the wife or the dog that had the hairdo.

The Black family didn't stop talking. They didn't stop meeting. They didn't stop phoning. They were insufferable. They never left you alone. But that was the point. They never left any of their own alone so how had this happened? Nobody had taken Molly's disappearance seriously. Nobody was genuinely worried. Until the letter. Molly's letter had sent shockwaves through the family. The letter was postmarked five weeks ago – she could be anywhere by now.

Bobby had gone over and over her words in his head since

the letter had arrived, trying to understand what it meant. She had said that they didn't need to worry about finding her anymore as if she was a burden to them, as if their long struggle with her was over. Bobby had heard about people disappearing. About places in India and Thailand where you go to live with spiritual leaders and renounce your identity. Molly didn't really want to disappear, did she? And if she did, how had things gotten this bad?

Naturally, the first thing each of the Blacks did when they read the letter was make it all about themselves. Uncle Mike wanted to call her in like a defective product recall. He spoke about her like a cat with an RFID chip in its collar and got completely irate when there was nobody he could call or no cheque he could write to miracle her back. Aunt Angela held a prayer circle in Glenmalure and Bobby's dad Even-Stephen analysed the letter for hidden messages in case Molly was under the influence of 'malign forces'.

They all spoke about the possibility of her joining a cult like it was just a matter of time. Bobby's mum Frances was only sorry she'd never had the chance to join one herself. But under all their bluster, an unspoken thread of fear coursed through the aunts and uncles. A sense that they'd been here before. They had just about pulled Uncle Danny from the brink and the older generation seemed wracked with fear that they'd lose Molly too. And for the first time Bobby saw that they might.

Bobby knew about grief. How it tricked you. How it sat deep inside you then came for you just when you weren't expecting it. Molly had spent the last ten years on the run. Somehow, now, her parents' deaths were catching up with her. Molly had saved Bobby from his grief. Where had he been when she had needed him? He had been so wrapped up in his own crisis that he'd let her slip from him. Molly had no parents, no siblings. The mismatched group of loons behind him on the plane were her safety net. They were all she had.

'Are you the pilot?'

Bobby had turned to face a small boy in a pilot's uniform and hat.

'Of course not. Clearly *you* are.'

The boy smiled widely and shook his head.

'Inna pilot but not this plane.'

'Oh I see, you're just a passenger this time?'

'Yeah. Inna passenger this time.'

A woman with hair sticking to her face at all angles scooped the boy up in her arms.

'I'd like to tell you that he got away from me, but I'm so exhausted I will happily allow my two-year old child to talk to strangers. On a plane at least.'

'His verbal reasoning skills are incredibly impressive for a two year old.'

'Parent?'

'Teacher.'

'That must be rewarding.'

Bobby stood.

'It is. It really is. Thanks.'

He didn't know why he added the thanks, but he felt unnaturally grateful to this stranger for understanding. He followed her back into the body of the plane. Up ahead he could see his unlikely congregation. Uncle John seemed to have awoken from his self-induced coma and was describing Bangkok's sex trafficking trade to the couple he had just stretched his legs across. The words PIMPS and OPIUM echoed loudly across the plane. The elderly lady's face was turning a pale green. She was gripping her husband's arm and saying his name over and over again.

'Listen, Stanley, what do you make of ISIS?'

Armed with the man's name, Uncle John turned in his seat to lean in closer to Stanley. A rush of panic filled Bobby from head to toe but he was caught behind B's biggest fan as she doled out peanuts. He bounced behind the air stewardess to incite her to speed up, but she continued even-paced and cautious, like she was administering IV drips to patients and not peanuts to passed-out passengers. From the other end of the plane, Uncle Danny emerged from behind the curtain.

When Bobby had agreed to go to Thailand, the trip had seemed like a comparative break from the funk he'd been in. But now he saw that the so-called extraction team consisted of nothing but liabilities. The line-up was an irate aunt with a broken ankle, a vacuous vlogger who Bobby had actively avoided for twenty years, a heavily sedated uncle on the verge of a pro-terrorism diatribe, a nervous wreck who could only grasp concepts which existed as functions in Excel, and at the last minute – and the absolute pièce de résistance – they'd had to replace Mike, the one reliable member of the team, with a long-term alcoholic.

'You've got to hand it to the ISIS lads. They made significant progress in a short space of time, didn't they? What do you think they are up to now?'

John went full whacko just as there was a hold-up at the peanut trolley. A couple wanted to understand the origins of the product. B's biggest fan was only too happy to oblige. By the time Bobby reached the scene, John's seat was empty. Up ahead, Danny was unevenly ushering John down the aisle expounding the importance of not getting a blood clot. Bobby was overcome with relief. He slipped into Uncle John's seat to give Stanley and his wife a break.

Glancing up, his uncles looked entirely out of place – two cumbersome beige figures bumping down the narrow aisle. However, despite their oddities he was suddenly filled with love for them. They were imperfect. But they were here. Trying to find the person they'd all accidentally let fall through the cracks.

26. LADY V

Bangkok, April 14th 2019

V closed the door to her suite and locked eyes with the minibar. Normally she would never do something so stupid. Minibars were the world's longest running scam. She had spent years inculcating the fear of god about them into her sons, who were now reluctant to even be in the same room as one, for fear of incurring some sort of cost. But V knew about self-preservation and right now she knew that she would only manage to keep sane if she was in a bath drinking something alcoholic. And since she was breaking a lifelong rule anyway, she reached for the mini-Champagne. Throwing her crutches on the bed, she changed into a robe. She was careful to avoid looking in the mirror.

Starvation wasn't how she remembered it. She used to rock up to shoots sustained only by Champagne and chewing gum. Now she was faint and furious. And was she imagining it or, without the exercise, was she already beginning to put on weight? In the bath she threw her cast up over the edge of the tub and let out a long deep breath.

The flight was over. The treacherous taxi ride through the streets teeming with people and pelleted by rain was over. She had been extricated from the Blacks who did not, it seemed, travel well. Between the plane and the terminal building John had turned beetroot and begun to evaporate through his linen suit. She hoped that the outfit was an anomaly and that the rest of his luggage was more low-key. He had arrived at Dublin Airport yesterday resembling a British colonialist having tea on a lawn in Delhi in 1926.

V took a swig of Champagne and it oozed into her system like liquid gold. It was worth every penny of the million dollars it probably cost. Still, her shoulders were hard as rocks and she had the added burden of knowing that she had to reassess her plan.

The original idea was that since she couldn't work because of her ankle anyway, V would come to Thailand with Mike for two weeks. The first week she'd put her feet up in the Shangri-La while Mike and the Nancy Drew crew found Molly. The Black family would stay in some budget hotel far away. V would of course *see* them. Once they found Molly, she would personally invite them to the Shangri-La for dinner on the outdoor terrace to celebrate. By the end of that first week, V would have a light glow from lounging by the riverside swimming pool and all the treatments she would avail of in the spa. She would order cocktails for the table and come across as generous and compassionate. Then she and Mike would fly to the Four Seasons in Koh Samui for the second week, packing the Nancy Drew crew off home.

The first spanner in the works had been the US delegation. At the last minute Mike had been called in to meet a major client from the US. But that wasn't even the worst of it. It turned out that B had made some sort of deal with the Shangri-La to do a live demo from their rooftop restaurant and in return the rest of the Black family could stay in the hotel for next to nothing. There was no choice now. V was part of the Nancy Drew crew.

Her phone beeped and she lunged for it, thinking perhaps it could be Mike checking in. Instead, it was a news alert about the doctor. V zoomed in on the picture. He was short and nowhere near as good-looking as the Griffith girl. Maybe he thought because he was a doctor, he might have a shot with her. V submerged deeper into the bath. She felt strangely protective of this girl she didn't know and vitriolic towards this predator stalking her. V's anger at the doctor was so strong she knew it was a lightning rod for other things too. Anger towards Molly for running away, for bringing them all out here on a wild goose chase. But the anger was laced with fear too.

V wasn't involved in finding Danny. She didn't get the late-night phone calls, she had never driven around cities in England looking for him, but she knew enough to know that when the others had found him it had been bad. So bad that John had become hyper-protective of the rest of them, behaving like a teacher on a school trip – constantly taking headcounts of them all.

No one ever talked about what had happened to Danny, what he would do for the rest of his life, if he'd live with his mother forever, if there was any future for him. They all just hoped against hope that he would somehow keep his head above water.

V stared momentarily at the marble surrounding her.

She had to remember – Molly wasn't Danny. Molly was a spoilt millennial who made a habit of running away. Molly had them following her around the world, questioning themselves, spending a fortune. She needed to be yanked back to reality. And V knew she was the one to do it. The Blacks were soft as brie.

Leaning lightly on her cast she hopped her good leg out of the bath. This time she forgot to avoid the mirror. The bathroom was covered in glass and all she could see was flesh. Her sharp hip bones and elegant clavicle had disappeared. Round and succulent, she looked like a hunk of meat. She shivered as she reached for the rest of the Champagne, dosing herself like she had dosed her children with Calpol – for general unease.

She hobbled into the bedroom and began unpacking one-pieces and sarongs she'd have no use for now. At the bottom of her bag she found the tattered red diary she'd thrown in at the last minute. She looked at it for a long time. She hadn't read it in years, and she had no idea if it would help Molly or make things worse. To V, the diary was a reminder of a time of pure terror. It sat there in the bottom of the empty bag like a foreboding totem, a reminder of what it felt like to be completely out of control. V drained her Champagne glass and threw the empty bag into the bottom of the wardrobe. She needed to get out of there.

At the spa, several ladies got to work on her at once, one soaking her good foot, another manicuring her fingers and a third massaging her shoulders. In the calm of the Urban Retreat, she began to formulate a new plan.

27. LADY V

Dublin, 1999

She was in the middle of a shoot when it happened first. Later she would become used to it. Later still she would become a complete expert in it – getting a physiotherapist to train her in pelvic floor exercises and setting up classes in the gym specifically to help pregnant women. But right now, with the bright lights melting her make-up and her fake husband's beard itching her cheek, she visibly jumped when she felt not just a trickle but a burst of urine escape her bladder. She hadn't even realized she needed to pee. The set was dusty from all the woodchip they were pretending to put together in their pretend house which they'd just got a pretend mortgage for. She'd sneezed and abruptly felt a surge of water coming out of her like a dam breaking on a river. No warning drops. No polite heads up. A FLOOD. A DELUGE. The inspiration for Noah's Ark. She stood stock still, unable to move.

Her first thought was Annabelle Black. With her wild red hair and her over-sharing, wearing all that velvet and maroon. When Annabelle had called up to the house last week, at first V had been intrigued. She'd always seen the Blacks in bulk. They seemed to V like a giant swarm of suburban vanilla, but Annabelle was different. Annabelle appeared in the newspaper and on the radio. She knew interesting people and did interesting things. Not interesting to V but artsy types rated her – she was a close personal friend of Terry Wogan. Annabelle had seemed to take an interest in V too, always approaching her at family events, asking her how she was. V wondered now if she wanted something from her. V wouldn't be giving her Sharon Corr's number if that's why she was here.

Annabelle had to run, she explained, as she rooted in the boot for something – she had to pick up Molly from the childminder before the child got cancer. The minder smoked sixty a day so Annabelle really tried to get her out of there before she hit the thirty-five to forty mark. The boot of her car was jammed full of Crazy Prices bags. V couldn't imagine Annabelle doing anything domestic, so she peered into the Toyota to see what Annabelle had bought. Cans of baked beans and fish fingers were visible through the plastic but there were exotic things in there too like a giant aubergine, couscous and several bottles of Chianti. V counted the bottle tops to tell Mike later.

'Look, I know this is strange, but no one told me about the peeing, and it knocked me for six. I wish I'd known what was coming so I thought I'd pop over in case.'

Annabelle passed V a plastic bag filled with something resembling industrial bandages. Annabelle was still talking, saying something about a play and the toilet and the fear and feeling alone. V hadn't a clue what she was blathering about until she saw the word in tiny print along the bottom of the package: incontinence. Annabelle moved around to the front seat and stopped with the door open.

'My mum was dead when I had Molly too. I didn't know if you knew that.'

V stood shell-shocked. She was immobilized by horror. The plastic bag of pads burned in her hands like a bomb. Annabelle was old. V was spritely. V was active. That wasn't going to happen to her. That only happened to middle-aged women. V wanted nothing to do with this package. She had to get rid of it; even touching it was sending her heartbeat sky high.

'I just thought I'd tell you that and also mention if you ever want to talk about anything – not just peeing yourself – just pick up the phone.'

Annabelle smiled softly, in a timid way that V had never seen before. After getting into the car, she started to back out of the drive. There was an added moment of alarm when she nearly reversed into a car turning into the estate.

The second Annabelle was out of view, V turned like lightning. Mike was due home any minute. She raced to the bin at the back of the house. Just before she buried the pads, a fleck of red caught her eye at the bottom of the bag. It was a small red notebook; probably a log of all the times the woman had peed herself. She grabbed it in case Annabelle had left it there by mistake, but when she opened it V found entries like a diary – all written to Molly. She didn't have time to hover, so she shoved it in her pocket promising herself she'd return it. She wrapped the pads in three Superquinn bags before putting them in the bin so that Mike wouldn't see the word INCONTINENCE.

Up until now, being pregnant had seemed all upside.

She had more ads in the last three months than she'd had in the last year. Dunnes Stores nightwear. Bank of Ireland mortgages. Vitamin supplements. If you wanted your brand to seem nurturing and heart-warming then a pregnant woman was the way to go. But now here she was, in the middle of a shoot, standing stock still as a stream from the deluge trickled down her thigh.

As she made her way through the studio to the bathroom, an uneasy feeling took over. She smiled politely at the cameraman, pointed towards the loo as she nodded at the make-up artist, but all the while her heart rate was quickening. She knew what the books said about what was coming: back pain, heartburn, indigestion, feet kicking into her ribs, losing control of her body and clearly of her bladder. Peeing her pants felt like a slippery slope. And she couldn't help but hold Annabel Black partly responsible. Why had Annabelle barged into her life like that? Arriving in a bluster, talking about incontinence, and offering V her phone number. V was nothing like Annabelle. Molly was a sweet girl but she was practically feral. She wore mismatched clothes and hung from trees and talked to herself. V's children wouldn't be like Molly. They'd always have clean hair and keep a cool distance from mess. They'd wear pale blue dungarees matched with white polo t-shirts – only OshKosh B'gosh.

V took a deep breath and held her underwear under the hand dryer. Within a few seconds they were dry. She took another deep breath and returned to the shoot. Annabelle might have been right about bladder control but that didn't mean V was anything like her. V was lucky – things came easy to her and parenting would be no different. She flashed her fake smile at her fake husband and pretended to sign their fake mortgage.

28. ANNE

Bangkok, April 15th 2019

If Anne had been on her own, she'd have walked there. She knew the hostel V had tracked down wasn't near but she always preferred walking in these situations. You had more control that way. You put on your good runners and brought a Dorling Kindersley guidebook complete with a pull-out map in case your phone packed up in the heat. You made progress. But after Uncle John had turned burgundy in the airport yesterday Anne had been too nervous to suggest walking, so instead, they had been sitting in a yellow-green taxi perspiring uncontrollably for thirty minutes.

Strangely enough Uncle Danny looked fresh-faced and fashionable beside her. His window was wound fully down, and he was leaning out like a dog, a giant smile on his face. His clothes looked brand new and he almost seemed young in a turquoise polo shirt and cream shorts. In the front, Uncle John was quizzing the taxi driver about what the different coloured taxis denoted. For some reason he was taking this information down in his notebook as if Thai taxi legislation was a pivotal clue in Molly's disappearance.

They pulled up to a hostel covered in Australians. Anne knew that the tanned blondes could be any nationality but whenever she saw anyone that relaxed, she automatically assumed they were from a different hemisphere to her. People were coming and going with a strange ease like they felt at home in the brightly painted communal space. Beyond the reception, a courtyard was covered in bunting, lanterns and bean bags. Vests and shorts were spread out across the grass tapping on phones and laptops.

Anne felt a pang of sadness for Uncle John. In his preparation speech he had painted a vivid and scarring picture of sex trafficking, modern slavery, poverty and drugs, the likes of which hadn't been seen since Nam. Anne's mum Angela had passed out at the image. Then this morning John had warned her and Danny again to hold onto their hats. They – the morning reconnaissance team – would be going straight into the lion's mouth, a den of iniquity which could only be prepared for by watching the darkest parts of *The Deer Hunter*. Instead, a male model glided by on an electric scooter offering shots of wheatgrass.

John broke into a little trot to catch up with him; Danny wandered out into the courtyard and Anne followed him. The doors were open to several of the dorms and they were extraordinarily tight. Rows and rows of bunk beds were squeezed up beside each other so that you could reach out and hold the person's hand in the bed next to you. She supposed that some people could sleep anywhere – that it was the bright communal space they liked, that they valued the company. Anne wouldn't be comfortable here herself, but she could see how a person might be. Molly certainly would.

'What do you mean privacy laws? My niece is missing.'

John's shout was audible in the courtyard. Anne turned to help him but was overcome by a strange sensation. She was startled to find she was about to vomit. She sprinted towards the bathroom and made it into a cubicle just in time. Her breakfast appeared in the toilet bowl. She sat on her hunkers for several minutes, looking on in shock – but then she shouldn't have been so surprised – of course, she'd get a tropical bug trailing Molly across Thailand. That was the dynamic of a lifetime.

She flushed the toilet, cleaned her hands and headed back to the reception. Clearly whatever she had, Uncle John had it too. Leaning on the reception desk for support, he was sweating so much he looked like he'd just walked out of the sea. It didn't help that he was immersed in a heated debate about international privacy law with the male model. The latter had an enthusiastic face like he was pumped to be debating the topic. The former looked like he was being choked. John's colour was rapidly alternating between a mild green and yesterday's burgundy.

'Privacy, man. I can't tell you who was or wasn't here. Big tech wants us to surrender our very essence to them. I can't be a cog in their wheel.'

'Jesus, that is exactly the kind of thing Molly would say.'

Anne took Uncle John's arm and thanked the model at reception. The taxi had taken a punt that they'd be back and waited outside. Grateful for the taxi man's prescience, Anne lowered Uncle John into the back seat. Patches of sweat were dotted across his khaki gear and she wondered if he needed to see a doctor. As her stomach lurched again, she realized she might need to see one too. She was filled with relief to see Danny stride through the reception and hop into the front seat of the car.

'The cleaning lady remembered Molly well. She said she was a very friendly girl – no surprise there.'

As the car pulled out into the road, Danny turned to read from the miniature notebook John had assigned to each of them.

'OK, so Molly stayed in the hostel from March 3rd to March 9th – she left shortly after she wrote us the letter, which as you recall was dated March 8th. Now, as to where she went after that is trickier, but at least now we know when she left Bangkok, so that is a start, right?'

Danny looked up from his notebook. Anne made a supreme effort not to portray her shock. That might have been the longest she had ever heard Uncle Danny speak. She looked across at Uncle John and was startled to find him staring misty eyed at Danny through his sweat-laden puffed-up eyes. He looked like he was about to have a stroke. Anne would have to text Lady V immediately. A doctor would have to meet them at the Shangri-La.

'You used the notebook, Danny. And to such wonderful effect. That means a great deal to me.'

John went green before passing out.

29. DANNY

Bangkok, April 16th 2019

Danny stood on the roof terrace of the hotel as darkness fell. Long low boats drifted down the river in front of him and behind him the pool shimmered turquoise. His inclination to hide whenever possible kicked in and he spotted a recliner in the corner under some trees. Sitting down he checked his recently hooked-up phone: 5.30 p.m.; 11.30 a.m. at home. Thirty minutes until he was to call Frank. Smiling waiters passed occasionally but largely it was quiet, so Danny closed his eyes and wondered how on earth he'd ended up on the other side of the world and when he'd tell his family the truth.

There'd been times before of course, countless, endless, unbearable periods of temporary sobriety or almost sobriety which all ended in heartbreak. There was no reason that this time would be any different except that, so far, it was. He'd had sponsors before. His family had informally filled the role too; Angela, Annabelle and John had all done stints calling him twice or three times a day, bringing him out for walks, ensuring he attended daily meetings. There'd been a brief stint after he came back from England when he thought maybe he could turn his life around. Then just before Annabelle died, he'd been nearing the idea too but for several years now it had seemed like all was lost. Until he'd met a former priest called Frank in the park and for some reason something changed.

When Molly had gone missing this time, Danny had been where he'd always been: on the side-lines, in a haze, underwater; several layers removed from anything. But then he'd dreamt about her. He'd seen her when she was small, leaping over buckets in an obstacle course that John had made for the nieces and nephews one unbearably hot summer. Danny dreamt that Molly had never changed. That she was still that little girl with the pink scrunchy, smiling up at her aunts and uncles, scanning the garden for her mum. Then when he woke, he realized with a start that he didn't know. He didn't know if she'd changed, what she was like or if she was OK because he didn't know where Molly was.

At first, he'd been gripped with panic and he had started mentally listing the bottles and where they were in the house but then another thought came to him; the thought of seeing Molly again. The thought of her scanning the garden, and not finding Annabelle, not finding anyone. He had reached for one of the unused phones in his drawer, managing to get it to work and called Frank. It was midday. And now he called Frank every day at midday. He'd been sober thirty-one days – a month today. It could change any second. It could all fall apart any minute but somehow so far it hadn't, and somehow he'd made it to Thailand and now there was the possibility that he might see Molly again.

When she looked around for Annabelle she wouldn't see her but if he could just hang in there then she might see him. 6 p.m. local time. 12 p.m. in Ireland. He tried Frank's phone. It went straight to voicemail. Danny breathed out slowly. A waiter passed with a tray of drinks.

On the morning of Annabelle's funeral, Molly wasn't ready. Danny and his siblings had stood in the kitchen in silence. They knew they had to give her time, but at what point would they acknowledge that Molly not being ready might not be about clothes or shoes but about the fact that she was not ready to attend the funeral of her only remaining parent? And at what point would somebody have to do something about it? They stood in a loose circle, holding a collective breath and not catching each other's eyes, each hoping the other wouldn't break because if they did then it would be tidal.

The problem was John. John was their splint. John held them all up, but he was cracking. They could almost see the dotted lines in his head connecting Bernard and now Annabelle and it was too much. At least with Bernard there had been a day or two after the heart attack to prepare, but this was a bolt of lightning too far, leaving their niece orphaned. What would happen to the house? Where would she live? Who would ask her how her day was? It wasn't just that someone was gone. Annabelle wasn't someone, she was an entire life force. Annabelle lit you up from the inside when you didn't even know you'd been turned off.

They had heard Molly's uncharacteristically quiet steps on the stairs. They followed her out the door in single file. They'd be late now. There was hardly enough time to get to the funeral home to see Annabelle laid out. So, they sped across the city in the jeep. Mike was driving with Frances in the front and John and Danny either side of Molly. A car pulled out in front of them and Mike swerved. Molly jolted and her freshly painted nail varnish smudged. A strange anxiety about the nail varnish seemed to make it hard for her to breathe and for the first time she looked up. It was clear that she didn't know who or what she was looking for, just that a desperate lack of control about everything was filling her. Mike was so surprised to hear Danny shout that he pulled over immediately.

John, Mike and Frances watched as Danny rooted through Molly's handbag. He'd seen her absentmindedly throw the nail varnish in there on the way out and thought it was an odd thing to bring to her mother's funeral. He found the small bottle of maroon red and calmly evened out the smudge with a light topcoat. As he painted Molly's nail Danny breathed slowly, deeply and loudly. His breath spread through the car until they were all doing it. They sat there waiting for the nail varnish to dry. They were each thinking that one of them would pull the trigger. That one of them would say that they needed to get going. That otherwise there would be no time for the funeral home. That they would have to go straight to the church. But no one said it because they realized now that they were not ready either. None of them was ready to see Annabelle dead so instead they sat in the bus lane breathing in unison.

Even on his darkest days Danny had managed to love his niece. He hadn't always been gone, or even if he was gone, he could come back. There were moments when he could come back. He wondered now how long this moment of clarity would be and if it would be enough.

He opened his eyes. A waiter was standing at the bottom of his recliner offering him a cocktail menu.

30. SHEENA

London, February 1st 2019

Everyone wanted the rain to stop. The shop assistant in the newsagent where she bought her morning banana. The patients who wandered to the end of the ward to stare out at its persistence. The nurses who considered sleeping in the hospital after night shifts rather than risk running to their cars in the downpour. But Sheena hoped it would never stop. The torrent beating down around them made the hospital feel insulated. Like a safe haven.

Between patients, she slipped into the stairwell to hear it clatter on the roof like nails shattering the glass. But the glass never did shatter. And something about that made her feel safe – the sense that the glass was always right on the edge of cracking but knowing that it never would. The door to the stairwell opened a flight or two below her. She held her breath but after a few steps, another door closed, and she was left alone with the clattering nails.

She wondered if Conor had changed his routine. She didn't remember seeing him so regularly before, but now it was like clockwork. If she didn't see him by the end of the day, he would appear as if out of nowhere around five o'clock. Was it him who was orchestrating their meetings or her? She knew that he had clinics on Tuesdays and Thursdays. Often he had an endoscopy but some days he would have a more complicated procedure like removing polyps or gall stones. On those days she might not see him until later. Until he sent a casual text about takeaway just when she was about to give up hope. Then he would call over with triple the amount of food necessary and they would fall asleep on the couch. It felt like something was building between them, but they hadn't even kissed.

The first time they met for coffee, she'd been her normal bubbly self. She'd asked him question after question, listening intently when he spoke about his family, his work, why he wanted to be a doctor, what he liked most about it. Sheena knew that people loved talking about themselves, and when you gave them the opportunity, they loved you for it. But about ten minutes in, he stopped mid-sentence and out of nowhere asked her how she coped working on the ICU. She batted it off lightly, but he remained silent. When, after a few minutes, he still hadn't said anything, she found herself rambling. She didn't mention the baby, but it hovered around every fake positive response she spewed. That night after she'd had another nightmare about the Christmas lights in the ward and the tiny movements the baby had made, she texted him. She said that the truth was – sometimes she didn't cope.

The next morning, she was mortified. She had never in her life sent a message like that. She wasn't dark and complicated. She was bright and breezy. She bounced. Her ponytail swung. She was the smiley ICU nurse. So, she didn't look at her phone. She showered and ate a slice of toast while chatting to her roommate who'd just come off a night shift and then walked the short distance to St George's. The next time she met Conor she would bounce and float and be who she always was.

Towards the end of that day, he was standing with a group of colleagues near the nurses' station. They were debating a patient's treatment. An older doctor was advocating for surgery, others disagreed. Conor looked up and caught her eye. Without any warning she felt tears swarming her insides. She immediately made for the stairwell, but he followed her. He held her firmly on both elbows and told her she was going to be fine. How did he know? How was he so sure? He'd experienced it himself. He made her feel like what she was going through was perfectly normal. He called it work-related secondary trauma – a form of PTSD. He told her about the six free sessions of counselling she was entitled to as a health care professional in the NHS and signed her up. It had only been three weeks, but she'd come to rely on his reassurance, on seeing him every day and the sense of safety he gave her.

Downstairs a door opened again and she was pulled out of her thoughts. The strides were quiet and irregular like whoever had entered the stairwell was taking them two or three at a time. She saw his carrot hair first. It was a glasses day. Most days he wore contacts but every few days his eyes needed a break and he wore dark frames. He bounded up the final flight. His expression changed as he spotted her. His transition from normal complexion to beetroot could be a genuine medical concern but hopefully it was just an indication that he liked her back. He reached into his pocket and before she had time to react a ball was flying at her head.

'JESUS, JESUS, I'm so sorry! I had no idea how far that would go.'

The sliotar missed her ear and bounced once before rolling around the landing. Sheena covered her laughing mouth as Conor chased it to no avail. He could not for the life of him seem to catch it. His white coat was trailing the ground with every near miss.

'Camogie? Didn't you say you used to play?' he yelled in explanation.

She put out her sneakered foot and stopped it dead just as he was bending down. He accidentally grabbed her calf then straightened up slowly like she was a police officer and she had told him not to make any sudden movements.

'For stress? Exercise can be really helpful. There is a club in Croydon. The Croydon Camogie Club.'

He was speaking so quietly and so sincerely that suddenly she knew. It wasn't just her. He had researched camogie clubs. He must have bought the ball or remembered to bring it from home. He had been thinking about her. He liked her too.

'I'd tell you to join my club but they only do ladies' football and I didn't know if you were into that.'

He was not tall for a guy, so they were at eye level when he stood. His eyes were bloodshot behind the dark frames. She wanted to reach out and take them off. She wanted to kiss his eyelids.

It seemed like at any moment he could move away. He could step back from her and lean against the handrail on the other side of the landing, but a moment passed, and he didn't move. He was so close she could smell faint sweat mixed with the Sure deodorant he kept in his locker.

'I've been thinking.'

He hadn't been looking at her but now he stole a glance.

'I'm a gastroenterologist – I can't keep bringing you takeaway. I'm practically breaking my Hippocratic Oath. What if I made you dinner some time? Something healthy.'

She didn't just want to have dinner with him. She wanted to talk to him late into the night. She wanted to hear about gall bladders and polyps. She wanted to take up ladies' football just so she could join his Gaelic club but there didn't seem to be a way to say yes to dinner that explained all this vehemently enough. So, she leant in and touched her lips to his. His lips were surprisingly soft, and it took a moment for him to kiss her back. When he did, he tasted sweet and familiar. She smiled in surprise when she realized what the taste was.

'Butterscotch!'

He laughed loudly in the echoey staircase.

'Werther's Original.'

He smiled before kissing her again. The ball slipped from his hand and bounced down the stairwell. It must have been raining all this time, but now in the silence of the back staircase, it was amplified – a million tiny nails chiming above them and now she really never wanted it to stop.

31. BOBBY

Bangkok, April 17th 2019

It was nearly 1 a.m. and Ned still hadn't shown up. Of all the people in all the world Bobby would least like to be encountering it was Ned Fortune. Not just encountering – dependent on. And of all the places he'd least have liked for this to happen, Titty Bar and Girls was up there. When Ned Fortune had posted a picture of him and Molly in Bangkok, he'd become their only lead, so Bobby knew they had to speak to him. But he still didn't understand how he'd found himself signed up to meet this joker in a grotty strip club with B of all people.

Bobby glanced at the bar. B seemed to have made friends with one of the topless waitresses. She was swinging her chest in circles so that the tassels crashed into B's face. B was laughing uproariously, and Bobby heard a judgemental sigh escape from his mouth. Bobby had no problem with the girls. He could even stomach the burly men who stood ominously in every corner presumably acting as some sort of pseudo security. It was the clientele that was the problem. He didn't know which were worse

– the gangs or the solo visitors. The gangs were loud, vest-wearing, tattooed oafs who had been drinking all day to get the courage to come to Titty Bar and Girls. Their vests were paired with tropical shorts and their arms vacillated between milk white and pig pink. The solo visitors were older and their dour faces eyed up girls a third their age. There were circles under their eyes and their hands were not always visible. Bobby was unnerved by the number of moustaches similar to his own. He shivered as he looked at his watch. After this drink he would call it a day. Ned Fortune wasn't worth this. Finding Molly wasn't even worth this.

'Does Ned Fortune know we're both gay?'

B returned with their drinks. Bobby didn't know if B was trying to put his best foot forward or if he was genuinely enjoying this but either way he was smiling.

'Do you mean by picking this place?'

Bobby sipped the electric bluc liquid that had landed in front of him. It was pure sugar and he winced as it trickled through his teeth.

'Yeah, like is he trolling us by asking to meet here? Because if he is, it's working. This place gives me the total heebie jeebies.'

Bobby was relieved to find that B wasn't enjoying this. He was worried B would have made a point of being open to any experience and say something annoying like, 'I'm just a yes person.'

'Let's just finish this and then go back to the hotel.'

'I'm not even sure he'll be able to tell us anything. I know your uncle John said in the briefing to follow up all leads – particularly witnesses who may know things that they aren't even aware of as being of interest – but Ned Fortune is the dregs of humanity.'

'Wow, you were really listening at the briefing.'

'Well, you always listen to other people's families, don't you? It's your own that don't stand a chance at getting through to you.'

Bobby took another sip of his drink. At least B knew that he wasn't a part of their family.

The Blacks thought differently. B had attended Black family events for as long as Bobby could remember. Communions, confirmations, birthdays, anniversaries, barbecues; even when Molly was away, the family wouldn't dream of excluding B. He glided confidently around family events helping himself to food and drink, acting like he knew everything about everyone (he did) and like everyone loved him (they did).

B was Molly's other half and Annabelle and Bernard's second son. Lady V and he shared snide jokes too mean for the rest of them. He knew YouTube stars that Blur and Oasis worshipped. He'd even managed to crack Anne – mainly by identifying when Molly was driving her up the wall, throwing his eyes up to heaven and getting her a glass of full fat Coke. B maintained an active email correspondence with Uncle John. Upon further investigation, Bobby had discovered the content of the correspondence was largely rap music suggestions. Uncle John had heard Wiz Khalifa's 'See You Again' on the radio and had just LOVED the sentiment behind it. B had helped him discover more artists in the rap genre. And since B had started his blog – *The Eco-Friendly Meat Eater* – Uncle Mike had become an avid follower. He saw it as a great antidote to the scourge on the world that was veganism. For decades Uncle Mike had put up with vegetarianism, but veganism was TOO FAR.

Safe to say that the Black family adored B. He was the gay son they wanted. The gay son they understood. A six-foot former rugby player coming out only confused them. When Bobby had come out, his aunts had invited him to all sorts of things they'd never have dreamt of asking him to before: opera at the National Concert Hall, shopping trips, afternoon tea. It was like he'd gotten his gay Equity card and was now in contention for new roles. Bobby knew from the moment he came out that if he were to get with B, everything would be squared away nicely for the family. It would all make sense to them. The two gay people they knew together and they would finally get what they'd always wanted: B as a legitimate son, nephew, brother, cousin. So Bobby had done the only sensible thing – avoided B like a rash.

It was easy as they had nothing in common. Bobby thought blogging was an embarrassing and transient pastime not to be confused with a profession. He thought using a letter to denote your name was a pretentious affectation that nobody should have pandered to – at least Veronica didn't hide her real name and – at least Bobby hoped – she didn't know they called her Lady V behind her back. Bobby had long established a distance from B and B had long respected it. Given this distance, he thought that maybe he should make an effort to be less of an arsehole.

'How are things with the Bitcoin tycoon?'

'Not great actually. He's avoiding my calls.'

Bobby panicked. This had not been his intention. He thought he was opening an innocuous line of chit-chat. He tried to quell what might rapidly become a personal conversation by staring straight into the blue sugar liquid, but B continued.

'He wasn't too happy when I told him I was coming to find Molly. He thinks we're co-dependent.'

This was *exactly* what Bobby didn't want. Conversations about co-dependency could only lead to deep meaningful conversations filled with drunken lay-person psychoanalysis. He never in his life thought he'd be happy to see Ned Fortune, but he had to hold himself back from embracing the creep when he sauntered towards them dressed as Jesus.

'Man, it's good to see you two. Sorry about the difficult circumstances.'

His posh accent grated on Bobby's ears. Ned Fortune claimed to have found inner peace in Bangkok but was just a privileged petty drug dealer servicing expats.

'Thanks very much for this, Ned. Listen, we are a bit tight on time here – do you know anything about where Molly is?'

'Yeah, man, I met her before she left for that place.'

He ran his hands through his long greasy hair.

'She was talking about disappearing. To an island, I think. Like an ashram.'

Bobby and B were silent. They knew this from her letter and yet hearing it verified was stark.

'Any idea where?'

'I don't know but I admire that girl. Leaving it all behind. She could just be like all the other girls? But she isn't, you know? I don't mind telling you that she really gets me going, man.'

Thankfully B seemed to realize that Bobby didn't take kindly to this admission. His arm shot out into the space between Bobby and Ned to stop whatever impeding action he might have considered taking. Vomiting was top of the list.

'OK, look, if you remember anything, can you text us?'

B shook his hand and Ned pulled it into his chest like some sort of gangster hug. Bobby started towards the exit. This seemed to elicit a concerted effort on the part of all the waitresses, who homed in on him, their tassels flying in his eyes. He emptied his pockets, spilling dollars onto their trays.

Even the warm humid air was a relief to Bobby when he finally escaped. He worried that B would pick up their earlier conversation about relationships and co-dependency when he caught up with him, but mercifully they walked back to the hotel in silence – both of them presumably preoccupied by the same thing. There were hundreds of islands in Thailand – over a thousand. Molly could be anywhere. Here they were on the other side of the world, in the same country as her but still no closer to finding her. Bobby had felt concerned before but now an eerie hopelessness filled him as he wondered what they'd do next. When they reached their floor of the Shangri-La, B finally broke the silence.

'Same place again tomorrow night?'

'We should bring Lady V on her crutches.'

'And your uncle John on a stretcher.'

Bobby closed the door behind him, appreciative that B had given him the opportunity to wrap up the interaction on friendly but not intimate terms. He was infinitely relieved he'd sprung for a single room and went immediately to the bathroom to shower Titty Bar and Girls off himself, before he began googling how to disappear in Thailand..

32. JOHN

Bangkok, April 18th 2019

When John woke again it was night-time. He had been in the hotel room for two days and had been unconscious for an alarming amount of that time. This wasn't how the trip was supposed to go. He wanted to be at the helm. He wanted to solve the problem at hand and return home triumphant with Molly safe and sound like nothing had ever happened. Like it was all a misunderstanding. Maybe they could even help the poor Griffith family find this evil doctor. From a distance. A nice safe distance with Molly curled up in the front room in Leopardstown drinking hot chocolate and talking to a nice Guard about whatever she'd seen. But instead John had been bed-ridden for two days. The hotel doctor said it wasn't even a bug. It was just high blood pressure that required rest and an adjustment of his medication. He swung his legs out of the bed. He needed to get out of the room.

It was only 11 p.m. but the hotel was already quiet. He could have gotten room service, but he didn't want to wake Danny, and, in the end, he was glad of the opportunity to stretch his legs. Making his way through the endless corridors, he passed smiling staff. They each stopped to bow to him with their hands together like mass. He paused to do the same back. He loved the bowing. He thought about trying it out back in Leopardstown; they'd get a real kick out of it at the tennis club. The lobby was a wide expanse of carved wood and greenery. He wasn't altogether sure, but he suspected that the only other body in the room was Anne. He could make out the back of her fair head in an armchair near the bar.

'Anne! Look at you there. It's great to stretch the legs, isn't it? I can't thank you enough for moving so quickly with the doctor. Thank goodness you were so fast. You never miss a beat. I haven't even checked in on your bug – I do apologize. I should have messaged on the chat room in the WhatsApp only I was asleep that whole time, would you believe? I hope B didn't catch your bug? Pity Bobby refused to share with him. He has a real bee in his bonnet about B, doesn't he? It's like that *Little Britain* sketch, "I'm the only gay in the village!" Do you remember that? Excuse me, young man – could we get a bottle of wine? What do you say, Anne, it might help kick the bug?'

He was glad to have caught the waiter as he passed through the lobby, but John had forgotten to do the bow, so he did one now and the waiter did another one back and they both chuckled – this could go on for days! A levity had come over John and he realized he should calm down a bit, he didn't want to send the blood pressure spiking again. But he was just so glad to feel better and be out of that room.

'Anne, you look well. Do you feel well?'

'I do actually.'

'I've been following the action on the wires. I hear the young men went to meet that dubious Ned fellow. Our V is something else, isn't she?'

'She is.'

'The way she tracked down the hostel and this Ned character. She's a real whizz on the internet.'

John picked up his glass to take another sip but was alarmed to see he had drunk most of his wine in the seconds since the waiter poured it. He put it back on the table.

'Isn't this just lovely? I love the way instead of your standard lamps all the lights look more like lanterns. And they do such a great line in greenery. You really feel like you're outside even when you are tucked up inside. Don't you? What's that smell do you think?'

'Incense.'

Anne was staring at her glass of Pinot Grigio with a glassy look in her eyes. He half wondered if she was drunk. She couldn't be, could she? This was Anne he was talking about.

'Sorry, Anne. That smell might not be helping your bug. I never thought. Do you think it's contagious what you have? Of course you don't feel like wine. I'm terribly sorry, don't you be drinking that now. I'll have the man get a cork for me and I can bring it to my room.'

John looked around for the waiter. The sight alone of the wine might make Anne feel worse but all the same he couldn't take the bottle to the room. Danny would discover it and it would be gone by morning. He would take it and stash it in one of the ferns.

'I'm pregnant.'

John was still half looking around for an appropriate

fern. He did a double take at the bottle and then at his niece. He nearly laughed, but stopped himself just in time. When he looked up at her, he noticed that her face was pale, and he saw something in her eyes that he had never even seen a glint of before – fear. He wondered what the appropriate way to comfort her was. A hug felt out of character but a pat on the back too typically avuncular. He could do better than that, couldn't he? He needed to do something because his niece looked like a deer in headlights. She was normally so solid, so steady, so reliable. But here she was, all at sea. He realized that the family poured so much energy into supporting those that couldn't keep upright that those who could keep themselves together got overlooked. He moved to the edge of the seat.

'Anne, this is wonderful news and Otis is such a nice young man.'

'Otis?'

Her pale face looked up at him. Lord. There was no way to get out of this. He would have to tell the truth.

'Oh Anne, I do apologize but after your friend – Mr Lift – visited, Mike mistakenly called him Otis – you know the elevator company Otis? They make most of the world's elevators and I got confused. I'm sorry. I am not being very helpful here, am I?'

He got a fright when he heard Anne laugh. Her entire armchair shuddered, and she reached out to hold his hand. It felt bizarrely soft, almost translucent like she had never even been outside. John knew his own hands were rough, so he tried not to squeeze Anne's pale silk ones too hard. She stared up at him laughing. His heart filled at the sound of it, and he wanted to wrap her in a big blanket.

'Stairs. His name is Alastair Stairs not Lift. Or Otis.'

Her fair hair had a slightly reddish tint in the bright light. Her skin was as white as could be, but somehow she didn't look as pale as before. Her cheeks were flushed from laughing and he felt a rush of love for her and a corresponding pain that he hadn't let her know this before now.

33. ANNE

Dublin, 2005

The number of rules broken in such a short space of time made Anne's shoulders stiffen and her jaw clench with unparalleled levels of anxiety. Annabelle had arrived at the school gates citing an emergency. She had bundled Anne into the car as if someone had died then inexplicably whisked her to the Shelbourne Hotel for afternoon tea on a Tuesday. She had ordered Champagne for two despite the fact that it was astronomically expensive, and that Anne was three years underage. The maître d' had given them the best seat in the house, in the bay window looking out over St Stephen's Green, because Annabelle had explained with a flourish that it was Anne's sixteenth birthday (it wasn't).

The day was unnaturally summery for March and the view would have been beautiful except for the stress of seeing Annabelle's beat-up Toyota pulled right up on the kerb impeding pedestrians. A policeman could approach at any moment. But the threat of the police was nothing compared to the impending wrath of Anne's mother. What if the school phoned Angela? Annabelle was notorious for giving Molly 'mental health days' but if Angela knew that Annabelle had pulled Anne out of school all hell would break loose. A trickle of sweat dripped down her neck into her school shirt. Anne glanced up at her aunt who squealed in delight as a four-tiered silver platter arrived at their table laden down with more food than Anne had eaten in the last month.

'Did I ever tell you about the time Molly's buggy broke at a drinks party in the Shelbourne bar? I was working on a play starring a young Liam Neeson. Now, this was before he shot to fame as Michael Collins of course but wasn't he just divine in that, could you cope with how gorgeous he was?'

Anne didn't know where to start. She could cope. She could absolutely cope but luckily it was a rhetorical question.

'I had organized a babysitter but of course that had fallen through at the last minute, so I brought Mol in in her old buggy. We weren't in the door a wet second before the buggy gives way, I mean completely collapses right at the foot of the director. Liam of course was lovely about it, but the director was one of those types – you know the kind – who genuinely wish that children were not a feature of human life? You know, they go around pretending there is basically no such thing and lose their minds if confronted with the reality? NOW of course I would tell him WHERE TO GO but at that time, I was still in that phase of my life where I was still trying to please everyone, you know, that godawful delusional state?'

Anne's heart was racing. She could barely process a word her aunt was saying but knew there was something wrong with the last bit. Pleasing people was the only way to get through life unscathed. That was about the only thing Anne knew for sure. You kept your head down and caused no trouble. Annabelle paused to take a sip of Champagne but waved a cucumber sandwich around in her other hand like a conductor's baton so as not to lose momentum.

Around them, Anne could sense middle-class ladies in cardigans struggle not to eavesdrop. Usually this would send Anne spiralling with embarrassment but with Annabelle she knew it was inevitable. Even if Annabelle wasn't a minor celebrity, you'd think she was. Her auburn hair cascaded in rich thick arcs over her shoulders. Her green eyes sat under powerful eyebrows, darker than her hair. She was all percussion – large rings tapped her glass, bangles clanked each other, and multiple necklaces bounced on her remarkably tanned chest. The cardigans weren't staring because Annabelle was loud, they were staring because she was hypnotic.

'So I'm there trying to keep Mol from climbing up the director's legs, Liam is trying to put the banjaxed buggy back together and then two gentlemen approach us from the bar. Now, you think Liam Neeson in *Michael Collins* is a hunk?'

This time Annabelle did pause but it seemed more for effect, so Anne didn't have time to clear up the misunderstanding that she was somchow obsessed with a middle-aged actor she only knew from History class when the teacher put *Michael Collins* on for the tenth time.

'Well, let's just say Liam and I looked up to see two American men who could only be described as DIVINE. Honestly, if Liam were here now, he'd say the same. One looked like Robert Redford and the other that doctor off *ER*, not the bald one, the other one.'

'Dr Ross?'

'Dr Ross! That's the one! Good woman, Anne. Exactly that.'

Annabelle beamed at Anne like Anne had just completed a cryptic maths theorem. Even though Anne knew that the excessive praise was just Annabelle being Annabelle, she let herself bathe in the prideful glow. She basked in being so close to such a bright light. Today for some inexplicable reason, Anne was the centre of Annabelle's focus and it was exhilarating.

'So they turn to us—'

Annabelle launched into an impression of what seemed like a cowboy from Texas.

'Mam, we can't help but notice that your stroller is a Maclaren Superdreamer pushchair model 400?'

The cardigans around them had stopped pretending not to listen. Annabelle must have realized this because she generously turned in her chair so the entire room could hear.

'Well, it turns out, aren't the gentlemen here to attend the WORLD GLOBAL FORUM of Maclaren pushchairs?'

Several cardigans murmured in excitement and one lady clapped.

'So Robert Redford kneels down and Dr Ross rolls up his sleeves and another man – this one is less good-looking – think the other doctor in *ER* – the bald one – gets out a screwdriver and they start fastening the buggy back together and talking about how sorry they are because the Maclaren is a superior make and we shouldn't have to experience this. In a jiffy the buggy is as good as new, Molly is squealing with delight, crawling all over the director who is dumbstruck, and Liam is up at the bar ordering a round of whiskeys for us all.'

Anne turned in the Venetian chair as the entire front room of the Shelbourne erupted into applause. Middle-aged women in pale pink and cream smiled from ear-to-ear. One woman was waving her hankie in the air like she was in Trafalgar Square on VE Day. Annabelle lowered her voice and winked at Anne as her fingers hovered between a scone and another sandwich.

'Well, that got quite out of hand.'

Suddenly as the women turned back to their tables, Anne was filled with a note of panic. The elaborate afternoon tea; the sun spilling into the Lord Mayor's Lounge; all Annabelle's energy focused on her; the light, happy feeling that was filling her; she didn't deserve it. It wasn't hers to have. What would Molly think? Even though she was down the country on some retreat she might be annoyed she'd missed out. Although that wasn't probable; Molly was a lot of things but jealous wasn't one of them. A worse thought struck Anne – maybe Annabelle did think it was Anne's birthday and Anne was accepting this very expensive tea under false pretences.

'Annabelle, do you mind me asking why you brought me here today?'

'Good question.'

Annabelle answered without looking up. She was having a difficult time deciding between the scone and the sandwich. In the end she put the sandwich directly into her mouth and the scone on her plate. She cut it in half and put an excessive amount of butter and jam on each side. She looked around for the waiter, pointing towards the jam, her mouth just about working off the sandwich.

'I was just worried that you did actually think it was my birthday and maybe I was accepting this tea under false pretences.'

'Your birthday is December 30th, my darling girl.'

Anne couldn't help but be touched that Annabelle knew her birthday.

'Do you ever miss your dad?'

Anne froze in the giant Venetian chair. All her senses heightened, and she could feel each tiny muscle from her toes to her scalp tighten. It was like Annabelle had dropped a bomb and it took Anne several seconds to check her body and realize that she hadn't been hit, that she had survived the mention of Gus. It took her another minute to realize that there was no one near her who would be affected by the bomb who she would have to pick up and put back together.

'People have good parts and bad parts to them, Anne. And just because they do bad things it doesn't make them all bad. So if you miss your dad or you hate your dad or you want to talk about your dad or you never ever want to talk about your dad, those things are all equally valid, but it must be hard to have to pretend he never existed.'

Anne knew from her face that Annabelle didn't need a response. She started pouring the neglected tea into the most beautiful china cups with a gold trim. The tea was a translucent copper. Anne took the cup Annabelle offered her and felt instant comfort just from holding it in her hands.

'This tea is just to say, I love you, Anne.'

Anne was surprised to find Annabelle staring directly at

her. She had no idea what to say back. She was completely overwhelmed. She couldn't remember a time in her life when she had been singled out like this. It didn't feel natural. Anne played a supporting role. She rowed in. She kept her head down. Annabelle smiled and seemed to forgive Anne when she responded by casting her eyes down and sipping her tea. Maybe Annabelle knew that it was the only way Anne could stop the tears that had welled up from seeping out. The tea was exceptional. Lapsang souchong. Anne made a mental note to check if Crazy Prices had it. With a flurry of courage she reached up for a slice of lemon drizzle cake and hoped that at home, her mother wasn't calling the Guards.

34. ANNE

Phuket, April 18th 2019

'I couldn't get us out today, but by god, by the time I was through with the poor devil on the other end of the line, we were on a flight tomorrow.'

Anne woke from a nap on the couch to find Uncle John pacing the living space of her suite. He grabbed a bag and started to stuff things in it. The bag happened to be B's and every item John packed was hotel property. He placed plastic-wrapped flip-flops on top of a robe that had Shangri-La clearly sown on it in gold thread.

'We will say that Helen is traumatized.'

Anne wondered what John was talking about.

'We'll say that she is insisting that I return home at once after my health episode and that you have kindly offered to accompany me. Then if anyone else offers to come too I will SHUT THEM DOWN.'

Uncle John shot his arm out in a karate chop like he would physically attack any member of his family who volunteered to accompany him home. He sat down on an armchair across from her.

'I might have to put on a bit of a show. Feign heart pain and weakness so you mustn't get a fright, OK?'

Anne attempted to sit up, but the sleepy sensation was nice. She tried to remember the longest conversation she'd ever had with John one-on-one before this but could only remember him congratulating her for never wearing leggings, which he thought were a scourge on society. Now he jumped from one topic to another, animatedly finding new problems he could solve.

'Of course, we'll have to be completely on our guard at this dinner tonight. There will be all manner of hurdles. For instance, shellfish – what if B makes shellfish? I will jump in of course and eat yours but doesn't everybody know you are mad for full fat Coke and, well, that's out for sure.'

Anne struggled not to laugh.

'Why?'

'The caffeine, Anne.'

John sat down in the armchair opposite her, rustling in his pocket for his mini-notebook.

'Some of these things I am more worried about than others, but I'll start with the most dangerous. Soft cheeses, undercooked meat, raw eggs, organ meat, caffeine – that's you, Anne – high-mercury fish, raw fish – look, will we just say no fish to be safe, Anne?'

Uncle John looked up from the list that he'd clearly found online, his pen hovering over the word fish, anxious to cross it off. His eyebrows were furrowed, like the question of the fish was the final detail in the negotiation of the Treaty of Versailles. His face was red, and his hairline had an overall sheen even in the air-conditioned hotel. Given his age, his hair should really be fully grey by now but large clumps of it were still dark brown.

He was wearing an old pair of loafers that he used to stock in his shop, replacing his own every alternate spring for the last thirty years. Anne could picture him wearing them on the beach in West Cork in the 1990s. One of those summers, walking barefoot up the lane, Bobby had stood on a thorn on the way home from the beach. Uncle John had carried him home on his back, then performed surgery on the thorn. He had sourced a needle and sterilized it, first with a flame then in some Poitín he'd found in the house. They had all stood around him, mesmerized as he warmed the area around the thorn in a makeshift footbath and eased it out with the needle. He wasn't any of their dads. He was all their dads. She couldn't let him leave without finding Molly. He needed to bring her home. Saving her, saving all of them, was who he was.

'You can't leave Thailand, Uncle John. What about Molly? Danny can come with me if you are worried, or Bobby.'

John sat back into the armchair and let out a sigh. The silence made Anne worry that he had given up hope; that the prospect of a trip up to some remote ashram, if they ever discovered where, was too much for him. But he couldn't give up; he was the family hero. He couldn't be broken because then the family would be broken. Anne would be fine on her own, she always had been.

'You are just as much my niece as Molly is, Anne. Just because you cause no trouble doesn't mean you don't deserve to be taken care of.'

Her instinct was to continue to fight him. To tell him she was fine. That Molly needed him more. But something in her desisted. A safe feeling came over her and she embraced it. Uncle John seemed to lose his franticness.

'Besides, Lady V has transformed into Jessica Fletcher and Danny has gone native. Bobby even seems to be working through whatever issue he has with poor B. They will be fine without us.'

'Thanks, Uncle John, but do we have to go back so suddenly? I will still be pregnant at home.'

She would need to find a way to communicate the development without saying the word. It felt so heavy, so final. She knew you couldn't be a little bit pregnant but that's how she felt – a tiny bit pregnant. One of these moments, it would hit her and she would have a meltdown. She – Anne Black – was pregnant. Pregnant, unmarried and the father was a slight English accountant who talked incessantly and whom she had only known for a matter of weeks. Unlikely didn't cover it. Unfathomable. Impossible. Only true a little bit. Only a small bit pregnant.

Suddenly it hit her that when she got back she would have her mother to contend with. That's when she'd really need John's help. Hopefully he'd intervene to ward off a séance with a bishop or a marathon set of novenas or whatever unmarried mothers had to do these days to appease fanatical Catholics. The thought of it exhausted her. Anne would really rather nap in the Shangri-La than be told she was going to hell.

'CHRIST ALMIGHTY, ANNE.'

Uncle John erupted from the couch like he was sitting on

an ejector seat. She wondered if his fake illness performance had commenced. If not, maybe she should be taking him home after all. His face was crimson.

'ZIKA, Anne. Those flies are still out there.'

He flung his arms out like Zika was sitting on the couch. Storming around the room, as if to tackle the imaginary virus, John launched into a rant about the latest World Health Organization thinking. He knew in his heart that they were keeping something from us. Anne had to turn away to stop herself from laughing. John recommenced his packing. He picked up a half-opened packet of crackers and stuffed them into B's Longchamp bag.

35. B

Bangkok, April 19th 2019

B hadn't exactly been looking forward to the 'LIVE DEMO' of the Eco-Friendly Meat Eater *Thailand special* – but, Christ, he hadn't realized how distressing the whole thing would turn out to be.

The first problem was the outfit. The hotel's marketing manager had insisted he wear an apron and a giant white chef's hat. The manager seemed to genuinely believe that no one would understand that B was cooking if he wasn't wearing the gear. Then there was the headset. The terrace wasn't all that big. B thought he could cook in the corner, record a quick demo, mention the hotel several times and uphold his end of the bargain. Instead, he looked like Britney Spears on the *Oops I Did It Again* tour, with a hands free mic the size of a plum too close to his mouth. The poor souls in Cambodia could probably hear him. And god knows they'd been through enough.

In addition to the mortifying rig-out, the barbecue was producing a strange amount of smoke, compressing the already desperately humid air. B could feel his camera-ready hair wilt and his shirt begin to stick to him. He was struggling to channel the curated version of himself he'd spent so long honing; his old shyness was creeping back up on him. This set of circumstances was the official living nightmare of a man with overactive sweat glands and a viral platform.

But the real issue was the audience. In B's vision of the evening, interested guests would wander up and ask him questions. A few might even feature on the video. A casual, relaxed atmosphere would pervade. Instead, a highly uncohesive group was dotted across the terrace in awkward clusters while B's voice BLARED over several tannoys no matter how quietly he tried to speak. A tour group of elderly Americans had arrived, and they were queuing with paper plates like B was a canteen lady dishing slop. A senior citizen named Hank was rolling on the balls of his feet at the top of the queue talking animatedly at him, while he desperately tried to change the settings on the gas grill to get a more even heat distribution. Hank was from Kansas City – the HOME of BBQ. The secret, he told B, was in the marination. Marinate your meat well and you couldn't go wrong. When Hank copped the no meat aspect of the barbecue he seemed to have a mild stroke.

B had to get the whole ordeal over with. He gave Danny the nod to start filming and began placing the vegetable skewers on the grill, detailing how he had parboiled the potatoes in advance. The prawns were Asian-inspired, soaked in chilli and lime. Here, he had a spiel prepared about how a big prawn could have a meaty quality to it, but Hank started heckling about barbecues meaning meat and meat only. Luckily Lady V gave him a dig with her crutch and Hank was so taken aback, either by her behaviour or her striking good looks, that he just stared in her direction, grasping his paper plate to his chest.

In the corner of his eye, B could see the rest of the Black tribe, one more eccentric than the next. Anne had arrived dressed for a formal funeral in a long-sleeved black top and black slacks not unlike Hillary Clinton's 2016 election attire. Despite her permanently pale skin, you could actually see heat trying to escape from her vac-packed outfit. John was following her around with a two-litre bottle of Evian, forcing her to drink straight from the bottle like she was about to step into a boxing ring. Every two minutes John sprayed anti-mosquito in her eyes. Now he was taking his safari hat off his sweaty head and forcing it on hers. When she reached for a prawn, John swiped it out of her hand violently. B was relieved John was going home; whatever about his blood pressure, he was acting ill in the head.

Over by the pool, Bobby had built himself an aggressively heterosexual perch. He was drinking a beer in his disgusting lace-up boots and reading a copy of *National Geographic*. Unnecessarily big headphones secured his moody teenager look. It made B want to vomit. Why Bobby ignored him was a mystery. Did he think two gays made a cabal? B himself also ignored Bobby but for a rational, mature reason: because he didn't want Bobby to think that B thought he was good-looking. Which he did. *Obviously*. He wasn't blind. The rugby scar on his eyelid made him look like a divine villain from a 1990s thriller where you weren't so sure you didn't want the killer to come get you after all. Somehow, he was even pulling off that hideous moustache.

B might not be a divine former rugby player but at

least he knew who he was. He didn't skulk around like an oppressed teenager. He didn't wear disgusting lace-up boots in deathly humid conditions to appear impervious to fashion or weather. B was evolved. B was functional. B could hold down a relationship. Couldn't he?

Right now, sweating over a barbecue in 73 per cent humidity, corralling another family's freak show in order to find someone who didn't want to be found, B suddenly wondered if Jeff might have been right. For whatever reason Molly had excommunicated herself from the world. And now B was jeopardizing a stable relationship for the whirlwind one he had with Molly. Molly lit up his life but maybe now she was about to blow it up too. And for what? B's heart started to race. When tonight's fiasco was over, he needed to try calling Jeff again.

From nowhere, festive music erupted. At first B presumed it was coming from a sound system, but he looked up to see a five-piece Mariachi band making their way across the terrace. The marketing manager had asked several times about putting a few fajitas on the barbecue but B hadn't paid any mind to it. Now the Mariachi five-piece were coming for the camera and B needed to exit the scenario before it became irretrievably embarrassing. He wrapped up the video in a hectic jumble of words, diving out of the shot before the wide hats took over. As he ran, B noticed Danny swaying his hips to the music.

B made a beeline for the cool of the poolside courtyard. It was starting to get dark, which felt like heaven-sent protection from the glare of the evening as a whole. Despite the heat and the stress, B smiled to himself as clusters of Americans talked incredulously about barbecuing vegetables like it was the second coming. The public side of things was sometimes a stretch, but he always loved the cooking.

'Hey, man.'

B was busy pulling his shirt and shorts from sweaty crevices where they didn't belong, so he hadn't seen Ned Fortune saunter onto the terrace in his Jesus pyjamas. His hair was still greasy, but he looked slightly less like a heroin addict.

'I remembered where she is.'

B looked up across the terrace to call them, but the Black family were already making their way over. If you didn't know them, you'd be frightened of them; a pack of sweaty zombies shuffling towards you. As well as the falling darkness, B realized that the weather was turning too. For the first time in his life, he prayed dearly for rain to relieve him of this ungodly clamminess.

'I wrote it down, in case I got fucked up on my way here.'

Ned held the paper out to the congregating group. Uncle John took it, and Ned added a 'Sir' and did a strange bow. Stranger still, John did a bow back. When John didn't read it out loud immediately, Lady V bashed him in the shin with her crutch. How would she go back to not having a weapon on her person? It suited her so well.

'Seedlings Eco Garden in Phuket.'

It began to pour rain from the high heavens but none of them moved. Beside B, Anne smelled so strongly of DEET, he worried that if she wandered too close to the barbecue she'd catch fire. John started talking about whether the rest of them were up to taking on the mantle now that his health had failed him. His speech had a ring of Dumbledore in King's Cross Station about it. B half expected him to produce Gryffindor's sword. Looking around the huddle gathered on the roof of the Bangkok Shangri-La, B couldn't help but feel a wave of love. These utterly ridiculous people only had one thing in common – they wanted to find Molly.

When the Mariachi band had finally stopped harassing their ears and the barbecue ordeal was well and truly over, B sat on the couch in the suite and weighed up his options. They'd agreed to sleep on any plans of trekking to an ashram but it was clear that Danny, Bobby and V would be going to find her. The option was still there: B could fly back to London tomorrow with Anne and John. He could put Jeff first and get on with his own life. He put his phone on speaker and kept pressing redial, but Jeff still wasn't answering. The repetition of the dial tone filled the room.

Even before Jeff, other people had said B and Molly's relationship was unhealthy. That he was leading Molly on in some way, that he was taking up all the time and energy she should have been spending on finding a life partner. Like a life partner was a golden ticket to happiness. And like you could only really be partners for life if you were romantically connected. There was always this suggestion that someday they'd have to move on; that someday they'd have to give each other up.

On the umpteenth ring, B stopped trying. Defeated, he stood and walked around the suite. Maybe Molly had decided that everyone else was right – that they did have to grow up and give each other up. He looked in the mirror. He knew he couldn't be sunburnt because he'd been consistently layered in Factor 50, so the bright pink of his baby face must be from the smoke and the sweat and stress of the night's high jinks. He looked so ridiculous he almost smiled.

Molly would have loved tonight. She would have charmed Hank, danced to the Mariachi band and somehow made the disjointed tribe on the terrace into the Brady Bunch. If Molly was still who she was before. But what if the old her was gone? What if he followed her to wherever she was now only to find out that she was done with him, with all of them? His heart ached at the thought. Even if she could live without him, he didn't think he could live without her. The thought was even more frightening than not finding her at all.

He caught sight of his Longchamp tote on the arm of the couch. It was full of hotel products. A branded hair dryer sat on top of a half-eaten packet of biscuits. He smiled – he didn't have Anne down for a looter. He turned off the lights of the suite, still unsure what he would do in the morning.

36. B

Dublin, 2003

'We really don't fit in here, do we?'

B stubbed a half-smoked cigarette out on the bench. He hated the taste. He hated the fuzzy feeling it left on his teeth. He hated how sick it made him the next day. He only liked the feeling it gave him when that guy in his year offered it to him, giving him a friendly nod of recognition that he'd never give him at school.

'Really?'

Molly's badly plucked eyebrows rose in surprise. B didn't think this was news, but a nervous smile appeared between her overly applied cherry lip gloss. He must not laugh at her. If it was hard for him to fit in, he knew it must be ten times harder for a girl. But she looked utterly ridiculous. In the glaring lights of the rugby pitch, her fake-tanned arms glowed jaundice. She was wearing a tank top with the word SASSY spelt out in faux diamonds. Pink glitter was scrawled across her cheeks. The glitter had started out at her temples but had formed two long paw prints down her face from when she was screaming the words to t.A.T.u.'s 'All the Things She Said' on the dancefloor earlier.

'Should we go home?'

Her face was scrunched up in concern like she had done something wrong. Like *she* was the one out of place, not the girls who at fourteen had gotten spray tans and blow-drys for the rugby club disco. Behind them, the music ramped up, blaring out of the emergency exit. A group of blue shirts and chinos started singing along. Their voices hadn't broken yet, so they squawked like provoked crows as they imitated 50 Cent, yelling across the yard about taking drugs and harassing women. B looked on morosely, but Molly was bent double. He wasn't sure what to think until she swayed back again, and her laughing face was caught by the floodlights.

'This is priceless. I'm going to liven things up.'

B panicked at the thought that she was going to accost the blue shirts and chinos, but she disappeared inside, slipping into the throng on the dancefloor.

Around him, the rugby stand was empty. Earlier, intertwined limbs had been dotted on alternating benches, but the cold had chased away couples once insulated by thimbles of vodka. B shivered himself now and pulled his forest green cord jacket tighter around him.

He knew he looked different, but he also knew that it wasn't a bad thing. A few people had complimented him on the jacket and a guy on the St Michael's Junior Cup team had crossed the dancefloor to ask him where he'd gotten his brown leather loafers (Arnotts). But still he felt outside it all. It wasn't just the clothes. It was what they found funny. It was the music they liked. It was who they wanted to be around, who they wanted to be. Everybody seemed to want the same things. B didn't want to be the exact same. But he didn't want to be the only one who was different either.

Then he thought of Molly. Molly wasn't the exact same. And when she tried to be, going on the bus into town to buy fake tan and squeezing her feet into heels that made her toes turn blue, she didn't care that she got it wrong. Molly was the last thing a fourteen year old boy seemed to want. She wasn't contained or sweet or compliant. Molly gave them piggy-backs through crowds at concerts. She challenged them to arm wrestles. She did an impression of Bill Clinton playing the saxophone while Hillary told him to shut up and bake cookies.

He knew that the boys in blue shirts would grow into the Mollys of this world. That one day they would wake up and see how funny and smart she was, but either way she didn't seem to care. How did she feel so OK just by being herself? Where did that come from? But he knew the answer even before he'd started wondering. The best part of the night would be piling into the Toyota at half eleven to tell Annabelle all the news. She always felt sorry for the chinos and fake tans. She became teary eyed at the thought of the normal lives they would go on to live. Molly and B, on the other hand, would light the world on fire. Annabelle saw B in a way that others, even others he knew loved him, couldn't quite see. When he was with Molly and Annabelle, it was like he was already that person. He was already lighting the world on fire.

B looked out across the pitch. It was such a peaceful sight that from this vantage point it'd almost be enough to make you take up rugby. There was a pause in the music so his laugh at the prospect was louder than he expected. Into the brief silence, the first few notes of 'Dancing Queen' rang out. He knew immediately what Molly had done. Dread filled him even before he heard the DJ call his name.

B didn't have to go inside. He could be proud of Molly for being eccentric without losing face himself. He sat still, holding his breath like a crime had been committed and he was about to be identified as a co-conspirator, until he realized the yard was empty. The blue shirts had disappeared into the sweaty mix, presumably looking for someone to rub up against.

On the short walk to the emergency exit, B imagined a clearing where only Molly stood manically trying to encourage people to dance to cringeworthy 1970s disco, but, as always, he had underestimated her. As he stood in the door he watched as girls in heels sprinted from the bathroom and from the hatch serving Club Orange. They made long human chains, handbags dangling on their elbows as they swarmed the dancefloor. The blue shirts and chinos were lined up against the walls, but they were tapping their feet too. The braver ones were even moving onto the floor and getting rewarded by fake-tanned arms looping around their crew cuts.

When Bobby walked onto the floor it was like a dam broke. It had just been announced that he would be the captain of the Junior Cup team next year. That made him a genuine celebrity. Jack Gleeson, the team's star kicker, was right behind him. They weren't just taller than the other blue shirts, they were bigger in every sense. Light brown hair flopped into Bobby's blue eyes and Jack Gleeson's smile was contagious. Things were easy for people like them. The world moulded around them, not the other way around. And this dancefloor was their empire. The dirty sweaty room elevated into euphoria and it was intoxicating. Jack was shy but everyone knew he could dance. All eyes were on him as he moved seamlessly, twirling Molly and digging Bobby in the ribs, slagging him for his tame shuffle. Molly had taken off her shoes. The floor could not be dirtier. It wasn't just the cigarettes and spilt soft drinks. It was years of sweat and grit and broken bottles. B would have to talk to her about it. She could genuinely get sepsis. But with her shoes off, she was spinning. She was twirling and bouncing. She radiated happiness. He felt a wave of love for her so strong he momentarily worried that it would burst out of him in some visible way.

B didn't move from the doorway. Molly knew that he couldn't join her. She knew that he cared too much what others thought of him to throw his hands up in the air and dance like he did with her and Annabelle around their kitchen. But that was OK. Molly looked up and caught his eye. She had spoken to him in a private language. It wasn't the language of fake tan and handbags or rugby and chinos. It was one that only they spoke. And it was better than any short-lived romance on the rugby stands. It was everything.

37. JOHN

Bangkok, April 20th 2019

He did the unthinkable and opened the minibar. Lady V had warned them all strenuously not to even *consider* taking a bottle of water from its money-hungry clutches but he was dying of thirst. The taxi would be here in fifteen minutes, he hadn't even left the air-conditioned room yet and already he could feel a layer of perspiration ready to encompass him when he stepped outside. He took out the contraband water, noticing that the bottle of wine from the other night was still in the fridge. He had been so dumbfounded by Anne's news, he'd forgotten to stash it in a fern. It would only confuse the staff when he went to pay. He called over his shoulder to Danny.

'Did you not want that wine?'

It was terrible to be so concerned about waste you'd rather give wine to an alcoholic.

'Look, John, there's something I've been meaning to tell you.'

John looked up in alarm. The bright daylight of the balcony shone on his little brother and Danny seemed strangely young. His face was trimmer than John remembered it. It didn't have its usual reddish tinge. His black hair was interspersed with discreet lines of silver compared to John's own badger-like mix of grey and brown. Thailand seemed to have the exact opposite effect on his brother as it had on himself. Danny was positively glowing. In his good M&S t-shirt and shorts he looked almost athletic. But his face was filled with concern.

'What is it, Danny?'

He didn't think he could take another shock. This trip was meant to be about Molly. Instead, every member of the family seemed to be having their own mini-crisis. And somehow John had emerged as the family's emotional guru guiding them through their breakdowns like Oprah. That woman was a rock of sense; a total exemplar of emotional navigation. She could get anyone through anything. John channelled her now.

'Back at home, I met a man called Frank. He used to be a priest.'

A lump formed in John's throat. This had been a long time coming. It was Danny's right to bring it up, but dread seeped up through John's loafers. Why now? He straightened up from the fridge.

'We've become friendly and a few weeks ago he asked me to come to the methadone clinic to talk to the patients about how I got sober.'

'But you're not sober.'

John realized his mistake. This wasn't about the past. This was just some mix up. He unclenched the fists he didn't even know he was gripping and strolled over to the couch to do a final check of his bag. His passport, money and his and

Anne's boarding passes were in his cleverly camouflaged flat bumbag under his jumper. He tapped his phone in its holster on the side of his belt and opened the front pocket of his bag to check on the spare copies of the boarding passes he liked to print out in case of loss or damage to the originals.

He eyed the letter he had written to Molly folded neatly on the bed. He had done three drafts. The first was eleven pages long. The third was thirteen. In the end he'd scrapped them all and told her just one single thing. He hoped to god it was the right thing. If he was her actual dad, would he have known just what to say? If he was Bernard, would it have come to him immediately, would he have been able to do a better job? He hoped not. He couldn't bear the thought of doing wrong by her. Of letting Bernard and Annabelle down. And yet there was something about leaving this to the others that felt right. He wanted Molly to come home too much. He had to fight his instinct to wrap her in cling film and keep her in the living room in Leopardstown where he could keep an eye on her for the rest of her life. He had to be there for her when she needed him. He couldn't be out there chasing her, willing her to come home. Instead, he needed to be her safety net, ready for when she wanted to come to him. He nodded to himself. That was quite good. It was like something Oprah would have said. He looked forward to telling Helen that one. He got a rush of excitement at the thought of seeing Helen. He couldn't wait to give her a great big hug and smell her T-Gel shampoo. He also couldn't wait to stop sweating profusely.

'Well, no, I *wasn't* sober.'

John stopped rearranging the contents of his bag. He had to pause a second to remember what they were talking about. When he did remember, he found himself holding his breath like he was underwater and couldn't for the life of him let go.

'So I thought I'd lay off the drink for a few days so I could go down there and talk to those poor souls and not let the old lad down and, well, I just kept on, you know, doing it like they say, day-by-day.'

'When was this?'

John's breath was pent now and he wanted desperately to release but he couldn't seem to. He realized how quickly he just snapped at Danny so tried to loosen his stance.

'Five weeks ago. I was so worried about Molly and all I could think about was Annabelle. All her visits to see me, the way she never let me out of her sight, and now here is Molly lost on the other side of the world with no Annabelle to find her.'

A car started beeping manically out on the street. Danny turned to take a look. It gave John a moment to catch his breath. He sat down on the chair behind him.

'It was you and Annabelle who found me, and I want you to know that I will find Molly, John, you can count on me.'

'You're sober.'

'I am.'

'But why didn't you tell us?'

'After everything I put you through, I couldn't raise your hopes again.'

Words failed John. He wasn't sure what the correct interaction was, so he held his hand out. He shook Danny's hand for several minutes, taking his brother in. His skin. His gait. His posture. It was all different. His eyes were alive where they'd been vacant and listless before. John wanted to be happy for him. He wanted to feel light and joyful and hopeful, but his body wouldn't let him. Something tightened within him and, despite his best wishes, all he felt was fear that this glimpse of his brother would be snatched away from him again like it had been so many times before.

'Well, you certainly look well, Danny.'

'I feel like I've just woken up. I feel like I've been asleep for thirty years.'

There was a knock at the door. But John didn't let Danny's hand go. Danny could fall apart again. He could have a drink tomorrow or that night or right after John left, but in this moment he had his baby brother back and it was almost more than he could bear. He pulled his brother in and hugged him close. He inhaled the fresh scent of Danny's clean hair and his clean shirt and his new self. He pulled away and picked up his bag on the way to the door.

'She reminds you of me, the missing girl in London, doesn't she?'

John turned in the hallway to face his brother.

'They all do. Every missing person poster. Every mother, father, brother on the TV looking for their loved one. I always thought—'

'You won't ever have to wonder about me again, John.'

John opened the door, tears streaming down his face. He wanted to believe his brother with every inch of his heart but again his body clenched, and his heart tightened like it was closing up to protect itself from some future pain.

Anne was standing at the end of the corridor. John waved goodbye to Danny and smiled as brightly as his body would allow. As he closed the door behind him, John realized that there was a lot of luck involved in who got lost and who got found. He wondered how you knew when your luck was up and, more importantly, how you were strong enough to keep your hopes up when luck was against you.

38. SHEENA

London, February 17th 2019

She'd started running again. She was nowhere near as fit as she'd been before, and she felt heavier, like she'd gained an extra dose of gravity, but each thump of the pavement felt epic. Before, she'd been light as a feather. Before, she'd had to hold back because she could keep going forever, she could fly. Now she was laden, now she was running as if always through mud and the funny thing was it almost felt better. Because now it was a miracle how far she could make it, now each pound of the pavement was a miracle pound forward.

Depression. That's what the counsellor had called it. Triggered by work-related trauma, but depression nonetheless. She knew that most families talked about these things now but hers didn't so she had no framework for how to start. She wanted to learn and grow and find a way to talk about what was engulfing her. She lapped Clapham Common over and over to get the courage to do it. She ran until her thighs hurt, until there was a dull pain in her chest and her face was red and her hairline sticky with sweat, despite the incessant rain.

The minute she rang the doorbell she realized that she should have texted beforehand. Who called to people's doors? This wasn't like home. It was central London on a Sunday night. She heard Conor pad down the stairs wondering aloud if any of his roommates had ordered takeaway. What would she say: I have depression? I am depressed? She almost turned to run but he opened the door just as she was about to flee.

If it wasn't for his bright red hair, she might not have recognized him. He wore a fluorescent yellow Gaelic jersey and too short white shorts and his glasses were an old pair she'd never seen before; large circles which changed the shape of his face entirely. His face flamed red underneath multiple patches of white where it looked like he'd rubbed cream on some spots.

'Oh my god, Sheena.'

It hit her: men care what they look like. She knew it was beyond old-fashioned to think that they didn't, to presume appearances were a female thing, but she realized now that that's what she'd thought. And now here she was embarrassing Conor, the one person in the world she'd least like to hurt. She'd been so wrapped up in her own problems that she had just presumed she could land in on him with hers. But he had his own life. He could have friends over or his brother who she knew lived in London. They hadn't even discussed dating properly; he could be seeing someone else. Or at the very least he could just want a night on the couch with his face cream in his Gaelic jersey. Either way, he didn't deserve to be accosted by someone who just wanted to get something off their chest on a rainy Sunday night.

'I'm so sorry, Conor, I should have called. I'm running anyway so I'll just keep going.'

This time she didn't wait. She turned in the rain and sprinted for the common. She could hear him calling her and now she was doubly stressed. Had running away been rude? He'd been so good to her these past few weeks; a real friend. The last thing she wanted was to upset him and she realized that's exactly what she'd done. She had barged into his life with her ten-tonne baggage and now she'd embarrassed him as well as everything else.

She thought she'd been running fast earlier, but now she raced. Now she hammered the pavement like it could take away the murky feelings that were dragging her down like a swamp. The rain was coming down in sheets around her and the common was empty. Eventually she spotted a bench at the far side, and she made for it. When she sat, she let her head fall between her legs.

'You know that for a knick knack to work you can't let the person see you?'

The bench rocked inordinately. Sheena looked up to see Conor slump beside her.

'You're meant to run away before they answer the door.'

He struggled to catch his breath. If his face had been red before, now it was crimson. He seemed to have forgotten the cream on his face and rain streaked lines of white down his cheeks. She didn't want to feel this way. She didn't want to feel immensely safe just because he was near. She didn't want to only feel hopeful again because he was here, but was that worse than being terrified and alone? Suddenly her phone buzzed on the bench between them and Conor looked up at her. She knew he'd noticed how often it rang; he may have even seen the name that popped up.

In the last week she'd started to ignore the calls. She kept her phone permanently on silent and hoped that maybe he would stop calling. Maybe he would forget about her and finally she could forget about what she'd done. She lay awake at night, counting how many times she'd raided the drugs cupboard in the last five weeks; nine, maybe ten? Each time she was sure it was the last, each time had felt like a dream, like it was someone else's hand reaching for the zopiclone or Xanax or codeine. It had been so easy that first day when it could still have been an accident, but now she was in something she couldn't seem to get out of. She knew she'd get caught. She felt it coming for her like when something heavy falls from the sky but hasn't landed yet. So she didn't look up. She wanted to tell him that she couldn't do it anymore but sometimes she wasn't sure what was worse – getting caught or letting him down. She was filled with dread and for the first time she wondered if she feared him.

'What is it, Sheena? You can tell me.'

Sheena's eyes were locked with Conor's and she knew that he could tell she was drowning. His eyes seemed to plead with her. For a moment she wondered if she could tell him. But how could she tell a doctor that she'd been stealing medication from the drugs cupboard? He'd have to report her. How could she explain it to anyone else when she couldn't explain it to herself?

'Depression.'

The word came out of her like a long exhale after being

underwater. She was a nurse. She was a medical professional and yet she couldn't explain the difficulty she had with the word. It wasn't the illness itself; it was associating it with herself. She felt deep empathy for people who suffered from depression; it just happened not to be her. It just happened that she was on the other side of things; she made people better, she brightened people's day; she was the smiley ICU nurse – and yet here she was; a dark weight tugging her down, an anchor deep inside her bringing her to her knees.

Conor pulled her into his arms and held her tight. She let the relief of saying the word take over. She let her entire body hang from its frame, and she sank into him.

'Things will get better. I promise. You will get through this. Come home with me. I'm cooking roast chicken. We can talk it all through, or not talk at all. Everything is going to be OK.'

They walked across the common. Her phone began buzzing again in her pocket. She was relieved Conor didn't ask who it was. With one hand she turned it off. She wasn't too far gone. She could still get out of this. Conor pulled her tighter to him and she let herself feel it; safe, hopeful and not alone.

39. BOBBY

Phuket, April 20th 2019

The strange thing was that none of them was drunk. They just seemed to have turned riotous with the heat or the humidity or the adventure of it all. Maybe it was the anticipation of seeing Molly. Tomorrow they would go to the Eco Garden, bring her home and years later they would all laugh about the time Molly fled to an ashram. It would be up there with the stint in Greece with the one-armed carpenter or when she broke up with the mayor of a small town in Poland and he put her in a jail cell. Maybe it had already started to be funny. He could feel it himself; a lightness had taken hold.

Bobby held back a few steps to ensure he was seeing things correctly. Danny had produced *Baywatch*-style biceps to haul V over his shoulder in a fireman's lift to get her up the hill. Danny smiled serenely despite V wriggling her entire body to whack B across the back of his legs with her crutches every time he goaded her.

'You had to know they'd get called Blur and Oasis.'

'Don't be ridiculous.'

'Come on. Damon and Liam? You were in a 1990s bubble when you named them, just admit it.'

Bobby had never seen anyone talk to V like this before. He had never even seen anyone look at her directly. From the wide smile on her face, she was enjoying it. She'd been in flying form all day – they all had. With Anne and John gone it was like the grown-ups had gone home. V had even sat beside them on the flight to Phuket. They'd played cards. Then when they'd arrived at the hostel, they'd all strolled down to the beach to drink watered-down cocktails. V had attempted to explain what Mike did for a living but after forty minutes they still couldn't understand. It had something to do with Americans.

Down by the beach there had been a steady stream of tourists but up the hill it was dark. The road was badly lit so Bobby couldn't be sure of what he was seeing but it was out before he could stop himself.

'Is that a tattoo?'

They had reached the top of the hill. Danny lowered V gently to the ground. Bobby bent down to get a better look.

'Is it a planet or something?'

He was tentative now that Lady V's smile had evaporated.

'It's a lone balloon blowing in the wind.'

Even V couldn't keep a straight face at this admission. She conceded a tight-lipped but definite smile. B erupted and Danny grinned ear-to-ear. He'd been chuckling in the corner of the bar all night like he was having the time of his life and Bobby supposed he might have been. Living with his Sudoku-obsessed ninety-two-year-old mother probably wasn't a barrel of laughs.

'Do you find that funny, BARNABY?'

B turned so quickly he could have got whiplash.

'Too far, Veronica. Too far.'

'I always have the last word, B. Always.'

V gave B one last jab with the crutch. Danny offered her his arm to lean on and they hobbled towards her six-person dorm. When V had found out that there were no private rooms left, she'd paid to keep an entire dorm empty for herself. Bobby thought her attitude to money was bizarre. She obsessed over small things but didn't blink an eye over monumental purchases. She had money but it was as if having it scared her. The woman seemed to have a genuine fear of minibars.

'Beer?'

Bobby strolled over to the outdoor bar. He nodded towards B who was standing by the door checking his phone. It was still early but there was no one by the pool. Dozens of sets of outdoor furniture suggested the place was teeming at other times of the year, but it was hard to imagine. It felt like a graveyard for plastic and aluminium.

'Still no word from the Bitcoin tycoon?'

'Not a peep.'

B was quiet, like the antics from only minutes ago were a performance.

'It must be hard for him to get used to what you have with Molly; he'll come around.'

'Do you think? It seems a bit dramatic to ghost the guy you live with.'

B lay back onto a sun lounger and took a swig of his beer.

'What happened with your ex – the guy who wore that stunning polo neck at Christmas?'

'Did he? Jesus, I don't remember that.'

'I never forget a polo neck.'

B's voice was so serious, Bobby couldn't help but laugh. After a minute he answered, 'He wanted kids.'

'And you don't.'

Bobby nodded. Up until this last year, Bobby's life had been on a clear track. He'd been saving a deposit for a house, the principal had nominated him for a Leadership training scheme, he was in a happy relationship. But the kids question had set something in motion inside him that he couldn't understand. It had unsettled something fundamental in him, almost dragging him back to the darkness of just before he'd come out.

'What age was Jack when he died? Fifteen? Sixteen?'

B sat calmly nursing his beer as if he hadn't just stepped on a landmine.

'Just turned sixteen.'

'You watched your best friend die when you were practically kids. It's much more rational not to want kids than to want them'

Bobby stared incredulously at B.

'What? You don't have to be Freud.'

The more times Bobby read Molly's letter the more he'd seen his own fear reflected in hers. She was so afraid of needing someone who she might one day lose, that she was willing to throw everything away. From a safe distance anyone could see how crazy this was. But Bobby wasn't at a safe distance. Wasn't that exactly the reason he didn't want things to work out with his ex? Why he couldn't imagine having kids? Why he'd given up rugby and tried to live as contained a life as possible?

The one person who seemed to know what was going on

in his head was the one person he had spent the last twenty years avoiding. They sat in silence. Bobby didn't know that B did a line in silence. He thought B was all bluster. That he was a fake, frivolous showboat who melded himself to others because he had no core to himself. But then Bobby had never taken the time to talk to him about anything much really. He was about to ask B to elaborate when B's phone pinged beside him on the sun lounger. Bobby was usually highly discreet so in hindsight he would wonder why he leant over so blatantly and read the message from B's boyfriend.

'You have made your choice. Best we end it here.'

40. BOBBY

Dublin, 2007

He didn't know why this was happening now. Why, out of nowhere, in the university car park he couldn't breathe. A weight was pressing down on his chest. He took the key out of the ignition and sat perfectly still. It was a normal grey October morning but with each progressing second, he felt like he was escalating into an uncontrollable panic, his body temperature rising, sweat seeping from him.

It wasn't the first time this had happened. Since he had started college in September, his heartbeat had begun to accelerate out of the blue. He'd seem to lose connection to his spiralling body, but up until now, it had always happened at night. Up until now, it had happened in a half-sleep nightmare which he could shake by jumping out of bed and running. He ran up and down the Strand at daybreak until his chest loosened, the weight lifted and eventually he could breathe again. After a cold shower he could return to a semi-normal state. He put it down to leaving school. He'd been a big fish in a small pond. He was having some sort of reckoning like a high school quarterback in small town America. But a chilling fear would shoot through him occasionally when he glimpsed what was deep down. It was over two years since Jack had died but still it haunted him like it was yesterday.

He took out his phone and asked her to come to the car park. He didn't know if she had lectures today, if she was even on campus, but he was desperate. Whatever this was, it was building, and he didn't know what would happen when it reached wherever it was going. He closed his eyes and imagined hanging on. He gripped the steering wheel until he could feel his knuckles whiten. He was focusing so hard on holding on that it was a few seconds before he realized the car door had opened. Molly was sitting in the passenger seat.

She was breathing slowly. He tried to imitate her, but it was like she was in a separate lane, a different track and no matter how hard he tried he couldn't get to her. He couldn't get back to normal. He jumped as he felt her hand on his. His knuckles shone white where he was still gripping the wheel with all his might. His breathing had quickened and now he was panting.

'Get out of the car.'

Obeying her, he stepped into the rain-soaked air. It wasn't actually raining, instead the rain had infiltrated the sky. It was disorienting and hard to see, like someone had thrown a damp towel over his face. Molly didn't get out of the car herself. Instead, she climbed awkwardly over the gearstick with her bird-like limbs and sat in the driving seat. Bobby walked round and got into the passenger seat. It occurred to him that he'd never actually seen Molly drive. He didn't even know if she had a licence. He figured she'd drive like a lunatic like Annabelle but instead the car pulled smoothly out onto the N11. He didn't ask where they were going, he didn't care. He closed his eyes and only opened them when the car stopped.

'We don't have any togs.'

'It's a Tuesday in October. Who's going to see? And if they do who on earth cares?'

Molly was already out of the car. She had pulled right up to the inlet. He watched as she marched in the rain towards the Forty Foot, her dirty blonde hair thrown up in a sprawling mess. She didn't have a coat and he realized she must have been in the middle of a lecture. She must have run to him. Left her coat, left her bag. Just like Molly not to care if she got robbed. Just like Molly to pull her jumper and t-shirt over her head in one go. Just like Molly to throw them on the waterside bench where they would surely get wet. But what did it matter? What did anything matter? She was running to the edge of the water in her black bra and purple knickers. She jumped. It was high tide and choppy. The water looked freezing; it looked heart-stopping. But his heart had already been stopped. Cold water couldn't hurt him now

He stripped to his boxers, a squalling wind tearing at his hair and awakening goose bumps. He couldn't bear to jump so he crept in down the railing, even though he knew that would make it harder. His breath stopped. His legs felt like they might be burning. He looked up but Molly was way out in the bay now. He took as deep a breath as he could muster and submerged himself. Tiny sharp nails pierced his skin. His breath constricted. But after a few seconds there was something else too. A slight release like the water had got in under his skin and unknotted him. One flash of OK-ness was enough. He started to swim towards it. His muscles responded and he got confidence from their strength; from the fact that his body seemed to know what it was doing.

The waves were strong, and he let himself be pushed and pulled. He turned onto his back and felt the water guide him. Suddenly, it felt like his body was flooded with air, his chest had loosened, and he could breathe again. The waves were lapping over his face, so it was a while before he understood that he was crying. He let himself go there. To the deep-down fear. He realized now that he had known for a long time. Somehow acknowledging it eased something further in him and he drank it in, tried to grasp onto it, bottle it for the times in the night when breathing seemed unreachable. It was minutes before he heard Molly calling him.

When he reached the rocks, he could see that she was already dressed but shivering, having had nothing to dry herself with. When he stumbled out, she hugged him tightly and used the sleeve of her jumper to dry his arms. He knew he was making her even wetter and yet he let her hold his soaking frame. They stood on the slippery walkway, the wind howling and the water choppy behind them. Had the wind been this loud before now or was it rising? The soaked clouds started to release their hold. The pellet-like noise of the sharp hail and the howling wind gave him cover. Maybe she wouldn't even hear him. His teeth were clinking against each other at a rate of knots but he managed to get the words out.

'I was in love with Jack.'

Despite the rain and the seawater, he knew for sure that they were tears this time because they were coming from deep in his chest.

'Oh Bobby.'

She held him so tight it almost hurt. She squeezed him like she was trying to squeeze the pain out of him.

'YOU'LL CATCH YOUR DEATH.'

They jumped in fright. Someone was yelling at them from the entrance to the inlet. An old man was pointing a stick at them. He looked like he'd wandered down from a mountain. He had a straggly beard and dirty wellies and was wielding the stick like he was corralling cattle. They tried to placate him, yelling back that they were fine, but he was hobbling towards them carrying something.

'You mad eejits. I wanted to ignore you but in all good conscience I couldn't and now you've made me miss the news.'

He threw the hard towels he'd been gripping at them.

'And now you'll have to come into the bloody house or you'll die.'

He had already turned and was making his way into the driveway of a large detached house. It was right in between the Sandycove inlet and the Forty Foot. The house was so big, Bobby wondered how on earth he had missed it before. It was old and not quite decrepit but getting there. The man stopped at the gate ushering them on angrily like they were late for an arranged appointment. Molly followed him like it was the most normal thing in the world to follow an old man into his house. Bobby was in all types of shock. He stooped to grab his clothes, awkwardly pulling on his jumper as he walked.

'What on earth are you doing canoodling in the sea in October?'

Molly reached the mountain man and laughed like they were old friends.

'Gosh, no, we weren't canoodling. I'm his cousin and he's gay.'

Bobby stopped dead. He expected Molly and the mountain man to do the same. He expected the sea to rise up or the wind to blow but the old man and Molly just kept walking to the house. Was that what he had told her? Was that what he was saying?

It wasn't just the man who looked like he'd wandered down from the mountains. His house was straight out of *Glenroe*. In the heart of the most affluent part of Dublin, the wallpaper was old-fashioned and homely. The hallway was lined with boots and it smelt like toast. Creeping in behind the others, Bobby could see that Molly had already taken off her Converse and propped them against the Aga like she lived there. The old man was putting a steel kettle on the hob when Bobby walked in. He threw another towel at Bobby and inexplicably murmured, 'Well, that's a relief.'

Bobby caught the towel and looked up at the stranger. Molly guided Bobby towards the Aga. She held his hands up towards the heat. It felt like sharp nails were piercing his skin again but this time it wasn't the cold, it was the sudden warmth he felt all over. It was relief.

41. B

Phuket, April 21st 2019

B hadn't for one moment believed that Molly had joined a cult. But Seedlings Eco Garden wasn't doing itself any favours. It was sealed off from a dirt road by high gates. Tall bushes and trees obscured any view in. A tiny hut blocked the entrance. The emaciated man occupying the welcome hut was smiling. He was smiling too much and refusing point blank to tell them if Molly was there.

Instead, he was offering to sell them seeds. Jars and jars of seeds lined the hut with miniature labels adorning each one. The emaciated man was talking about them half in practical terms, half in magical speak. It seemed like some of them would grow into viable foodstuffs and others would transform your soul.

As they were wont to do, each of the Blacks was dealing with the situation differently. Danny was listening intently to the man explain the difference between Thai Holy Basil, Thai Sweet Basil, Thai Hoary Basil, Thai Red Basil and Thai Lemon Basil. Lady V's crutches were hovering over the glass jars in an unnerving fashion like she was about to sweep them off the rickety shelves and send them crashing to the dirt floor in one fell swoop. Bobby was snooping around the hut in his disgusting boots, which to be fair had suddenly upped in practicality, given the filth of the place. B took a moment to survey the situation and work out how best to approach it. They'd come this far. It seemed that B might even have sacrificed his relationship to find Molly. He would not let them fall at the final hurdle.

If this place was a cult then B wasn't totally unprepared. He had gone through a phase of listening to every podcast ever made about cults. It was hardly a degree in psychology, but it would have to do. He knew about the sex ones, the drug ones, the ones with the leaders who killed everyone in one tragic but – you had to hand it to them – very efficient swoop, but seeds were a first.

He knew that it was vital to remain at least visibly calm. Cults often had front organizations that pretended to be neutral resources – hence the goddamn seeds. Jesus, it was all becoming apparent. One cult he'd read about had been sued loads of times and that's how the families of cult members had found out what went on in there. Why hadn't B looked into this more before they'd just rocked up? He should have checked the court records. Had he learnt nothing from his Netflix true crime binges?

He only remembered now that he was in this dirt hut that before you approached the cult you were meant to educate yourself in their particular practices. You had to know all the things they believed and crucially you had to speak about their beliefs positively. It said online that Seedlings Eco Garden empowered individuals by helping them fertilize their greatest seed of all – their soul. The

Blacks would never be able to keep their cynicism at bay long enough to pretend to buy into that. But B knew how to construct whatever persona the situation required. His confidence was gaining. He was nothing if not a chameleon. This was his moment. He was perfectly poised to handle this. It could have come from the podcasts, but it might just be instinct – there was one thing he knew for sure. Whatever they did, they mustn't act hastily.

It was at that moment that he spotted Lady V. She'd left the hut and was hopping on her crutches towards the other side of the compound. She must have known she was on borrowed time because she was swinging her casted leg in massive swoops, flying by miserable-looking plots tended to by miserable-looking people. In the distance he could make out a hut with a sign saying 'Meditation Sanctuary'. It seemed like V had placed her bets on Molly being there because she was making a beeline for it like it was the try line on the last day of the Six Nations.

B needed to change tack immediately. Lady V had gone rogue, and although he knew from his research that storming the cult aggressively was absolutely the wrong approach, he had to adapt. He had to make sure that the seed-selling emaciated cult front man didn't spot her and call some alert which activated rabid dogs and mobilized the miserable cult members tending to the miserable plots.

'I'll take them. I'll take them all.'

Danny, Bobby and the emaciated seed seller looked up as if noticing him for the first time. B produced endless baht notes and poured them out on the counter.

'But I need to know in detail how to plant each one.'

The emaciated seed seller lit up: How did B know? It

was not about which seeds you chose to grow but how you brought them into this world. As the man delved into detail about giving birth to plants by combining equal parts peat moss, loam and sand in a bucket, his accent miraculously transformed. At the beginning of their interaction, he was babbling a mix of sing-song Thai and the Queen's English but suddenly now he smacked of a New York taxi driver.

B was so busy distracting this absolute cad at the desk that he didn't see V walk back into the hut. Her face was drained. B had to do a double take to register that there were tears streaking down her face.

'Let's go.'

B was in such shock he forgot to take his seeds. Even the ones that would cure his soul.

42. LADY V

Phuket, April 21st 2019

After all this time, there she was. In a hovel at the back of a dirty cult. On her own, with her back to V, Molly's legs were crossed, and her hair was unbearably greasy. V figured that Molly would see her and they'd go from there, but she hadn't turned around so now V just stood in the doorway of this makeshift shack like she hadn't been looking for her niece for weeks. Like the whole purpose of being here wasn't to grab her and run for the hills.

V had spent the entire journey picturing what she would do when she finally found Molly. She would be foaming at the mouth with anger. She would have to stop herself from yanking Molly's dank ponytail and manhandling her out of the lotus position. For a while she had considered telling Molly that she'd broken her ankle in Thailand to make her feel bad, but the others would probably reveal the embarrassing truth. Still, V could intimate that it was the distraction of Molly's disappearance that had led to her accident and subsequent pain and inconvenience.

Lady V had imagined the other cult members too. She figured she would have to shoot daggers at some guru in a dress who spewed nonsense about respecting Molly's spiritual journey. She had practised the firm grip she would need to keep on her niece's arm so as not to be waylaid by Westerners who had 'found themselves' and fake high priests who were really just sexual predators. But none of the gardeners had batted an eyelid as she high-tailed it across the compound. And now that she had her eyes on the prize, V was struggling to revive her anger. She tried to channel the weeks of certainty about what needed to be done and why.

On the drive into the godforsaken wilds of Thailand, she had peered out the window at the alternate scenes of paradise and shambolic chaos and marvelled at the fact that she had continued with the whole escapade in the first place. At every moment she had been on the brink of pulling the plug. When Mike couldn't go. When John and Anne left. Nobody would have been surprised. Bobby and B were the real candidates for this job anyway and at every juncture she still half expected to pack it in, but something had been propelling her. She wondered if maybe it was her competitive nature. By running away, Molly had set them a challenge and V couldn't let her win. Or it could have been pure curiosity. Molly's behaviour was so completely foreign to V. The audacity and pure selfishness it took to cut yourself off, the naïve belief that going to the other side of the world to pick organic soybeans would somehow make everything better. It was so bat shit crazy that V half wondered if she had just wanted to see it for herself.

Whatever had been propelling her all this time and all

this way, she knew it was different from what motivated the Blacks. The Blacks took it as a given that you would follow your niece halfway around the world. They spent their lives talking over each other, complaining behind each other's backs, begrudging attendance at communions, confirmations, birthdays and anniversaries, but god forbid one of the pack would go missing.

V often wondered what it would have been like to grow up in a family like the Blacks. Her mother died young so maybe that shrunk her own family down to size. But even still, they had always felt contained, separate in some way. After she met Mike, she had tried to bring her own family closer together, to emulate what the Blacks had, but her siblings weren't constitutionally built for that level of blind closeness. Instead, it was the Blacks who had brought her into their frustrating but infinitely safe cocoon. Despite all her protests, the Blacks had made her feel part of something. How had someone like Molly – so at the epicentre of the Blacks family – lost her footing?

It was then that V noticed the dirt. A layer of grime covered the uneven boards Molly sat on. There was constant movement, mainly of small insects, but in the corner of her eye V could make out at least one cockroach. Who would choose to live in this squalor? How desperate did you have to be to think that this was the solution to anything? V expected a lot of things when she found Molly, but she had not accounted for this sinking feeling in her chest. This sudden unease that she'd read the whole situation wrong – that she was in over her head.

Molly's shoulder blades protruded from her light muslin robe like sharp rods and it looked like she might be shivering. V's eyes moved down Molly's back to her non-existent hips. Molly was vanishing like she had shrunken into herself. It was warm but the rain showers had been constant too. If Molly had got stranded in a rain shower, she might have caught a cold – or worse, pneumonia. And who would know? Who would mind her? Liam and Damon came into V's mind. What if they fell apart? Who would pick them up? Who would have the patience to travel around the world and tell them they weren't alone? The Blacks. The Blacks would be there for her boys in a way that she hadn't understood she needed them to be. But why didn't Molly know that?

All this time, V had been wrong. Molly wasn't selfish and spoilt. She wasn't footloose and flighty. Molly thought she was alone. She kept running away because she didn't think she had anyone left. V was beginning to understand; it wasn't anger or her competitive nature that had propelled her here. In all the moments she had spent irate at the whole fiasco she had failed to recognize how much she loved her niece. Now she saw that Molly didn't need to be yanked out by her dank ponytail. She needed someone to take her in their arms, hold her tight and tell her she was not lost, she was not untethered. But V was not that person. She reached into her pocket. She placed John's letter on the ground and hobbled out the falling-down door.

43. JOHN

Dublin, 1989

Bernard's face was pained. He was trying to hide it, but he had worn his heart on his sleeve since he was a child and John knew that he was fighting back tears. They sat in silence in the snug in Toner's where they'd come since they were young men. Back when they wouldn't have dreamt of this kind of pain – when they hadn't even known that they'd wanted children, let alone how much it would hurt to lose one.

John knew this was the last time. He knew it without even talking to Helen about it. They couldn't go through another miscarriage. He didn't even think he could cope with the trying again. The hoping and wishing, holding their breath, the two of them pretending they weren't watching and silently celebrating a day without bleeding only to delve into a deep depression that they tried desperately to hide from each other when Helen's period did eventually arrive.

'She'll be yours too.'

John was startled to see that Bernard was crying. He made no attempt to wipe his face, he just stared at his older brother over their untouched pints willing him to understand. John knew now why Bernard waited so long to speak. Bernard had known that John would bat him off. That he would tell Bernard not to be ridiculous but that was not what Bernard wanted. He needed to be able to help John in some way. He had to be able to help him.

They were to be twins. Cousin twins. Only a few months apart. Boys or girls (despite Annabelle's unfounded insistence that she was having a girl), they would go to the same school and wear matching clothes. They'd feel at home in each other's houses and not blink an eye when it was an aunt or an uncle instead of their parent at the school gates. They'd spend their holidays together in West Cork. They'd fight and crawl and scream and cry and giggle and they'd be thick as thieves.

'She'll be all of ours – yours and Helen's too.'

John didn't want Bernard to feel that he had to share their baby. He wanted Bernard to know that there was no part of him, no tiny part of him that begrudged him and Annabelle. If anything, it was the opposite. Now more than ever, this baby was all that mattered. John hadn't even wanted Bernard to come out tonight – Annabelle was well into her third trimester.

Annabelle had wanted to do a home birth. Bernard could have been brought around to the idea, but when she told John, his face had paled first white then green. She had booked into Holles Street the next day. John knew that most pregnancies were straight forward and nothing would happen to Annabelle, but after everything Helen had been through, he couldn't help but worry. He had to stop himself from calling Annabelle at odd hours of the day to make sure she was feeling OK. He already loved his brother's baby more than he could have fathomed possible. And he would do everything he could to mind that baby for the rest of his life.

'I know, Bernard. I love that little girl very much already.'

John jumped as Bernard threw his arms around his shoulders. John wanted to tell him not to be daft. He wanted to find the energy to make a joke or fob Bernard off. He hadn't hugged his brother since he was a child. If ever. But he felt Bernard's tears on the side of his head and decided to give in to the swell that had been chasing him. He hugged Bernard back and let his brother take the whole weight of him.

44. JOHN

Bangkok, April 2019

Molly Black, you were born in a storm. Hail and wind and thunder and lightning and we never thought we'd get Annabelle to the hospital. But we did and you changed our whole world. You were the first, you see. You were never just Bernard and Annabelle's. You belonged to us all from the start.

Your father was a great man. A warm, kind and thoroughly decent man. But there is a reason why we all still draw such strength from your mum. It's because when Bernard died, Annabelle could have shut up shop. She could have made sure you were alive and well but kept a safe distance from the painful business of life. But she didn't. She dived right back in. She rose and fell with it. Sometimes the falls are devastating. But Mol, your mum taught us that the highs are worth it.

You don't have to come home. Just know that you have a home to come to. Forever and Always.

Love,
Your Uncle John

PART THREE

45. SHEENA

London, March 1st 2019
The night of the disappearance

She knew he was angry, but she couldn't stop smiling. He was pacing and cursing, but it bounced off her. His anger couldn't get inside her. She was like those rocks you learnt about in Geography class. Some of them were soft and got worn down by rain but others held their ground. Limestone was a soft one – she couldn't think of any of the hard ones – but she knew that she had gone from being a soft one to a hard one. She needed to find a way to explain to him – to make him understand that she was OK now, that she was going to be OK. That she felt light again. Light and bubbly and like she could bounce again.

'Sleep with whoever you want, just help me out with this one thing.'

He'd come from a party, and at first, he'd been jokey and flirty. He'd placed his hands on her hips. His aftershave was piney and intoxicating. He was happy about Roscommon Conor, he said. Delighted for her but it didn't mean she had to let him down. A door opened somewhere on the street and his hands dropped from her hips. He scowled in anger as he turned away and she felt a pang of guilt.

The drink would sustain her. It would help her hold her ground. That's what she'd told herself when she was getting ready to meet him, as she'd downed vodka after vodka to get the courage to tell him that she wasn't going to do what he'd asked anymore. She tried to loop her arms around his neck and pull him back, but he was already walking away. She followed him for what felt like an age. She wasn't going to steal any more drugs for him, but they could still be friends, couldn't they?

The truth was, the more she worked with the counsellor and the more time she spent with Conor, the more unreal the whole thing felt. It was like she'd been in a trance, like she'd been sleepwalking. If it had been anyone else, she wouldn't have even come close to doing something so stupid, so out of character. But he was different. He was the first boy she'd ever loved. And he'd seemed to love her back in a way. Or at least he'd always been kind to her. And then when she moved over to London, he was the only person she'd known from home. The only person who knew about apple drops from Morrissey's pub. Who understood that her parents would never in a million years be visiting her – that London was more foreign to them than the desert. Who understood that slightly restless feeling that came over her on Sundays when she didn't quite know what to do without her family bustling around her, a roast in the oven and her mum cleaning everything that moved.

She knew that it was all in her head. She knew that he was seeing someone else. But late at night he'd come over and things would slip into a grey territory. They'd watch movies for hours and he'd rest his head on her shoulder. It would get so late that it seemed to make sense for him to stay over. They'd sleep in the same bed but get up in the morning and pretend that spooning all night meant nothing. He'd kiss her forehead before he left, and she would have to remind herself that he was going home to someone else. That there was nothing real there.

He stopped walking. They'd reached the canal. It was gushing like it was about to overflow and she realized it must be the rain. She slipped slightly and wondered how drunk she was. The grass was soaked through, and she slipped again, holding out both arms to get her balance. They'd walked for almost half an hour now. She would struggle to find her way back to the tube. But he would make sure she got home OK. They were friends. They could still be friends, couldn't they? She picked her way carefully towards him.

'We can be friends.'

She hiccupped and let out a little laugh. He moved close towards her, and she smiled. His jaw was chiselled, and his light brown curls flopped on his forehead. God, he was handsome, but she was impermeable. That was the word! Impermeable was the word and that was what she was. She was marble and no rain could get through. This whole thing would end and then it would be like it had never happened, that the medication had never left the drugs cupboard. She had Roscommon Conor. She was training for another marathon. She felt her heels rise like she would one day soon start to bounce again. She looked up into the clear black sky. It had even stopped raining.

'We were never friends, Sheena.'

He was speaking so low she struggled to hear him over the rushing water of the canal, and even then, she couldn't have heard him right. She felt herself slip and reached out to grab his shirt. He pulled her hand away.

'I used you. When I wanted to feel good about myself, I got anything I wanted from you – even pills for a while.'

She tried to remember him as he was, the boy she'd had a paralysing crush on. The boy with light curls who'd bought her apple drops from Morrissey's pub. But when she sought out his green-brown eyes she realized that boy was gone.

'And you were a fucking idiot to let me.'

Jeff turned and walked back into the darkness.

46. DANNY

Phuket, April 22nd 2019

Danny slipped quietly out of the hostel. He closed the gate behind him only to open it again to let a cat in. He began walking down the hill. Bobby was further up the hill trying to find better wifi, B was in the village asking locals for information and V was sitting on a sun lounger staring blankly at the sea. No one had been brave enough to ask her exactly what had happened at the Eco Garden. Why they weren't all celebrating, why they'd come all this way only to leave Molly weeding a garden in Thailand. But whatever she had seen had made V question everything, including whether or not they should have come at all. The only thing they were all sure of was that no one knew what to do next.

Danny looked up at the grey sky. There were no clouds but no blue either, just an ash-coloured mass above him that looked full of rain but felt warm all the same. He knew that most people loved holidays. That holidays were the highlight of most people's year. And it wasn't just rich people. Even people with no money went on several holidays a year these days, but Danny had never much understood it. Getting on a packed Ryanair plane with people who lived down the road from you, just to sit in an apartment next to more people from home, traipsing down strips of English pubs looking for imported Guinness and decent sausages. Your baggage getting lost, the stress of not speaking the language, people not understanding you and maybe you were accidentally rude without meaning it. Then coming home burnt to a crisp and putting photos on Facebook for your neighbours to like. Danny preferred to drink normal Guinness and sausages and not have to worry about sun cream. But now as he made his way down the hill, he realized that it wasn't just the pictures people came away for. It was the sky and the sea and the warmth that hung in the air when the piercing heat of the sun passed, effortlessly relaxing his shoulders and making him feel like he didn't have to work so hard at everything.

He walked along the seafront in the lazy afternoon heat. He took in the laughter of backpackers lounging in cafés, their long limbs spread out around them. Despite the fading sun, little kids were making sandcastles with grey clay, their squeals of excitement reaching the walkway. Locals selling t-shirts and trinkets nodded at him like the hard sell of the day was over. He smiled back, grateful to be able to catch their eyes, to connect with people in a way he hadn't in years. He took off his shoes and walked onto the sand. He waded into the water and felt the sea tickle his toes.

He thought about the day in the Phoenix Park when he'd met Frank. That day he'd clung desperately to a window of temporary respite from the terror. He'd grasped at that fleeting moment of OK-ness like it was the stag or the mist or Frank that held the possibility of survival and if any of those things changed even a tiny bit then he'd be lost again. But he was beginning to realize that it wasn't the stag or the mist or Frank. Just like it wasn't the water on his toes or the warm air on his arms now. It was him. The OK-ness was somewhere in him and he had to learn to find it when he needed it. He had to find a way to look inside instead of clinging to something outside him, desperately hoping a stag wouldn't move.

Being far away didn't solve anything but he saw what holidaymakers saw now: sometimes it helped. The different colours and weather and faces made you see how you could be different too. He wondered if there was any possible way in which he could stay here. Here on the other side of the world where he caught people's eyes, where the air was warm and gentle water glided over his toes.

'MOLLY!'

Danny turned to see B shouting at the top of his lungs. He was sprinting across the beach. Danny followed his voice. Standing at the other end of the beach was a small figure, thin and bird-like. Molly moved slowly towards B but she was tentative. She smiled but it was a pained half-smile and suddenly Danny knew. She didn't want to see them. She wished they hadn't come.

'Are you OK? Is that place a cult? This episode was a wild one even for you. How did you find us?'

B was elated when he reached Molly, asking her question after question.

Molly quietly explained how she'd got John's letter. How she figured someone in the Eco Garden had opened an outer envelope where the postage would have been. But her fellow gardeners seemed genuinely not to know about any letter, so she'd come into the village. But it wasn't to come home with them, it was to say goodbye.

A giant weight pressed on Danny's chest and he felt like he might not be able to breathe. It was this; this feeling of being knocked over by a bus that made being sober seem an impossible feat. How could he have forgotten? You get to feel all the good things, but you have to feel the unbearable things too.

'Christ, Molly, do you have any idea what you've put us through? Sending cryptic letters, fleeing to the other side of the world? Your family has been worried sick.'

Molly put her thin hand on B's arm but he shook it off. Danny knew what it was like to be that person. The person everyone is trying to save, the person who lets everyone down. And he knew too what it was like to need space. To desperately need to be somewhere else to work things out instead of on the main stage in front of everyone, your every misstep breaking everyone's heart. He wanted to intervene somehow to stop what was happening and yet he stood in the water, his feet sinking into the wet sand. Family was sometimes simultaneously not enough and too much. You needed them and there were times when what you needed was not to need them.

'What the hell did you mean in your letter – that we don't have to find you anymore?'

Molly considered the question, answering quietly.

'I thought that maybe I needed to go off the grid, disappear. I guess I had gotten kind of desperate, but then I heard about this Eco Garden—'

B cut her off.

'Why do you have to be on the other side of the world to find yourself? Are there no gardens you can weed in England? Or Scotland or Wales? For god's sake, the whole of Ireland is ONE BIG WEED.'

Molly stood silently while B's voice reached its highest octave and suddenly it hit Danny. On the outside, B had it together and Molly was a mess. On the outside, B saved Molly and B never needed Molly. But suddenly Danny saw that it wasn't that simple.

'I love you, B. You're my best friend in the world, but I have to work through some stuff, and I have to do it on my own.'

Molly reached out to hug B but he didn't grip her back, he only stood limply in her arms. As she began walking away, B turned to say something after her but decided against it. Instead, his whole frame curled over and tears rolled down his face.

Danny wasn't sure how long he'd been standing in the water, but the tide must have come in because it was almost up to his knees. B looked hopelessly out towards the sea like he'd known Danny was there all along. Danny made his way towards B unsure how to save him from feeling so much when Danny himself was only learning to feel again. And he wasn't at all sure if he could handle it.

47. ANNE

Dublin, April 23rd 2019

She wasn't *not* telling Alastair about the baby. And she wasn't in denial either – although she could see how you might be – the whole thing was nuts, totally unbelievable except for the clear scientific proof that this was how it happened, and that it had in fact happened to Anne.

She had thought that she'd get a taxi straight to his house and blurt it out immediately, but when they landed she was exhausted, so she decided she'd shower first. Then she wasn't altogether sure that Alistair would answer her calls after what had happened on the N11, so she decided she'd leave it until she was back in the office. But when they returned to work the Tuesday after the bank holiday everything was different.

Alastair was part of a gang now. The audit team had gone out over the Easter weekend and Alastair had emerged as some sort of mascot. He'd surprised them with his drinking stamina and impressed them with historical quips. It turned out the plague was a big hit. Greg and Tonia were the ringleaders of the gang, but it wasn't them she was worried about. Alastair seemed to have formed a special friendship with Rowena Powell.

Little Rowena Powell with her skinny ankles and her petite pumps with the bow on them. The girl couldn't be older than twenty-four. She giggled mercilessly at absolutely everything and made a big point of not drinking caffeine. What was she trying to prove? It's not heroin. 'Can I have decaf?' she would ask in her annoyingly quiet voice. At the end of every day on that job in Ennis, she had looked sympathetically at the four empty Coke cans that lined Anne's desk like she understood that addiction was a disease not a choice.

Worse than ignoring Anne, worse than acting hurt and betrayed, Alastair was perfectly friendly. He came straight over to her to ask her how she was, whether they'd found Molly, how she was coping with the jet lag and whether she'd like a cup of tea. He interacted with her in a formal, mature way as if to show her up for throwing a tantrum on the N11. Anne was struck mute. While he spewed nonsense, her brain went into overdrive about how she could possibly broach the subject. Would she ask him to step outside? But that might give him the satisfaction of thinking she wanted to apologize. Should she write it down on a post-it and pass it to him? Suddenly a wave of nausea rose up through her and she reached around the desk for the dry crackers that seemed to help.

'Oi, Stairs, you on a tea run or what, mate?'

Greg, who was from Leitrim, was attempting some sort of Cockney lad impression. Alastair responded in a thick midlands accent.

'Hold your horses, boss!'

This seemed to be a 'bit' they did, and the office erupted around them. Anne suspected that the escalation of her nausea had nothing to do with the pregnancy but rather this mortifying social interaction.

'Excuse me, Anne!'

Between leaving her desk and getting to the kitchen, Alastair was stopped several times like a celebrity on a red carpet. Rowena Powell called after him to remind him that hers would be decaf in a voice like she was doing an impression of a mouse. Anne was sure Rowena was an imposter. She was probably a lout outside of work and had assumed this meek caffeine-free persona to lure poor Alastair in. The girl probably mainlined Lucozade late into the night and smoked actual cigarettes. Anne flinched as Rowena turned towards her and gave her a nervous smile. Anne had been burning a hole in the back of her head and didn't have the energy to pretend she wasn't.

Alastair emerged from the kitchen with a tray of mugs. No one had even known his name two weeks ago and now he was dropping by people's desks making individualized jokes, smiling like a complete eejit. He would probably be the life and soul of the picnic this Friday.

The company picnic happened every year in the Iveagh Gardens and every year Anne dreaded it like a hole in the head but now it would be unbearable. Alastair and his new pals would probably share a rug. He'd wear something mortifying like shorts and they'd all gather around him like he was some sort of comic genius and Anne would probably be spewing in a bush. It was pure spite, but she could not tell him at all. People did that. She could go the whole nine months and just sit quietly getting on with actual work while he performed like a monkey for these mindless idiots.

'He's been arrested.'

Anne looked up to see a crowd forming by the TV. People were getting up from their desks. Someone turned up the volume. The doctor's bright red hair was visible in between the white shirts of policemen. He was short so the police towered over him but still you could see him move towards the squad car. Anne gravitated towards the screen. She couldn't make out exactly what was happening, but someone was saying that they couldn't arrest him; they'd no evidence he was there that night, they could only bring him in for questioning. Someone else wondered why a stunning girl like her would have been seen dead with a guy like him. The word creep echoed around the group. The crowd surrounding the screen were all in agreement: the doctor was dodgy. Anne's heart began to race. Did that mean they had found Molly? Had she known something after all? Anne checked her phone, but the screen was blank, the family thread quiet for once.

Anne pictured Molly's wide smile. Her relaxed nature, the fact that nothing seemed to irritate her. The way she sang 'Don't Cry for Me Argentina' out of key while driving. Or how she counted in fives under her breath when she was stressed. How when she was home you ended up eating egg yolk after egg yolk for breakfast because Molly loved the white of the egg. Maybe Molly wasn't attractive because she was magnetic. Maybe she was attractive because she was herself.

After witnessing her parents' marriage implode, Anne had

decided that her life would be insulated from mess. Even if it meant living life on the side-lines, shut out from others, then fine, Anne knew there were far worse things. Molly did the exact opposite – she threw herself into the world, she let herself get battered. And up until now Anne had thought that Molly brought chaos on herself, that that's what you got for all the adventures: hurt.

But maybe it wasn't just Molly; maybe it was impossible to keep life out. Anne had been careful all her life not to get too close to anyone, not to form attachments or court chaos, but she'd opened the door a crack and now an entire world of mess had fallen in. She was pregnant and she barely knew the father. Worse than that, it seemed she couldn't even bring herself to tell him.

It had been creeping up on her like she knew it would; the reality of the situation. Its tentacles had formed during the half sleep on the flight and cleaning the flat had only kept the panic at bay; now it engulfed her. Where would the baby live? Would she and Alastair take turns ferrying him or her between them? Christ, would Alastair move in? Would she have to tell Joel the lodger to move out? At least she wouldn't find pieces of sweetcorn in tiny crevices around the kitchen anymore, or would she? Maybe Alastair was an absolute fiend for corn. Because, in case she forgot, she didn't know the father of her out-of-wedlock child FROM ADAM. And if that wasn't frightening enough, she'd have her mother to deal with. She'd have to hear about Jesus Christ our lord and saviour and all his thoughts on what women should and shouldn't do and what Matthew and Paul and all the apostles thought. It may as well be speaking in tongues, but she'd have to sit there and listen because she was a good girl and Killian was a million miles away and her dad was worse than dead. Her heart began racing now and her face became flushed.

Suddenly her heart ached with longing for Molly. If she knew that Anne was pregnant, she would go around in a bluster doing impractical things like buying gross tea and suggesting cloth nappies, but it would be a comforting bluster. She wouldn't even pick up on Anne's minor snipes, she'd just take them as a given like she had since they were small. For all the ways Anne found Molly annoying, she realized that Molly was the only person who actually never seemed annoyed by Anne.

Anne had spent years keeping a mental tab of how different she and Molly were. Molly was fun. Molly was spontaneous. Molly ate anything, did anything, went anywhere with anyone. Anne was none of those things. Anne kept a virtual ruler with her at all times to measure herself against her cousin. She thought that was how everyone saw them – like they only existed in contrast to each other. But Molly had never compared them.

Anne had looked forward to being grown up so she could choose to unlink herself from her cousin. And that's what she'd done, but now she realized that of all the people in all the world she wanted right now, it was Molly. And it seemed like Molly was finally, fully gone. Anne's stomach wound in a knot so tight she knew it wasn't morning sickness. It wasn't jet lag or exhaustion, it was the pain of missing Molly and realizing too late.

'That poor girl. Maybe we could do a whip around to help with the search?'

Fucking Rowena Powell.

'That is such a great idea, Ro-Ro.'

Alastair jumped like a flash to get a giant envelope. Anne went to the bathroom to vomit.

48. LADY V

Phuket, April 23rd 2019

V set out early for the Eco Garden. She knew the others would follow, that they'd attempt an intervention, that they'd plead with Molly to come back so V had to get there first. She'd finally understood why Molly was in that godawful place and knew now that yanking her out of the lotus position wasn't going to solve anything.

Molly had to work through her grief or else it would chase her forever. The others didn't want to hear that; they wanted to wrap her in a blanket and force feed her lasagne, but V knew that her niece was right. There were some hells you had to go through by yourself, and nobody could save you from them. She gripped the tattered red diary. She wondered if it would be comforting to know how loved you were or unbearably painful to understand just how much you'd lost. She hoped it was the former.

She hopped awkwardly along a silt outcrop of land next to water. You couldn't call it a beach. Grey clay barely covered plastic bottles and shopping bags. From where she walked, she could see the real beach, the one the authorities invested in. By the real beach there was a walkway lined with restaurants and beauticians where Australians ate Pad Thai and got massages. But here on the silty edge of the water, there were no Australians, just a delivery boy waiting on a moped at the back of a grocer.

She stopped on her crutches for a minute and pulled her hair out of its ponytail. Swathes of wet black hair cooled her back. This morning for the first time in years, she had noticed streaks of grey running through it. Her Friday morning appointment at the hairdresser was so set in stone that she had entirely forgotten that without it she would have a head of silver. V rarely thought about her mother and never once thought them alike. But this morning, there was a glimpse of her in the mirror and for only the second time in her life, V had had a pang of longing for the stoic calmness she'd emitted, for the sense of safety that had been innate in her mother's presence.

When V had moved to Dublin at eighteen, she may as well have gone to the moon as far as her family were concerned. And when she'd become a model, she had leapt into a different universe altogether. There was such a big gap between herself and her mother that when she'd died, V hadn't longed for the conversations they'd had but mildly missed those that had never happened. There was no indication that that would ever change. She had no idea that a time would come when the loss of her mother would envelop her, dragging her down into a darkness she didn't know possible.

The nurses kept saying it was baby blues, that the hormones were at her, but if anything, that had made it worse. It downplayed what was happening to her as some general concept that other people took in their stride. Whatever was happening to V was terrifying and completely paralysing.

It started out with tears. Night, noon and morning, but that she could handle. It was the fear that crippled her. A deep dread that encompassed her. Dread at the sound of their cries, dread at the exhaustion that there seemed no end to. It was only then that she realized all her mother had gone through, how little V had understood and how much she wanted her mum to be there deep in her bones. Her quiet, decent mother had done this six times. The first time she would have faced the debilitating fear alone. Five more times she would have faced the exhaustion, the colic, the reflux and the relentlessness of breastfeeding. V had no idea. All those years in Dublin, she thought she had outgrown her mother, surpassed her in some fundamental way. She had met important people, eaten in expensive restaurants, appeared on TV. She thought that her mother's world was small, her accomplishments minimal. But all this time, it was the opposite. Her mother was a quiet superhero who must have had an inner strength that V had started to suspect she didn't have.

After the birth of the twins, all she'd wanted in the entire world was her mother to walk into their over-the-top house with its pillars and colonnades and jeeps in the driveway. She wanted to ask her practical things that would have been second nature to her mother, like how to wind Liam whose burps were like gold dust, or how to stop Damon's reflux, which was making him throw up in the night. But more than that, she desperately wanted her mother to take her into her arms and tell her that she would get through it. That she would emerge from this black cloud. That she was able for it. That there wasn't something fundamentally wrong with her.

Instead, the person who told her all these things was Annabelle. It was Annabelle who organized a rota of help, tagging Helen, Angela and Frances in to take the boys at alternating hours. It was Annabelle who got into the bed beside her. Annabelle who held her despite her leaking breasts and unwashed hair. How had V forgotten this?

She hadn't forgotten it of course. She had blocked it out. Even now, on a pot-holed road in Thailand nearly twenty years later, the pure fear of that time still sent shivers through her. Even though her boys were six feet tall, healthy and well, all the ways in which things could have gone wrong still seized her physically. By blocking it out she had been able to keep a safe distance from it, to not fall apart. But blocking it out also involved recasting Annabelle. If Annabelle was a flighty, foolish artsy type then V wouldn't feel her absence so much. But the truth was that Annabelle had saved her. The least she could do now was give her daughter a small part of her mum. And hope that it might just be enough.

V arrived at the gates to the garden. The seed hut was empty, so she wandered in. Laughter took her by surprise, and she saw a group huddled around a long-haired guy in a bright yellow vest. He was holding a stick in one hand and a shrub in the other and saying something about plant propagation. Beyond him, people in hippy gear were piling into an open topped flatbed, some of them wearing floppy gardening hats, others holding hoes. V hobbled into what looked like a nursery, ramshackle wooden frames marking out various plots of overgrown leaves. She slumped onto a bench. It was only then that she realized that the annoying ache she'd been feeling in her cast was in fact an agonizing pain. She tried to get at her foot to dislodge a stone but couldn't reach. Her exposed foot was covered in dust and the rest of her body ached from carrying the dead weight of her leg. She caught a whiff of herself and laughed out loud. She absolutely stank.

'V, is that you?'

Molly peeked out of a row marked 'Microbes'.

Molly had none of Annabelle's features. She was a golden-streaked brunette where Annabelle's dark red locks were legendary. But she'd always reminded V of Annabelle. It wasn't physical. It wasn't her eyes or her bone structure, it was just the feeling you got when you saw her; an inexplicable warmth. But for the first time since V had known her niece, Molly didn't exude warmth. She stood stock still in the dust, and she was tense. She was wary and V was filled with sadness.

V was reminded of when Molly was a child, how she was a strange mix of outgoing and shy. It was like she wasn't sure if her natural inclination for pure unfettered enjoyment was OK. V had often watched her in John and Helen's back garden playing alone, talking softly into the silence. Not to herself but to a world that was so clearly there. To people and things in her head which seemed to bring her endless joy. Had she lost that? Is that what grief did to you? Was her inner world too sad to go to now?

Molly sidled tentatively towards the bench and sat down beside V. She was wearing those wide pants that girls her age wore. She looked like an extra in *Raiders of the Lost Ark*.

'I can't go home.'

Molly was resolute and V knew she was on a tight rope – one wrong step and Molly might be lost to them forever.

'I understand. I just need to speak to you before I go, if that's OK?'

V had made it sound like she knew what she wanted to say but all her certainty of what the right thing was had evaporated the instant she'd seen her thin, vulnerable niece in the back of the tiny hovel. She knew she couldn't fervently take on a new life philosophy and drink the Kool-Aid as fully as Frances had after Annabelle died. She would never be naturally warm and soft like Helen. But there must be a way for her to explain to Molly what she didn't seem to know: that she wasn't alone. Even though she'd lost the two people she was supposed to belong to, she wasn't untethered. V was relieved when Molly broke the silence.

'What happened to your leg?'

V looked at the dirty cast and suddenly wondered why on earth she'd bothered lying. Smelly, sweating and dusty on a bench in an Eco Garden in Thailand, it was hard to remember why she cared what some young guy she didn't even know thought of her, why she'd been so afraid of not being who she once was.

'I slipped and fell on the treadmill.'

Molly didn't blink an eye.

'And you came all this way for me with your leg in a cast. B told me how much trouble I've caused, I'm sorry.'

'Didn't you know we'd come for you, Molly?'

Molly's wide eyes looked up at her and V suddenly knew

that she didn't know. That she was lost and frightened and alone.

'I thought I'd used up all my coupons.'

V's face must have portrayed her confusion because Molly continued quietly.

'Like maybe everyone has a certain number of coupons allocated to them for help and support and with Mum and Dad gone and all the times I've messed up that maybe I'd used up all my coupons.'

'Well, frankly so did I.'

It was a relief to laugh.

'But it doesn't work like that. Coupons are for Tesco, Molly. Families don't have coupons. I hope things work out for you here. I really do, but the grief, the loneliness, the fear – it will come again. It always does, and when it does we'll be there. We will always be there.'

V looked to her niece and tried to sear what she was saying into her brain, but Molly was fidgeting. Molly held one of her wrists with the thin fingers of her other hand and suddenly V could feel her grief like it had happened yesterday. She realized that was because that's probably what it felt like for Molly. She'd been too young to fully process her dad's death and too afraid to process Annabelle's. So, she'd run. She'd run and run until it had caught up with her, and now she was feeling it all in one fell swoop like being hit by a truck.

They sat without speaking while V wondered desperately what words could soften such a brutal blow. Molly reminded them all of Annabelle – of her warmth and love – but who was there to remind Molly?

'You remind me of her – of your mum.'

Molly looked up at V.

'Not her hair or her looks but the way she made us feel. The way she cared for everyone and saw them for who they really were? That's what you do. Annabelle seemed to have a sixth sense about when people needed help. She sought us out. She never let anyone fall through the cracks. So travel the world, stay away for long stints, but never leave us forever, OK? The world is too hard for us to lose another Annabelle.'

V reached out and held her niece's filthy hand. Molly reluctantly let V hold it. V realized that if Molly really was staying, they would have to make sure she was at least contactable. V could buy an extra phone and give it to the least crazy of the gardeners just in case. She scanned the hippies for a suitable candidate. She watched as a new group arrived back in the open-topped flatbed. This group had pitchforks and they began moving a hill of what looked like dead hay. One of the group was moving faster than the others. He moved the dead hay with the strength of an ox, and he was familiar. V wondered if her eyes were deceiving her.

'Is that Danny?'

'He's been here since 5 a.m.'

V did a double take as Danny looked up and waved at them. He stuck the fork into the hay and started towards them. His white t-shirt brought out his recent tan and he had an alert air about him. As he got closer V could see that his eyes were green. Had they always been this clear? She realized that she honestly could not remember ever seeing his eyes before, like they had never made eye contact. But it wasn't that. It was that his eyes were always downcast, and when they weren't looking down, they were glassy, like he wasn't really there. But this morning in the Eco Garden in Phuket, in his white shirt with his tanned arms, he had never seemed more alive.

'What on earth has happened to you?'

Danny laughed at V's unintentional bark.

'I'm sober.'

'Jesus Christ.'

'I'm going to stay.'

'Sober?'

'Sober but also, if Molly will let me, I'm going to stay here in Phuket.'

V's first thought was of the phone. She could buy an extra phone for Danny. Then she realized how crazy the idea was. They were dropping like flies. But before she could protest, Danny crouched on the silt in front of them.

'Molly, I know you can't come home. I know you're in the middle of something and maybe you don't want your family around you, but you see sometimes a man falls down a hole.'

His beautiful green eyes were bright. Did any of the other Blacks have these emeralds? Where had they been all this time? Could the drink have dulled them or was it just the puffed-out red around them?

'The walls are so steep he can't get out. Then a doctor passes by. The man asks him for help so the doctor writes a prescription, throws it down in the hole. Then a priest comes along, right? He writes out a prayer, throws it down in the hole and moves on. But then his friend comes over.'

Danny's face had never been more intent. Whatever was bringing him alive like this, whatever had made him leap back into the world like it wasn't all over, like there was still something worth fighting for, whatever it was, it was contagious. V was revved up like she had been on the stepper at the gym all morning.

'Then his friend jumps in the hole. And your first instinct is to say what an idiot, right? Because now they are both bloody stuck down the hole. But then the friend says, "Yeah, but I've been down here before and I know the way out." I'm that person, Molly. I know the way out.'

V and Molly were struck dumb. They stared at this man they'd known almost all their lives. He hadn't just changed physically. He was a different person. A person who'd come close to the brink and was barrelling back into the world, wiser than any of them. This wasn't just him saving Molly, he was saving himself. V didn't know exactly what Danny had been through, but she knew enough to know that, like her, it was Annabelle who'd caught him before he fell through the cracks. And now they were here to do the same for Molly. V had been the beneficiary of the Black family safety net. So had Danny. Now it was their turn. Now they were the safety net.

'But if you don't want me here, I'll leave.'

Danny sat on his hunkers while he waited for Molly to respond. V wondered if all this time he'd been secretly going to the gym because he was very fit for a man who only a month ago could have died of alcoholism. V closed her eyes and hoped against hope that Molly said yes.

'What about the family?'

Danny took this as a yes and smiled widely.

'I'll deal with them.'

V reached out for their hands and together they lifted her

up. She considered opening her arms to hug her brother-in-law or her niece, but it might be so out of character they'd get a fright. She settled for a pat on the shoulder, and even then, she noted the surprise in both their faces. She started towards the exit, getting back into the swing of her crutches. She turned at the gate of the nursery.

'That story was beautiful, Danny. Was it from the Bible?'

'A kind of modern-day Bible.'

Danny winked.

'*The West Wing*.'

Molly let out an involuntary laugh, and for a moment V could see her. Not the protruding bones or the greasy hair or the baggy pants but the girl in the garden talking to herself. She wasn't all gone. Suddenly Molly ran towards V and hugged her. Despite her shock, V remembered why she'd come in the first place.

In the rising heat of midday, V slipped the diary into Molly's pocket. She hoped against hope that the comfort of knowing how loved she was would outweigh the pain of learning just how much she'd lost.

49. ANNABELLE

June 1989

Dear Molly,

There has been a terrible mistake. We got through the big event safe and sound, then there were a few blurry days, but now out of nowhere we've been sent home. When I gripped the nice nurse at the door of Holles Street in terror, she told me that you and I just needed to get to know each other. So I'll start here: my name is Annabelle and I am your mum.

For a long time, I thought I was a tall person. My parents told me I was the guts of six foot but then a few years ago I got measured and I wasn't a grain of rice taller than five foot five. Can you believe that? It tells you all you need to know about my parents – they genuinely thought I was six feet tall.

There were no rules in my house growing up. Instead, there were vehement beliefs to live by. My mother taught me to always carry spare knickers because you never know when you might have to run away. That is my first piece of advice to you, my darling girl. It has saved my neck more times than I care to remember.

Other key things to know about me include that I once saw Terry Wogan on a bus. What happened was, I was very tired after a day of painting sets, so I wasn't paying much attention when a familiar man sat down beside me. I thought to myself, god, I really don't feel like talking to anyone, but it would be awfully rude to ignore this man who I clearly know. I smiled and asked him how he was. He said he was very well, and we chatted from RTE all the way to your uncle John's house in Leopardstown. When I was about to get off, I finally admitted that I couldn't quite place him. I thought maybe he had studied with Bernard or dated your aunt Frances. He very kindly explained that I recognized him from the TV but that he, on the other hand, hadn't a clue who I was. Can you believe it? What a nice man.

I have long been dogged with a wart on my left hand. I tried chopping it off with a kitchen knife, but it bled everywhere and then I forgot to clean the knife. Then Bernard licked it thinking it was strawberry jam. Isn't that awful? I'm glad to get that off my chest.

In relation to God, I'm all for him. Say, for instance, I was at a dinner party and the Pope was there – I would absolutely chat away to him. I'd ask him how he cleans that big ring and if he ever puts his red shoes up with a bottle of Chianti in St Peter's Basilica. I'd give him just as much time as I would, say, a hairdresser or a bin man (both of whom are undervalued magicians).

My own personal religion is baths. I believe deeply and wholeheartedly in baths. Baths in winter. Baths in summer. Baths when you are down in the dumps, baths when you are on top of the world. If you find yourself in an emergency where a bath is not available, a hot water bottle can give you enough comfort to tide you over until your next bath.

I think you might be my new hot water bottle (but don't worry, I don't use you to heat up my toes). You spent all day today next to my heart but now it's 4 a.m. and I've just rolled you onto the bed after your feed. Bottle – as my milk never showed up for the big performance. The less kind nurses tell me you will be malnourished, deprived and deeply unhappy because of this. But you are lying here beside me in the bed, your little arms reaching up above you and your legs outstretched like a drunk sailor. (Soother in of course because if I'm going to be cast as a degenerate mother I may as well get the perks.)

Bernard is lying on the other side of you snoring peacefully like the world hasn't changed immeasurably. Like we didn't just bring a whole other person into this mixed-up world. I on the other hand haven't slept in days. I feel like I've just been injected with a giant horse dose of adrenaline.

I've got to admit to you, my darling girl, that I'm struggling. Do you know the way athletes do a lap of honour after winning a race? Well, after the marathon that is labour it turns out that instead of a lap of honour, the lap of motherhood is one of continuous fear, self-doubt and judgement from every seat in the arena.

I think I will get better at it. But at the moment it seems I am not Mother Earth. I break all the rules. I feed you whenever you like. I rock you and let you fall asleep on my chest. I keep you in the bed with me but I'll nip that in the bud when you are in your late forties (fifty max).

Maybe by then you'll have your own children, and it will be useful to hear how your own mother didn't feel cut out for this either. Maybe like me, you will be terrified of the little bundle whose hopes and dreams you hold in your suddenly inadequate hands. And I will be there to tell you that, despite their starched uniforms and stereotypical casting (matronly and always from Drogheda), the less kind nurses are wrong. Your in-laws are wrong. The other mothers at the playgroup are wrong. You haven't failed. Not one bit. Because I have decided, just now at 4 in the morning on this humid night, that it's not about the soother or breastfeeding or the sterilization (which, by the way, I think is far too much faff to bother with). It is just about looking in your big blue eyes and telling you I love you. Always and forever.

Mum
XXX

50. JOHN

Dublin, April 24th 2019

When word finally did come from Thailand, it made absolutely no sense. At first, John thought it was his fault for not understanding what Bobby was saying. He'd gotten into quite a tizzy that morning about the annual street party. The party happened every year on the third Sunday in May. It had taken place through thunder and lightning. It had even hung on to that date when Mrs Brady's daughter from number 38 had gotten married the day before. The entire extended Brady family had come back from Wicklow to attend and brought wedding cake for the whole street.

Now after thirty-four years, Proinsias Murtagh had suddenly taken an interest in the event. He wanted to move the street party to coincide with Earth Day. Well, John had googled Earth Day and it was just the other day – they had missed it for this year anyway. It would mean cancelling the May event and waiting another year to hold the outdoor event in an entirely unpredictable month weather-wise. AND they'd be competing with the big man upstairs coming back from the dead and that rigmarole could fall on any Sunday depending on the moon. What was the old hippy thinking? The flyers had already been round-robined by the street council so there was no chance of the party changing dates, but it had really gotten under John's skin. He'd been on to various council members all morning to make sure Murtagh's campaign would go no further.

So when the phone rang he had his spiel at the ready, but it turned out to be Bobby calling long distance from Thailand. That was another factor driving up John's blood pressure. The cost of the call. With every minute he could feel his blood pressure rising but on the other end of the line Bobby was hmming and hawing and joking and laughing like he was a millionaire.

Everything Bobby said was confusing. They'd found Molly but she wasn't coming back. And Danny had joined the cult. Was he hearing him right? After a few too many minutes of casual chat John got firm with the boy.

'Bobby, I need you to confirm certain aspects of your account for me.'

He wished he had a pen. He would have liked to write this down.

'Molly has not joined a cult.'

'Molly has not joined a cult.'

'And you are telling me that not only is Molly *staying* in this gardening centre place, but Danny is refusing to return as well.'

'I wouldn't say refusing, Uncle John, he is just happy here and is going to stay till the end of the summer.'

'You are not going to like this line of questioning, but I have to ask – have you or any other members of our party taken mushrooms or any other natural or synthetic substance which may have narcotic qualities thus rendering your judgement of the situation impaired?'

The gravity of his words brought Helen into the hallway in her housecoat. Her face was scrunched up in concern. John knew he wouldn't get a straight answer, but it was annoying how long Bobby laughed for.

'I shouldn't laugh. I know how tough this must be to hear. But we aren't on drugs. We came all this way to find Molly and I'm afraid she doesn't want to come home.'

John stood holding the phone. For once in his life, he was at a loss. There was always something to be done, some practical fix for any problem he faced. All they had to do was find Molly. All they had to do was get her home and keep her safe, and yet somehow, deep down, he knew that this time there was nothing he could do. He couldn't fix this. His heart sank and he felt completely and utterly powerless.

'At least we know she's safe.'

Bobby must have sensed John's heart sink because he rushed to reassure him. 'Danny will be with her now. He told us about being sober, can you believe it? You must be really proud.'

John looked up at Helen. His face must have fallen because she came rushing to him thinking that something was wrong. Bobby made it sound so simple. Like sobriety was a switch and it had been flipped. John tried to feel the same but all he felt was fear. Fear that Molly had slipped from them for good this time and fear that now that Danny was finally found he could get lost again at any moment. A thought struck John: this was life. You'd be mad to think you'd any control over it.

'Look, I better go. We'll give you and the family a full debrief when we get back.'

Bobby was starting to say his goodbyes on the other end of the line, which was at least good for the poor lad's phone bill. John knew that the debrief comment was only meant as a little gift to him but still the thought of an AGM gave him a lift.

'Good point, Bobby. Send me your flight details and I will make sure to rally the family approximately two days later for a debrief. Helen is signalling to me here that she will make those sausages wrapped in bacon that you like. No, sorry, she is saying they are more a winter food, it will be mini-quiches.'

'OK, excellent. Good to have a heads up on the food we'll be having. Oh, and Uncle John? Thank you.'

'For what?'

'For whatever you wrote in that letter. It was you that brought her back to us.'

Helen put her arms around John's shoulders, and he was grateful for the scaffolding. Normally he was terrified that napping would propel him further into old age but he would need a lie down after this.

It was only when he lay down on the bed and closed his eyes that he remembered Sheena Griffith. He had to find out if the doctor had been with her that night. He rose from the bed and made his way back down the stairs wondering how on earth he'd contact Seedlings Eco Garden in Phuket.

51. BOBBY

British Airways Flight, April 26th 2019

Despite the abject failure of their mission, the mood on the way to the airport was jovial, like they knew they had to distract themselves from what was really happening. It helped that Lady V admitted everything in the taxi. The first-class flights, the proposed second week in the Four Seasons in Koh Samui. The fact that she had had no intention of partaking in the search but had instead memorized the treatment list in the spa at the Shangri-La. B started calling her 'Bold as Brass Ronnie', which she claimed to hate but smiled at, nonetheless. The more she revealed the more she laughed. It turned out she hadn't broken her ankle by slipping on a wet floor but had fallen off a treadmill. Then she pulled up her Nike leggings and explained how she'd gotten the tattoo of a balloon floating away to impress a poet ex-boyfriend who ended up dumping her for a TG4 weather girl. Still, she wouldn't tell them which member of Boyzone she'd dated. (Bobby was beginning to suspect it was Mikey.)

V's jet-black hair was no longer pulled back in a vice grip

but hung loose over her shoulders. It had frizzed up in the humidity and curled slightly on the fringes of her face but somehow this made her even prettier, more human pretty than robot pretty. She looked young. Vital and energetic despite the crutches. Bobby wouldn't dream of saying it to her but the teeny tiny bit of weight she'd put on suited her too. Her face looked less like a collection of perfectly shaped facial features and more like a person. He wasn't sure what had happened between her and Molly, but it was clear that it had softened her somehow. She was altogether a less scary person.

Bobby himself had only had a few minutes with Molly. They'd stopped at the Eco Garden on their way to the airport and dropped the rest of Danny's things into the hut where he'd be staying. Bobby had thought that V would be the voice of reason, that she'd insist Molly come home, that she'd talk sense into Danny, but she was all on for leaving half the family in an Eco Garden in Thailand. The only concession she'd demanded was leaving an obscene number of phones with them in case of emergency. That and the fact that she was so disturbed by how greasy Molly's hair was, it seemed like at any moment she would whip out some Pantene and offer to wash it herself.

Bobby wasn't sure what to say but any lingering doubts he might have had were aired by B whose normally cool exterior was replaced by an unsure and agitated one. It was clear to all of them that B was terrified of losing Molly. And the one moment Bobby had had with his cousin, he'd realized just how close they'd come to that. She mentioned offhand how she had planned to go to a remote forest where you can leave all your belongings and 'take time out of the world' but someone had told her about the Eco Garden and she thought she'd try it first. Once he realized how close she was to walking away for good, Bobby saw that the way things had ended, with Molly safe with her uncle and contactable – it wasn't so bad after all. Although he knew he'd have a tough time explaining that to the rest of the family.

Halfway through the flight, Bobby noticed that the light above B's seat was on. He walked to the back of the plane and sweet-talked two gin and tonics out of the air stewardess. While she was rustling up some ice, Bobby thought how strange it was that he was actively trying to hang out with B after all these years of avoiding him like the plague. Then he realized. All this time, Bobby thought it was him who had been avoiding B, but now it hit him: B avoided Bobby too.

'Do you avoid me?'

Bobby placed the gin and tonics on B's tray table standing over him in shock at this realization.

'Yes. Just like you avoid me.'

Bobby slid into the seat knowing he hadn't a leg to stand on. They each took a swig of their drinks. It seemed that neither of them was willing to buckle. B's screen was showing an old episode of *Modern Family* and they both glanced at a goat running around a backyard without sound. Eventually B gave in. He looked at his watch.

'Well, we have another godforsaken six hours so you may as well tell me why.'

Bobby was only halfway through the first gin and tonic but the air stewardess popped four more in front of him. He looked up at her with what he knew to be his most charming smile, but her eyes were fixed on B. She winked and a blush flared up across his translucent skin. Even his strawberry blond hair seemed to glow crimson.

'Because of that.'

'Because people recognize me?'

'No, because people love you. The whole world now, but before then, my family has always been besotted by you.'

'You don't like me because your family like me?'

B spoke so calmly that Bobby had to laugh. Where anybody else would be annoyed by such irrationality, B just seemed mildly amused. It was like he'd had the stuffing knocked out of him and now he was just going with whatever punches came next.

'I was worried that the minute I came out the whole family would just presume we'd get together. It was still at the time where if people found out you were gay, the first thing they'd say is that their cousin Richard is gay so a) they are super cool with you being gay and b) given you have the same orientation it would make sense for you to get with Richard immediately.'

'True.'

B reached over to take the other half of the cans and mini-glasses of ice.

'But you haven't met cousin Richard. He's divine.'

Bobby laughed.

'There is a third option, you know, Bobby? Other than us getting married or being mortal enemies. We could be friends. You do realize that is possible?'

'You must think I'm such an idiot.'

'No, I just figured you thought I was too gay to hang around with – that I'd ruin the "is he or isn't he?" aggressively straight vibe you've got going on.'

'Aggressively straight? Jesus, is that the vibe I give off?'

Bobby finished the second gin and tonic and felt the first drink starting to ease his muscles. He wondered why he had been so uptight. All these years, B had been nothing but nice to him, and Bobby had avoided getting to know him just because it would make his family happy. The chip on his shoulder was beginning to get heavy. It would have been nice if all these years they could have been, as B had suggested, friends. With Molly gone, he could do with one. Maybe it wasn't too late to try.

'In all the commotion of finding Molly, I never asked – how are you doing? Are you and the Bitcoin tycoon or whatever he is really broken up?'

'I don't think so. He's probably right; I guess I can't jump on a plane every time Molly gets green fingers.'

B downed his G&T.

'I see you shaved the tash. Was it because you fitted in so well in Titty Bar and Girls?'

'That was one creepy mirror.'

They laughed as the curtain from first class opened. Two glasses of Champagne on a silver tray hovered in an air steward's hand. The note read: 'To the plebs in economy, love Bold as Brass Ronnie'. B had fallen asleep again before Bobby remembered that he'd never found out why B avoided him too.

52. ANNE

Dublin, April 26th 2019

It was worse than shorts. Alastair Stairs was wearing a dickie bow with braces. He had set up a table with a gingham tablecloth and was jovially constructing jugs of Pimm's. He was chopping cucumber and fielding compliments on the dickie bow like he was a social animal. And it was working. The partners were flocking to his mint-scented stand, popping strawberries in their mouths and saying loudly how inventive he was – how quirky and fun the idea was. Anne was hiding behind a birch tree, nursing a lemonade and shooting him daggers.

Anne treated the annual spring picnic like she did everything else – thoroughly and with serious preparation. Normally at these things she would have a plan of attack. She had an Excel spreadsheet detailing her colleagues' spouses' and children's names. Ideally, she liked to have one titbit about each person's personal life like, 'Hello, Mike, how is Peter finding the origami?', or, 'Is Nancy still playing the saxophone?' Failing a personalized titbit, she would ask detailed questions about their children's education which was of utmost importance to them all. Then she'd compliment spouses on their shoes because this worked for men and women. She was diligent and thorough at socializing like she was at everything else. But today she didn't care. Today, for the first time in a long time, it felt like her own life was more important than work. What the baby wanted trumped everything. And the baby wanted to hide behind a birch tree nursing a lemonade.

The band started up in the tent and Anne looked at her watch. She had subjected herself to an hour and a half of this inanity. Given the circumstances, this seemed plenty. She downed the rest of the sugary lemon and made her way through the bushes. Her lunchtime walks here had paid off. She knew a route to a secret gate that meant she wouldn't have to pass through the masses. The minute she had decided she could abandon ship she started to fantasize about her evening. The first treat would be taking this dress off. She knew that she wasn't even nearly showing, that the baby was tinier than a pea, but it didn't feel that way. She craved loose jumpers and leggings. She craved curling up with hot water bottles. It would be nothing short of strange to have a bath in such warm weather but that was exactly what she would do. If she had learnt anything from her aunt Annabelle, it was that there wasn't much a bath and a hot water bottle couldn't fix. She just hoped Joel the lodger wasn't home cooking corn on the cob. Would it bother her so much if it was a different vegetable? It stuck in his teeth when he smiled at her.

'I can't bear it any longer.'

Anne stumbled in fright. For several seconds she was sure she would be able to regain her balance, but the rough terrain got the better of her and she fell bum-first into a bush. She turned to look back at the Pimm's table where she was sure Alastair had been stationed seconds ago. How had he gotten to her so fast? She expected him to help her up, but it seemed he hadn't even noticed that she was in a heap in the bushes, her yellow M&S dress fanned around her. Alastair seemed to be on a track and was unwilling to acknowledge anything that would force him to veer off. Including Anne falling into a bush.

'I've been trying to be normal, but I just can't. I need to tell you something.'

Anne tried to stand but one of her high heels had twisted half off and to be quite honest the bush was surprisingly comfortable, so she sank back into it. Alastair's hairline was moist and an actual bead of sweat rolled down to his eye. He must have been roasting in his tweed trousers. There was no outlet for air because he was locked in by the braces and the buttoned-up dickie-bowed shirt. The hot day must have taken him by surprise and now he had to tell her about Rowena Powell. Suddenly she felt warm towards him. It was not his fault she had a meltdown on the N11. And Rowena Powell wasn't a bad person. The caffeine thing was just annoying but each to their own. They would be very happy together.

'I love you, Anne. I know that's not what you want to hear but I just find myself totally unbearably excited to see you, and when you were away I felt so sad.'

Anne was shocked by the laughter that erupted out of her involuntarily. She couldn't help it. Alastair was a nervous wreck. He was so on edge that he was up on his tippy toes leaning forward, his ears pricked like she might say something, and he didn't want to miss it. She knew that laughter was a completely inappropriate response, but it was just that she was so used to being the awkward party in any social interaction that she didn't know what to do if you were on the other end. She was trying to say something supportive, but the laughter was rippling through her and the bush was shaking. Eventually she reached her arm out.

'You might have helped me out of the bush before you proclaimed your love for me.'

'Oh my goodness, yes of course.'

He grabbed her arm and pulled her vertical. He apologized profusely like he had only just noticed that she was sitting in a bush. How bad *was* his eyesight? She hoped it wasn't genetic. Lord knows what other genetic flaws the man would pass on. But as she took in his expectant face she was overcome with the most uncharacteristic wave of excitement. Sure, the man had terrible eyesight but think of all the other things she would learn about him on this adventure.

'It's good you love me because we are having a baby together.'

'Excuse me?'

'Now, you don't need to worry at all. You can be as involved or not as you like. Gosh, you look a little peaky, would you like to sit in this bush? It's actually quite comfortable.'

Even though it was her who had suggested it, she was still surprised when he lowered himself into the dent she had left in the bush. They were ruining the integrity of a perfectly good bush. Some park keeper would be crestfallen on Monday morning.

'Look, you take your time there, I'm sure you must be in shock and you don't need to say anything now.'

She was touched by how, despite his speechlessness, he still clung to her hand. He murmured something but she missed it, so she leant into the bush to hear.

'This is the best thing that has ever happened to me.'

Could the daft man be crying? She planned to tell him to pull himself together but couldn't help but feel tingles of warmth shoot up through her. She would almost cry herself if she was that type of person. A roar went up from the tent where it seemed karaoke had started. Greg and Tonia were doing a rendition of 'The Time of My Life' and it was genuine head-in-the-oven stuff. The entire gang was singing along like infantile youths. But worse still was Rowena Powell standing on the side-lines judging them like a caffeine-free mouse. Suddenly Anne remembered the entire problem with telling him in the first place.

'What about Rowena Powell?'

'What about her?'

'Well, it seemed like you two had struck up a friendship of sorts?'

The minute she said it she realized how stupid it sounded. What was she accusing him of? Making a colleague tea? It wasn't even real tea. Her thinly veiled flash of jealousy seemed to inject him with a dose of energy. He jumped up from the bush.

'Let's get out of here.'

'What about the Pimm's station?'

'Fuck the Pimm's station.'

He seemed startled that fuck had come out of his mouth and giggled like a schoolboy. Jesus Christ, maybe she loved him too. She leant in to kiss him and felt his entire body relax in relief. He put his arm around her as they walked to the gate.

'Rowena Powell of all people, Anne. She makes such a big deal about caffeine. You'd think it was heroin.'

53. ANNABELLE

July 1989

Dear Molly,

I know I'm not a conventional parent. And I know that isn't always a good thing. I shouldn't have brought you to Neary's last week to meet Pat O'Shaughnessy. I forgot he was a drunk. I thought he was on the milder end of alcoholism like F. Scott Fitzgerald but it turns out he is closer to Hemingway. He spilt half a pint of Guinness on your babygro and we had to sit on the bus all the way home with you smelling like a brewery while old ladies with blue hair dye scowled at us.

And that time we ran out of nappies wasn't good. I had to wrap you in a towel until Crazy Prices opened at 9. The night I left you backstage when I was asked to do a last-minute job at the Abbey was questionable. You were snoring benignly until the costume lady started to accessorize you with feather boas and dusty velvet curtains. Your little sneezes could be heard from the eves! In hindsight that was a bit of a lark. But given all the things I've done wrong I wanted to tell you about the things we are getting right – you and me.

Walking. We walk to the ends of the earth. Or at least to the Crumlin junction. Rain, hail or sunshine we march off in the morning and I narrate the lives of our fellow boulevardiers for you. There is the woman who walks her cat on a leash who we call Deirdre. She smells like dead flower water, but we like her. We try to nod to her, but she is having none of it. There is the tall man with the scar across his face whose origins we speculate on every day. You think it's a straightforward agricultural accident. I think he has recently returned from Australia where a shark got him right on the cheek. That or he is a Russian spy. Then there is Sad Sam who walks down our street kicking stones and never raising his head. Sometimes we simply can't cope with how sad he is. We are very concerned that he is being bullied. Sometimes we follow him. Far behind, mind, but just to make sure there isn't a big bully waiting for him at the playground.

Another thing we get right is singing. I don't mean to be critical, but you aren't great at talking. It's really tricky that you aren't able to respond to my musings. They tell me this defect could go on for another two years. Thank Christ we have musicals. I perform West End numbers and you stare wide-eyed. You cry if I'm out of my range, so I guess that is feedback of sorts. At the moment we are perfecting *Evita*. I don't want to boast but I fill 'Another Suitcase in Another Hall' with a level of poignancy I believe really hits home with you. You lie quietly on the bed like you relate on a deep level to being abandoned by a revolving door of lovers in Buenos Aires in the 1930s.

Then when we get bored of walking or singing, we like to talk about Mako – the imaginary baby in Japan. I tell you how you are so loved. You are so so loved. You are the most loved baby in Europe. But unfortunately, there is a REALLY cute baby in Japan who is VERY loved, so you just missed out on most loved baby in the world. We try to imagine the ways in which Mako is better than you. I'd say it's the eyelashes. They say he has eyelashes so long you could sweep the floor with them. You think it's a classic case of baby sexism. That Mako won over the panel simply by being a boy.

All joking aside there is one thing we can agree that we got right. Boy, did we pick the right dad for you, my darling girl. I was up for having a baby. I thought it was a lark I could get on board with, but your dad has loved you in his stalwart, consistent way since the moment you appeared as a prospect on the distant horizon. Like me – he knew you'd be a girl. He has been talking about walking you up the aisle like it's the first step you will take. (Which it won't be, by the way. I'm hoping you'll be an anti-establishment lesbian.)

I know that when people see your dad and me, they see me first. I take up all the space. I bluster around changing the energy, letting loose whatever is in my head. They think he's quiet and sweet. But your dad is our superpower. He is calm in all the ways I am frenetic. He is even in all the ways I'm high and low. And he is kind. And never forget that there are few things more important in life than kindness. So, we chose well, my darling girl.

I like to think of it that way. That you and I have always been best friends. That we conspired before you even existed because that's how it feels – like you've always been a part of me. Like a second heart. Or rather persistent psoriasis.

Love,
Mum
X X X

54. THE FAMILY

Dublin, April 27th 2019

Uncle John got the date wrong. Instead of two days after V and Bobby's return, we were all squashed up in the lounge before their plane had even landed. The truth only emerged when all the mini-quiches had been eaten and Uncle Mike was snoring in an armchair that he had insisted on pulling into the heart of the war room. We weren't best pleased to be held captive in the den, but at least now that it was nearly summer Blur was wearing flip-flops which provided adequate aeration to negate his athlete's foot.

If we were annoyed, lord only knew how Bobby would take being shipped straight from the plane to the AGM. We didn't even consider that Lady V would show up, so we didn't know our arse from our elbow when she bounced in on her crutches, smiling broadly. V smiling was like seeing an inanimate object move; like a vase erupting in anger or a table coughing. She was wearing white shorts and her jet-black hair hung loose around her face. Her light tan made her look about twenty-five. She opened her arms to hug anyone in her path and a few people gripped onto her like they had been waiting years for this and wanted to get their money's worth. Helen produced a second batch of mini-quiches, which she had been squirrelling away like a snake. Mike woke up and was the only person in Dublin 18 who didn't have a mild stroke when V kissed his forehead and sat on the side of his armchair with her arm around him like a teenager. Even Granny looked up but could only be briefly torn away from her Sudoku. Eventually we were in our natural state – crushed together in a tiny room discussing the intimate details of each other's lives.

'In this kind of situation there can be a temptation to fire out questions willy-nilly and lose key facts. I've taken the liberty of writing out the things we already know. Bobby and Veronica, we'd be grateful if you could fill in the blanks for us.'

Uncle John's latest purchase was a flipchart. He had more coloured pens than facts but wanted to use the full spectrum of colours so had written some fairly obvious information on the chart. Things would have to be pretty dire for us to have forgotten Molly's name. But it was up there along with her date of birth and eye colour. Her hair colour was conspicuously missing because no one knew what shade it was at the best of times. The flipchart also listed members of the search party like they needed to be immortalized after returning from the moon.

'As requested on the internet chat room, I hope that each member of the family has prepared a question in advance so we can go around the room in an orderly fashion.'

Predictably nobody waited for him to enact his orderly fashion. Several people jumped in with questions and he started madly flipping to fresh pages on the flipchart to capture them all, murmuring that this mayhem was exactly what he was trying to avoid.

'How did she get there and what is she living off?' (Even-Stephen)

'Is she eating OK?' (Aunt Helen)

'Has she found our lord and saviour Jesus Christ and has she given any thought to coming to live in Glenmalure? There is a wonderfully diverse community there now.' (Aunt Angela)

Presumably this meant a suspected Protestant lived one town over.

'B's partner Jeff booked her flight. She is paid a stipend for watering weeds. She looks like she hasn't eaten a meal since the nineties and absolutely not under any circumstances will she move to Glenmalure.' Bobby paused. 'Sorry, Angela.'

It was only when we were all focused on Bobby that we noticed that he'd shaved his moustache. The relief was palpable. At least we'd overcome that horror.

'What about the doctor?' (Oasis)

'I can field this one.'

John started turning pages on the flipchart until he found one that read 'Sighting of the Doctor??'

'Molly lost her phone.'

Several people groaned and Lady V cackled loudly.

'But thanks to Veronica's ingenuity I was able to contact Danny. Unfortunately, Molly never saw the doctor; the only person she saw outside that night was B's – now I believe ex- – boyfriend, the imaginary money billionaire.'

'When is Molly coming home?'

Most of us hadn't even noticed Anne hiding behind

the flipchart. We'd noticed Alastair all right because he was hovering beside Uncle John like an assistant handing him different coloured markers. He must have survived Cinemagate. He seemed absolutely riveted to be here.

'Does she not realize we need her?'

Perched on the windowsill in one of her signature M&S polyester work dresses Anne looked distraught. An outburst from Anne was an unusual occurrence at the best of times and an outburst which seemed favourably skewed towards Molly was downright baffling. Most of the time it seemed like Anne could barely stand Molly. She rolled her eyes at her adventures and steered clear of her drama. They were like two vastly different flavours of Tayto crisps reluctantly caught in the same multipack. But today she looked upset. In fact, she looked a grey-ish green like she had eaten something funny.

The door knocked so we didn't get to explore Anne's pallor. Uncle John did a quick headcount, but we were all there. Nobody moved. It was like we were cutting drugs and there was about to be a police raid. We all looked at Alastair. As our last known external visitor, we held him responsible, but he sat stock still, as confused as the rest of us. Finally, John nodded the all clear to Helen and she opened the front door. A man with long grey hair stood in the hall in luminous cycling shorts, sandals and socks. There wasn't enough room for him to come inside the rammed den, so he stood in the doorway peering in at us spread across the floor stuck like glue to each other.

'What is that?'

We were all shocked by Uncle John's uncharacteristic bark and craned our necks to see that the man was carrying a pie with radioactive green material seeping onto the plate below it.

'Key Lime Pie.'

The stranger had a receding hairline but white-ish hair sprouted in uneven patches all over his face.

'Did your wife make it?'

'No, I made it.'

We stared from one late middle-aged man to another trying to process the bizarre interaction.

'What's it for?'

'You and your family. I didn't realize your niece was missing. Fionnuala in 76 told me. Did you find her?'

The stranger didn't ask this empathetically but in an accusatory roar. John's face was filled with suspicion.

'Yes.'

The tension between them was nail biting. It was like the *Kardashians* for old people.

'That's good then.'

Our proper upbringing had us crawling in our skin for John to say thank you. After more suspicious glances John finally succumbed.

'Thank you, Proinsias, and thank you for the pie.'

The sandal man handed the pie to Helen and abruptly turned in the doorway and let himself out.

Uncle Mike jumped forward in his chair like a child.

'What on earth was that?'

'A peace offering of sorts.'

Uncle John looked emotional, and we were all dying to hear more, but, most out of character, he began to wrap up the meeting early. He folded the sheets over to the front page of the flipchart and handed his utensils to Alastair. The rest of us followed suit and started to unfurl our limbs from each other. We were thinking about the mini-quiches as we headed for the door. Given she had squirrelled some away before, no doubt Helen had a third batch hiding somewhere. She was sneaky like that.

Emerging from the cramped den, Blur asked Bobby in front of everyone how he was coping with his anxiety. Despite the public interrogation, Bobby seemed touched and started telling him about alternate nostril breathing. Oasis wondered aloud why nobody had even mentioned Uncle Danny. Lady V hugged him close and said that it turned out that after all these years Danny was the one person in the family we didn't need to worry about. We were nearly in the kitchen before we heard the yelling from the laptop.

'HANG ON.'

We all hovered in the front hall. Killian's tanned face appeared on the screen. For no apparent reason he had no shirt on. It was hard to make out what he was saying until Alastair held the laptop up above our heads.

'So Molly saw this billionaire person talking to the nurse that night? And then he buys Molly a flight to Thailand the next day? Does no one else find that a bit suspicious?'

A car alarm blared outside but we were all too busy connecting the dots to wonder if it was one of ours. A smell of burning emanated from the kitchen but even Helen didn't move.

'The Griffith girl.'

John spoke first but it was Mike who took out his phone.

'We need to tell the Guards.'

'And the police in the UK.'

'Bobby, does B know that this Jeff character paid for Molly's flight?'

Killian was pacing the screen of the laptop now like ground control managing a military operation.

'God, I don't know, she only mentioned it to me briefly before we flew.'

'You need to call B immediately.'

'I will but before I do – what are we accusing Jeff of?'

Bobby held his hands out to calm the sudden frenzy. He seemed to be asking us all.

The car alarm went off. We followed John and Mike to the hall. John started searching in a drawer until he found a piece of paper with the detective's number on it.

'Knowing more than he is letting on.'

In the background we could hear Alastair introducing himself to Killian. Then a beautiful kimonoed girl appeared on the screen, and this time, Killian hung up on us.

55. B

London, April 27th 2019

On the plane B had been in a bubble, safe from the reality of break-ups and press tours. But as he stepped off the Heathrow Express at Paddington, the cold of a predictably grey London brought him back to reality. As he made his way back to Soho, B didn't know how to feel about what he was walking into.

The melancholy stayed with him until he turned the key in the door and saw Jeff's stuff. Jeff might not be answering his calls, but he hadn't changed the locks and his every belonging was still there. B hadn't been sure how he felt until he had stepped over the threshold, but his immediate relief told him everything he needed to know. He wanted this relationship. He wanted the calm predictability of his grown-up life, his beautiful Moroccan tiles and his quiet financial wizard. Reassured, he stepped into a long hot shower, crept into clean sheets and slept like a log.

When he woke it was evening. He knew that Jeff would be home from his daily errands by now but still he stayed in bed. Rain was battering down on the Velux and he lay there looking at the dark sky and thinking about Molly. He was still reeling from her decision to stay. He didn't understand what she could do there that she couldn't here. He knew it was self-centred but it felt like she was punishing him for moving on. And yet as they'd left the gardening cult, he could see something about it was different. Something about *her* was different. He was beginning to wonder if all this time he thought she'd needed him more than he needed her when actually it was the other way around.

From now on, he would bury himself in boring domesticity. He would cook. He would wear tracksuits (nice ones) and give Jeff all his attention. He would listen to him properly. He wouldn't take him for granted as background noise. He would appreciate his safe normalcy. He would get more involved in Jeff's work, learn about cryptocurrency. There was a documentary about it on Netflix he'd been meaning to watch.

The apartment was dim. The days had been getting longer before he left London but today the rain made it feel like night was closing in early. The living room was an empty blue hue. Jeff must have got held up with work. It happened sometimes – even on the weekend. Even overnight once or twice. B turned on all the lamps and flipped on the TV. *Mean Girls* was on and he got all the way up until Lindsay Lohan turned mean before he started to worry. He flicked to Sky News in case something had happened. A train crash, a fire in the tube. Or something wonderfully banal like a strike.

His ears were alert for the tinkle of a key in the lock so when the buzzer sounded B got a fright. It was a few seconds before he had the wherewithal to wonder why on earth Jeff had rung the buzzer. But then it came to him:

they were breaking up after all. Jeff had decided to give B fair warning for whatever would ensue. He had left his stuff there because it was B who was moving out. Jesus, of course. Jeff had probably expected him to have spent the afternoon packing. He stood now, uncertain what to do. Should he start packing to show Jeff that he knew he meant business, or should he plead his case?

He was about to run to their room to at least change out of sweats when the buzzer sounded again. Was Jeff going to break up with him via the intercom? That would make a good story at least. He walked over to the door and buzzed him in without talking to buy himself time. Then he realized that all this time he didn't have his phone on him. He ran to their room and grabbed at his hold-all from Thailand, looking for the phone. There at the bottom of the bag he saw, of all things, five missed calls from Bobby. Christ, the guy had gone from hating him to ringing him obsessively. But nothing from Jeff. B threw the phone on the bed and, eyeing up the bag, had an idea.

He dragged the bag, half-packed, to the door. That should gain him some leverage – he could point to it as evidence that he knew how serious the Molly situation was. He was taking Jeff's message seriously – he was ready to move out if he had to. He was pulling on jeans when there was a knock at the door. The guy wasn't even using the key to his own apartment. B had had bad break-ups but this looked to be that worst kind – where the other person was so keen to get away from you that they were calm and gave you space like you were a nutjob they just wanted rid of.

'Let yourself in, for god's sake!' he yelled as he ran to the door, answering it angrily now. If he had known it was going to be this acrimonious, he would have slipped the Le Creuset coffee mugs into his bag.

Two men stood in the doorway. Despite their plain clothes B knew immediately that they were the police.

56. ANNABELLE

July 1989

Dear Molly,

Your dad says I've created a monster, that you now expect Broadway-level entertainment 24/7, but I don't know why you should expect any less. How can you be expected to stare at inanimate objects for hours without knowing their back story?

The monkey that floats above your playmat has had a string of unsuccessful romances. He longs to settle down in a semi D in Kimmage but can't raise the capital because of the unpredictable nature of playmat work. The cloth dolls that the Spanish teacher from school brought back from Mexico are enjoying their time in Dublin but they find the food unbearably bland. They were asking you yesterday about the limp tasteless cabbage served with a hunk of dried-out ham. You said you were on a liquid diet. Let's see how long that lasts, the snippy one with the eyebrows said. The little rabbit with the button eyes? Used to be a heroin addict.

Other news in our world: Mako is still as cute as ever (Bernard is not impressed by this game either, but I tell him you are a realist – you want to know the truth). You used the F word about him today but I've got to tell you people love fat babies. What else? Sad Sam – the boy on the other end of the road – is definitely getting bullied. We followed him yesterday and saw him buy a very large ice cream en route home. Comfort eating. He didn't even look happy. You and I are discussing what our best approach will be. I'd like to write a really nasty note to the bully but you say grown women writing horrible notes to eleven year olds is inappropriate. So I will settle for us hiding outside the playground and shooting horrible stares at anyone who resembles a bully.

I've also started to bring you further afield. We go on long walks in Wicklow and the air fills our lungs and makes us feel rejuvenated again. A few days ago on one of these romps, I realized I needed to pee. There was no one around and I somehow managed to crouch down for a quick wee with you strapped to me. Then would you believe it I found a Kleenex in my coat pocket. What luck! I'm never one of those organized types with tissues handy. But then after, I didn't want to litter so I folded the peed-on Kleenex and put it in my coat pocket thinking I'd throw it out but of course I forgot. And, when I got home I realized that it wasn't actually my coat I was wearing – it was Bernard's. So when Bernard got home and reached instinctively for the tissue he keeps in his jacket pocket, I screamed like he'd produced arsenic and told him its origins. But do you know what he did? He blew his nose in it anyway and laughed like it was all a big joke.

If I can tell you something as appalling as that then I can tell you my biggest secret of all. Between you and me, Mol, I've started writing. I've felt the urge for years, this sense that a play was bursting to get out of me, whole scenes playing out in my head, but I could never translate them to the page. I could get the words down OK, but I couldn't seem to communicate the deep feeling that I had in my bones. These people who were alive in my head would come out flat on the page. Until now. It's like something has clicked, like I've nothing to lose anymore by just pouring it all out there.

I have you to thank for that, my darling girl. What's there to lose by writing when I got all I ever wanted from this mixed-up world when I got you? (And a man who sneezes in my wee.)

Love,
Mum
XXX

57. BOBBY

Glenmalure Vistas, May 3rd 2019

Families were like countries. They had diplomatic back channels through which sensitive information was passed. And that was how Bobby found out that Anne was pregnant; through a diplomatic back channel organized to diffuse a diplomatic incident. Even though Anne wasn't even twelve weeks yet and none of the rest of the family knew, John had negotiated that Bobby be let in on the news. He argued that Bobby's high approval rating among the aunts might help get Angela on side. V was let in because, since their return, she and Bobby were treated like family elders or victors of the Hunger Games, allowed to decide the future fate of the family. So that was how Bobby found himself in Glenmalure Vistas on a Friday afternoon nervously waiting for the door to open in order to convince Aunt Angela that her daughter wasn't going to hell.

The motley crew had pulled up to the gates after school in Uncle John's Skoda. Bobby had walked slowly through the schoolyard, straightening his tie and trying to emphasize his height to shake off the feeling that he was ten again.

But squeezing into the back of the car with Anne was too familiar and he was right back to summers in West Cork and fights to sit in the front. Obviously he'd have let her win this time, but she had insisted on staying in the back with Alastair while the new Lady V glowed in the front. She was out of her cast and it seemed she was out of gymwear and make-up too. She was wearing a loose shirt and jeans with bright white pumps. She was getting younger by the day.

Anne, on the other hand, was pea green and for the first time Bobby started to take this madcap quest seriously. Given that his own parents were furious that he wasn't popping out children with another man, it was hard to believe that unmarried pregnancy was still an issue. He thought the market for sin and shame had firmly shut up shop. So, when he saw Anne's tangle twister face, Bobby was suddenly glad he'd come. He wouldn't take so much as a Hail Mary from Angela – if they ever got out of Tallaght. Uncle John's sense of direction was dire.

'Look at that mad woman following her dog, what kind of a person gets led by their dog?'

They stared out the window at the lights. To be fair to Uncle John he couldn't see her stick. But still it was a struggle to keep the conversation on the straight and narrow.

'I do apologize. I have great respect for the blind community.'

When they eventually arrived, Bobby was mesmerized by Glenmalure Vistas. He had seen the reports on the news about ghost estates and figured that Aunt Angela lived in a half-finished shell where drifters and wild cats roamed rampantly. He had thought it would be made up of a few ageing oddballs who'd been dumped there by their kids and some young parents who'd bought here during the boom and were now stranded in a suburban wasteland about to lose their minds.

Given that he presumed his aunt lived in a post-apocalyptic hellhole, he felt bad that he'd never visited her. But now they were here, and it was a kind of Stepford bliss. It was absolutely miles away from anywhere but there were wide patches of well-landscaped greenery, trees that would grow into miniature forests, and playgrounds with that spongey floor that kids could nail themselves on and still be fine. The houses were toy house replicas not about to win any architecture awards but bright and cheery all the same.

As discussed on the drive, John was to ring the doorbell. For some reason this was a key detail. Perhaps it was felt that someone else might do it wrong. Bobby and V stood behind the main trio like bodyguards about to jump in if things got out of hand. Alastair Stairs was laden down with flowers and chocolates. He had a bottle of Champagne waiting in the back of the Skoda depending on how things panned out. Anne had had to stop him from bringing a Bible as a gesture of goodwill. But before they had a chance to execute the doorbell plan, the door shot open.

'I saw you through the window!'

An older man with a shock of white hair, an impressive moustache and wire-rimmed glasses opened the door. There was a moment of silence before John apologized for getting the wrong house and they all turned on the doorstep. All except Anne who remained rooted to the ground. Given she had visited her own mother before, she was certain that this was her house. Peering beyond the moustachioed man in the doorway, Bobby began to notice Aunt Angela-style artefacts in the hall; religious trinkets and homely colours lined the hallway.

'No, no, this is absolutely Angela's house, I am merely her gentleman caller.'

The gentleman caller had an American accent and much to all their surprise he roared laughing. He was old but strikingly attractive. His skin was a rich brown and his pupils so dilated that his eyes looked black. He was wearing a crisp shirt and tie under a sweater vest that Bobby reckoned Alastair Stairs might be coveting. His trousers were pulled up to his ribs, giving a good view of dazzlingly white Nikes which Uncle John was examining like only a professional shoe salesman would. The man's silky moustache was making Bobby regret getting rid of his own.

'Do come in!'

Maybe it was the Nikes but he moved like a much younger man. He had a lift in his step as he bounced down the hall calling Angela. They all followed him into the kitchen where Aunt Angela had her head in the oven. Bobby resisted the urge to joke that she must have already heard the news. He settled for a look at Lady V who either had the same thought or could at least appreciate the bizarre nature of the situation. Angela seemed to have missed their arrival because for several seconds the yellow Marigolds remained rustling in the browning foam of the oven cleaner.

'Jesus, Angela, take your head out of there, the fumes from that stuff are lethal.'

Angela didn't seem at all surprised to hear John's voice and they slipped into light bickering about the poisonous nature of the oven cleaner versus the need to get right in there to get a good scrub. Still, she let him pull her up from her crouch and they kissed on the cheek in the middle of this apparent argument. Bobby had an unexpected pang of longing for that kind of unconscious relationship, for someone who knew you blind, who walks into your house like they live here too. He had a pang of longing for Molly. But there was always Anne. He had made a pact with himself to stop forgetting Anne. He looked for her in the huddle by the kitchen door. She looked tiny. So small and concerned. He had an urge to go over and hug her but was relieved to see Alastair reach his arm around her.

John started moving around the kitchen punching appliances and the woodwork aggressively, listing what he would replace and what he could simply repair. He mentioned how he had a toolbox in the car and for a few moments it seemed like light DIY was the reason they were here in the first place. The older gentleman had the kettle on and was preparing the most beautiful tray of fine china. It was so fancy that there was even a folded tablecloth on the tray.

'Could I interest anyone in a gin and tonic? Ange and I usually wait until six o'clock but I'm sure we could make an exception for company.'

This was too much. The motley crew all looked to Angela, who seemed to realize she needed to provide at least some explanation, if not for the wildly attractive gentleman caller then at least for her wildly out-of-character daytime aperitifs.

'Dr Hassan is my neighbour in number 36.'

'Can you believe my luck to have a neighbour as wonderful as Angela?'

The family's silence intimated that they could believe it. Bobby looked around for someone to take the baton but the group was struck dumb. Anne and Alastair looked like they hadn't even noticed the drink or the gentleman caller but were just desperate to get their secret out. Uncle John looked angry that Aunt Angela had integrated into the community to the point of having visitors despite the fact that he had never visited her himself. Lady V was clearly about to burst at the thought of Angela's secret life drinking G&Ts with the most handsome septuagenarian she'd ever seen. Suddenly Bobby remembered the reason he had been brought on board in the first place and jumped in to fulfil his role.

'Absolutely. Aunt Angela is a marvellous person and I'd say she is a wonderful neighbour.'

'Jesus H Christ, Anne.'

Uncle John dropped the toaster he had been inspecting and jumped in front of Anne like he had just seen a sniper get a lock on her. He tried to murmur but we all heard him say how he'd only just realized that the fumes of the oven cleaner would be TREACHEROUS to her condition as he ushered her out of the room. We all followed him into the toy house living room, with Dr Hassan bouncing behind in his Nikes with the beautiful tray. Bobby wondered if he should warn him of the impending catastrophe, but Anne had blurted it out before the rest of them had even managed to sit down. If the unusual company and the daytime alcohol had surprised their oddly assorted group, nothing came close to their shock at Aunt Angela's response.

'What wonderful news.'

Bobby only realized after Aunt Angela had spoken that

he had closed his eyes, which in hindsight was truly bizarre. What had he expected to witness? An exorcism? He opened them now to see Dr Hassan spring out of his seat.

'Now tea is definitely the wrong choice! I'll go next door and get the gin, and a soda pop for you, Anne!'

They all watched out the window as he waved excitedly while running across the grass. Even Uncle John was silent as they all sat in shock. At Angela's response to the news? At the elderly moustachioed man sprinting across the lawn to get gin to celebrate Anne's pregnancy?

Bobby glanced up to see how the others were coping with the mayhem and noticed for the first time in the silence how different Aunt Angela looked. She appeared younger but he realized that strangely it was because she had stopped dying her hair. Her light brown frizz had become a healthier silver and it had taken ten years off her. He thought he spotted a tiny bit of rouge on her cheeks and he felt a swell of affection for her. They'd written her off. Banished her to a ghost estate and forgotten about her. But after all these years her eyes looked bright again. V broke the silence.

'Does this mean you are happy about the news, Angela?'

'You all think I'm a religious nut. I know that. But since Gus left—'

There was a sharp intake of breath at the mention of his name like someone had just said FUCK.

'—God has been there for me. And for me religion isn't a noose. It isn't all the things you can't do. It's all the love and hope that God helps you find when you are at the depths of your own despair. I can be religious and still like my gay nephew best.'

She paused to give Bobby a nod and he couldn't help but

feel a buzz of pride. It had long been suspected that he was the favourite, but it was nice to have confirmation.

'I can be Catholic and still help the Muslim women in the estate raise their children any way they see fit, and I can be overcome with emotion that my only daughter is about to have a baby with what seems like a lovely young man.'

Aunt Angela turned her gaze directly at Anne.

'I haven't been much of a mum to you, Anne. I lost myself when your father left. But these last few years in Glenmalure Vistas and in particular the last few months getting to know these asylum seekers from all over the world, I have found my calling. I'm just sorry it took me so long.'

'The asylum seekers they relocated? They relocated them here?'

Lady V was the only one putting the dots together.

'Yes, Dr Hassan was the top cardiologist in Aleppo. My neighbours are such lovely people, Veronica, and they've really opened my eyes.'

Anne was not a crier. But clearly Alastair was. He had welled up and was snorting loudly in a disgusting pink armchair. Anne sat still. Bobby knew that the suspicious look on her face wasn't for lack of empathy. She was nervous. Cautious of the change in her mother, mentioning her dad's name, not hiding behind the Bible so she didn't have to come up with her own response system. Drinking gin and tonics in the afternoon. And she was allowed to be cautious. After all these years she had built her own survival mechanism and it would take time for that mechanism to include Angela again. But Alastair couldn't help himself; he embraced Angela warmly, the chocolates and flowers squashing in between them. In the confusion Bobby accidentally hugged Dr Hassan too who had appeared out of the bushes with a bottle of Bombay Sapphire and a Coke for Anne.

By the time they left two hours later, Bobby, Lady V and Dr Hassan were tipsy, and an array of smiling people had arrived to wave on the delegation. In the car on the way home, their motley group sat in silence; in shell shock at the idyllic Glenmalure Vistas, the devilishly handsome elderly Syrian man and the beautiful children running on the grass, but safe in the knowledge that nobody thought that Anne was going to hell.

58. B

London, May 7th 2019

When the doorbell rang this time, B was prepared. The police had been back several times. Always with no warning. Always with more details. Since they'd first called with concerns over Jeff's involvement in Sheena's case, they had tracked his passport to the Dominican Republic. Then they'd unravelled his Bitcoin empire to find an amateur drug ring for public school bankers. B stood over the asparagus risotto taking a minute to steady himself. He inhaled the lemon zest he had just added. Whatever they revealed this time, he would calmly accept it like he had everything else. He would stay locked in the apartment and cook food until the freezer exploded or he got kicked out. Exhaling, he walked to the door.

There could no longer be any doubt about the colour of her hair. It hadn't struck him in Thailand, but in the muted grey of the hallway, Molly's hair was a definite shade of blonde. Characteristically messy and slightly too long but beautifully sun kissed. There were streaks of sweat on the denim shirt slung over her shoulder like she had been using it as a towel to wipe under her armpits. B stood in the doorway in shock.

'You came back.'

Molly hugged his crumpled tracksuit. She smelt of sweat and Skittles. B breathed her in and swallowed back tears of relief.

'Of course I did. We've had our share of bad break-ups but dating a secret drug-dealer who flees to the Caribbean is a first.'

Molly stood back from the hug but squeezed his hand and kept holding it as she stepped inside.

'I forgot how beautiful this place is, B.'

He looked around at the leather couches and expensive rugs and was suddenly embarrassed. He wondered what on earth had happened. How could he have lived with someone and find out he barely knew him at all? What did that say about him? All these years he had prided himself on one thing – on knowing exactly who he was. He wore his self-awareness as a badge of honour. But it turned out he knew the constructed B: the viral vlogger, the man with the Moroccan tiles. He followed Molly into the kitchen. He turned off the heat on the risotto and turned to face her. He wasn't sure where to start.

Jeff had worked in finance – that much was true. He'd started on the futures desk of a big trading company, just like he'd told B. The policeman had explained that most of them took uppers and downers in that line of business – it was the only way to regulate their bodies so they could entertain clients late into the night and be up again at 5 a.m. They set their alarms for fifteen-minute naps in bathroom stalls at lunch and popped pills when they needed to. Somewhere along the line it seemed that Jeff had become the point guy; sourcing drugs for everyone on the payroll. He'd realized he could make more money as a white-collar drug dealer than he ever could on the futures desk. So, he switched lanes. He transferred from hard commodities to pharmaceuticals.

Clean drugs, the policeman told him; what wealthy types wanted now was a civilized relief from reality: Xanax, codeine, sleeping tablets; drugs that if found in your cupboard could be explained away. B had looked up in surprise as the officer mentioned as an aside that he thought cocaine's reputation had suffered from its portrayal in *The Wolf of Wall Street* which had made it seem dated and crass. Without pausing to let B take in his use of the word crass, the policeman went on to explain that to go with their middle-class drugs they wanted a middle-class drug dealer. A drug dealer you could invite to your wine and cheese night. A drug dealer you'd have in your book club. And that was where Jeff came in. He already had all the contacts. He was quiet and polite and discreet and expensive. Now in the stillness of their expensive apartment, B looked at Molly and wondered where to start.

'Jeff wasn't who I thought he was.'

B was taken aback by the shake in his voice, yet he knew why it was there. Jeff had blindsided him, but B wasn't without fault. He'd been so wrapped up in the apartment and his book that he'd fallen in love with a version of the truth that worked and never really looked under the hood.

'Who *is*?'

He laughed at Molly's characteristically benevolent response.

'You're not annoyed with me?'

'For trusting someone? Of course not. Are you still annoyed with me for running away?'

'You're Molly Black. You always run away.'

He was trying to be funny, but he saw he had hit a nerve. Molly moved back into the living room and sat down. She stared at the teal rug.

'Jeff knew I'd be happy to run, that I wouldn't ask any questions.'

'You aren't to blame, Molly. And at least it worked out for you. You're happy there, right?'

'The happiest I've been in a long time.'

Molly smiled and B felt a pang of guilt. He'd been so high and mighty in Thailand; sure that he was the one who had his life sorted and that Molly needed saving. When here he was – blindsided and clueless. He cringed at the thought of it.

'Now my mess has dragged you back.'

'Of course I came back, B. Is it stupid to ask how you are doing?'

B let out a sigh. He had spent countless nights around dinner tables, nudging friends for details of horrible break-ups. He wanted the gory details when affairs were caught on baby monitors or burner phones revealed sexy pictures. His jaw dropped when engagements ended abruptly, or marriages were annulled after revelations discovered on honeymoons. He'd felt pity for these people, safe in the knowledge that that kind of thing would never happen to him. He was different. He was self-aware. He grabbed a cushion and covered his face with it, murky grossness filling his insides. He felt vaguely nauseous all the time lately. He wondered if this was what pregnancy felt like.

'Do you need me to remind you of all the nutjobs I've dated?'

Molly slipped out of her shoes and curled up on the couch. Even though she smelt of the sweat her shirt hadn't soaked up properly, her presence beside him made everything less awful.

'Luckily I had a front row seat.'

B removed the cushion and gladly received a hug from her. They sat entangled for several seconds, her bird-like arms enveloping his cherub pudge. He was overwhelmed by how grateful he was to see her.

'Unless. You aren't dating the crazy guy selling seeds at your cult, are you?'

'Jeb? No, but he isn't crazy. He was involved in an altercation which left a man dead in Nova Scotia in 1984 but he's really calmed down now.'

Despite himself, B laughed but Molly suddenly looked serious.

'B, Jeff may have been trying to get rid of me, but he accidentally saved me. I wish I could say the same for Sheena. There was something going on between them that night, I know there was. They were fighting – he was angry with her. Jeff was from a small town in Galway, right? So was Sheena. Maybe they knew each other?'

'Even if they were from the same town, Molly – Ireland is smaller than South Carolina, and more incestuous. We all know each other. Given he was the Irish Pablo Escobar, that nice nurse was probably just buying drugs from him.'

B was ashamed to admit it, but he hadn't thought twice about that poor girl. He'd been so wrapped up in how he'd been deceived that he hadn't wondered who else might have been hurt. Jeff was long gone and there was no indication that he knew this missing nurse. There was nothing linking them except Molly's vague recollection of seeing them on a street in Islington on the rainiest night of the year. For all they knew he was giving her directions. But when B looked up, he realized that Molly wasn't going to let this go.

Molly was carefree. She floated and glided on top of situations. She never got too close to anything. But there was something about this girl she'd never met that was tugging on her. In the half light of the muted apartment, B realized what it was. Molly had been in too many dangerous situations to count; she'd been in the wrong place at the wrong time and let her curiosity fuel countless dodgy situations. Molly felt responsible for Sheena Griffith because she could have been her.

'OK, let's go to the police – we can at least tell them what you saw.'

B pulled on jeans and a t-shirt while Molly threw some water on her face. From the bathroom he could hear her humming a familiar tune and B welled up. It was *Evita*, 'Another Suitcase in Another Hall'. The familiarity of the song, of her presence, filled him with relief. B turned off the lights while Molly helped herself to one of his jackets hanging in the hallway.

'Did you use your jean shirt to wipe the sweat from under your arms?'

'What else would I use?'

They shuddered into laughter.

They were halfway down the stairs when B's phone beeped a news alert: a woman's body had been found in the canal.

59. MOLLY

London, May 8th 2019

She hadn't packed for the weather. In her memory, London was a cold wet place and the prospect of it being warm hadn't even dawned on her. The heat was rising up through her legs as if her tight black jeans were melting. She was still wearing the blue jean shirt she'd shown up at B's in and now she waved it in front of her face as an ineffective fan. She knew that her clothes made her look out of place. Like she was still out from the night before. Which she was – the night before just happened to have been months ago.

Sheena Griffith's dress had caught on a nail under an empty barge. Molly and B had watched all night on TV as a blurred image of the body of a girl they'd never met was pulled from the water. Molly had to remind herself how wet it had been. That it had rained for weeks. That the canal had burst its banks, that the grass had been soaked through, that the water had gushed in a frightening way. Because standing on the edge of the canal on this sunny May day it was impossible to imagine slippery banks, gushing water, a woman drowning.

Children in shorts held the hands of mums in summer dresses. Dads led fleets of bikes, which flew by with a hair's breadth between them and the edge of the canal. The whole place felt so safe, like nothing could go wrong, like disaster was an impossibility. A perfect storm had to happen for Sheena Griffith to lose her life. Molly's whole life had been a perfect storm, so why was she the one standing on the bank? Sheena Griffith was a nurse. She was consistent and reliable. She could be counted on. The only thing Molly could be counted on was to run away.

Molly wondered now if it had ever worked? Sometimes. Sometimes being on the move had helped distract her from the emptiness, from the sensation that there was no home to go back to. But when her friends had started to build their own homes, there were fewer and fewer house shares where there was always a couch. And when B had settled down, it had shaken her to think that she was the only one running. So, she'd gone one step further this time. She had pre-emptively cut herself off in case that was what was about to happen. In case there was nowhere left for her to call home. And somehow, for the first time in a long time, she'd ended up somewhere that felt like home. Something about the combination of people, being outside all day, watching the garden develop and following the seasons. It made her feel part of something, rooted and peaceful. She wanted to go back to the Eco Garden, to leave all this mess behind. She'd done all she could do. She'd told the police what she knew. She'd been there for B after a catastrophic break-up and yet something was holding her back from getting on a flight.

A jogger brushed past her. The smell of sweat and deodorant filling the air. In her pocket, her mum's diary burned like it was alive. Reading her mum's words was like getting a colour video of a blurry black and white image; you knew the content, but you'd forgotten all the important parts. It was like knowing someone had green eyes but forgetting how they sparkled; the difference between knowing the sky was blue and seeing it stretch out in front of you, cloudless and vivid. She knew that her mum was fun and warm and caring, but she'd forgotten what it felt like to be at the centre of all that warmth. To feel lit up from the inside, and to be the one to light her up too.

She wondered what her parents would tell her to do if they were here now and before she knew it a gush of warmth enveloped her. Her dad's old fleece embracing her, inhaling his perpetual smell of pencils and chalk. Her mum's pure delight in every tiny thing Molly did. The curiosity and deep interest in the world that kept her afloat even after everything that had happened. Molly looked at the calm canal. She watched the children running and the cyclists speeding. V had said that Molly was like Annabelle. She wondered if that was true.

The police had been grateful to Molly for her statement. They'd been polite and helpful and professional, but CCTV footage showed that Jeff was gone by the time Sheena fell. Technically he was in the clear. They couldn't even book him on the drugs because there was no extradition treaty between the Dominican Republic and the UK. Molly knew there wouldn't be diplomatic negotiations over a petty drug dealer, but it seemed impossible that the last person who'd seen Sheena alive could flee and that was it. She'd left the police station crest-fallen.

The TV channels had all shown footage of the doctor. They'd shown the rows of cameras outside his house and how his knees weakened when he heard the news. Molly knew grief. It was the one thing she knew backwards, and the doctor was drowning in it. It was ridiculous to feel so much for someone you'd never met but her heart ached for him. He loved that girl and at the very least he deserved to know what had happened the night she died.

She had to do something. She didn't know what, but Annabelle didn't let anyone fall through the cracks. And Molly, she hoped, was like her mum.

60. ANNABELLE

August 1989

Dear Molly,

There has been a bit of a mix up. When your father came home from work this evening, he found me crying inconsolably on the kitchen floor. He immediately searched the room for you, but you were perfect, sitting in your little bouncer, giving me what I took to be a very sympathetic look. Your father was not so sympathetic when he discovered what ailed me.

It all started out very normal. In recent weeks, I had been reading to you. I started with *Peter Rabbit* and *Alice in Wonderland*, but you got bored of children's stories, so I branched out. We moved on to Jane Austen, but like Jane you got fed up being told how important marriage was. And rightly so. Then, we moved on to the Russians. You found them much more interesting. You preferred Tolstoy to Dostoevsky although we DID stop reading when Anna Karenina got to the train station. We agreed that she probably got herself the Russian equivalent of a nice big muffin, had a nice warm cup of tea and went home to bed with a hot water bottle. But the thing was, I hadn't read *One Day in the Life of Ivan Denisovich* before, so I didn't know which parts to edit.

Now of course in hindsight, the fact that it was set in a Soviet gulag in the 1950s should have been a red flag, but once I'd started there was no way I could have stopped. You wouldn't have let me. You were gripped. I sat on the kitchen floor leaning against the cabinets and read to you all day. It was just poor timing that Bernard came in when you and I were deep into discussion about what life was all about. Poor Ivan was so hungry and so cold. He was so cold, Molly, that you and I shivered at the thought of the poor man. What is so wrong about crying uncontrollably for someone detained in a Russian gulag in the 1950s? They had had a TERRIBLE time.

When Bernard got over his fright and confirmed that nothing was actually wrong with you or me physically, that we were just having an existential crisis, god bless the man, he sat down on the floor beside us. He opened a bottle of red wine and we sat there long into the evening making funny faces at you and holding you as tight as you'd let us. Now you are both asleep and I am listening to your alternating breaths. You are in sync like you have always breathed together.

Bernard says that we have to build you to be stronger than we are ourselves. That you need to have a better filter between yourself and the world than we do. He didn't mention the word shoes because even I know I shouldn't have given that homeless woman mine, but the truth is I quite LIKE walking barefoot and it was a beautiful summer's day. But that's beside the point. I know I feel too much. But what other way is there to live in this crazy world than to throw yourself into it?

I just crept down to the kitchen to retrieve the offending book. I plan to finish it late into the night while you and your dad are sleeping and if I cry my eyes out then so be it. I'd rather feel all the things than nothing at all.

Love always and maybe a bit too much,
Mum
X X X

61. BOBBY

Dublin, May 10th 2019

Bobby wasn't much into anniversaries. He tried to forget this one and every year he almost did. Every year he avoided it, right up until the day itself when he always woke knowing. Every year when his eyes opened, he knew immediately that Jack had died on this day. So, he did all the things his mindfulness course had taught him. He let it in. He tried to feel it like a wave washing over him, but when that wave went tidal, he ran. He ran and ran until he found himself in town. He wandered up Grafton Street in the early morning light and watched vans and trucks unload their goods. He walked through the park as the cold of the morning broke, warming up to a genuine heat. He found himself outside the church.

It wasn't early anymore. Maybe 10, 10.30. Probably around the time the funeral had been. There wasn't a reason why he hadn't been back here since. He hadn't avoided it. Church just didn't brush up against his normal life in the way that it had done when he was a kid with school masses and priests for teachers, with confession and then the funeral.

No one had asked too much of Bobby after that. It seemed like they expected him not to believe in anything anymore, but the truth was he didn't know what he believed.

He stepped down into the cool of the lobby. After the run and the warming morning, he was glad of the cold emitting from the stone. He looked down at his clothes. He was wearing grey tracksuit bottoms and an old sailing t-shirt, but God wasn't supposed to care, right? He pushed through the doors to the church and found it silent. Mesmerizingly silent. It was empty except for one old woman sitting in the front row. Bobby sat down at the back remembering too late about bowing to the altar, but, like the clothes, he figured God would understand.

He willed it to come over him now; the grief, the sadness. He willed it to come to him now instead of surprising him. Instead of creeping up on him when he wasn't ready for it, but all there was of Jack in this moment was happiness. All there was were early mornings freezing in Dun Laoghaire teaching kids sailing, endless summer afternoons aimlessly wandering around Sandymount Green looking for something to do, someone to meet, some adventure to begin. All there was, it seemed, was time. In his memory they were forever bored, with nothing to do but mess around on their bikes, walk from one person's house to another looking for something to do. All that time and now there was none. No more time.

'Bobby.'

He hadn't realized he'd closed his eyes and now they were doing something funny when he tried to open them. Light was streaming in and he saw stars before he saw her. He'd thought she was old. An old woman in the front row of a church but that wasn't what she was. She wasn't old. She was vibrant. She was a raving atheist.

'Mum, what are you doing here?'

She didn't seem at all surprised to see him. She made her way to a small enclave where she put some coins into a box and lit three candles.

'I'm always here on Jack's anniversary.'

Bowing in the direction of the altar she walked towards the door. Bobby sat there a minute or two before he followed her. She was waiting at the entrance and he nearly choked when he saw that she had a cigarette in her mouth. She took a long puff and started walking. Bobby watched his mother cross the empty road to the park. She was layered in light shawls but underneath she wore quite a smart linen dress. Something left over from her old life no doubt. Something from when she was her, as Bobby saw her.

They circled the green in silence a few times before they sat. The park was busy now. The playground was teeming with activity, little voices laughing, howling and crying, all forming a chorus of aliveness that was instantly reassuring.

'Can I help?'

When his mother finally spoke, he realized how long she had been trying to do just that. How many different ways she had phrased it, how many different times she had broached it, how much she cared, how hard it was for her to see him suffer. And yet he didn't have an answer.

'I don't know how, but yes.'

'You loved him.'

'You knew.'

'Only suspected.'

Frances had finished her cigarette, but she held the butt

in one hand away from her shawl as she pulled off another layer. Bobby looked at his mother properly for the first time in a long time. Her hair was up in a chignon, and she was still pretty. She'd been tenacious once, he knew that. His grandmother and uncles had told him about the scholarship she'd won to UCD, about the part-time jobs she'd worked to get her law degree, how proud they'd all been. Even Grandad who wasn't entirely sure about girls and college smiled broadly in the photo of her graduation. She'd been this person that made sense to him, someone he'd looked up to until she'd given it all up. Become a phony, and for what?

'Is that why you don't want children? Because of what happened to Jack?'

Christ, this again. He tried to contain his irritation, but it was out before he could stop himself. He snapped.

'Why do you care so much about me having kids?'

He expected her to flinch as he raised his voice, but instead, she laughed.

'Bobby, I owe you an apology. Imagine me – who claims to be an enlightened feminist – weighing in on whether my son should have children or not? After years of being appalled by the corrosive myth – entrenched by the patriarchy, by the way – that any sense of purpose in life equates to procreation, then I make a big deal about it when my son doesn't want children.'

Bobby was surprised by a sudden sense of relief; by how good it was to hear his mother acknowledge how inappropriate the intrusion into his personal life was. A thought occurred to him.

'Maybe that's why you are plaguing me about it. Because

women have been interrogated about it for so long you want to give your son a dose of it.'

Inadvertently he let out a laugh.

'Maybe it's progress.'

'Gosh, well, either way, I owe you a sincere apology.'

His mother turned to look at him.

'It's actually nothing to do with kids, Bobby. In the months and even years after Jack's death you turned in on yourself. I don't know how much you remember but you didn't want to leave the house. Even now, it seems like you are just existing – that you are frightened of anything that comes too close to living.'

Bobby's chest was constricting and despite himself he felt tears rise to his eyes.

'I'm worried you'll do what I did when I lost Bernard and Annabelle. Be afraid to feel too much so you run away from anything that might hurt you. Kids, a relationship, sometimes even rugby seems too painful a reminder of your life before Jack. And it's a pity. Not because you were good. But because you loved rugby.'

Frances paused and looked out across the grass.

'I know. Because that's what I did. I loved the Law Library. I loved mounting a defence and fighting a case. But I didn't know how to be the person I was before they died. Losing Bernard was one thing, but losing Annabelle as well was too much. She was the great love of my life.'

He looked up at his mother. All these years, he'd felt like she didn't understand him and now he wondered if it was the other way round – he hadn't understood her. And if that was the case then it would be his fault. She had tried; it was him that couldn't stand the new version of her. Him that didn't think parents were allowed to change and now here he was wondering who she'd been all these years.

'Good god, Bobby, don't look so shocked. You are such a closet conservative. But no, I'm not a lesbian.'

Bobby hadn't been thinking along those lines but laughed now at the thought – maybe he *was* a closet conservative.

'I had the good fortune of meeting someone who saw me exactly as I am. A friend. *The* friend. The great love of my life.'

'You knew Annabelle before Bernard, right?'

'I introduced them.'

Bobby looked at his mother's rings and realized that once they had sat on plumper fingers. Once they had held tight to her, but now they twisted and turned loosely.

'I met her in Greek and Roman Civilization. She brought Homer and Socrates to life like they were sitting at the table next to us. And even in college she wrote these whacky plays. When I brought my nerdy younger brother to see one of them, he was gone.'

'What do you mean?'

'Oh, he would have been in love with her forever whether she knew it or not, but as luck would have it, they ended up teaching at the same school and she got to see how wonderful he was.'

'Nobody talks about Bernard much.'

'No. They don't. We should try but it hurts deep and hard.'

'Still?'

'Still.'

Bobby leant his face back to the sky. So, this was it. It was to be this hard and you just had to find a way to survive it. Or the opposite. You had to enjoy it to the maximum to honour those that were gone. But how did you find the energy? How did you keep going?

India, he realized. Yoga. His mother leaving the Bar. Her new weird friends and all the talk of auras. That was all survival. Bernard and Annabelle's deaths had crushed something in her, and she'd had to start again, become someone else just to continue to exist. He looked across at her and felt a sympathy he didn't know why he hadn't felt before. Why should she be any less fallible than him? He reached out and held her hand. She gripped it hard.

'What are we going to do, Mum?'

'Just keep going, love. That's all we can do.'

They sat watching the city come slowly to life before them, holding on to each other with all their might.

62. LADY V

Dublin, May 15th 2019

Camilla had won an award. Ireland's best small-to-medium modelling agency in the boutique category. The lucky thing was that she actually had to bring it into town today for another purpose entirely, so the girls were able to take a look. Then once it was produced from her handbag and suitably fawned over, it happened to stay on the table. Imelda nipped to the loo and texted V and Jacqui emojis of monkeys with their hands over their faces. Oblivious, Camilla ordered Champagne and Jacqui kissed the maître d' who came over with a bouquet of flowers for each of them.

V felt like she was seeing all this from afar, as if she were underwater. It seemed suddenly that there was something big and unmovable between her and her friends. She tried to snap out of it, to come back to reality – her reality – the reality that her friends were moving fluidly in, but it seemed like she had entirely forgotten how to play her part.

Imelda returned from the bathroom, her eyes wide. She moved her mouth almost imperceptibly, but they all received the message. One of their nemeses was at the corner table. The only question was which one. There was the prop who'd cheated on Jacqui after the 2009 grand slam in Cardiff. There was Camilla's dentist who'd extracted the wrong tooth but only admitted it after the rotten tooth fell out during a commercial for the Irish Tourism Board. There was the TG4 weather girl who had stolen the boyfriend V had gotten the tattoo for; the surgeon who'd put more silicon in Imelda's left boob and made her lopsided. There were countless rival models from their heyday and social columnists they had love/hate relationships with. Then there were the younger models who didn't bear thinking about. Mike liked to joke that V and her friends kept a book of all the people they hated – it was the Dublin area phonebook. He'd laugh for hours and then stare in disbelief when Damon asked him what a phonebook was.

V looked around the linen-clad room. Marcel, the owner, had just arrived and was dropping by tables air kissing groups of middle-aged women. The women around them were coiffured and coutured. They wore kitten heels and matching handbags. Their outfits resembled mothers of the bride ensembles brought out again for a birthday or a school reunion.

V looked around her own table. At Imelda's hat which had its own chair, at Jacqui's pale pink lipstick which matched her elegant dress, at Camilla's award. She felt a deep pang of affection for these women she'd come up through the ranks with. Who, despite divorces and business failures and the deaths of loved ones, had woken up this morning and gone to the hairdresser, who'd carefully applied bronzer and drawn on lip liner. She admired their brave faces and battleworn armour, but it was becoming clear to her that this wasn't who she was anymore.

For years, V had felt an excruciating anxiety in the lead up to the bill for these lunches arriving. Far from lessening when she became wealthy, her money-related anxiety only seemed to amplify. She had tried various tactics to quell it: taking out lump sums of cash as a physical reminder that she could afford it, eating next to nothing to reduce the final bill. But she'd never lost the niggling anxiety about money and for the first time today she wondered if that was actually OK. She had thought that eventually she'd get used to the finery – that that was what people did – but what if this just wasn't how she wanted to spend her time or her money? What if she wasn't interested in comparing notes on how the surgeon who'd put more silicon in Imelda's left boob had lost all his money and now lived in a bedsit in Rathmines or spreading rumours that the TG4 weather girl sold meth? What if she hated Marcel's creepy kisses and fell in love with dresses in Tesco?

She looked down at her yellow sun dress. She had popped into Tesco to get athlete's foot powder for Damon and seen the dress in the far aisle. Normally she'd never have bought clothes in a supermarket but this morning she'd wondered, why not? Then when she got home, she'd thrown on some pumps because when she'd seen the heels in the cupboard she'd wondered who she'd be breaking her ankle for again. Her hair fell loose over her shoulders because she didn't feel the need to keep it pulled to within an inch of her skull anymore.

When it had been her turn to debrief, when they'd heard what Camilla had worn to the award ceremony, guessed which member of Westlife Imelda was doing the interiors for (Mark), how Jacqui was opening a boutique in Ranelagh, V had considered telling them the truth. When they'd asked, she had considered breaking the unspoken pact of actually telling them how she was. She thought about telling them that breaking her ankle had made her see that she exercised compulsively – that she was addicted to it; how gaining weight made her feel like she'd no control and that terrified her. About her sudden fear at possibly losing Molly and everything it brought up; her unprocessed grief over Annabelle; her dark secret about her post-natal terror. But they'd built their friendship on an image of themselves. They'd overcome challenges by saving face and it wouldn't work to drop it now. She was changing but they weren't and they didn't have to. They seemed to be doing just fine the way they were. If the ordeal with Molly had taught her anything, it was that you had to do what worked for you. You had to keep your own boat afloat, whatever that meant for you.

It felt like she had been tugging on one end of a rope in a tug of war and suddenly she realized that she didn't have to. She didn't have to pull anymore. She didn't have to drop hints about how successful the business was. She didn't have to sculpt her arms every day like she might be on the cover of *IMAGE* magazine again. She wouldn't be on the cover of *IMAGE* again and much to her surprise this thought made her smile. It was a relief.

After lunch the girls would stroll tipsy up Grafton Street for their quarterly competition of who could burn through their credit card fastest in Brown Thomas. They would crowd around a thousand euro handbag wondering if Imelda's husband would divorce her for buying it even though she made twice as much money as him. They didn't have a language for being the breadwinner, so they just repeated their mothers' narrative. When the lunch was over V didn't make a big deal about leaving. She invented an excuse and made sure to give each of her friends long hugs and excessive air kisses.

She hadn't been on a bus since the 1990s. It turned out you needed some sort of jump card to get on, but once she was sorted, she climbed to the top and watched the city out the front window. As the 46A sped along she peered down at the canal. She took in the red-brick houses of Donnybrook; she looked into the rugby club Bobby had raised trophies for. She remembered the joy she'd taken in bus rides when she'd first moved to Dublin and she wondered what her life would have been like if it hadn't been shaped by her physical appearance. If instead of modelling, she'd waitressed or worked in a bookshop. Would she have different friends? Would she think differently? Was it too late to try not to be defined by it? She got off the bus at Leopardstown.

'Veronica, what a lovely surprise!'

Helen stood in the doorway in an apron that said 'May the Forks Be with You'. V was pretty sure Helen had never seen *Star Wars*. It would have been a gift from one of her beloved students no doubt. Helen's skin was slack but somehow appealing, soft in a way that made you want to touch it. V realized that her hair was actually dark like her own. If asked, V would have told you that Helen was mousy. But sure enough as she looked straight at her sister-in-law, Helen's hair was a rich black with beautiful strands of silver running through it. She had the same thought about Helen that she had about Danny on the beach in Thailand – had she ever really looked at the Blacks? Where had she been all this time? What had she been seeing?

'I was wondering if I could help with the street party preparations?'

'That's so kind of you, Veronica. Come in.'

She could hear the others in the kitchen. She stepped into the room as Even-Stephen was earnestly going through the pros and cons of whether to pre-wrap the knives and forks in paper napkins or put them unwrapped in baskets. John and Frances were taking this dilemma seriously. One consideration was wind. If they wrapped the cutlery then napkins would be less likely to blow all over the street. But wrapping them meant having an equal number of knives and forks and did everyone really need a knife? They were a few short. Standing in the doorway, V watched them debate where the wind would be coming from on Sunday.

She thought about all the times her boys had been in this house. All the street parties and family meetings and graduations and communions. The warm hustle and bustle the Black family had created for her boys. The kettle always on. Someone always willing to give you a lift or collect you. The expectation that you would stay for dinner. The knowledge that they'd come for you. To Liverpool or Thailand or anywhere else they needed to. The terrifying thought came to her that she might cry. If one of them thanked her for coming or pulled out a chair for her, she might explode, so she pre-empted their kindness and jumped into the discussion.

'If you pair the knives and forks, Stephen, I'll wrap them in the napkins.'

If they were surprised to see her, they hid it well.

'Marvellous, Veronica, pop yourself down there. What I'll do now is I'll make the tea because we can't let our energy fall flat when there is still so much to do.'

V sat down beside her brother-in-law as the kettle started its low hum. Helen was telling John to focus strictly on the tea and not to come near her domain. He was making a big deal of calling her sergeant and not stepping over an imaginary line. Even-Stephen was singing, and Frances caught her eye over the knives and forks.

'I love your dress.'

V couldn't help but smile. It was not the role she'd ever have chosen for herself but in the semi D in Leopardstown with the Black family around her, she was no longer playing a part. She was just herself.

63. B

Shannon Airport, May 17th 2019

B had never been to Shannon Airport before. Embarrassingly he'd barely crossed the River Shannon. Early in life, he and Molly had decided that adventure lay further afield. Excitement meant big cities and warm climates, but as they'd driven west from the airport to Galway that morning, they'd been mesmerized. Ireland was annoying like that – the weather was always good when you happened to be home. Molly and B factually knew that annual rainfall this side of the country was epic, that they'd barely last a weekend in rural Ireland, and yet here it was: green fields, stone walls, blue sky and an altogether familiar feeling that they didn't know they'd been missing. They'd been silent in the car, nervous about what they were doing and unsure if it would make any difference.

The church was packed. People were dotted behind pillars, in doorways and behind confession boxes. Sheena Griffith played camogie. It seemed that just before she went missing, she had signed up to play for a club in London. People called her the smiley ICU nurse. Every detail aimed at summing up her life had the opposite effect on Molly and B. For them, she was being brought to life for the first time as her coffin lay in front of them. The priest kept stressing how hard it was to communicate her vibrancy, her pure energy, her bounce. But it was her father whose plain words brought them to their knees.

He looked uncomfortable in his navy suit. He was pulling at it like the suit was the main problem, not the funeral or the coffin or his daughter's death. And maybe that was wise. Maybe it was safer to pull at your collar or to straighten the seams of your trousers than look at the simple wooden box and try to take it in.

He spoke slowly; he loved his daughter; he and his wife were grateful for all the support the community had given them. He guessed that sometimes accidents just happened. Beside him, B felt Molly's whole body tense when Sheena's father said the word accident.

Molly and B had spent several hours pacing the apartment, unsure what to do. They didn't even know what extra information they had – if any. It was probable that Sheena's family knew Jeff – since he was from the same town. The police would have told them by now that he'd been with her. What good would knowing they'd been fighting do? This poor family had lost their daughter, what business did they have showing up, making things worse? Or did her family have a right to know? They'd decided in the end that the family had enough on their plate but that if the time was right – if it seemed like he wanted to know – they'd tell the doctor. He could decide what to do with the information.

Sheena's father turned to look at the coffin but stopped.

His mouth was open, but he closed it again and instead stood looking at the wooden box. There was a moment when it seemed like one of his brothers or a nephew might come up to help him, but they decided among themselves not to rise. Molly and B held each other's hands. They let his pain wash over them and tried to absorb some of it. Given they'd never met Sheena, B couldn't explain quite how sad they felt. Were they mourning Sheena or were they thinking about Bernard and Annabelle? B wondered if their sadness was actually something else: relief at having managed to hold on and gratefulness that they had each other.

Outside the church, there were vague attempts among the crowd to chat, to say how beautiful the service was, but mostly there was silence. The sun shone on their faces and Molly and B absorbed all they had learnt about this girl they never knew. When they finally spotted the doctor, his face was red and tears streamed down through his freckles. B was suddenly filled with dread. Where would they start? What were they even going to say? B looked behind him and wondered if it was too late to get out of this, but Molly stepped forward.

'I'm sorry to bother you. I'm Molly, this is B. Do you mind if we speak to you for a minute?'

Molly tentatively touched the doctor's elbow and he nodded. They shuffled away from the throng to a patch of grass under a cherry blossom tree. If it hadn't been a funeral, the scene would have been idyllic.

'There was a man with Sheena that night. We wondered if you knew anything about him?'

The doctor had been in a daze but suddenly he was alert, his eyes jumping between B and Molly.

'You're the person who saw them together? Do you know him?'

B looked up from where he'd been eyeballing the fallen blossoms on the ground. He felt a lurch of guilt. Not really, he wanted to say. It seemed they hadn't known him at all. Reluctantly B nodded and the doctor continued.

'They were both from here and I guess they'd known each other all their lives. Her family tried to contact him but now it seems he's gone to the Caribbean, and no one can track him down. I know it was an accident. I know they have CCTV footage that guy Jeff was calling her over and over and she wouldn't tell me why. I feel like I'm losing my mind. Do you think they were seeing each other?'

B's breath involuntarily constricted. The thought hadn't even occurred to him that Jeff could have been seeing Sheena as well as everything else. Molly tried to reassure the doctor.

'I honestly don't know, but you aren't losing your mind. There was definitely something going on. They were arguing. Could she have been buying drugs? It turns out he was a dealer.'

The doctor was quiet for a moment like he wasn't sure whether to go on. He lowered his voice and looked around him.

'Sheena had been suffering from depression. After I heard that Jeff dealt drugs, I wondered a few times – the way he called her incessantly – if he'd been pressuring her to take medication from the hospital for him.'

B felt the bottom fall from his stomach. He was just beginning to process how little he knew about Jeff. He'd tried to take in the drugs thing – it wasn't great, but people did drugs, people sold drugs, that didn't make Jeff irrevocably bad. All this time, B had been following Molly on her mad hunch, just happy to have her back and pleased to try to help the police, but here it was plain as day: Jeff hadn't fled because he was a two-bit drug dealer, he'd fled because he'd taken advantage of a vulnerable young woman. Up until now this whole thing had felt like an unpleasant dream but now it was a nightmare. A woman was dead. Who knew what had happened between them that night at the canal? All they knew was that they were at her funeral and Jeff was on the run.

'You loved her.'

B was momentarily startled by Molly's frankness with this stranger but then that was Molly. She had a way with people that you couldn't teach. You couldn't emulate it or explain it. She was warm and genuine because she was herself. Who, B wondered, was he? A person who'd lived with a con. A person who'd seen Moroccan tiles and fancy furniture and never looked past Jeff's cool exterior to see anything else. The doctor held Molly's gaze like she was the only person who could see him. As they hugged, B nodded his goodbyes and walked towards the car. He felt like he'd been punched in the gut.

When they pulled up to Departures, neither of them moved. They'd done what they'd come there to do. They'd done all they could. And yet they were far from relieved. They sat in the airport car park and gazed at the planes taking off. B tried to distract himself from his wrenching gut by turning on the radio, but it was like going into a time warp. The most recent songs were from the 1970s and the commentary was parochial. The radio host was giving a detailed account of a steak he'd eaten at a communion recently and congratulating the butcher on a fantastic slaughter.

It was warm and they'd both rolled down their windows. B looked at Molly's profile as she stared out the open window. Although she was smartly dressed in black, she was still Molly. She had strings around her thin wrist that looked like a friendship bracelet that an eight year old would make, and her handbag was a tote from the gardening cult.

B wondered how he could possibly explain himself. It was he who'd trusted Jeff, him who'd moved in with a guy he'd barely known.

'Molly, I don't know how I let this happen.'

'Life is brutal.'

Molly turned to face him, and B was surprised to see her smile softly.

'Sometimes it is painfully, unacceptably brutal. Sometimes you trust someone, and they let you down. Sometimes they aren't who they say they are and then they flee to the Dominican Republic. Sometimes they go and die.'

Molly looked out the windscreen, but it was clear she wasn't looking at the few disparate passengers leaving the airport. B leant his head on the steering wheel and took in Molly's deflated figure in the front seat. He wondered if this was it. If she'd finally had the stuffing knocked out of her; if they both had. They wanted to trust the world, they'd wanted to light it up, but they were all out of spark.

'Did you put this on?'

Molly's hunched figure shot up straight and her ponytail wiped towards him. B turned up the radio to hear what she was talking about.

'No, I swear.'

'This is ridiculous.'

Molly unbuckled her seatbelt. Once outside she threw her head up to heaven and shouted, 'Mum, you are RELENTLESS.'

A few elderly Americans jumped in fright as they passed at the other side of the car park. B followed her out of the car. They'd missed the beginning, so ABBA was already halfway through asking them to take a chance. If it *was* Annabelle who'd pulled some strings at Riverside FM then she sure had picked her moment. B wasn't sure if Molly was angry or happy, but she began not quite to dance but to throw her body around like she was a freshly washed jumper that needed to be wrung out.

B closed his eyes and let the hurt and embarrassment of the last few weeks fall to his feet and he began to move them like his life depended on it. He was jogging on the spot like he was at the gym in his funeral suit but somehow it was helping. ABBA were crescendoing and they rose with it, throwing their bodies around and taking alternate lines, leaning into the imaginary mic. The car park was practically empty but for possibly the first time in his entire life B didn't think he cared what anyone else thought. He twirled and threw his hands up in the air and it was leaving him; the pain and confusion of the last few weeks was leaving him and all he would be left with would be jumping up and down with Molly in a car park. As ABBA began to fade out, Molly began to climb onto the roof of the car. B started to tell her to stop but joined her instead.

'Fucking Ireland.'

From the roof of the car, they could make out the estuary.

The sun was bleeding out lengthwise across the water, no sign of setting.

'It's bloody stunning.'

Out of breath they stared transfixed. B tried to inhale the fresh air and hold this moment, sitting with Molly on the roof of a car looking out over the sun engulfing the water before she left and everything changed again.

B wondered what would happen next. He didn't know what the situation was with the flat, if Jeff was still paying the mortgage, but either way, B knew he'd be moving out the minute he got back to London. He tried but couldn't remember what it had been like to live there with Jeff, the two of them playing house; it seemed like a trance. There was always work – the book was selling well, and now he could throw himself into the next one.

A burning part of him wanted to ask Molly to come back with him, to go back to the dive in Finsbury Park, to go back to faking phone calls trying to get all the things he had now: book deals, sponsorship and success but no Molly. But he knew that he'd have to do things differently this time.

He – they – had constructed someone who moved easily in the world – who blended and moulded to whatever the situation required, but he was beginning to realize that maybe you weren't supposed to be able to adapt to every situation. There was no construct that could protect you from the harsh realities of life. Despite how successful the construct had been, he knew he'd need to start from scratch this time. To drop the airs and graces and see what the world thought of him as he was – overactive sweat glands and all. And this time – like Molly had discovered – he'd have to do the work on his own.

'I can't get past the fact that her family, the doctor – that no one may ever know exactly what happened that night. What Jeff was saying to her, what had gone on between them.'

Molly stared into the distance. He was sure that Sheena's family wanted answers, but ever since she'd shown up on his doorstep B had increasingly understood why Molly was so desperate to know too. She needed to know why this girl who'd gone missing on the same night as her had made one bad decision and ended up dead. When Molly had made so many bad decisions and had somehow ended up alive, looking at a sunset. He tried to think of how he could make things better but there was only one person who'd know how to fix this.

'What would your mum do?'

'Well, let's see, which of her beliefs could help in this situation?'

Molly spread her fingers as she began listing options.

'Always carry spare knickers in case you need to run away. Baths solve everything.'

'Don't tune out during the musical interlude – the audience is still looking at you,' B chimed in, glad for a moment of levity. But after a pause the mood turned sombre again.

'There are few things more important in life than kindness.'

'It's better to feel all the things than feel nothing at all,' Molly whispered and they sat silently wondering if that last one was true.

'Of course, it would have been easier for Mum.'

B looked at Molly in confusion.

'Because she would have taken a lover from the Dominican Republic in London in the seventies so she'd just call him up. They would have the whole thing sorted in a few days and next Christmas Hector and his family would come to stay for a month.'

B leant back and tried a laugh, but it was hollow. Everything was hollow. A woman was dead and it seemed there was nothing anyone could do.

'Wait, that's it.'

B heard a thud and looked up to see Molly jump off the car.

'Fine, so there is no extradition from the Dominican Republic.'

She began pacing the car park. She stopped mid-pace and smiled up at B.

'But have you ever heard of a country that didn't have an Irish pub?'

Molly's eyes twinkled and B suddenly saw that the spark wasn't gone after all.

64. JOHN

Dublin, May 17th 2019

John didn't tell Helen where he went when he left the house in case she got too happy about it and wouldn't let him stop. But for the moment he was thoroughly enjoying his daily walk on the pier. Maybe all the more for the secrecy. He'd been inspired by Dr Hassan and bought a pair of top-of-the-line runners. He had conducted research both in-store and online and chosen the ASICS GEL-KAYANO 2600; a model he'd recommend to anyone, being himself an expert in the shoe industry. The professional athlete gear made him feel like he was walking on air. He left the house in the morning in shorts and a t-shirt like he hadn't a care in the world even though he was the chair of the biggest street party in the Dun Laoghaire Rathdown region and the event itself was a mere forty-eight hours away. To distract himself he popped his earphones in and listened to the woman whose name was just like Lizzy but with an O. He rounded the Lep Inn, crossed over the N11, passed St John of Gods, through Monkstown and over the bridge to the sea. The truth was, he *was* feeling Good As Hell.

The pier you walked said a lot about you. He had nothing against East Pier walkers but he himself was a West Pier man. He felt the East Pier was for tourists, people who sauntered, people who liked ice cream – the kind of people who stayed in bed after 9 a.m. West Pier people were hardier. They didn't mind the rough gravel and the occasional weeds. That was just the type of people they were. When he got to the end of the pier he slid through the small gap in the wall to the other side of the harbour.

The sea was even more beautiful than usual today. A blue beyond imagining. It wasn't choppy but not too still either. Out here he could see the entire city all the way to Howth Head. He wasn't sure if the pure happiness he felt when he got there was from looking out at the shimmering sea or if it was endorphins from all the walking. He wondered if this was what the fat spandex cyclists felt. If so then he was sorry he'd put them down. So what if they looked like luminous sausages? Everybody deserved to feel this energized.

He had been on his perch at the bottom of the pier when he'd found out. He had been looking out to sea when he'd heard the girl was dead. Of course, he'd known that was probably the case weeks ago but still his heart sank. He knew he had no right to feel as sad as he did. In some way he felt ashamed, like he was taking the grief that rightfully belonged to her family. But deep down he knew the grief was a sort of guilt. A guilt that he'd got his girl back and they hadn't – even if Molly wasn't the type of person you ever fully got to keep.

Her flight back to Thailand was booked for tonight. It would be Thailand for a few months but then it would be somewhere else then somewhere else again. He wondered if she would always be wandering. If that was her way of coping or if one day somewhere would feel safe enough to stop. He understood that people had to find their own way in the world but here he was with all this time on his hands, all this energy, and if only he could explain that it wasn't just her needing him – that families are like jigsaws – two parts have to fit; he needed her too. If only it was like when she was small.

After Bernard died, John had offered to pick Molly up from school every Friday. After a few weeks, he'd insisted that he could handle Anne, Bobby and Killian too, so every Friday at half two they all piled into the back of the car and for three hours the world was their oyster. They'd no homework on a Friday so John knew he had it easier than their minder Elaine who smelt like cabbage. In the winter they would go to Rathmines for McDonald's followed by a movie in the Stella or the Classic. The kids would run around the empty cinema high on Coke and Fanta or cuddle into him sleepy after the long day. He could still remember the tears the day Mufasa died in the Classic in October of '94 – the children's and his own. It was an awful shock.

Then in the summer, they'd bring a football to the park or visit the zoo. John still remembered how he felt at the end of those days. You'd think he'd be sad after he dropped them home, but the elation lasted for days. He'd find himself repeating funny things they'd said for Helen all weekend or doing impressions in the shop on Monday. Molly with her scraggly hair, talking to herself in her bright coloured cycling shorts. Bobby always looking for something to throw, kick or catch, sprinting across the Phoenix Park when they got out of the car like a dog let off a leash. Killian following him in awe and Anne quietly looking on, worried. Always worried. But maybe that was changing.

John could see her almost trying to find something to worry about these days and the beautiful truth was that she couldn't find much. Even if she couldn't quite make peace with Angela yet, Alastair was a regular in Glenmalure Vistas. Dr Hassan, it turned out, was a master baker and the two of them were competing in crumbles. Anne craved crumbles and ate them night, noon and morning. Rhubarb, apple, blackcurrant – the interesting thing was that it seemed the fruit didn't matter, it was the way the fruit juice made the crumble soggy. She had explained this to Helen, who wanted in on the act and was at home currently combining apples and home-grown strawberries in an attempt to get the edge on Dr Hassan and Alastair.

As John sat now feeling the warm breeze on his face, he wondered what role an uncle could play when a newborn baby arrived. Mums and aunts seemed obvious helpers, their presence secured, but John wanted to help too. He'd already gone a bit mad in Tony Kealy's baby equipment shop. Anne and Alastair had agreed that he could buy them a buggy but once you were up at the shop you saw that there was a swathe of gizmos and you wanted to order them in advance. He didn't want to freak Anne out so he got them all delivered to Leopardstown and he just kept them in the back bedroom ready to drip feed her bouncers and mobiles and cots when the time was right. But he didn't just want to buy them things, he wanted to be around, to help out, to feel purposeful. He wondered if it would be helpful if he made up a nice daybed in the back bedroom for Anne for when they came to visit; she and Alastair could nap while he and Helen minded the baby.

He had Molly's room set up too – he always did. He'd redecorated it since she'd last been home. Now it was a cool white with grey lamps. IKEA's finest. He did a weekly hoover and dust and most evenings he peeked his head in just to make sure it was all set. Molly kept some old clothes and various papers from college in the drawers and John and Helen both cherished the postcards she sent. Helen had bought a corkboard and tacked them on with multi-coloured pins. It didn't matter that she was rarely there anymore; what mattered was that it would be there when she needed it.

He thought then of the other room. The one he had stored all his hopes and dreams for daughters in. Maybe Anne and Molly in some small way *were* his girls. Moved on and out there in the world but still with rooms at home. The thought made him smile. And now there would be a baby, a grand-niece or nephew. A little bundle to hold and burp and teach to walk and talk and dance and be proud of.

His phone vibrated in his pocket. It was B's number.

'B, wonderful to hear from you – I've just been listening to Beyoncé's *Lemonade* here – it's even richer when you consider the context. That Jay-Z is a bit of a bastard, isn't he?'

'Uncle John, it's me, Molly.'

John's heart filled.

'Oh Molly, you are very good to ring me before you leave. What an ordeal you have been through. I'm sure the funeral was awfully sad. Are you all set for your flight tonight?'

There was silence on the other end of the line, and it

sounded like she was already at the airport. He thought he heard a plane taking off in the background. A thought struck him.

'Mol, have you finished your mum's diary yet?'

Again, he was met with silence and this time he feared he'd put his foot in it.

'I've been afraid to. I know I've already lost her, but it feels like I'll lose her again when I finish reading.'

John's heart ached. He tried with all his might not to ask her to come back to Dublin. He scrunched his face up and closed his eyes and somehow managed not to burst. He wondered if he'd ever be able to let her go fully. He didn't think so, but maybe that was how it was meant to be when you loved someone so much.

A flock of seagulls made a dive for the water. The birds were invading the city, becoming increasingly aggressive and attacking people unprovoked. There was widespread concern over what to do about them, but John could never hate them. He knew they reminded Molly of home. And that meant that no matter where she ended up at least she knew her home was here. He gathered his breath and told her to have a safe flight.

'Wait, Uncle John, I was ringing about a friend of yours. Well, maybe not a friend, but didn't you sell shoes to a criminal who fled to the Caribbean and started an Irish bar?'

Actually, there were two, but John hoped she meant the gentleman who'd evaded taxes in the UK, not the one who'd lit his wife on fire. Although the latter did have excellent taste in a seasonal summer brogue.

'Yes, my pocket book is quite international and includes

both the upper echelons of society and those in more compromised legal situations.'

'Did any of the criminals end up in the Dominican Republic by any chance?'

John breathed a sigh of relief. The arsonist/murderer was in Trinidad and Tobago.

'Yes. Up until I retired, I sent Harold a pair of loafers every year to his Irish bar in the Dominican Republic. I know he never paid taxes to the Queen but he was awfully polite and always paid for postage.'

'Do you think he'd like to make amends?'

65. ANNABELLE

August 1989

My darling girl,

News just in. The competition was rigged. All this time, Mako's eyelashes were fake. Glued onto the poor Japanese baby's face – can you believe it? But the upshot is that you are now officially the most loved baby in the world. Reporters have been flocking to the house, but you are handling the attention stoically. It's almost as if nothing has changed. You fall asleep despite the limelight. You drool unselfconsciously across furniture. You lie on your playmat talking to the flying monkey about his dream of owning the semi D in Kimmage.

It's early morning and it's still dark. All summer, the sun would start flooding in from 5 a.m. or even 4.30 some days but a sudden shift has happened. There was no bluish hue to signal the slow end of summer – instead the darkness simply refused to lift this morning. I've turned on all the lamps and the most marvellous opera is on the radio. You've fallen back asleep and I do plan to, but I can't take my eyes off you.

At the beginning when you came, I was in shell shock, terrified of the responsibility, sure that I would let you down. Then the summer became an odd mix of these moments of complete terror when I'd wake in the night sure I'd lost you in my bed and other moments of pure boredom standing in my nightgown sterilizing bottles (which you know I abhor). Now the summer is coming to an end and I'll have to leave you soon. I'll have to go back to my students and snatching free periods to write. So now I have a new fear.

I will never have this time with you again. I will never have this moment here at 5 a.m. when the entire city feels still and I get to look at your puffed-out cheeks and soft lips and hear your tiny breaths which are the most reassuring sound on the planet. The terror mixed with boredom consumed so much of my energy this summer and now it's over.

From this moment on, I will do nothing but enjoy you. I will dance around the kitchen with you. I will sing at the top of my lungs to you. I will tickle you until you keel over. I will do nothing but enjoy you, love of my life.

I have so much to thank you for, Molly, but one thing I never could have expected. All this time I've been annoyed with my own mother. Annoyed with her for not telling me how hard this is, for dying and leaving me. But you've made me realize something. She couldn't possibly have left me. I love you so much that dead or alive you will never not be loved by me. My love will be a part of you forever and always because you are a part of me forever and always. So I too must still have my mum's love. You haven't just given me a new love of my life – you've given my own mum back to me.

Love forever and always,
Mum
XXX

66. THE FAMILY

Dublin, May 19th 2019

This must be what it feels like to compete in the Olympics. This nervous adrenaline must be what fires up football teams before the World Cup. We have all put so much into today, and now that the street party is finally here, we are determined that it exceeds all expectations. That's why we were so surprised when the hippy from next door was let into the preparation area. We looked to Helen when he arrived in the kitchen in his socks and sandals, but she nodded solemnly like they had an understanding.

'It's days like this when neighbourhoods are defined. What kind of a neighbourhood do we want to pass on to our children?'

Uncle John stared into the distance of his suburban garden as he started his pre-war speech. None of us mentioned that John had no children because he did. We were his children. The only problem was that not one of us would be able to afford a house in this or any other neighbourhood until we were well into our fifties – if ever. But that was beside the point. This was the most important day of Uncle John's year. And we would be here for him no matter how tense things got. No matter how bad the rush on sausage rolls was. No matter how aggressive Tony in 42 and Bill in 39 got during the tug of war. No matter how irate Fionnuala in 24 got when Fionnuala in 76 inevitably won best bake for her raspberry scones. No matter what happened, we were determined that the street party would be a roaring success.

'Who is that lad? He's a bit old for a caterer, isn't he?'

The hippy pointed at Dr Hassan, who was arranging fried dough balls soaked in honey on a plate that Helen was holding.

'He was the last neuroscientist out of war-torn Aleppo and is a close family friend.'

The bench shuddered as Uncle Mike jumped to defend Dr Hassan. He hadn't anticipated how big his belly was and it made the table bounce. We all held our hands out to steady the five thousand sausage rolls covering the table. But then Mike remembered he'd forgotten the most important thing so he jumped up again.

'He went to HARVARD.'

'I am a cardiologist and I studied at Yale but thank you, Mike.'

Dr Hassan had been baking for the street party for days. He was wearing a #NotInGlenmalure t-shirt. Last week a reporter for RTE had asked Angela how the refugees had impacted her community. She had looked at him for several minutes before telling him that the refugees WERE her community. She said that his question perpetuated the culture of 'them' and 'us' that had riddled this country since the civil war. Well, not anymore, she had said, raising her voice. Not in Glenmalure! Since then, Angela had become a global icon for inclusion. Niall Horan had retweeted the video and #NotInGlenmalure was trending.

'Mike, if you would please sit down, we can go through the timeline one more time.

'1 p.m.: Introduction and special welcome to new members of the community.

'1.30 p.m.: Food and drink will be served.

'2.30 p.m.: Games and competitions to begin.'

When Uncle John started listing the outdoor games, we all looked down into our laps. It didn't matter which app you favoured – Met Éireann, AccuWeather, the BBC, even the Norwegian Meteorological Institute app – they all said the same thing: rain was coming. It was forecast for 1 p.m. but ominous grey clouds indicated that elsewhere across the city it had already started to pour. He hadn't told John, but Mike had secretly bought a hundred ponchos in the euro discount store just in case.

'When I call out the task you are responsible for, please say your name loudly. Best garden competition.'

'Veronica.'

'Best traditional bake.'

'Angela.'

'Best gluten-free bake.'

'ALASTAIR.'

The table shuddered as Alastair's enthusiasm erupted in the corner by the napkins.

'Giant Jenga – am I saying that right? I really don't know about this one.'

'Proinsias Murtagh, and I promise, John, it's a real hoot, give it a chance.'

'Tug of war.'

'Mike.'

'Sack race WITH responsibility for ensuring bags are returned to their owners after the event.'

'Bobby.'

'Egg and spoon race.'

'Molly.'

With hindsight we would all wonder why Dr Hassan was so excited given that he'd never met Molly. But maybe our reaction gave him a fright because somehow the plate slipped from his hand. We all turned from a soaking Molly standing in the doorway to the dance Helen and Dr Hassan were doing to save the honey dough balls. Most of them landed on the floor but then, as if from nowhere, B appeared and snatched the last sticky golden round. He stared at us all, suspended in silence, then popped it in his mouth.

'Delicious.'

The table erupted into applause as we leapt to our feet. We gravitated to Molly's sodden figure, but Anne elbowed us all out of the way. She held onto Molly's thin frame so tightly it looked like she would break. And for so long that the rest of us had to settle for pats on the head and kisses blown from afar. While we queued to hug B, the hippy neighbour gravitated to Dr Hassan.

'Do you know who this is?'

Dr Hassan handed him a honey dough ball.

'The niece who ran away?'

'Ah yes, their Molly.'

'Their Molly.'

It wasn't just rain. There was hail and wind and at one point someone swore they'd seen lightning, but it turned out Tony in 42 had just electrocuted himself stringing up Christmas lights. It didn't deter him from the tug of war, though, and the electrocution might have swung it for him because he pulled Bill from 39, sloshing in the rain, over the line. The Fionnualas made peace when it was clear that Syrian baklava and semolina and almond cake were superior to any hard-as-rock scones. There was one major fracas when Uncle Mike produced the ponchos and the old hippy went around shouting SINGLE USE and LANDFILL in people's faces until every wearer agreed to reuse their soaking wet plastic ponchos as coats every year until they died.

A man who looked like he'd lived outside for a century – his skin as rough as sandpaper – arrived in a shiny purple tracksuit. Despite his elderly age and weathered appearance he won the sack race and the egg and spoon race before Uncle John spotted him. He embraced the stranger who'd saved his brother like it was Danny himself who had shown up, and the rest of us murmured Frank to each other in explanation. Frank went on to win the over-sixties' sprint and drank a gallon of Fanta before saying his goodbyes and breaking into a jog home.

As the games came to an end, a weak, watery sunshine that seemed isolated to the cul-de-sac sprung up around us. The apps had said it would stop raining, but no one had expected sunshine. Despite Bobby's best efforts, sacks and hula hoops littered the street. Kids high on baklava roved around on bikes and scooters, looking like monsters, their face paint dripped down into chocolate-covered smiles. The muddy adults in their multicoloured plastic ponchos hurriedly drank Jacob's Creek from soggy paper cups before the cups fell apart.

Bobby, B and Molly sat on the wet footpath laughing as Alastair and Anne recounted how Alastair had declared his love for Anne. Alastair dived into a bush to illustrate. Molly tried to defend Rowena Powell, who, when you thought about it, had done absolutely nothing wrong except drink weak tea. Helen, Angela and Frances were lounging in deckchairs listening to V, perched on a wall detailing how she'd fallen off the treadmill. Frances tested V's newfound familiarity with her sisters-in-law by asking about Boyzone, but V politely said she still couldn't say which member she'd had the liaison with. On the green, the old hippy was trying to get Dr Hassan to pronounce Proinsias correctly and lobbying him to join an Irish-speaking wing of Extinction Rebellion, claiming he would pick up Irish in no time. Which was probably true – Dr Hassan already spoke four languages.

Over by the food stand, John's phone pinged. He nodded at B who signalled for Molly to follow. They huddled together by the side lane, but John spoke so loudly that we all heard what was said. John's friend the tax dodger had tracked down B's ex. Jeff had stressed again what we all knew from the CCTV – that he hadn't seen Sheena fall, that he'd been long gone by then. But he did say she'd given him some pills. He said she was only one of many sources; that he hadn't forced her into anything.

'I know he was pressuring her that night. And even if he wasn't –how about the fact that he fled the country despite being the last known witness to a supposed friend's death? If he did nothing wrong, then why did he take off to the Caribbean?'

'Because you're right, Molly – he knows that morally he

did something wrong – and the jumped-up coward thinks he's a criminal mastermind wanted internationally for selling pills to bankers. But I can tell you this.'

John reached out his arms, resting one arm on each of their shoulders. He was short so he had to stretch to reach B. Normally so sure and confident, B looked deflated under John's weight.

'He won't get away with it. It's unclear what the police can do next but at least Jeff will have to answer to someone. I have an address for him, and my contact is willing to speak to her parents, to ask this Jeff character whatever they want to know. Technically in the clear or not – her family and the doctor and the whole town will know what that lad did. He will live his whole life unable to return home unless he shows up at her parents' door to tell the truth and beg forgiveness. That is, if they want anything to do with him; it may be hard for them to believe anything he says given he pulled a runner.'

B and Molly stood in silence under Uncle John's human tent. Looking at B, it was clear that he wouldn't know what or who to believe for a long time.

When a grey darkness began to descend, we eventually moved inside carrying sodden paper plates, half-eaten cakes and cups of Coke with sausages floating in them but no excess ponchos as everyone had dutifully brought theirs home to reuse. The last of the weak sun shone partway up the stairs as Uncle John carried Molly's sham of a bag up to her room. When she reached the top of the stairs, Molly peered in the door of her bedroom. Inadvertently we had all followed her and now we stood huddled on the landing and dotted down the stairs.

The athlete's foot was back so Blur stood barefoot on the landing eating a sausage roll. Beside him, Helen flinched as flakes of sausage roll pastry littered the good upstairs carpet. The battery on Granny's iPad had died so she looked up from her Sudoku for the first time since 2010. It was not clear if she liked what she saw; she glared at us suspiciously. Even-Stephen was bringing her up to speed on who everyone was in case she'd forgotten. From the doorway of the bathroom, inexplicably Alastair was taking photos of everyone. Uncle Mike was peering into bedrooms and Lady V was yanking him back by his poncho. Anne was on the top step and for the first time in a long time she didn't look peaky. In fact, she looked a million dollars, her bright pink dress covered by the yellow poncho she was still obediently sporting. Aunt Frances stood on the middle step leaning on Bobby whose sturdy frame supported her. Bobby was in his old rugby club hoodie – someone said he'd taken up coaching. And at the bottom of the stairs, Angela was laughing at something Dr Hassan had said.

Molly turned in the doorway to face us. It had been made very clear to us that she was going back to Thailand. V had even offered to pay for her flight. That was where she needed to be for a while, and everyone had accepted it. But that didn't stop us being happy to see her. Her sun-bleached hair was messy and too long, her jeans were ripped and her bones too visible, but she was home. It wouldn't be forever, it mightn't even be for long, but for now Molly Black was home. And if she ever forgot that she had a home to come to again, now she knew that we'd follow her to the ends of the earth to remind her.

Uncle John pulled Molly into his arms. We all followed,

huddling them from all angles. In the epicentre of the hug Alastair Stairs beamed and Blur took the opportunity to pinch anyone within arm's reach. Squirming, we broke apart, Uncle Mike chasing Blur down the stairs for pinching his bum. Oasis was asking Helen if she'd secreted any mini-food away and the rest of us groaned at the mere thought of more food.

'One last thing,' Uncle John called from the landing. Towering over us, he looked like a dictator holding court over his charges. 'Please put a note in your diary. We will be having an AGM next Sunday.'

'Christ almighty, the girl is home – she is right there. What do we need another meeting for?' Uncle Mike yelled up the banisters. He had Blur in a headlock.

'It takes a village to raise a baby, Mike.'

'To do what?'

The last of the sausage roll still in his mouth, Blur looked up as Uncle Mike released the headlock in shock. Blur seemed to be the only one of us who didn't hear what John had just let slip. John himself was suddenly backtracking on the landing saying something about village spirit, but immediately all eyes were on Molly. Now we knew why she was home: she was pregnant. You had to hand it to her; there was never a dull moment when she was around. But picking up on our glances, Molly yelled, 'Don't look at me!'

She laughed loudly like her being pregnant was the funniest idea in the world. We searched the landing for Lady V – who knew what age she was? She could be anything from thirty-five to fifty.

'Christ on a spoon, it's Anne.'

No one knew who had phoned Killian, but somehow his

kimonoed torso was suspended mid-air on a selfie stick at the bottom of the stairs.

'YES! It's me! It's me! I mean, it's us! We're pregnant.'

Alastair Stairs erupted from the melee as we stared on in amazement. We searched the crowd for Anne and were surprised to find her rolling around laughing. It took her several minutes to stop laughing long enough to nod confirmation that Killian's wild assertion was true.

It was Molly who moved first. She ran back up the stairs and into her room grabbing something from her bag. She returned with a small red book and handed it to Anne. They embraced and we were surprised to see tears in both their eyes when they finally broke apart. We couldn't hear what they were saying because Uncle Mike had suddenly erupted into tears, murmuring over and over again, 'The beauty of new life.'

In the centre of us all, Anne beamed. She didn't flinch or shy away, instead she smiled as we all hugged her. John nearly collapsed with relief against the banisters when Anne looked up to him with a forgiving smile. And from the ground where Alastair's phone had fallen in the commotion, Killian seemed to have put on a shirt.

'To be fair, that was worth calling me in the middle of the night for.'

67. DANNY

Phuket, May 19th 2019

Danny hung up the phone. It was the third phone call he'd had that night. Anne and Alastair first, then Molly and John. Then his mother had managed to tear herself away from her Sudoku to FaceTime him, but it turned out she didn't want to tell him she missed him like the others had, she just wanted to ask him if Syria was on the north side near Swords.

A soft breeze blew across Danny's face as he sat down. His hut was elevated slightly and his legs dangled off the small bamboo porch. Around him, all was still. Even the cicadas with their loud cricket-like noise seemed to have died down for the night. In the dark he could make out the high banana plants he would be taking a team to harvest tomorrow. They would take a machete to the toughly packed sheaths and jump out of the way as the bundle of green bananas fell to the ground.

He looked down at his tanned legs. He barely recognized them. His bare feet were worn and hardened but they felt alive. His hands were callused and cracked but they were living and breathing too. Every part of him felt alive. He stood to go back inside but stopped a moment to look out across the gardens one more time. Even in the dark, as far as he could see there was only green and with it a fresh balmy air. It was the most beautiful sight he'd ever seen. He soaked it in.

He'd learnt that you could disappear in an instant. Before your own eyes. In Liverpool or London or sitting at the kitchen table in your own home. But now he knew something else too. He crept quietly along the bamboo, back into the hut. With a bit of luck, no matter how lost you get, it's possible to find yourself again.

EPILOGUE: ANNABELLE

June 1999

Before Molly was born Annabelle had hated feet. The look of them. The smell. The way balls of fluff gathered in crevices and wiry hairs sprouted out of men's pale toes. She enjoyed telling people that she thought all feet should be cut off, or at least legally kept out of sight. Even a brief glimpse or whiff of them made her stomach turn. But then Molly arrived. The soles of Molly's tiny feet were as soft as a pillow, her tiny toes barely looked like toes and Annabelle thought she could just eat them.

A sharp kick landed at the bottom of Annabelle's spine. Molly's feet were no longer tiny. The soles were tough from when she insisted on walking barefoot in West Cork. Her toenails were sharp and were sometimes badly painted pink or black depending on the babysitter. After basketball and ballet and long jump and karate her feet smelt sweaty just like everyone else's but still Annabelle clutched at the offending foot and held onto it for dear life.

When she awoke next Molly was gone. Someone would have been here; Frances probably. Molly would have had a nice breakfast. Bobby might have shared his pop tarts with her.

Annabelle made her way down the stairs. She caught sight of herself in the mirror and was surprised to see that she was somewhat normally dressed. She felt like she had five oversized coats on. Instead, there she was in loose trousers and a t-shirt Bernard had got in the lost and found at his school. Grey and lifeless, she looked as dead as Bernard. Except her cascading hair, which looked frightfully alive. She wondered if somehow her hair hadn't heard the news.

When she reached the kitchen, she saw it on the calendar. It was circled many times: the end of year play. End of year, that must mean June, but Annabelle could have sworn it was still winter. She wanted to tell someone that the year hadn't ended – the world had.

She knew enough to shower. She was ready when they arrived. Frances in her best suit and chignon and Stephen driving. Annabelle had come to accept that she was underwater, that she was under a thick layer of fog, but still it was disconcerting to be outside her house. She watched familiar places slide by through the window as if she was seeing them for the first time. Everything was different but of course she knew it wasn't. It was her. She was different.

They had saved a place for her. Not too far back and not too close to the front either. It was near the edge of the aisle in case she needed to escape, and she had a pang of gratitude for whoever had thought all that through. At whoever had arrived early to get just the right spot. It could have been any of them because they were all here. John and Helen were in the row behind her with a camera and video recorder. Angela was on one side of her and Stephen and

Frances the other. Mike was in front with a frighteningly good-looking girl who looked vaguely familiar. Annabelle felt half imprisoned and half safeguarded but veered swiftly towards the latter when she began to register the sad smiles of other mothers and the various hands reaching out to squeeze her arm. It was only when the school hall went dark that she could breathe again. She closed her eyes and willed herself not to cry. But she knew that if she did then at least Molly wouldn't be able to see her.

The stage lights suddenly shone bright and a rickety curtain pulled open in haphazard fits and starts. Annabelle didn't remember what the play was, she didn't know what part Molly had and she couldn't recall her practising around the house. She couldn't remember anything of the time since Bernard's death. She could barely hold in her head how long it had been. Was it seven weeks or eight? It filled her with fear that she might be expected to exist again, that she'd have to be in this world in any real sense again now that she was fundamentally broken. If she had to exist again then she'd have to answer real questions like how she'd support Molly, how she'd pay the mortgage. Was writing just a pipe dream now? Suddenly she heard Molly's voice.

Molly stood at the front of the stage reading from what looked like it had once been a box of cornflakes but was now a script meticulously covered in tin foil. Her hair was braided into a French plait and she wore an oversized white shirt with a bow tie. It took Annabelle a moment to register that she was speaking in a thick Southern American drawl. For a mad moment, Annabelle wondered if the play was *Cat on a Hot Tin Roof* and then she remembered that the children were nine.

'Cinderell-ER was washing them gone darn tooting floors ALL day and lord but she was bored.'

A shot of nerves pummelled Annabelle. What was Molly doing? Why wasn't she taking her role as narrator seriously? Was she desperately trying to get her mother's attention? Her father had died and now her mother was a zombie – was the poor child terrified of losing her too? Children are resilient, the doctor had told her. Children bounce back. What about her, she'd wanted to ask? Would she ever come back?

The audience erupted into laughter and Molly glanced up. Her eyes shone and suddenly Annabelle could see that she was scanning the audience. She was searching for Annabelle but because of the dark she couldn't see her. Annabelle, on the other hand, could see her daughter's every feature. Her light brown hair, her scrawny elbows sticking out of her oversized shirt, her wide smile, and suddenly she knew exactly what Molly was doing. She was having fun. Annabelle looked on in disbelief wondering at this human who was made from her and like her in so many ways but also not like her too, and it was those ways – the ways in which Molly was so completely herself – that were nothing short of magical. When Annabelle was nine, she'd taken herself so seriously she had thought she was Laurence Olivier. Molly only wanted to laugh.

The little girl playing Cinderella seemed to have no interest in the play. She seemed genuinely concerned about rubbing a stain off the floor. Bobby arrived on stage carrying a tin foil sword. The boy looked terrified. He hovered over Cinderella as if trying to catch her attention while Molly continued to paraphrase the text in a cowgirl drawl.

'The Prince, he was a nice fellER but personally I wouldn't get too worked up over a boy.'

'AMEN, Molly!'

Parents were whooping and hollering, and one mother let out a wolf whistle. In all the hubbub Bobby seemed to forget his line. In the chair beside Annabelle, Frances was twisting and turning. She couldn't look but suddenly there was B dressed as a pudgy mouse, putrid red with embarrassment but whispering the Prince's lines across the stage. Bobby followed his cue and finally their class were shuffling off the stage and the next class was ambling on to do *Little Red Riding Hood*. In the huddle leaving the stage Annabelle spotted Anne who'd stood stock still as a tree the whole time. Annabelle must remember to tell her how convincing she was – she'd captured the melancholic essence of a weeping willow beautifully. B lingered by the curtains. Even though he was quaking with nerves it was clear that he'd loved being on stage. Bobby fled the stage like it might eat him.

What was the teacher thinking making poor Bobby go through that? Never had anyone wanted to play a mouse in a play more than Bobby. And never had anyone wanted to play a prince more than Barnaby Eustice – he just didn't know it yet. He needed someone to take him under their wing and show him what he was capable of. Next year she would have to direct the play herself.

Next year. The thought struck her as strange. It was the first time it had dawned on her that there would be a next year and the thought didn't fill her with dread. She stood and, thanks to her well-chosen seat, was out of the hall like a shot.

The school was like a maze, but she could hear them. Giddy from their performance the kids were milling around backstage unaware that they could be heard from the hall almost better than the children on stage. That was something she'd have to address next year. Next year. The prospect was suddenly a genuine possibility, shining bright like a mirage. Annabelle didn't care if it disappeared. For one moment, this moment, she felt like she might exist next year, and it was Molly who'd made her see this. Her light-hearted funny girl who didn't care what people thought, who simply wanted to laugh. Annabelle scanned the hairsprayed heads looking for the plait, wondering who had done her daughter's hair, who had meticulously covered the cereal box in tin foil, and she fought back tears at these tiny kindnesses, at the army of family and friends who were silently knitting a safety net while she hung on by a thread.

'MUM!'

Annabelle turned around. Molly was already down the corridor, but she was running back now, sprinting towards her, and Annabelle forgot how fast her daughter was. She almost told her to be quiet, to think of the class on stage now. She almost asked her if she was frightened of losing her, if she thought her mother would be broken forever. If she was resilient, if she was going to be OK. But instead, she ran towards her daughter and when they collided Annabelle held her as tightly as she possibly could. Next year she would learn to do a French plait, next year she would wrap the script in tin foil, next year she'd exist.

ACKNOWLEDGEMENTS

This novel would not be in your hands today if it wasn't for my incredible and steadfast agents Emily Harris and Sheila Crowley. I want to thank them for their continued support and invaluable editorial input. Thanks are also due to Abbie Greaves, formerly of Curtis Brown, who first read my work and encouraged me to keep writing.

I am indebted to the two wonderful editors who worked on this book – Clare Gordon and Madeleine O'Shea – who made the book better at every turn. I would also like to thank Kate Appleton, Amy Watson, Sophie Whitehead, Declan Heeney and all the team at Head of Zeus and Gill Hess for all their work promoting and distributing the book. My sincere thanks to Nina Elstad for designing such a beautiful cover.

There's Been a Little Incident is a love letter to the friends and family who keep us afloat when things get tough. I could never have written such a novel if I wasn't blessed with friends and family who, when I felt like I was hanging on by a thread, took up knitting. My extended family have filled my life with love, security, and fun. A particular thanks is due to my cousin Nell, whose support is constant, and to my wonderful aunts who seem to have a sixth sense about when to pick up the phone.

Like Molly and B, I am blessed to have lifelong friends with whom I've enjoyed countless adventures. My deepest thanks to The Original Band, Mates and my London support network Holmes Road and Girls, Girls, Girls. A particular thanks is due to those friends who were early readers of the book and provided invaluable feedback: Eavan, Alice T, Jenny, Claire, Hannah, Aileen and Emma G. A special thanks to Carla, Ciara and Trina for being by my side every day on the wild ride that is parenting, to Lucy for the lifesaving yoga, to David Lee for all the laughs, to Rachel Anderson for the much-needed sartorial help and to Lynn for letting me pick her brains about being a nurse in the ICU.

I won the lottery when it came to in-laws. Catherine, Eamonn, Colm and Raquel are an incredible source of support and I feel blessed to be part of the Sheehy family. I would also like to thank my wonderful sister-in-law, Emma – the highlight of my week is Wednesday pizza night with you and my beloved nephews Harry and Lenny. I am deeply grateful to an honoury member of our family – our childminder Priscila Aparecida dos Santos Dornelas – whose love and compassion we will never forget. Thank you to all the team at Press Up who let me work in their offices, hotel rooms and restaurants and have always shown me great support.

This book is dedicated to my parents and my brother,

who believed I would be wonderful before I could hold my own head up. It is of course sad that my beautiful and fun-loving mum is no longer here to see the rest of our adventure unfold, but the truth is we had enough happiness for a lifetime, and we'll never lose the love she wrapped us in. Dad and Matt – you are the constants that make it all possible. Thanks for always knowing exactly what I will order in a restaurant.

And finally, to the loves of my life. I read a lot of books. I've written some too. But never have I come across two characters as wonderful as my husband Brian and our daughter Kate. You are constant sources of wonder, surprise and fun and it is the great privilege of my life that I get to spend every day with you.

READING GROUP QUESTIONS

1. *Grief was always coming for her. Waiting until she couldn't move. Until there was nowhere to hide.* How does the novel present the experience of grief? Did you learn anything about the grieving process from reading it?

2. Of the whole cast of characters in *There's Been a Little Incident*, who is your favourite and why?

3. What do you think of the method of inserting text message conversations and letters throughout the novel? Does this way of constructing a narrative about Molly from different perspectives help us to better understand her decision to run away?

4. What do you think of the way the author represents family life? Does any of *There's Been a Little Incident* feel familiar to your own experiences?

5. *Who did Molly belong to now that B was moving on? Who did she belong to so much that sometimes they got confused between her needs and their own?* What do you make of Molly's need to 'belong' to someone?

6. The Black family often find themselves in less-than-ideal situations, which leads to some very humorous moments. Did you have a favourite funny scene, and why did this one stand out to you?